SO-AFT-629

THE SUMMER OF U

Books by Holly Chamberlin

LIVING SINGLE

THE SUMMER OF US

Published by Kensington Publishing Corporation

THE SUMMER OF US

Holly Chamberlin

KENSINGTON BOOKS
http://www.kensingtonbooks.com

All characters in this publication are fictitious, and any resemblance to real persons, living or dead, is purely coincidental.

KENSINGTON BOOKS are published by

Kensington Publishing Corp.
850 Third Avenue
New York, NY 10022

Copyright © 2004 by Elise Smith

All rights reserved. No part of this book may be reproduced in any form or by any means without the prior written consent of the Publisher, excepting brief quotes used in reviews.

If you purchased this book without a cover, you should be aware that this book is stolen property. It was reported as "unsold and destroyed" to the Publisher and neither the Author nor the Publisher has received any payment for this "stripped book."

All Kensington Titles, Imprints, and Distributed Lines are available at special quantity discounts for bulk purchases for sales promotions, premiums, fund-raising, and educational or institutional use.

Special book excerpts or customized printings can also be created to fit specific needs. For details, write or phone the office of the Kensington special sales manager: Kensington Publishing Corp., 850 Third Avenue, New York, NY 10022, attn: Special Sales Department, Phone: 1-800-221-2647.

Strapless and the S logo are trademarks of Kensington Publishing Corp.

Kensington and the K logo Reg. U.S. Pat & TM Off

ISBN: 0-7582-0145-1

First Kensington trade paperback printing: May 2004
10 9 8 7 6 5 4 3 2 1

Printed in the United States of America

As always, for Stephen.
And this time, also for Joey.

Acknowledgments

The author would like to thank Jack and Betty for their indispensable companionship and love, and the Animal Rescue League of Boston for introducing them to her.

She would also like to thank her editor, John Scognamiglio, for his enduring faith and support.

Finally, with a full heart, she would like to welcome Ella Carol Nelson to this world!

May

Gincy
The Go-to Girl

The crisis was discovered at four forty-five in the afternoon. Fifteen minutes before ninety-nine percent of the staff hurried out of the building to enjoy their sixteen-hour vacation.

My boss, Mr. Bill Kelly, Kell for short, was frazzled. He didn't handle crises well. What he did do well was delegate responsibility.

He came tearing into the center of our office area, what little hair he had on end, plaid shirttails untucked.

"Listen up, people. We have a problem. The idiots at the copy shop lost our proposal and we've got to recreate it. Now. It's got to be at the printer's tonight."

I watched the predictable reactions of my colleagues.

Curran, the senior designer, slipped out of the room backwards.

Norton, the copy editor, suddenly found the piece of blank paper he was holding extremely interesting.

Vera, the administrative assistant for our division, feigned a sudden hacking cough.

"Kell," she gasped, "I wish I could help, but I think I'm really sick. If I don't get home and into bed soon . . ."

Kell turned to me. "Gincy, you'll stay, right?"

"It's gotta get done," I said, shooting my coworkers a look of disgust. "I'm here."

That's me. The go-to girl. Virginia Marie Gannon.

I guess I got my work ethic from my father, though our choices of work couldn't be more different.

Dad manages a hardware store, the small, privately owned kind that monsters like Home Depot have mostly put out of business.

I'm the senior editor of the monthly publication sent to subscribers of a public television station here in Boston.

Come to think of it, I'm not sure how much of a choice my father had when it came to a career. He didn't go to college. When I was about twelve I heard a rumor from a cousin that he'd never even finished high school.

To this day I don't know the truth about that. I'd never ask Dad straight out. It would embarrass him, and though my parents aren't my favorite people in the world, I treat them with respect.

It's what you do. Work hard and respect your parents. In that way, I'm a typical Gannon. In other ways? Not so much.

Anyway, the job got done and at six thirty-five I left our office on Bowdoin Street.

By the time I raced through the door of George, An American Cafe, it was almost seven o'clock. The place was a cemetery.

"Where is everybody?" I barked to the dimly lit room. "There's nobody here!"

A dark-haired girl about my age stepped away from the bar. I noticed she had breasts the size of Pamela Anderson's. Almost.

How can you not notice something like that?

"Uh, hello?" she said. "We're here. Me and—Clare, right?"

Another girl, a blond one, all clean and healthy-looking, like she could star in a soap ad shot at a mountain spring or something, slipped off a barstool and joined the first girl. She nodded and looked at me warily.

Okay, maybe she had a reason to. I'd caught a glimpse of my hair in the window before charging through the door. It was pretty wild. I think I'd forgotten to comb it that morning.

I had, however, remembered to wash it. Which was more than I'd done the day before when I'd been up since four A.M. working on a report for Kell the Inefficient. Next thing I knew it was eight-thirty and if I'd stopped to shower I would have been late for a nine o'clock meeting.

You know how it is.

"So," I said. "I thought there was supposed to be a meeting here tonight. You know, to hook up with roommates. For a summer place. In Oak Bluffs."

"There was a meeting," the dark-haired one drawled, "but it seems it was over at, like, six-oh-five. By the time I got here at six-thirty, everyone had already hooked up."

She nodded toward the girl next to her. "Except for Clare. And me. I'm Danielle, by the way."

"Hey. Gincy."

"That's an unusual name," Danielle said flatly.

"Yeah," I answered flatly. "It is."

The one named Clare stuck out her hand and I stared at it. She let it drop.

"One girl told me all the good houses are taken," she said. She sounded apologetic. "I think you're supposed to rent them by February or March and then look for housemates. Not the other way around. I didn't know."

I propped my fists on my hips. What there was of them.

I tend toward the skinny.

"Crap," I said. "Well I didn't know, either!"

Danielle heaved this big dramatic sigh. "None of us did," she said. "I guess."

I was seriously disappointed. I really wanted the summer to be something special.

And then, inspiration struck.

"Wait," I said. "All of the good houses might be taken but that doesn't mean there aren't still bad houses to rent. Right?"

"I suppose," Clare said doubtfully.

"A bad house?" Danielle rolled her eyes. I noted she was wearing a lot of eye makeup. Personally, I'd owned the same tube of mascara for three years. "See, I don't like the sound of that," she went on. "That means, like, a bathtub but no shower, right? Ceiling fans but no central air?"

I guffawed.

Ms. Fresh Mountain Air tried to hide a smile. "It might be worth taking a look," she said. "I . . . I kind of had my heart set on this."

There was a beat of silence and then I said, "Well, what's it gonna be? Are we going to do this or what?"

"Well, I'm not spending the entire summer in the city," Danielle declared fiercely. "The grime is murder on my skin. And speaking of murder, I just read in the *Globe* that street crime has like, tripled from last year. And you know how they get in the hot weather."

I narrowed my eyes. "How who gets?"

Danielle looked at me incredulously. "Duh. Criminals?"

Okay, I thought. *But I'm watching closely for any signs of bigotry.*

"I'm allergic to cigarette smoke," Clare said suddenly.

I eyed her keenly.

"Well," she admitted, "not allergic, exactly. It's just that I don't like it. It gives me headaches."

Danielle nodded. "And cigarette smoke stinks up my hair, not to mention my clothes. No smoking in the house. Agreed?"

I considered this.

Truth was, I wasn't a big smoker. I was kind of a social smoker. A wimpy smoker. It was the only thing about me that was wimpy. I could live with a no-smoking rule.

Still, I kind of hated to let things go.

I kind of liked to win. It was one of my more obnoxious traits.

"What about on the porch?" I countered. "If there is one. Or in the yard?"

Danielle and Clare discussed this with eye language and then Danielle nodded. "All right. But if the smell starts getting in the house . . ."

"Yeah, yeah, fine. Anyway, we're jumping ahead making house rules before we even have a house."

Clare didn't answer but checked her watch for about the tenth time.

"Hot date?" I asked.

She blushed and hefted off a barstool what I realized was a

suit in a plastic dry-
He's working late t
home before he do

I didn't at all kn
the rules later."

"Good, because
eight," Danielle sa

She suggested a
cursion to the Vi
listings we found
with an Oak Bluf

After we'd ex
couple left and I
and a plate of na
fee I'd drunk were eating away at the lining
could hear them munching.

So could the bartender, who after a particularly loud growl
gave me a funny look.

I smiled sweetly. "If you could hurry with those nachos?"

I'd always hated snobs.

Maybe because I grew up among people whose idea of culture
was a monster-truck rally followed by super-sized sugar drinks at
the local DQ.

I was pretty sure half of the residents of my hometown—which
I not so fondly called DeadlySpore, New Hampshire—were related. I guessed for some people, inbreeding was a goal; incest,
something to kill the slow passing of rural time.

The evidence was clear, at least to me. Every single class in our
local grammar school and high school had at least one member
of the extensive Brown family.

Maggie Sullivan was a Brown.

Bobby Manigan was a Brown.

Petey Ming, who looked as Asian as his last name, was a Brown;
I don't know how, exactly, but he was.

Basically, you threw a rock, you hit a Brown.

Note to the uninformed: Rock-throwing was a sport of choice

re, as was name-calling, merciless
whole wheat bread instead of Wonder
e-giving.
e, ever participated in any of these sports
d spectator.

r back as I can remember, say from about the age
t different from the infuriatingly dim-witted mo-
y, do morons come in any other kind?—who popu-
e neighborhood where I lived from the time of my birth
day I left MooseDroppings, New Hampshire for school in
ton, Massachusetts.

Addison University. Ah, the haven for wanna-be artistes. (Yeah, use the French pronunciation here.)

Also known as losers.

That's not fair. Not everyone who went to Addison was a loser.

Sure, some started out that way and just perfected the role over time. Everybody knew these kids. Every high school had them. Kids who blustered and swaggered about their Hollywood-style future and somehow, in the end, came running home, proverbial tail between proverbial legs, to take a job tending bar at the local dive. For the rest of their lives.

Other kids started their freshman year at Addison bright-eyed and truly, touchingly optimistic about preparing for a life in The Arts. Then they became losers, usually by the middle of their sophomore year, when they realized they had absolutely no artistic talent whatsoever.

Losers or posers, or a fascinating combination of both.

Me? I started at Addison an eighteen-year-old combination of loser and poser. Pretty impressive, I'd say. Not everyone can pull off such a loathsome personality at so young an age.

Even more impressive—and rare—is that by the end of my four years of higher learning (you know, higher as in "wanna toke, man?"), I was neither a loser nor a poser.

(See? I know how to use neither/nor, either/or. Losers don't know anything about good grammar. They spell grammar "grammer." Posers don't give a crap about good grammar. They have sycophants write their stories for them.)

So, if neither poser nor loser after four years of dopey seminars on the latest fad in acting methods (taught by people whose one and only claim to fame was a television commercial for deodorant) and ridiculously unhelpful internships at the tiny offices of sadly illiterate neighborhood newspapers (whose staff always included a totally bored party boy at the switchboard) and far too many theme parties (such as, Come as Your Favorite Living South American Philosopher!), what, then, was I?

One: Highly unemployable and not proud of it. That made me not a poser.

Two: Possessed of a substandard college education and embarrassed by it. That made me not a loser. And explained my desire to teach myself the rules of grammar.

Still, I knew that if I had to do it all over again—what a joke!—I'd probably be the same jerk I was the first time around. I doubted I'd be enrolled in Harvard or Brown or Northeastern, even knowing at eighteen what I now knew at the ripe old age of twenty-nine.

And counting. Thirty loomed.

Not that calendar year, but on the first day of the next. I missed being the first baby born in WormSlime by three minutes. Nancy Harrison, married to a Brown, delivered a bouncing baby boy at 12:02 A.M., to the eternal frustration of my mother.

I wasn't sure she'd ever forgiven me for being late, let alone for being born.

Anyway, turning twenty-nine had made me think. About age and accomplishment and roads not taken. Yet. The reality was that I'd been working since I was nine, baby-sitting, mowing lawns, running errands for the elderly neighbors.

And then I'd put myself through college.

And then I'd gone on to develop a not-so-terrible career in public television.

Don't get me wrong. I loved to work, even if I didn't have any major assets, liquid or otherwise, to show for my dedication. Student loans ate most of my salary; rent ate another large portion.

The fact was that I was tired. Really tired.

And so I determined that in those last months of relative, if not starry-eyed, youth, I was going to have some fun. Meet a bunch of cute guys. Stay out all night. Sleep all day, at least on the weekends.

Before getting back down to work.

Sitting there all alone at the bar, sipping a beer, I determined to rent a house on Oak Bluffs even if it was the rattiest dump imaginable.

And even if I had to share it with the odd couple.

The blond one, Clare. She looked as if she'd stepped out of the pages of an Eddie Bauer catalog, all scrubbed and healthy. I doubted we had anything at all in common.

And worse, the Pampered Princess, Danielle. With her red nails and her gold necklaces. Seriously not the kind of person who could be my friend.

But then again, who was? I could count my female friends on a fingerless hand.

The nachos finally arrived. I dug right in, slopping guacamole on my shirt. My tummy quieted immediately.

Gincy, I told myself, *this is going to be one hell of a summer.*

Clare
She Can't Say No

I never said no to Win. I wasn't sure I knew how.

"So, get the low-fat milk," he went on, his voice slightly distorted by his speakerphone. "And Clare, sweetie? If you could also pick up my black suit, that'd be great. It won't be ready until five-thirty, but that shouldn't be a problem for you, right?"

Plus, I hadn't told him about the summer house. I didn't want to pick a fight over something as silly as dry cleaning when I knew a truly big fight was to come.

"Sure," I said, folding clean laundry while I held the portable phone between my shoulder and chin. "No problem."

"Thanks, sweetie. You know, with your afternoons free—"

"They're not free, Win," I replied, automatically. We'd been through this so many times. "I have to grade papers and review lesson plans and then there's housework and—"

Win chuckled his indulgent chuckle. "Okay, okay, I get it. Sorry, sweetie. Look, I've got to run. See you later. Oh," he added, as if just remembering. "I probably won't be home until at least nine so grab some dinner for yourself, okay?"

Win lowered his voice; now it held a note of long-suffering. "I have to take this client out for drinks after work. You know how it is."

No. I didn't know how anything was.

But I was beginning to figure things out.

"Sure," I said. "Bye."

We hung up and I finished folding and putting away the laundry. The simple task always gave me a feeling of accomplishment. At least something in this world was clean, neatly folded, and put away just where it had always belonged.

Like my so-called life?

I never could say no to Win, not even at the beginning of our relationship.

To be honest, Win had never asked me to do anything dreadful or dishonest or criminal.

He wasn't abusive. Not in any common sense of the term.

It was just—it was just that he was powerful and I was . . .

Not powerful.

But not stupid, either.

See, I'd finally come to understand that Win had power over me because I allowed him to have power over me.

I'd given it to him from the moment we'd met just over ten years earlier. I hadn't known what I was doing, not really.

And if I had?

At eighteen years of age I welcomed Win—a strong-willed, decisive, career-focused man—into my life with a sigh of relief. Not a literal sigh, you understand.

But having Win around made things easier for me. For example, in spite of my parents and professors pressuring me to think seriously about my future, I had no idea what I wanted to do or be until Win helped me decide on a career in teaching.

I liked being a teacher, very much. What was more, I was a good teacher. I was dedicated and sometimes even inspired. At least, my fifth graders at York, Braddock and Roget seemed to like me.

Win, it seemed, knew me when I didn't even know myself.

There were other reasons for my falling in love with Win Carrington.

I knew he wanted someday to be married and have a family, and I wanted those things, too.

My mother, who'd never worked outside the home, having married just out of college, urged on our budding relationship. Maybe she recognized in Win something of my father, a man who was a stellar family man if you looked at it in terms of financial support.

My father.

Daddy had always loved me, in a formal, distant sort of way. But he never paid much attention to me for the simple reason that I wasn't a boy. James, five years my senior, and Philip, two years older, were his major concerns.

His heirs.

Daddy was so old-fashioned he almost seemed like a character straight out of a Victorian novel. But he was all too real. And quite early on he assigned me to my mother.

His two girls.

Mother chose my clothes and took me to Girl Scout meetings while Daddy brought my two brothers to his beautiful office at the University of Michigan Medical Center where he was chief of urology.

Mother attended my ballet recitals while Daddy took my brothers on fishing trips up north.

Mother taught me how to sew and knit while Daddy encouraged the boys to excel in school and sports.

Nothing changed this dynamic until I started to date Win. Suddenly, I became visible to my father. Suddenly, I was worth his personal attention.

And the more Win achieved, the higher in Daddy's esteem I rose. At least it seemed that way to me.

When Win was accepted at Harvard Law, Daddy took us all to Chicago for the weekend.

When Win made Law Review, Daddy gave me a big fat check, as if I'd been the winner of the prize.

And when Win was offered a partner-track position at the law firm of Datz, Parrish and Kelleher, Daddy treated us both to a weekend at Canyon Ranch in the Berkshires.

Everything was just fine.

Still, not long before that May evening when I committed myself to spending a good part of the summer with two strangers, and in spite of my father's gifts and approbation, something inside me began to change.

I felt as if I was waking up. I felt as if I was falling asleep.

And for someone who was known for her even keel, this was frightening.

I'd feel terribly restless, then lethargic; full of nervous energy, then barely able to get out of bed.

My favorite pastimes, like knitting and power-walking along the river, suddenly held no interest.

I started to screen all calls so that I wouldn't have to fake a good humor.

I lost what little sex drive I'd had.

Clare Jean Wellman. I'd always been the girl who was so pleasant and easy to please.

But suddenly, I felt all discontent.

And angry. But I wasn't sure why.

Sad, too, but I couldn't identify the source of the sadness.

Win didn't seem to notice my altered mood and behavior. At least, he didn't say anything to me about it. I guess I was grateful for that. Strange, but true.

I was grateful for his oblivion, or what passed for it.

I started searching out articles in popular women's magazines on mood swings and hormonal shifts, on something astrologers call the Saturn Return, and finally, on depression.

But members of the Wellman family didn't go to therapy.

Besides, I asked myself time and again, why did I need therapy? I had a steady job, a good family, a nice home.

I had Win.

Maybe, I came to think, there's nothing wrong with me.

Maybe . . .

And then, one day while flipping through a magazine called *New England Homes,* I saw a promotional article about Martha's Vineyard and it occurred to me, just like that, that I could go away for a while.

By myself. At least, without Win.

Classes ended in mid-June and the fall semester didn't start until after Labor Day.

Why did I have to stay in Boston when I could be somewhere closer to nature?

I missed spending time in the country and being by the water. It wasn't my choice to live in a big city. But Win had made his decision, New York or Boston, and I'd chosen Boston as the lesser of two urban evils.

A summer in the heat of the city? Or a summer by the seashore?

Besides, Win worked such dreadfully long hours and I knew he'd be starting a major case sometime in August, which meant we wouldn't be able to take a vacation together anytime soon.

The idea was tantalizing. Going away without Win.

I felt as if I had a dirty, thrilling secret.

For two days I did nothing more but fantasize about spending part of the summer without Win.

And then I saw a sign taped to a streetlight, a sign advertising the housemate event at George.

And there it was. Just like that I made a verbal commitment to share a summer house in Oak Bluffs with two strangers.

What had I done?

I asked myself this question over and over again on the way home to our spacious loft on Harrison Avenue in the South End. It became a chant in my head, matching my footfalls: *What have I done, oh, what have I done.*

I passed a tiny, bustling restaurant called The Dish on the corner of Shawmut. It was a balmy evening and several diners were seated at the small tables on the sidewalk.

At one table sat a woman alone, her pug resting at her feet. She was about forty-five and simply dressed; she looked content and relaxed.

I could never do that, I thought. *Eat alone at a restaurant.*

Or could I?

I spent an awful lot of time alone for someone with a live-in boyfriend.

It would be nice, I thought, *to work up the nerve to actually do more on my own, like enjoy a warm spring evening at a friendly local restaurant.*

The woman caught my eye as I passed, and smiled. I returned her smile, awkwardly, and walked on.

Courage, Clare, I told myself. *Taking this house for the summer is a step in the right direction. It's a step toward independence.*

That's what you want, right?

Independence?

But what does Win want for you? a teeny voice questioned.

He wouldn't be pleased with my plan, that much I knew for sure. The real question was: Would I have the nerve to stand up to his desires?

In other words, would I have the nerve to say no to him and yes to me?

I stopped at Foodie's, a midsized market across from the big cathedral, for Win's milk and for something prepared for my dinner.

And as I waited for the plastic container of macaroni and cheese, I thought about the two women who'd likely be my housemates.

Danielle seemed okay. She was a bit flashier than most of the people I knew but she seemed like a nice person.

I liked nice people.

Niceness, I'd always thought, was an underrated quality.

Gincy?

Well, I was a bit worried about her. About how we'd get along. Already I could sense that she was a bit pugilistic. Kind of a trouble-maker. Kind of wild.

Maybe, I thought, *I should reserve any further judgment until we all meet again.*

I paid for the groceries and, juggling a white plastic bag and Win's dry-cleaned suit, headed over to Harrison Avenue.

All anxiety aside, I was excited. On some level I really didn't care what Win thought about my plan. And that brought a sense of freedom, something I don't think I'd ever felt before.

I took a deep breath and for a moment imagined I was on the beach, alone with the stars and moon and pounding black surf.

My life suddenly seemed very scary.

And quite possibly, very wonderful.

Danielle
She Likes Herself

I t wasn't my fault that I was late for the meeting.

I mean, in the business world, what meeting ever starts exactly on time?

I'll tell you. None. Not many.

I'd been the senior administrative assistant at the Boston offices of a large construction firm for seven years and I'd seen my share of meetings.

Not even engineers, known for being all precise and focused, are on time for meetings. Not always.

So who would expect a meeting of random twenty- and thirty-somethings with some money to spend on a nice summer vacation—a meeting held at a totally casual bar like George—to begin exactly at six o'clock?

Please.

Most people in my office, located near Northeastern's attentuated urban campus, didn't even leave the building until at least six-thirty. So they told me because I made sure to be out of there no later than five. I didn't make enough money to work until seven.

That was my husband's job.

At least, it would be when I found him.

Anyway, I left the office that day at five on the dot, per usual, giving myself plenty of time to take a leisurely stroll through the mall on my way from Huntington Avenue over to Boylston Street, almost up by the Gardens. It was a very nice day in late May and for a moment I considered avoiding a shortcut through the mall in favor of a bit of fresh air.

And then a disgusting bus roared by, belching thick black smoke, while I waited for a traffic light, and I thought: *What? I should destroy my lungs more than they're already destroyed by this foul city air?*

No thank you.

I suppose I didn't have to walk through the entire mall. It did take me out of my way.

And I suppose I didn't actually have to detour upstairs. But I did and that's when it happened. I saw the cutest pair of slides in the window of Nine West and they just called out to me.

"Danielle Leers!" they cried. "Look at us! Just imagine yourself wearing us to dinner at Davio's."

Well, as any self-respecting woman will tell you, when a pair of fabulous shoes cries out to you, you march right inside the shop and you try them on.

Of course, the slides looked spectacular on my feet, especially with the Raspberry Royale I was wearing on my toenails.

Sure, once summer came I'd be wearing Sassy Strawberry, but I was expert enough to know my color matches—without the help of *InStyle* magazine.

I bought the slides. And when I left the store, feeling that special after-purchase glow, I suddenly remembered that I'd forgotten all about the summer-house rental meeting.

I checked my watch to see it was already six and, with a shrug, headed off toward the closest exit. I figured it was better for me to stick to the streets if I were to make the meeting at all.

Which I didn't. Because by the time I got to George the meeting was over and everyone was hooked up with housemates but for me and two other girls who'd come in late.

Well, long story short the three of us decided to just go to the Vineyard and hope to find something decent to rent.

So there I was, committed to sharing a house—well, at least to trying to find a house—with two total strangers.

Neither of whom seemed anything like me at all.

Maybe, I thought, that was a good thing.

Maybe it would be fun to hang out with the one named Clare. She was okay. Her clothes were a bit bland but at least her hair was nicely, though simply, done. And she had a boyfriend, so she'd be no competition.

Though I did wonder why she was renting a house without said boyfriend.

The other one, Gincy? I wasn't so sure about her. The girl's hair was a disaster. And she hadn't been wearing any jewelry. Unless you counted ratty little silver studs in her ears as jewelry. Which I did not.

Still, she'd be no competition, either. No man I'd want to date would ever in his right mind want to date that mess of a girl.

In the end, it didn't really matter how well I got along with my two housemates. I wasn't renting a summer house to make new girlfriends.

Actually, I'd never been much for girlfriends.

True, I kept in touch with a few girls I grew up with in Oyster Bay. That's on Long Island, part of New York. We e-mailed on occasion and I saw them whenever I went home to visit my family.

But I didn't have a lot in common with Amy and Michelle and Rachel. Not only because they were all married and I wasn't.

I'd kind of been different from the start.

Like, I was the only one of the group to leave home for college.

While Amy and Rachel attended a local community college and Michelle made the commute to and from New York University every day (her parents didn't want her to live in the dorms), I went off to Boston University and majored in communications with a minor in art history.

For four years I flew home to Long Island for holidays and for summers and, though I always had a nice time, I was always happy to get back to Boston and my own life.

Then, as graduation drew closer, it became clear that my parents assumed I'd be returning home to find a job in New York.

I rebelled against the notion.

I loved my family. But I didn't want to start my so-called adult life under their gaze. They'd given me enough grief about going to Boston for college, but I'd stuck to my guns. I'd needed to be alone, to grow.

And there was just no way I could go home after those four years.

My privacy had become too important.

Amy, Michelle, and Rachel were each married by the age of twenty-three.

My father hinted that maybe I might want to marry, too.

My mother wondered what was wrong with those stiff New Englanders that they couldn't tell a lovely young woman when they saw one.

Honestly, I was in no hurry to marry. At first.

Which brings me back to the summer house. I had chosen to rent a place in Oak Bluffs because I couldn't afford to take a house on Nantucket or one of the super-expensive areas of the Vineyard, like Edgartown.

I knew I could ask my parents for money. They'd give it to me, but first they'd try to get me to drop the idea of a house and come home for a few weeks that summer.

And I didn't want to do that. Their love could be so overwhelming. I'd never stopped being afraid that I would get lost in their emphatic embrace.

And it was someone else's embrace that interested me.

I was taking a summer house in the first place because it was time to find a husband.

A husband worthy of Danielle Sarah Leers.

Who was Danielle Sarah Leers that fateful summer? Let me tell you a bit about her.

Height: five feet, four inches tall. Just right.

Coloring: medium olive complexion, brown eyes, and perfectly arched eyebrows, thanks to Studio Salon.

Hair: thick and dark brown; I liked to wear it to my shoulders and it was always perfectly groomed.

Figure: some had called me voluptuous. Others said that I resembled a young Sophia Loren.

Or a Catherine Zeta-Jones.

Or, on one of my best days, a Jennifer Lopez.

Really. People told me this. You can ask my mother.

Once, a very long time ago, a guy had the nerve to tell me I was a smidgen too fat. I told him to take a leap. What I looked like was my business and my business only. He tried to backpedal and claim he meant the fat remark as a compliment, but it was too late. He was history in my book.

See, I'd always believed that self-esteem was a very good quality to have. I owed mine to my parents. They taught me early on that I was beautiful and intelligent and entirely worthy of happiness and love and social success.

They taught, and I listened. I might not have listened so well all the time at school, especially during geography and social studies—like I've ever had my day ruined by not being able to find, I don't know, Uruguay, on a map! But at home I listened very carefully.

It wasn't that I was full of myself. I'd known girls who were full of themselves and they were just insufferable. Insufferable was, is, and always will be unacceptable. But I did advocate feeling good about myself. Feeling worthy of good things.

Why not?

As my grandmother was fond of saying, "You're dead a long time."

Think about it.

Anyway, I didn't worry obsessively about an extra pound or two. I knew I was beautiful with or without the pound.

And I didn't tolerate anything less than total gentlemanly behavior from men.

I went for regular massages and facials and had a manicure and pedicure every two weeks. Once, someone at the office asked me why I bothered to have my toenails done during the winter.

"It's not sandal weather," she pointed out. "No one sees your toes."

"Correction," I replied. "I see my toes. And I'm the one that matters."

Since high school I'd worn only yellow gold, never silver. Not that I hated silver; it's just that I'd decided to have a trademark, a signature style. And I'd learned early on that every woman should have a personal jeweler, someone she trusted.

Every woman, I believed, should have a lot of things all for herself. It all came back to self-esteem.

It all came back to self-respect.

It made me want to scream when I saw women allowing themselves to be trampled by men who wanted them to pay for their own dinner, men who didn't call when they said they were going to call, men who wore sweatpants in public.

I thought: *What is the world coming to when this bad behavior is allowed?*

Here was the thing: You gave men an inch, they took a mile. You had to set boundaries. You had to make them play by the rules. And if they didn't want to play by the rules, they were out of the game. Period.

I considered myself a good person.

I donated the previous season's clothes to a homeless shelter. You know, the mistakes, the pieces you just shouldn't have bought.

Not that I made many mistakes.

At the end of each year I wrote a check to the Women's Lunch Place.

"When you have as much as we do," my father often said, "you should give a little back."

Someday, I'd think, *when I have children, I'll teach them what my parents taught me. I'll make sure they're proud and strong and generous, and then happiness and success will follow.*

At least, that's what I was told should happen. Sometimes I had my doubts about the happiness part. Not that I talked about those doubts or anything.

Though I had doubts, I did have faith, of a sort. My family didn't keep kosher or go to synagogue, but on the high holy days we did gather for the special meals. The women cooked and the men sang and read some prayers.

Most of which I didn't understand because I'd never taken Hebrew in school.

Please. There was enough in life to keep track of, what with a job and a social life.

Still, I'd always felt that tradition was important and vowed that when I married, my husband and I would instill the importance of tradition in our children.

Back again to the topic of a husband.

I had a plan once, a long time ago, to meet Mr. Right by the age of twenty-five or so.

Maybe it wasn't so much of a plan as a felt certainty. I just never thought I wouldn't meet Mr. Right by my midtwenties.

But there I was, twenty-nine and single. And turning thirty that summer, August tenth.

Thirty.

I could hardly believe it.

Suddenly, I was very, very aware that many of the other women on the streets of Boston were younger than me. I took to scrutinizing them, the clarity of their skin, the thickness of their hair, the brightness of their teeth, the firmness of their flesh.

Rivals. Dangerous rivals.

Not that I'd lost confidence in myself, but . . .

Face it. Thirty is old for a woman.

Danielle, I told myself, *it's high time you got down to business. It's high time you tied the knot.*

Marriage was a sign of maturity, right? It said to the world, "Look, I'm an adult. I can talk about mortgages and gutters and snowblowers and property taxes and in-laws and school systems and life insurance with the best of them. With my parents."

Marriage was an end to childhood or a prolonged adolescence or something.

It was an end to something.

Well, I was ready to put an end to something.

I was ready to be an adult.
I was ready to join the club.
Now, all I had to do was find Mr. Right.
No big deal, I told myself. He was out there somewhere.
And he was going to love me in my new slides.

Clare

Nothing Can Stop Her

Win wasn't happy about the summer house.

I hadn't expected him to be. Still, his disapproval scared me a little.

Win would never hit me. It wasn't that. It was the look in his eye, the steely look, the look that seemed to cut me off from his consideration.

We were in the expensive, state-of-the-art kitchen Win had chosen for our expensive, state-of-the-art new home.

"If you're worried about the money," I said, "I'll pay for the house out of my parents' allowance."

The look intensified. "Don't ever doubt my capacity to support the both of us," he said, in a low, cold voice. "I'm the man in this relationship. Don't ever forget that."

What could I say? I turned away from him, picked up a dish towel, and began to dry the silverware.

"Clare, why do you insist on doing the dishes by hand?" Win sounded exasperated. "We have a Bosch to do that."

I whirled around. "You're always too busy to spend time with me anyway. What does it matter if I go away for a while?"

Or if I like to wash the dishes myself?

"It matters because—" Win stopped. Changed tactics.

Now his voice would be cajoling. Calculated to calm.

He came close and put his hand on my shoulder. "Sweetie, why don't you go home, spend the summer with your mother."

Why? So she can keep an eye on me?

"I'm taking the house." I moved out from under his touch. "You can't stop me from doing this, Win."

Win took a deep breath before delivering his prediction. "Mark my words, Clare, you'll regret this. But you know what? If you don't want to take my advice, fine. I'm just trying to stop you from making a big mistake."

You're just trying to stop me from living my life.

Win went back to his laptop, to some document he had to review for work. I went into the bedroom and sat on the edge of the bed.

It occurred to me again that I was so alone. I had no friends other than the wives of some of Win's colleagues.

And they weren't really friends. Not the kind I remembered from grammar school, the close friends, the kind you giggled with, the kind who knew your family almost as well as you did, the kind who knew how you liked to eat ice cream straight from the container.

An hour later, Win came to bed. I was under the covers, still in my clothes. We didn't speak.

Don't ever go to bed angry. That was one of my mother's favorite pieces of relationship advice. She swore she and Daddy had never gone to bed without first making up.

I thought she was lying.

Gincy
You Can Never Go Home

I don't know why I called home.
It's not like my parents ever called me.

Hardly ever.

It's not like I really had anything to say to them.

Stuff about my job, they didn't understand. Stuff about my personal life, I didn't want them to know. Not that anything so steamy was going on at the moment.

Still.

I called from the office the next afternoon, using my calling card. I wasn't in the habit of abusing the office phone or e-mail or copy machines, unlike some people whose names I will not mention.

For instance, my office buddy Sally. She was kind of an after-work friend, too, though at that point we hadn't hung out often. Only three times. And she'd instigated each of those drunken evenings.

Good kid, in spite of her carefully calculated tough-as-nails appearance.

"Mom? It's Gincy. Calling from Boston."

Had to rub that in, didn't you? My better self shook its head, ashamed.

"Hello, Virginia," replied my grim mother. "Is anything wrong? I hope you don't need money because we just don't have any to send you, what with—"

I rolled my eyes for the benefit of nobody. "Mom! No, I don't want money. God. Can we please just have a normal conversation? Jeez."

"I wish you wouldn't use that language, Virginia. You know how I feel about bad language."

Yeah, I thought. *Which is why it pours out of my mouth when we talk. Can't help it, Mom. That's what you do to me.*

"How are you, Mom," I said, shoving aside the urge to staple my hand to the desk. It would take my mind off the pain of this conversation. "How's Dad?"

"Oh, we're fine, what would be wrong, except for the money—"

"How's Tommy?"

My brother, just twenty-five, had forgone college for an exciting life as a check-out boy at the local Harriman's, a giant food store. We'd never gotten along, even when we were kids. Tommy had a mean streak. And, worse, though he acted plenty dumb, I suspected he was actually fairly bright. Just lazy. And I abhorred laziness.

Mom sighed. "Seeing some piece of trash he picked up in TreeStump. That town produces more garbage—"

Of course, nothing was ever Tommy's fault. His slutty girlfriend, the bad-influence best friend, the cops who had nothing better to do than arrest a young boy just sowing his wild oats. They were all to blame for Tommy's miserable life.

"Oh!" my mother was saying. "I do have some news."

The basement flooded again because you're too cheap to install a French drain or whatever it's called that prevents the flooding of basements?

"You remember your cousin Jody?"

How could I not? The kid had been a poop-throwing terror.

"Uh, yeah, Mom. I used to baby-sit her."

"Oh, yes. Well, she's dropping out of high school to have a baby!"

Now there's an interesting career choice, I noted.

"Who's the father?" I asked, as if I would know the little shit. "Is she getting married?"

"Well, of course, Virginia! Uncle Mike wouldn't dream of letting his daughter live in sin or his grandchild be a bastard. What can you be thinking? FrogPiddle is not the big city, you know."

There was absolutely nothing I could say to all that, so I radically changed the subject. "Guess what, Mom? I'm renting a house on Martha's Vineyard for the summer. With two other women. Right by the beach. A house."

There was silence for a moment.

Then: "Does that mean you won't come home for Jody's wedding?"

And there it was.

What had I expected? My mother to be happy for me?

"Put Dad on, Mom."

The conversation with my father was brief. I told him about my plans.

"Guess we won't see you this summer, then," he commented. "You be careful all on your own out there on some island."

Yeah, Dad, I'll watch for sea monsters. I hear they rise from the deep with every full moon . . .

"I'll be fine, Dad."

I always am.

I hung up and rubbed my eyes. Damn flourescent lights. And in the middle of the buzzing office, phones ringing, computers dinging, voices calling, I suddenly felt very, very alone.

And then, there was Sally. In all her chopped, purple-haired splendor.

"Hey," she said, staring at the bulletin board above and behind my head. "You want to grab a beer after work?"

I noted a new nose piercing.

"Sure," I said. "Thanks."

Danielle

The Single Daughter

The call wasn't as bad as I'd expected.

My mother lamented and wailed a little, but after I assured her that Martha's Vineyard was popular with eligible bachelors—not only gay men—she accepted my summer plans with a sigh.

"At least," she said, "you won't be wasting your time, having fun to no purpose. Danielle, I'm so glad you've decided to settle down and get married."

"Well," I said, nerves tightening, "I do have to find the man first, Mom."

"Ppff!" my mother sounded. I could picture the flip of her plump hand in the air, dismissing the silly little obstacle. "Like that will be a problem? Look at you! You're gorgeous. Any man in his right mind would die to marry you."

In his right mind.

Note to self: Watch out for lunatics.

"Thanks, Mom. Is Dad there?"

The very first thing he said was: "You know, your mother would love if you came home for a couple of weeks this summer. You can't do that?"

There it was. The guilt.

"I signed a lease, Dad," I lied. "Besides—"

"You know, David will want to see you. Him and that fiancée, what's her name?"

"Roberta."

Why had Dad always pretended to forget the names of every one of David's girlfriends?

"Maybe David will come and visit me on the Vineyard," I added, knowing Dad had at least one more guilt card up his sleeve.

"What about your poor old dad, did you think of him?" my father said, his tone now half-teasing. "You don't love him anymore? You found someone else you love more than your father?"

This was always the killer. I was my Daddy's little girl, though unlike lots of other females I'd tried hard never to take advantage of that.

"Oh, Dad, of course not. You know you'll always be number one with me. It's just that—"

"Danielle, go, have a good time. I'm only being silly, just joking around. You're a young woman, a beautiful girl, you should be out having fun."

"I'll be home for my birthday," I said, tears prickling my eyes. "In August. For a weekend."

"My little girl, thirty years old." Dad sighed. "You're making me an old man!"

"You're not old, Dad," I said, thinking: *My dad isn't old, is he?* Sixty-five. That wasn't old by modern standards, was it?

"Well, I'm getting old, and thank God. You know why?"

The comfort of the familiar. Also, the dread.

"Because if you weren't getting old you'd be dead," I recited.

Dad chuckled. "Exactly right! Now, go, have fun at the beach."

I promised I would try.

Gincy

Inauspicious Start

I suppose we could have taken the plunge and rented a house sight unseen.

Trusted the broker. Believed her tall tales.

In the end it wouldn't have mattered much. By the time we were ready to rent, all that remained on the market for summer was crap. At least in Oak Bluffs.

Our broker mentioned a few little compounds on the Tisbury Great Pond. No electricity. Dubious plumbing. Spectacular views. Lots of peace and quiet.

"We're not interested in peace and quiet," Danielle announced. Turning to me and Clare, she whispered, "And the only view that interests me is the view of a well-muscled, masculine chest!"

It hadn't taken me long to notice that on occasion Danielle lapsed into romance-novel language.

The weather didn't help sell us on the place, either. The day was chilly, wet, and gray. I'd neglected to wear a jacket over my short-sleeved T-shirt. My arms were prickled with goosebumps.

I wondered: Was the Vineyard worth the grief? It wasn't like it was easy to get to, compared to say, the Cape. First we had to take a bus to Falmouth and from there, the ferry to Oak Bluffs.

Maybe, I thought, I should just bag the whole idea of a summer place and spend weekends and days off taking day trips in a rental car to places like Sturbridge Village and the Louisa May Alcott house in Concord. Or was it Lexington?

Oh, yeah. Like I was gonna have some dirty fun in any of those places.

"Girls, not for nothin'," Terri was saying, "but listen to me. I'm not just tawkin for tawkin over heah. You don't have a choice, this late. You take this or, believe me, you'll be sayin', my gawd, we should'uv listened to Terri."

"Are you from Brooklyn?" I asked.

"Yeah, so?" Terri looked at me warily, like I was going to rat her out on some old neighborhood crime.

I shrugged. "Just wondering. I like to see if I can place accents."

"What accent? Anyways, do we have a deal? Huh?"

It could have gone either way. I mean, the house was pretty lousy even by my low standards. A lacy Victorian folly? No way. More like a shack gone to seed.

Two minuscule bedrooms, more glorified closets than actual rooms. Which was interesting, as there were no closets. A refrigerator circa 1965 or so. A smell of must so heavy we'd be airing out the place for months to come. A couch that even I wouldn't sit on without first spreading a clean sheet. And spraying several cans of Febreze.

The good thing about the house? It was in Oak Bluffs.

And Oak Bluffs was a pretty funky place. It had a history of Revivalism, which had something to do with the Methodists, a group that scared the bejesus out of Catholics and the more mainstream Protestant types.

Revivalism and all it meant somehow led to a profusion of late-nineteenth-century wooden houses built in the Carpenter Gothic style, and to the growing popularity of Oak Bluffs as a vacation spot for the average, middle-class American.

I didn't know how the history all worked but I did know that Oak Bluffs still featured a vibrant and affluent African-American community.

And that it had a lot of bars.

Danielle wrinkled her nose. "The kitchen is kind of dirty."

"I can clean it," Clare said promptly. "I mean, it has to be done."

"How much cooking are we going to do, anyway?" I said. "I'm thinking we'll be hanging out most of the time."

Where are you getting the money for all that hanging out? an annoying little voice in my head asked.

Shut up, I told it.

Danielle had another problem. "The paint's all peely."

"On the outside. Who cares?"

"Uh, maybe it's got lead in it?"

"And you're going to sit around eating paint chips?" I shot back.

"I'm just pointing out."

Terri shrugged.

"The bathroom is awfully small," Clare noted, tapping her chin with a finger.

"We'll use it one at a time," I replied.

Terri sighed. "Lookit, whaddaya gonna do? It ain't a palace. You can afford a palace, you don't come to Oak Bluffs. This is all I'm sayin'."

"That's all she saying, Clare. Danielle. Come on," I urged, even though I was still a bit unsure how I felt about taking the plunge.

Let's consider this again, Gincy. Summer weekends on the beach? Or a week in FernSpore to attend the wedding of a pregnant teen and other similarly high-class family functions?

What, was I crazy?

"Are we going to do this or not?" I said.

We stood on the tiny, rickety porch, looking at each other with tentative expressions, when suddenly, Danielle's eyes darted over my shoulder, and before I could move out of the way, she gripped my arm. Her long, painted nails were like razors.

"Ow!" I cried, yanking away. "God, you're like Vampira! Watch it with those talons."

"Sorry," she mumbled, eyes still fixed at a point down the street. "Girls, you just have to see this. Oh. Oh. Oh."

"What?" I asked irritably, turning to see what had caught her eye.

And there It was. God's gift to women. And men. Freakin' everything with eyes.

At least, the physical ideal. And in bike shorts, too. Damn.

"Oh, that just can't be real," I said. "Can it?"

The guy was coming our way and had seen us gaping at him. He didn't seem to mind the attention, if his grin and attitudinal strut were any indication.

Broad shoulders, trim waist, flat stomach, muscled legs, and, you just knew, a great butt.

"He is pretty handsome," Miss Perfect-with-a-Boyfriend said.

"Pretty handsome?" I shrieked. "Are we looking at the same guy? He's the sexiest thing I've ever seen!"

"Not a thing," Clare corrected. "A person. And yes. He is sexy."

Danielle winked and the Adonis winked back. "Hetero. Definitely."

"So?" Terri prodded with a loud clack of her gum.

What was she doing on the Vineyard anyway? Shouldn't she be filming *My Cousin Vinny Part II*?

"You want the house or not? You don't want, I've got a nice young couple who might just be interested. I—"

"We'll take it," Clare blurted. Then she looked at me and Danielle with her big baby blues. "Right?"

Danielle looked at me and nodded. "Right."

Take the plunge, Gincy.

Finalize a major decision based on a hot guy's butt.

Now there's maturity.

"Well, kids," I said, "let the fun begin."

Gincy
Three Girls in a Tub

Needless to say, phone service wasn't included in the deal. Neither were towels and bed linens.

The result was that on the first weekend of our venture, the three of us were loaded down like pack mules: Danielle with matching everything Louis Vuitton (I had to ask); Clare with assorted Vera Bradley, from ditty bag to duffel (I had to ask about that, too); and me with a monstrous blue canvas backpack a cousin had used on various hiking trips (until he fell off a mountain, conveniently leaving his pack behind) and a big black garbage bag tied in a double knot.

The bus was crowded and hot. When it came time to board the ferry, I raced to grab us three seats on deck. Danielle balked at being exposed to the "weather." I reminded her of the smelly first leg of our journey and pointed out that the day was sunny and dry.

She caved and put on a wide-brimmed straw hat she pulled—miraculously uncrumpled—from one of her many bags.

"Well," she said brightly. "So."

"Here we are." Clare smiled tentatively.

I looked from one to the other of my roommates. Disaster from right to left.

What were we thinking, three strangers hooking up for an entire summer?

"Is this going to be the level of conversation this summer?" I asked. "Because if it is, I'm thinking we should make a deal right now. No talking. Ever. Except for essential commands, like 'toss me a beer.' "

Danielle sighed magnificently. "Oh, Gincy. Please. It's just first-date jitters. Except that we're not on an actual date."

"Right," Clare said, looking suddenly all sincere. "We just have to rely on the art of conversation. You know, make appropriate small talk. That will lead to a deeper intimacy."

"We're not in therapy here, you know," I snapped. "And I'm not happy about the 'intimacy' word. Ever. Don't expect me to get all weepy and reveal a dark inner secret about my childhood. Even if I had any dark inner secrets, which I don't. Just so you know."

Clare blushed very pink and stood up from the whitewashed slatted bench on which we sat. "I think I'll go inside—"

Danielle reached for Clare's arm. "Oh, honey, sit down. Gincy's just teasing."

Reluctantly, Clare sat and I shot her a half smile of apology.

"What Clare means, Gincy," Danielle said pointedly, "is that to get a good conversation going among strangers you start with the basics. You know. What's your favorite TV show. Or movie. How do you like your martinis. Who's your favorite designer. How many brothers and sisters do you have. Stuff like that."

"*The Honeymooners. Cool Hand Luke.* Gin, onions, shaken not stirred. What designer? One brother."

"Name?"

"Tommy."

"Older or younger?"

"Younger."

"Are you close?"

"No. He asks too many questions."

Danielle beamed. "See how easy that was? Now we know something about you. Okay, my turn. I love, love, love *Legally Blond,* the first and second movies."

Figures, I thought. *Did this chick even go to college?*

"TV, that's easy. *Will & Grace* because of Grace's clothes, though she's far too skinny—I mean, you can count her ribs!"

And that was a problem Danielle did not have to worry about.

"Martini," she went on. "Lemon or raspberry vodka with olives."

Ugh. Adulterated martinis disgusted me.

Danielle cocked her head and pouted. "The designer question is a tough one," she said. "Where do I begin? I'll just say it depends on my mood. And the season. And how much money I can spend, of course."

Of course. My own clothing budget was—well, it was pretty much nonexistent.

"Siblings: one brother. His name is David and he's thirty-six. He's very handsome and he's a doctor and he's engaged. It'll be a late spring wedding. And I'd better be one of the bridesmaids. And that's me!"

I shrugged. No big surprises from Danielle.

"Clare?" I said, without a trace of challenge in my voice. I still felt kind of bad about scaring her.

"Oh," she said, as if surprised she had been included in the silly game. "Okay. Well, I don't watch TV much. But I guess if I had to say . . . I guess I'd say *Murder, She Wrote.* Remember, with Angela Lansbury as Jessica Fletcher? It's on a cable channel. Repeats, of course."

Clare's favorite TV show featured a widowed senior citizen? Okay. Maybe Danielle did have a point about simple questions revealing complex clues to the self.

"How nice," Danielle said blandly, crossing her already tanned legs. Maybe they just looked so tan because of the white shorts she was wearing. I made a mental note to check her bathroom supplies for spray-on tan.

"That's very . . . nice."

Clare seemed oblivious to our dismay. "I have several favorite movies," she went on. "I'm not sure I could pick just one. Each one has its own merits, of course."

"I'm sure they do, honey. Just pick one from, say, the top ten. Off the top of your head. Just, you know, without thinking."

Did Clare ever speak without, you know, thinking? I wondered.

"Well, all right. Then, *It's a Wonderful Life*. And *On Golden Pond.*"

"Fine. Martini preference?" *And don't say chocolate,* I warned silently.

"I don't drink martinis. And I don't really pay attention to designers."

Here, Clare pulled lightly on the fabric of her short-sleeved, pink polo shirt. "I mean, I buy quality clothes that never go out of fashion. Classics, I guess. Usually from Talbots. L.L. Bean. Sometimes Ann Taylor. But I only go shopping twice a year. There are always so many other things to do, you know?"

Danielle lowered her massive white sunglasses and peered warily at Clare. "Like what?" she said.

"Well, like read. Or knit. I love to knit. Or grade papers. Or power-walk along the river. Or do the chores, like pick up Win's suits and shirts from the dry cleaners and buy the groceries. And handwrite letters to my family back in Michigan, which is so much more personal than typing. And—"

"We get it," I said. Danielle looked too horror-stricken to stop the madness. "What about siblings?"

"I have two older brothers, James and Philip. James is an orthopedic surgeon. He's married and has a two-year-old named James, Jr."

How original, I thought nastily. *And how self-congratulatory.*

Not that I ever had strong opinions or anything.

"And Philip?" Danielle inquired.

"Philip is a communications director for a big pharmaceutical company."

"Is there a Mrs. Philip?"

Clare's eyes shifted to the horizon. "Well, yes, but . . ."

"But what?" Danielle asked eagerly.

Ah, I thought. Watch what you say around this one. She craves juicy gossip.

"Well, she asked for a separation, but Philip hasn't agreed to it yet. She said Philip spends too much time at the office and not enough at home, with her. But he's the one who makes the money." Clare turned back to us, pleading in her voice. "Doesn't she understand that he's only doing what he has to do?"

"Maybe," I said, "he doesn't have to do it so excessively. Maybe she'd like it better if they had less money but more intimacy."

What the hell was I saying?

Clare shook her head. "But they're trying to have a baby. And babies cost lots of money these days."

"Yeah," I snapped, "if you treat them like freakin' royalty. When I was a kid—"

"Does Mrs. Philip have a career?" Danielle asked, cutting off what was sure to have been a tirade on one of my pet subjects.

"No. She married Philip right after she graduated from college. She's only twenty-five. She's been home trying to get pregnant."

I swear Clare delivered that bit of information without a trace of sarcasm.

Danielle cleared her throat and adjusted her hat, which, as far as I could see, didn't need adjusting.

"Unless I'm seriously out of touch with contemporary culture," I said, "Mrs. Philip needs Mr. Philip at home with her for that particular task. What does she do while she's waiting for him to show up?"

"She runs errands, I suppose. They have a housekeeper. I don't know. Maybe she volunteers." Clare lowered her voice, as if anyone cared about this silly exchange. "Honestly? I think I'd go out of my mind if I didn't have a job to go to. If I weren't being productive somehow."

Danielle sighed. "No wonder your brother spends so much time at the office. Honey, don't take offense, but I think what Mrs. Philip needs isn't Mr. Philip, it's a life. Of her own. Now, before it's too late. That's just my opinion."

"There's never been a divorce in the Wellman family," Clare retorted, as if that put an end to that discussion.

Which it did, because then there was a lull in the chatter. Lulls drive me nuts. They make me feel like I'm failing to hold up my part of the social bargain. They make me feel responsible for everyone's entertainment.

Okay, I thought, standing and stretching. Now what?

"I'm going to get a soda," I said, suddenly eager to be alone. "Does anyone—"

But I wasn't about to get away so easily.

"Here," Danielle said. "I've got bottled water for everyone. Sit down, Gincy. I have another fun question."

Grudgingly, I sat. And accepted the free water. Free stuff was good.

"What's the question?" Clare looked as dubious as I felt.

"Okay. Here goes. Who's the most recent person you've had a sex dream about?" Danielle looked as if she was dying to share her own juicy nocturnal adventures.

I was not. But she wanted conversation? She was going to get conversation.

"That's easy," I said, wiping water from my chin with the back of my hand. "Hank Hill."

"Excuse me, what?" she said. "Hank Hill? As in the 'star' of *King of the Hill*? Hank Hill the cartoon character with the saggy gut and bad glasses?"

"Look, it was a dream, okay?" I shrugged elaborately. "You can't help what you dream. Your head gets all weird when you sleep."

"His character is very upstanding," Clare offered. "Except for always wanting to kick people's asses, he's very socially acceptable."

"I thought you didn't watch TV?"

"Well, not a lot of TV. See, Win stays late at work several times a week so, well, I guess lately I've gotten into the habit of watching TV while I eat dinner. It's—It's not so lonely that way."

You don't have to apologize for watching TV, I almost said. But didn't.

"Was he good?" Danielle asked.

"What?"

"Was he good in bed?" Danielle repeated. "Was the dream worth it?"

"Oh. Well," I admitted, "nothing actually happened. You know, sexually. It was more like I was attracted to this guy and then I realized he was Hank Hill, but a real guy, not a cartoon. He was a teacher in a boarding school. So was I, come to think of it. And then he had a nervous breakdown."

"Before anything sexual could happen?" Clare asked.

She looked truly interested in my answer. Maybe she had a secret crush on Hank Hill.

Hmmm.

Jessica Fletcher, New England-based mystery writer and amateur sleuth, and Hank Hill, a tall Texan specializing in propane and propane accessories.

Interesting.

"Right," I confirmed.

Danielle sighed. "Gincy, honey, you are one weird chick. Clare, your turn."

Clare squirmed in her seat. "Oh, this is silly," she said, "but I had a dream once about Niles, from *Frasier*. It was very romantic. He was a total gentleman. He never even took off his suit jacket. We didn't, you know. We just had dinner."

"Niles Crane is no Hank Hill," I pointed out. "I'll take a T-shirt over a suit jacket any day."

"Am I the only one on this bench who actually has sex dreams that involve actual sex?" Danielle demanded.

"Okay, kiddo," I said, "let's have it. Who have you been boinking in REM sleep? You've been dying to tell us since this conversation started. Spill."

Danielle preened. "Well," she said, "I had a totally hot dream about Dr. Phil. He was a-ma-zing. First—"

"The bald TV psychiatrist?" I blurted.

"Now you're making fun of bald? You fantasize about a cartoon character."

"He's also kind of fat," Clare said.

"And this from the girl who fantasizes about a nonexistent

person," Danielle said. "A TV character. Niles Crane isn't real. Dr. Phil is."

And so the journey passed. It took only about forty-five minutes but it felt much, much longer.

If this is what friendship is about, I thought, maybe I should throw myself overboard now.

Gincy
She Is What She Is

That evening, after having unpacked and picked up a few basic groceries, the three of us decided to go to a popular restaurant called Truce and to split up after dinner. In case any one of us wanted to do something the others didn't.

Danielle came out of the bathroom with hair bigger than any I'd ever seen on Jennifer Lopez.

"Whoa!" I said, feeling my own measly mop.

Someone had told me that if I bothered to style it I could look very gamine. I knew what that meant but I pretended not to know. Sometimes I can be quite perverse.

"I didn't know you had that much hair!"

"It looks real, doesn't it?" Danielle beamed. "It's a hairpiece! Isn't it fantastic?"

Clare didn't look so sure. "Why are you wearing a hairpiece?" she asked.

"Why aren't you wearing a hairpiece?" Danielle shot back.

Clare? In a hairpiece? Miss straight-and-shiny pageboy, Miss Eddie Bauer catalogue model? I was curious to hear what she had to say.

"Because it's kind of much. That's just my opinion," she added quickly.

Always the peacemaker. The girl needs to cause some trouble, I thought. It would do her a world of good.

Danielle took a sip of the pinkish martini I handed her before retorting. "It's a legitimate accessory. And it wasn't inexpensive."

"I'm sure. It's just that, well, I'd be embarrassed to wear a hairpiece."

"Why?" Danielle demanded. "Why would you be embarrassed if it made you look gorgeous and glamorous?"

"Well, still." Clare kind of squeaked. "I don't think I could be seen in public that way."

"What way? Gorgeous and glamorous? Well, honey, that's your problem."

"I'm naturally suspicious of artifice," Clare admitted.

I grinned. The poor kid. "I wonder. Can you be artificially suspicious of artifice?"

"What's natural, anyway?" Danielle said. "Besides, I don't know, nature. Trees and flowers and rocks. You can't tell me that every decision a person makes isn't about artifice. About selling something, getting a message across."

Clare took a sip of orange juice before speaking. "A starving woman in Ethiopia who has to decide whether to share her family's tiny bit of food with another woman's dying baby isn't thinking about getting a message across. She's thinking about how she'll survive another day in such a dreadful life."

"Well, okay," Danielle admitted, "so let's just talk about people like us, privileged people, people who aren't starving, people who aren't living in refugee tents."

"People choose to wear L.L. Bean instead of Prada," I said, enjoying myself mid-Martini, "because they want everyone to know they're about comfort. Or, I don't know, family values. Vacations on Nantucket with the sailboat and the perfect blond children. Tomatoes and corn on the cob. Weekends in Maine at the family camp. Blueberry pie. Maple syrup."

"I don't dress to send a message to anyone," Clare protested. "I dress for me. I like to be comfortable."

"But your L.L. Bean ensemble is a costume anyway," Danielle said. "A uniform."

"It is not! I've never worn a uniform in my life! Except for my Girl Scout uniform."

Danielle sighed magnificently. "Don't get me started on those uniforms. Anyway, I am so tired of this conversation. Look, all I'm saying is that men appreciate a little artifice. It makes them feel the woman went out of her way to impress them."

"Some men, maybe," Clare said. Self-righteously? "Not the kind of man I want to be with."

Now it was my turn to sigh dramatically. "God, you are boring, Clare."

BANG!

I jumped at the sudden loud noise. Clare had slammed the glass bottle of orange juice on the counter; juice was running down the outside of the bottle and pooling.

"How dare you say that about me!" she cried. "You know nothing about me, nothing! Until a few weeks ago you didn't even know I existed. How can you possibly have the right to judge me?"

It was not the reaction I had expected.

"Hey, look, I'm sorry. I was just goofing around. I thought, you know, you'd just tell me to go stuff myself."

Clare hung her head and I saw her taking a deliberate deep breath. Danielle raised her perfectly arched eyebrows at me.

"Fine," Clare said then. "But I don't think calling people 'boring' is funny. I am the way I am for a reason. For a lot of reasons. I—"

"Okay," I said. "I got it. Really."

A cell phone rang just then.

"It's me," Clare declared, reaching into the pocket of her chino shorts. "It's Win. Hello?"

Danielle and I watched her hurry out onto the raggedy porch.

"Well," Danielle drawled, "there's more to that girl than meets the eye."

Gincy

All by Her Lonesome Lone

"**M**orning, sleepyhead," Danielle singsonged. "I was just about to show Clare my dating system. Grab a cup of coffee and I'll show you, too."

I dragged myself into the kitchen and poured a cup of coffee from the old perk pot we'd found under the sink.

"Who made this?" I grumbled.

I didn't know about my roomies, but I'd been out very late the night before, flirting heavily with a guy at a bar with a crappy pool table. Things were going great until I beat him, in itself a minor miracle as I suck at pool.

Some men just can't handle a strong woman.

"It's too watery," I went on. "And what do you mean you have a system? Why do you need a system to meet men?"

"Duh! It's not a system to meet men. Men are all over the place. The world is lousy with men. It's a system to weed out the losers. To separate the wheat from the chaff. To evaluate potential husbands."

I grunted. Pre-coffee was also pre–witty reply.

"Okay," Clare said musingly. "But it sounds like an awful lot of work."

"Do the work up front and you won't have to do it on the back end."

"The back end?" Clare asked.

"Yes. After the wedding. Make sure they're properly trained right from the start and you avoid problems down the line."

"Men aren't dogs, Danielle," I said, sitting next to Clare at the kitchen table. "Well. You know what I mean.".

Clare shrugged. "I'm kind of curious about this system. Can we see it?"

Danielle looked oh-so-smug. "Of course. You can adopt my basic structure and tailor it to your own particular needs."

And she proceeded to walk us through a binder full of lists and charts. By page five, my eyes had glazed over but Clare, oddly, seemed still interested.

"Under 'Style,' see," Danielle was pointing out, "I've included 'Hair' (natural color & texture, cut, maintenance); 'Clothing' (casual, office wear, formal)—absolutely no white socks except on the tennis court!"

"What about at the gym?" I said.

"Oh. Well, that's okay. As long as I don't have to see them. Or wash them. Anyway, here's 'Personal Grooming' (cologne, nails—length & cleanliness, breath, etc.), and—"

"You're unbelievable!" I burst out, caffeine all kicked in. "You know that?"

Danielle beamed. "I know. Let me tell you, my method is fool-proof. Also, look, I rate his 'Relationship Quotient.' For example: Has he been in a long-term relationship? If so, how long-term was it and why did it end? Has he ever been married? Etcetera."

"What if he doesn't tell you right up front about his past?" Clare asked.

"Well, then I ask him. Of course. I have a right to know."

"And he has a right not to tell," I countered.

"Fine. Then he's not the right man for me. Full disclosure is very important."

A date is not a court of law, I thought, but all I said was: "But—"

"But nothing, Gincy. End of story. He's history. Now, would you like to hear the rest of my categories? I'm always refining the system."

"Uh, no thanks. That's okay." I got up and left my roommates poring over the binder.

I wondered as I walked down the porch steps and headed toward the beach. What had I gotten myself into with these two? They were so totally unlike me. I couldn't imagine we'd get through the summer without a major meltdown.

Truth is, I'd never been very good at making or keeping friends, male or female. I'm not really sure why.

My best friend in grammar school was a doofus named Mark. We were an odd pair, to be sure; Mark chubby and klutzy, me skinny and speedy. But it worked, our friendship, especially since we shared a general cynicism none of the other kids in DeerPlop seemed to have.

When Mark's family moved away just before seventh grade, I was down for about a week until one day I realized I didn't even remember Mark's last name.

Maybe I was just unfit for true friendship. I didn't know.

In sophomore year of high school I struck up a sort of buddyship with the new girl in town, Kathy O'Connell. I never found out why her divorced mother had dragged them both to WormSlime, New Hampshire, where there was virtually no career opportunity of any kind.

But there was Kathy and she was wild. I mean, really bad. I liked her immediately and she liked me. Maybe because I sort of worshipped her. Kathy was who I wanted to be but didn't have the nerve to be. Anyway, I was like her acolyte or something, the driver of the getaway car, her personal assistant in mischief and crime.

Our brief and totally unequal friendship came to a crashing halt when Kathy schemed to break into the Kmart out on the highway one night and see what she could make off with. She was especially interested in the electronics, which she then planned to sell.

I just couldn't go along with her plan. I was ashamed of my cowardice but also kind of proud of my ability to distinguish right from wrong. Kathy was disgusted with me, called me every foul name in the book, and told me never to even look at her again. I kept my promise, which wasn't hard because she was arrested while stuffing a Nikon camera down her pants, and sent off to a juvenile detention center in BarfVille.

Soon after, her mother moved on, ostensibly to be closer to her wayward daughter.

For the rest of high school, I remained pretty much a loner. It didn't bother me. Occasionally I'd go to a movie with some kids, but most of the time I hung at the crummy little library where I could go online on its crummy little computer and pore over its crummy little collection of books on art and film.

Once, I went on a date with a guy home from college for spring break. I don't know why. I wasn't really attracted to him but it seemed an interesting thing to do. It wasn't.

Ah, the ocean. And sand. And a few teeny, white puffy clouds. A view. A vista.

I took a deep, cleansing breath of the fresh morning air. I loved living in the city but the great outdoors definitely had its benefits. Still, I'd stick to the beach, I vowed, plopping down on the sand, still slightly damp with dew. There was plenty of nature back in HorsePoop, New Hampshire, but I was never going back there.

And I wasn't the only one who'd made that vow.

I closed my eyes, let the sun warm my upturned face, and remembered.

When I was a senior in high school I got a letter from a guy named Mark Tremaine. It took me a moment to realize the letter was from my old friend, and not just some prank or misdirected mail. Mark wanted me to know that he'd come out of the closet. I was happy for him for about a minute and then tossed the letter on my mess of a desk. I never saw it again. And it was the last I ever heard from Mark.

When I got to college, I finally experienced the artificial

frenzy of oh-my-god-best-friend-dom. For the first two years of college I had a new best friend approximately every three weeks. Nothing stuck. Probably a good thing.

By junior year I was back to spending a lot of my time alone and enjoying it. After four years at Addison I graduated with nothing more than a handful of passing acquaintances.

Throughout my twenties I continued this habit of not forming or keeping close relationships.

I dated my share of guys but bailed on the few who seemed interested in sticking around.

The office provided a pool of people from whom I could chose companions for the sole purpose of a drink after work. Sally was a fairly recent addition to that list of drinking buddies, and while I liked hanging out with her a couple of hours a week—she was good for a laugh and a verbal wrangle—I never saw us becoming real friends.

Whatever real friends were.

Maybe, I thought, gazing out at the glittering ocean, *I'm a social freak.* Or maybe I was meant to be close—really close—to just one or two people during the course of my lifetime.

If so, I hadn't met that person or those people yet. Clare and Danielle were just not going to fit the bill.

The sun was getting hotter by the minute. It was going to be a scorcher and I'd forgotten to pack sunblock. That was one thing Danielle and Clare were good for. Borrowing things from.

Not that my roomies were horrible or anything. They were okay. A bit odd, but who wasn't? We just had the usual living-with-strangers stuff to work out. Each of us came with a bundle of habits acquired over almost thirty years. That meant approximately ninety years of habits all told, a lot of crap crammed into one leaky old house.

Clare, for example, was very, very neat. Maybe it had something to do with her Midwestern values. I didn't know. I'd never been further west than Chicago. I suspected Danielle and I might be witnessing a borderline obsession with cleanliness.

Danielle, on the other hand, was completely averse to the most basic cleaning chores. The girl had had a housekeeper all her childhood, still had one for her small one-bedroom apartment in Boston.

Wash a dish? Damp mop a floor? Ew. You paid people to do that. Like, maids.

Me? Well, I'd been told by former college suitemates that living with me was like living with a frat guy. I could see why some people would make the comparison.

I did on occasion leave the lights on all night. I did sometimes blare music at odd hours. I did tend to sing loudly and badly in the shower. And once I did forget to put the top back on a container of sour cream.

I still didn't think that one isolated incident should have earned me the nickname Moldy.

Maybe that was the deciding factor. Because come graduation I vowed that I would never, ever have another roommate again. Since then, most of my income had gone toward rent—in other words, down a black hole—but at least I had my privacy and independence.

Except for this summer.

I started back for the house, thinking now of breakfast and a shower. And hoping Danielle wasn't hogging the bathroom. And that Clare hadn't finished the Cheerios.

Well, I thought, as I walked under the strengthening sun, *it doesn't much matter what I think of my roomies or how well we get along. I've signed a lease and now I'm stuck with them.*

Suddenly, I remembered one of my father's many favorite clichés. "When life gives you lemons," he'd tell me, like when I'd get assigned a lousy science lab partner, "make lemonade."

I grinned. With Danielle and Clare as my roommates, I'd need lots and lots of sugar.

Gincy
Musical Sheets

Though I loved the sun and sand, I'd never been much for lazing around on the beach. I'm too full of nervous energy for laying flat in public.

Unless, of course, I'm hung over.

But I agreed to hang with my roomies for a while later that morning while they sunbathed on the Oak Bluffs Town Beach. What else did I have to do?

Face it, Gincy, I told myself, throwing a threadbare towel in a backpack, you're a workaholic. If you're not working, you want to be working.

My father, I thought, *would be so proud. If he really knew anything about me.*

We found a relatively empty section of beach and settled in, Danielle on her plush beach towel and matching chair; Clare on a bright blue mat; and me on half an old sheet.

I watched as Danielle shrugged out of her belted terry cover-up.

"What the hell are you wearing!" I cried. "You look like a World War Two poster girl, you know that? What's-her-name, Lana Turner. You're poured into that bathing suit. And what's up with the torpedo bra?"

Danielle rolled her eyes. "It's a retro look. It's very popular this year. I'm supposed to look like Ava Gardner. Mimi Van Doren. Marilyn Monroe. And it's more a late-forties, early-fifties look, post–World War Two. Have you ever read a fashion magazine in your life?"

"No," I lied. "Never."

They didn't need to know I bought and read, cover to cover, every September issue of *Vogue, Bazaar, Elle,* and *Marie Claire.* It was cultural research, that's all.

"I think you look nice," Clare told Danielle. "I could never wear a white bathing suit, though. I'm too pale. And since I don't allow myself to tan . . ."

"Let me guess," I said, eyeing Clare's navy, one-piece, conservative tank suit. "L.L. Bean?"

"At least I didn't raid my brother's underwear drawer this morning!" Clare retorted.

Danielle whooped with delight.

I was wearing my standard beach fare. A thin tank top and a pair of boys' boxer shorts. With a thong underneath. You know. For modesty.

I grinned. "Touché."

"Why don't you try one of the super-advanced self-tanning lotions?" Danielle said to Clare.

For the next few minutes my roomies discussed the merits and pitfalls of various expensive beauty products. I slathered on more drugstore-brand sunblock and watched a chunky, middle-aged, fish-belly white guy in a teeny Speedo-type bathing suit play Frisbee with a girl I seriously hoped was his daughter and not his girlfriend.

Men. You can't live with them, you can't . . .

"I was thinking," I said, interrupting my roomies' deep discussion. "We should talk about what happens when someone wants to bring a guy home for the night."

Danielle nodded. "Good point. We have only two bedrooms. As it is, we rotate getting the couch. Okay. So if someone brings home a guy, I say she should get the second bedroom for the night. And the girl she's displacing takes the couch or shares the first bedroom with the girl who's got the first bedroom for the night. According to the schedule."

"That could get messy," Clare said. "The way I see it, the girl who's been displaced should get a substitute night alone in the second bedroom since she lost her turn to the girl with the unexpected guy."

Danielle scrunched up her nose. "What?"

"Or," Clare went on, "this is a better idea. Each girl is assigned a particular night when she can bring home a guy and use the second bedroom. That way there are no surprises!"

"But what if I don't meet a guy on my appointed night?" Danielle argued.

"Then you forfeit," Clare said matter-of-factly. "It's only fair."

"It's only a freakin' fascist state is what it is," I commented, reasonably.

"Why does it even matter to you, Clare? You've got a live-in boyfriend back home!"

"Yeah, are you planning on fooling around behind his back?" I said. "You don't seem the type."

"No, of course not! And I'm not the type. But—"

"So, stay out of it. Let me and Dani handle the sexual logistics."

"Danielle. It's Danielle, not Dani."

"Whatever." I stood and stretched. The sun on my shoulders felt electrifying. "I'm going for a swim," I announced. "Nobody touch my Snowballs."

Clare
The Root of All Evil

I couldn't sleep.

Danielle was snoring lightly in the other bedroom; Gincy was passed out on the couch in the minuscule living room. Usually, a few hours at the beach tires me enormously, but for some reason I found myself staring wide-eyed at the dingy white ceiling.

And worrying. About everything.

Maybe Win was right, I thought. *Maybe my renting this house is a big waste of hard-earned money.*

What would I know about real value?

Money had never been an issue in my life until then. Meaning that until renting the house with Gincy and Danielle, I'd never had to think about things like paying bills and sharing expenses. First my parents, and then Win, had taken care of those matters.

And there was something I hadn't told my roommates. My parents supplemented my fairly small income with a monthly check. Though I religiously deposited each check, the fact was that the money was there if I needed it.

My father had made sure I knew that the monthly supplement was part of my inheritance; that when he died, my portion of his estate would be that much smaller. Still, I didn't feel comfortable letting anyone but Win know about my financial arrangements.

Anyway, that summer I was writing checks of my own for pretty much the first time. A fairly hefty sum each month to the owners of the little house in Oak Bluffs, sent off via Terri at People's Properties. It was both satisfying and slightly scary, sealing the envelope and knowing that my portion of the house was secured.

What I hadn't considered before signing the lease was that unless the entire amount of rent was paid on time, our right to the entire house was jeopardized. All three names were on the lease. Clare Jean Wellman. Danielle Sarah Leers. And Virginia Marie Gannon.

And Gincy had been late with the first installment of rent. She apologized and explained she'd had to get an advance on her salary, but still. It annoyed me. I wondered if she realized what was at stake. Her carelessness could have ruined the summer for us all.

But I'd kept my feelings to myself, something I was very good at. Mostly. I just couldn't keep quiet whenever Danielle insisted we chip in for a housekeeper, a luxury Gincy clearly couldn't afford and one I didn't think necessary.

It was about time Gincy learned how to clean up after herself.

And Danielle, who knew all about cleaning by watching her housekeeper, simply had to pull on a pair of rubber gloves and get busy.

Clare, I told myself, *you're becoming a grumpy old lady.* I shook out the crumpled sheet and turned on my side, still hoping to catch an hour of real rest. I'd worked myself into a bit of a state.

And another thing, I told the ugly papered wall. *I simply refuse to split the grocery bill in three equal parts when Gincy routinely brings home those disgusting pink-and-white Snowballs which I wouldn't eat if I were starving to death.*

Danielle agreed with me on that issue, though she was the one who suggested the three-way split in the beginning. I don't think she had any better idea than I did about what constituted Gincy's diet. The girl ate junk food by the pound and yet was skinny as a rail.

I sighed, tossed off the sheet, and got out of bed. A nap just wasn't going to happen. I tiptoed past Danielle's room; she was still out cold. Downstairs I crept into the kitchen, hoping not to wake Gincy, who was collapsed on the couch, mouth open, legs dangling.

She looked silly.

I smiled.

Okay. So far, things hadn't been as bad as they could have been with my roommates.

But I wondered when I would start to have fun.

Danielle
Bad Things and Good People

My paternal grandmother was a very wise woman.

"Sometimes," she would say, "God tests us.

"He challenges our faith in Him by putting terrible obstacles to happiness in our way.

"He tests our inner strength by forcing us to face trials of spirit and patience and perseverance.

"He urges us to meet those trials and overcome those obstacles and be the best people we can be.

"And when we do," Grandma Leers would say, "we are rewarded. Not necessarily in this lifetime but definitely in the next."

This was what I added to her words of wisdom: "If I'm going to be rewarded for tolerating slobs and enduring cretins, I want to be rewarded now. In this life. In a big way."

This was another addendum: "Sometimes, there is no reward. Sometimes bad things happen to good people. And no matter how much faith and patience and other superhuman qualities you display, you still get screwed in the end."

That fateful summer, God decided to test me by putting Gincy Gannon in my path. What I ever did to annoy Him, I didn't know.

Gincy Gannon was beginning to convince me that God had a sick sense of humor.

My midafternoon beauty rest was very refreshing. I felt really wonderful. Until I joined my roommates in the kitchen.

"What are you wearing?" I demanded, stopping short at the entrance.

Clare looked at me quizzically.

"Not you," I said. "You! Gincy. What's that you're wearing?"

Gincy looked up from the Sno Ball she was eating with a fierce concentration. "What? I didn't hear—"

I pointed with a trembling finger.

"That's my T-shirt. And it's got—Sno Ball!—all over it!"

Gincy wiped her hands on her shorts and peered down at her flat chest. "Oh. Sorry. I didn't bring enough clothes for the weekend. I found this—"

"In my dresser drawer!"

"Jeez, don't shout. Yeah. Look, I'm sorry, I'll wash it—"

"You'll buy me a new one is what you'll do, missy!"

"What? It's a lousy T-shirt!" Gincy protested.

"It's a hundred-and-fifty-dollar Ralph Lauren T-shirt, you moron!" I screamed. "And you got that disgusting Sno Ball all over it."

Gincy pulled the shirt away from her chest. "It's not Sno Ball," she pointed out. "It's hot sauce. I had chili for lunch. And it's not all over. It kind of makes a pattern. An abstract pattern. You could say it's art. Hey, I could borrow more of your shirts and spill stuff and we could market a whole line of T-shirts and make some real money!"

Clare looked downright afraid. But I was too drained to continue the argument. Instead, I sank into a chair.

An herbal wrap, I thought. *I need an herbal wrap because of this girl.*

Clare
Other People's Children

I don't understand why people can't treat other people with respect.

That's what I was taught to do. It's not all that hard, either. Respect for other people and their feelings and their property quickly becomes second nature.

Danielle didn't even claim it was an accident that she had eaten one of my nonfat yogurts for breakfast that Sunday morning. I came shuffling into the teeny kitchen and opened the old refrigerator—the one I'd thoroughly scrubbed—only to find the last of my yogurts gone.

Confused, I turned around to ask my roommates if they'd seen it.

Gincy was sucking down black coffee from a chipped ceramic mug, her feet up on the Formica kitchen table.

Danielle, dressed in a black silk robe, was sitting next to her, licking a spoon covered with raspberry yogurt. In one hand was a container that clearly read "nonfat."

"That's my yogurt!" I cried.

Danielle shrugged. "I just thought I'd give it a try. You can have one of my low-fats."

"But I don't want one of your low-fats," I protested. "I want *my* yogurt."

"You don't have to be so fussy," she snapped. "Just eat the stupid low-fat. There are, like, three flavors in there."

"Low-fat is not the same as nonfat," I said.

Gincy muttered, "Somebody needs to get laid."

I slammed the refrigerator and turned on her, furious. "Shut up!" I shouted. "Every word out of your mouth is foul! Don't you ever just—just—"

"Just shut up? Rarely. Sorry."

I clapped my hands to the sides of my head. Since when had I become so dramatic? "Oh, this fighting is killing me! Aren't we supposed to act like a family?"

"What do you think we've been doing?" Danielle laughed, got up, and tossed the spoon in the sink. "Doesn't your family argue? Don't they act like freaked-out lunatics every time someone won't get off the phone or out of the bathroom fast enough?"

"No. No they don't."

"What, is everyone all polite and stuff?" Gincy asked with a snort.

"Yes," I told her. *Unlike you.*

Danielle came over to where I stood and took my hand. I tried to pull it away but Danielle hung on.

"Clare, honey," she said. "Maybe things are different where you come from. You know. Out there. But where I grew up, it's normal for a family to scream and yell and slam doors."

"And hate each other and call each other toilet scum and douche bags," Gincy added enthusiastically, reaching for the half-empty coffeepot.

"That's what family is all about, honey. Love. Unconditional love. It's where you can hang your hat and throw silverware and where you and your cousins can pee in the pool—"

"And projectile vomit after drinking your uncle's secret beer supply." Gincy laughed. "Once, my cousin Mikey hit the side of the garage from the back steps. It was like fifteen or twenty feet!"

For a moment I just stared at them. My roommates. I was stuck with them for an entire summer.

And then I burst out crying.

"I guess she's not a morning person," Gincy whispered loudly as Danielle finally let go of my hand.

June

Gincy
Guys and Dolls

Kell had asked us to come to a quick meet-and-greet session at which the new director of daytime programming would be introduced.

Everyone from our department showed up but Sally.

I snatched a bagel from the tray of goodies provided for the occasion and poured a third cup of coffee. Then some bigwig named Weinstein introduced Rick Luongo.

Mr. Luongo seemed a bit embarrassed by the fuss, and after mumbling something about "looking forward" and "teamwork," he melted into the crowd of about twenty.

I spotted him again just before leaving the conference room. He was shoving a jelly donut into his mouth. Powdered sugar covered his chin and a big blob of raspberry jelly was about to plop onto his tie.

Hiding a smile, I returned to my office. Anyone who was brave enough to eat a jelly donut in public, on the first day at a new job, couldn't be all bad.

Later that morning, Sally stopped by.

"Have you met the new guy?" I asked. "I didn't see you at the meeting this morning."

"I was late." Sally made an ugly face. "And I met him later. He's just like all the rest of the corporate scum."

"How do you know?" I asked, not really expecting a sensible answer.

Sally was so predictable.

"Uh, he's wearing a tie? And a blazer. A navy blazer."

I decided to give her a hard time. "His tie was sort of funky. Those abstract patterns? Well, if you look real close, they're not abstract at all. They're puppies."

I wasn't kidding about that. Rick Luongo wasn't exactly Mr. GQ, at least in terms of his clothing.

Sally snorted. "A typical man. Using his tie as a conversation piece. Tie as penis is what it really is. He lures you in with his pathetic wit and the next thing you know—"

"His mother gave it to him," I said. "I asked."

I was lying, of course, but . . .

Sally glowered and folded her arms across her chest.

No matter how hard Sally argued, I wasn't going over to her side.

Something about this Rick guy struck me as okay. In spite of the nerdy outfit, which now boasted a jelly stain.

I think it was his face. His entire manner, actually. There was something open about him. And, okay, he was pretty damn good-looking in a slightly swarthy male sort of way.

The kind of way that makes you think of Mediterranean beaches, salty skin, and fresh-caught calamari for lunch.

"Whatever," I said to Sally.

She huffed and walked out of my office.

Sally hated men and it wasn't because she was a lesbian. I've known plenty of straight chicks who loathed and despised men and enough gay women who thought that, on the whole, men were no better or worse than women. But Sally did happen to be gay, openly and proudly so.

It didn't bother me that she was gay. So what?

What bothered me was when she got in a mood that dictated the only topic worthy of discussion was Being Gay. For obvious reasons, I had little to contribute to those so-called discussions.

After a half hour of her ranting about rights and privileges and identity crises, I was bored and angry.

Sometimes just angry.

Like a few nights before Rick Luongo's debut. We were at Jillian's, shooting pool. Sally sucked, by the way, even worse than I did. And she was rattling on about gay this and gay that. Like the right to get married and job discrimination and blah, blah, blah.

Now, I was all for legalizing gay marriages, and job discrimination of any kind made me sick, but all I was trying to do was have a good time. Not change the world.

"Can we please, please talk about something else?" I begged, after missing yet another shot. "There's more to life than being gay, you know."

"We are our sexuality," Sally responded. "Our sexuality defines us."

"If it defines us, why don't I talk only about how great it is being hetero?" I asked cleverly.

Forgetting that Sally had an answer for everything.

"Because you're the majority," she replied with an utterly annoying air of superiority. "Or so you say. The world is the way you made it, not the way we would make it if we could. You don't need to talk about your sexuality. The world as it exists *is* your sexuality."

You know what, I thought, not for the first time, resting my forehead against the pool cue, *I just don't have enough schooling, formal or informal, to argue this sort of thing.*

And I definitely don't have the patience.

"Fine, whatever," I said, giving up. "I'm the enemy. Now, just shoot. I want to wrap up this game before midnight."

Since I'd been hanging out with Sally, I'd been thinking a lot about the whole gay thing. I mean, things had really changed in the past ten years. All the good stuff—the relative tolerance on the streets of major cities, programs for gay teens dealing with the horrors of coming out—all that was great.

But some stuff struck me as odd. For example, one day while watching MTV it hit me that contemporary pop culture was insinuating that women having sex with women was totally common.

And I don't mean hot Bunny-on-Bunny action for the voyeuristic pleasure of balding straight men in paisley silk bathrobes.

I mean, one average straight girl and another average straight girl deciding to date each other rather than the two cute guys in Accounting, even though they'd never dated women before and weren't considering coming out of any closet because they'd never been in any closet.

Music, magazines, TV, and books—the voices of every medium said it was no big deal to suddenly decide, hey, I really like her, I think I'll have sex with her.

Even if you'd never had a homosexual thought in your life.

But I thought it was a big deal. I found it a huge deal to suddenly develop a passion for a body part you'd otherwise never had a passion for.

I mean—a vagina? Suddenly, that often leaky, smelly . . . thing was something you wanted to touch on someone else? I didn't think so. Not for me, anyway. You could count me out of the lesbian sex thing.

Sure, I admitted, I might really like another woman, as in maybe sort of have a crush on her, in the way you look up to someone who is totally more talented than you are.

Like, if I ever met Hillary Rodham Clinton I might gush and make a fool of myself in the presence of so much talent and intellect and incredible loving patience.

Bill was one lucky man and Chelsea one lucky daughter.

And don't get me started on Mother Theresa.

But were those feelings romantic? No. Well, maybe in the capital R sense of the word.

But were those feelings sexual? No they were not. Not in any sense of the word. Ever.

At least, not for me. God knows I didn't want to offend anybody by speaking for them.

Just like I didn't want anybody else speaking for me. Like

telling me that if all factors were in place—like luck and tim-ing—I might someday have sex with another woman. No big deal.

No, thank you. Not happening.

And neither was work. I'd been sitting at my desk for almost ten minutes by then, staring blankly at the computer screen, on which neon spirals danced.

Damn, I thought. *Focus, Gincy.*

But it was no use. Sally had pissed me off with her automatic dismissal of Rick Luongo. And now all I could think about was how, when she wasn't hating men, Sally was assuming that a lot of the heterosexual women around her were lying to themselves about their sexuality.

How would Sally feel, I wondered, if I assumed that she was lying to herself about being a lesbian? Huh? How would she feel?

She would feel royally pissed off, and she'd have a right to be.

Royally pissed off is how I felt when she gave me the lifted eye-brow, that same smug expression I used to see on my mother when she wanted to imply that she knew better than I did about myself. That I was too blind and stupid or young and naive to know anything better than she did. That no matter what I said or avowed or claimed, it was worthless, it was wrong, it was stupid.

I groaned and clutched my head. Nice. Now I was obsessing about my mother. At work. On sacred turf. And it was all Sally's fault!

My mother. Ellen Marie Gannon.

The way I saw it, my mother assumed I was a failure because she wanted me to be a failure, for a whole bundle of sick, self-serving reasons, only one of which was that she was a failure and misery loves company. Mom wanted me to be what she needed me to be.

Of course, I knew that if I ever confronted her with my knowl-edge, she'd deny everything.

My mother, I'd realized, was similar to Sally in a way neither would ever have imagined. See, though she'd never come right out and said it, I knew that Sally assumed I was gay.

Why? Because she wanted me to be gay. She wanted to be right about me. She wanted me to be what she needed me to be. Her lesbian buddy.

Why does she need me to be lesbian? I thought, truly puzzled. *I'm already her buddy. Jeez. Talk about selfish.*

Back to work. Determinedly, I opened a file that needed attention that morning. A draft of a presentation. And I stared at it, seeing only a collection of letters.

Damn that Sally! And my mother. And their assuming things about me.

Fine. If they could assume, so could I. I could assume—in my less generous, darker moods—that they were both smug, self-centered, pathetic losers.

I'm not, I'd tell Mom, *slinking home to YellowBelly, New Hampshire, shamed and beaten, to wither away the rest of my days in trailer-park misery.*

And I'd tell Sally, *Look, kiddo, I am so not going to have a eureka! moment and discover that lo!, I am gay. At least not until you have a eureka! moment and discover that lo!, you are straight.*

I squinted hard at the document open on the screen before me.

Fine. Back to work.

Sally and Mom would just have to deal with my reality. In spite of their best efforts to convert me, I was not going to succumb to either of them.

Ever.

Clare

The End of an Era

Iknew something was wrong the moment I walked through the front door.

Win was home and it was only six-thirty. Usually he didn't appear until almost eight.

"Hi," I said warily. "What's wrong?"

Win grinned. "Nothing's wrong. Why?"

"Because you're never home this early."

"Aren't you happy to see your boyfriend?"

"Of course. I didn't mean that."

Win opened his arms and, dutifully, I went into his embrace. *Sex,* I thought. *He wants sex.*

But he didn't. Win stepped away and said, "Come sit down, Clare. Over here, on the couch."

I sat and Win perched next to me. Without preamble, he took a small black ring box from the front pocket of his suit pants.

"I want you to marry me, Clare," he said. "I want you to be my wife."

What Win wants, all about Win . . .

Not, "Clare, will you please marry me? I would like to be your husband. Would you like to be my wife?"

"You haven't asked me," I said.

I eyed the ring box in Win's hand as if it were a can of coiled snakes.

"Yes, I did," he cried. "I just did! What do you mean?"

I sighed. I'd spent so many years explaining . . .

"You told me what you wanted. You didn't ask what I wanted. I get to say yes or no. That's the way it goes."

Let him indulge me, his silly little fiancée.

"Of course, sweetie," Win said soothingly. "I'm sorry. So: Clare Wellman, will you marry me?"

"It's so—so sudden," I mumbled.

"Sweetie, we've been together for ten years, this is not sudden!"

"But we haven't even talked about getting married. I—"

Win eyed me oddly. "Hey, I thought you girls liked to be surprised. I thought you girls wanted the romance."

You girls . . .

A question kept nagging at me: *Why is he doing this now? Why now?*

And an answer kept flashing.

He thinks you're slipping away.

He thinks he's losing his control.

He's trying to reel you back in.

He knows you can't say no.

"Besides," Win was saying then, "let's face it, Clare, we're not getting any younger. You're almost thirty and if we want to have kids, which of course we do, then we'd better get moving. Am I right? You know I'm right."

"You're right," I said.

You're always right.

"Of course I'm right. Now . . ."

Win handed me the ring box with a look of such anticipation I almost burst out laughing. Almost.

Like he didn't know what I would say.

I opened the box.

"It's beautiful," I said.

It was. But the ring wasn't my style. It wasn't me.

Win should have known that.

"I knew you'd love it," he said, jumping to his feet, a man with a mission. "So, I'm thinking sometime soon. Say, September."

"September!" I felt sick to my stomach. "No, Win, that's too soon, there's no time to—"

"Oh, come on, sweetie. You're a whiz at getting things organized. Plus, your mom can help, and your friends . . ."

"But the fall semester starts September tenth," I argued. "How can we take a honeymoon? I'll need to go back to work."

"I'm sure the school will give you a leave of absence," Win said smoothly. "Or a sabbatical. Isn't that what you teachers call it? After all, it's not every day a girl gets married!"

More weakly, I said, "But you start that big case in August. It'll never be over by September. How can you get away . . ."

Win reached out to stroke my hair. I winced at his barely perceptible touch.

"Sweetie, I'll work it all out, don't worry about a thing. All you need to do is have fun planning the wedding. Okay?"

I nodded, hardly aware of the motion. Win talked on and I tuned out.

What friends? What friends will help out? Maybe I don't want help. Maybe I don't want—

"So, are we set?" Win's voice, intruding. "September? Late September. Hey, you'd better start calling around now, book the church and a place for the reception, and, you know, whatever else needs to be done. You girls know these things."

I stared at the huge diamond ring on my finger and felt only disbelief. What was happening to me?

And then Win was on the phone.

"Mrs. Wellman? Hey, it's Win. No, nothing's wrong. In fact, we have some big news. Hang on. Clare, sweetie, pick up the other receiver, okay?"

Numbly, I did. And we announced our engagement to my family.

Danielle

When You Least Expect It

Things were going swimmingly.

I'd lined up a date for Friday night. Saturday was open but I was planning on dinner at Lucca's and then drinks at the club next door. With any luck I'd meet someone before the end of the night and line up a date for the following weekend.

And then I met him. Coincidentally, unplanned, a surprise.

Here's how it happened.

The sun was high and bright and I had a sudden, intense craving for an ice cream cone.

Intense cravings should always be satisfied.

So, carrying my beach bag equipped for a lazy afternoon of sunning, and wearing my broad-brimmed straw hat, I first headed to this tiny little place called SusieQ's for a cone.

The line was long, which gave me plenty of time to decide what flavor I wanted. Peach? Mocha Java? Or maybe decadent Chocolate Supreme!

Suddenly, my hat was knocked forward over my eyes. I let out a little scream. I mean, who knew what deviant was trying to blind me before he grabbed me and my overflowing bag!

"I'm so sorry!" a male voice said. "Can I—"

"No, I can—" I righted my hat and with a deep breath looked at the person now standing before me, a look of sincere apology on his face.

"I'm sorry," he repeated. "I was standing behind you and I— Well, I'm not used to judging the circumference of, uh, that kind of hat. Not that there's anything wrong with it," he added hastily.

I considered him keenly before replying. Physically, he wasn't my usual type—dark hair and eyes, clean-shaven, not too tall— but I was woman enough to appreciate masculine beauty in any form.

His wild hair was light brown, randomly streaked by the sun. His eyes were an amazing light blue-green, like Richard Burton's eyes, intense, penetrating, framed by dark lashes. He hadn't shaved in a few days; his stubbly beard was blond and brown and red. And he was tall, at least six-two.

Very nice.

"That's all right," I said graciously. "I forgive you."

Mr. Sunkissed smiled back. "At least let me buy you an ice cream for any trouble I caused."

Ah, a gentleman!

I graciously accepted.

By that time we were near the head of the line and I'd had plenty of time to note his clothing. Nothing spectacular. A dark T-shirt, jeans, and, oddly for the weather, work boots. He was clean and the jeans fit very nicely, but overall, he was too casually put together for my taste.

"What'll it be?" he said when we reached the window.

"A peach cone, please," I said.

Mr. Sunkissed also asked the server for a gallon of cherry-vanilla.

"For my dad," he explained. "It's his favorite. He doesn't get around too well anymore so I stop here when I can and get a supply."

"Oh, how nice," I said. A respectful son. Good sign. "So, your father is vacationing with you?"

Mr. Sunkissed handed me the cone and I noticed large, well-sculpted hands. Then he took his package from the server and we stepped out of the line.

"No," he said, "we live here year-round. In Chilmark. But you're here on vacation?"

I told him I lived in Boston and had rented a house with two other girls. Before he could reply, his beeper went off. He checked it and, with a frown, told me he had to get going.

"I'm sorry, again," he said, grinning. "About the hat."

"That's quite all right. It was nice talking to you."

There was a moment of awkward silence, Mr. Sunkissed poised to run off, my cone beginning to melt over my fingers.

"Well," he said, "maybe I'll see you around town again."

I nodded and he dashed off. I watched as he got into a black pickup truck and drove away.

I didn't even ask his name, I realized. Not that it mattered. I could never get serious about a guy who drove a pickup truck.

With a shrug, I headed toward the beach.

Gincy

The Ship and the Ocean

Danielle was curled up on the couch, busily at work updating her husband-hunting schedule.

"So far, so good," she murmured. "Three dates down; a second date with bachelor #2; two new prospects on board, not counting Mr. Pickup Truck . . ."

"You're rapacious," I blurted, tossing aside the week-old copy of the *Globe* I'd never had time to read. "You're like a starving cat working its way through a bowl of tuna fish covered in heavy cream."

"That reminds me," Danielle said, closing her account book. "I'm hungry! Who wants to go to lunch?"

Clare came into the living room from the kitchen. "I do. There's nothing in the fridge."

"And, we can't meet men in our own kitchen," Danielle pointed out, grabbing her purse. "Not that it matters for our bride-to-be!"

Clare gave a half smile. "I've got the keys," she said. "Are you coming, Gincy?"

I was. We wound up at the Beachcomber. Someone had left a copy of *Esquire* on the next table. Danielle began to leaf through it.

"Ha!" she cried. "You've got to see this ad!"

She passed it around. It was a full-page ad for penis enhance-ment. A larger penis, it seems, was guaranteed to "get the job done."

"Do you think that's how men really think about sex?" Clare seemed disturbed. "That it's all about 'getting the job done'?"

Danielle shrugged. "I don't know. Maybe the ad is saying that men don't really care about women, just getting done what they have to get done to make the women continue to have sex with them. I guess."

"All men care about is getting off," I declared. From experi-ence. "If they can get off without getting the job done, that's even better."

"Oh, Gincy," Clare protested. "That's not true!"

Danielle returned to studying the full-page ad. "So," she said, musingly, "you think 'getting the job done' means giving a woman an orgasm?"

"Yeah. I think."

"But you don't need a big penis to do that!" she cried. "You don't need a penis at all!"

"True. So maybe they mean getting the job done is the whole sex act. The whole shebang, start to finish. God, who writes these ads, anyway?"

Clare seemed very interested in her crab salad.

"Why should any of this be surprising?" Danielle said, tossing the magazine to the floor. "Isn't that what men are really all about? Fixing broken car parts. Solving messy plumbing prob-lems. Seeking leverage. Building decks. Grilling hamburgers. Punching out bad guys. Getting the job done. Don't talk and muse and ponder. Just do something. Just get it done."

Clare put down her fork suddenly. "That makes men sound so simple," she said. Was she upset by this? "So easy to understand."

"They are simple," I said. "They're right out there, getting the job done. End of story. Nothing complicated about it."

"But every man is different," Clare protested. "Every man's an individual!"

"Okay, to some extent," Danielle admitted. "But ask a cross

section of men what they want in life and they'll all say, 'to get the job done.' I guarantee it."

"I don't know . . ." Clare said.

"Women, on the other hand—"

I clapped my hands to my head. "Oh, boy, here we go."

Danielle smirked. "We are unclassifiable. We fit no one mold. We are complex and ever-changing."

"We sound highly annoying," I said.

"Chameleon-like. Seasonal. Cycling with the moon. Rising and falling with the tides."

I pretended to gag. Clare winced.

Poor Clare. Half the time she didn't know what to make of us.

"I think I'm going to be sick," I said. "Like, seasick. I want stability. I want my feet planted firmly on the ground. Maybe that's why I don't have any women friends. I'm enough of a woman for me to handle."

Danielle rolled her eyes. "Okay, we'll change the subject."

Then she leaned toward Clare, eyes gleaming. "So, Clare, are you totally psyched about the wedding?"

Clare twisted her massive engagement ring, right to left, left to right. It almost freakin' blinded me.

"Well, you know. I guess. I mean—"

"Having doubts?"

Clare looked at me, horrified. "Of course not! Why would you say that?"

"Did you hear how you answered Dani's question? Talk about equivocation."

"It's Danielle. Clare, honey, don't worry. Every bride feels overwhelmed. But I'll tell you what. This is your lucky day. I'll be your wedding planner! No charge, of course, except an invitation to the big event. How's that? Feel better?"

Clare managed a small smile. I thought she looked sick, but Danielle was elated.

"Excellent! Let's get started right away. There's so much to do! Okay, we know it's an early fall wedding. Hmm. Tricky. The weather could go any which way. I'd go with an indoor reception and as for the dress, well, let me do some research. No short sleeves, but maybe sleeveless, with some sort of bolero jacket or wrap for modesty in the church—do you want a church ceremony?—and—"

I dug into my burger.

Clare picked listlessly at her meal.

Danielle chatted on.

Danielle
Love American Style

Oak Bluffs may be chock-full of vacationers, foreigners, outsiders, but still, it's a small town.

I was pondering the selection of bath oils in the window of a charmingly old-fashioned pharmacy when the door to the shop opened and who should walk out but Mr. Pickup Truck.

"Well, hello," I said brightly, as he caught my eye. "Remember me? We met in line at SusieQ's."

"Of course I remember you." He laughed. "I almost knocked your hat to the ground."

I favored him with a dazzling smile. "As you can see, I'm wearing a much smaller brim today."

"It's pretty," he said. "Your hat."

This guy was too cute.

"Thank you."

"So," he asked, shoving a small white bag into the back pocket of his jeans. "What's your name?"

I extended my hand, and he took it promptly. His skin was rough but not in an icky way. His hand, as I'd noticed the first time we met, was wide; his fingers were thick but not at all fat.

A very manly hand, I thought. *Strong and manly.*

"Danielle Leers," I told him.

"Hi, Danielle. I'm Chris Childs."

We released hands.

"What kind of name is Childs?" I asked.

Chris looked puzzled. "It's my name," he said, finally, laughing.

"Oh, I mean, is it Irish or—"

Chris shrugged. "My family is Protestant. My dad says our ancestors came over from England. I don't know how the name came about. You could ask the town librarian, though. She's into genealogy."

My heart sank. Rats. Christian and a pickup truck. Totally all-American.

Oh, well, no one was perfect.

"Oh, no, that's all right," I said, with a less-dazzling smile. "I was just wondering."

Where did we go from there?

"My family's lived on the Vineyard forever," Chris said, though I hadn't asked. "Well, for a long time. Generations."

"Oh. My family lives on Long Island," I told him. "My great grandparents came from Europe. Poland, mostly. They lived in Brooklyn and then their kids moved out to the Island. Some went to New Jersey, but we don't talk to them anymore."

Chris looked puzzled. "Because they live in New Jersey?"

"Oh, no," I assured him. "Because they didn't invite any of us on Long Island to their son's Bar Mitzvah."

"I've never been to Long Island," Chris said, skipping right over the reference to my family feud. "I hear the beaches are great."

"They are. Just beautiful. Next time you're in New York you should try to get out to the Island."

Chris kind of shuffled from foot to foot.

"Well," he said, with an endearingly tentative smile, "I've only been to New York once. Most of the time I was in Manhattan. But I did get to the Bronx Zoo one day. The Big Apple. It was interesting. Boy. But it wasn't my thing. I could never live there, you know?"

Not really, I admitted silently.

Who wouldn't want to live in Manhattan? Or at least visit every month or so? The shops, the restaurants, the museums, the galleries . . .

I felt city-lust rear up through me right then and there. *Carrie Bradshaw,* I called silently, *wait for me!*

"So," Chris said abruptly, as if he'd sensed my silence was maybe not a good thing. "I have to be going. My dad is waiting for his medicine. So, bye."

"Okay," I said, sorry to see him go but not knowing how our conversation could recover from the Manhattan crisis. "Bye."

"Bye." He walked off a few feet and then turned. I was still looking after him. I wonder if that surprised him. "There's a storm watch tonight," he called. "If you're out on the water this evening, well, be careful."

"Oh," I said, with a little wave. "Okay. Thanks."

He didn't have to know that boats other than ferries and I were not close friends.

Chris waved back and off he went. I continued to watch.

What. A. Hottie. I'd never seen a guy look so excellent in jeans. Never.

Now, I thought, turning back to the body-oil display, *if only I could meet an eligible man, real husband material, an urban guy, a professional, who looks like Chris.*

Wow.

I'd be in heaven.

Gincy
Mr. Romance

He cornered me in the break room.

Well, not cornered.

It was more like he was pouring a cup of coffee for himself when I walked in and got a can of soda from the fridge.

"Hey."

"Hey," I replied. "Jeez, watch—!"

"Oops." Rick grabbed a handful of paper towels and mopped up the coffee that had sloshed on the counter when he'd replaced the pot on the burner. Then he tossed the wad of wet towels at the garbage can.

They landed on the floor with a plop.

"I'll get it," I said. "You're a menace, Rick."

He laughed and blew on his coffee. "Yeah, I know. But, see? I'm trying not to burn myself."

"Good boy."

I was on my way out of the room when he said, "Hey, Gincy, can I ask you a question?"

I turned back and shrugged. "Sure. Ask away."

"I was wondering. Would you like to go out sometime?"

Now that was the last thing I'd expected to hear from Rick Luongo.

"With you?" I blurted.

"Yes."

"To do what?"

Rick shrugged; I noted a wet spot on his tie where coffee had splashed. *Why,* I wondered, *does he even bother with ties?*

"I don't know. Whatever you like to do on a date."

I glanced into the hall. No one coming. Good. This was weird.

"You want me to go out on a date with you," I repeated. Just to be sure.

"Yes," Rick said, with a big smile. "That's the idea."

"But we work together."

"True. But I'm not your boss. We're in different departments."

"It could be awkward. No matter what happens."

"Life is awkward."

He had a point there. And he had great hair, all dark and wavy, and a sexy, slightly rapacious smile.

Hmm. Kind of like a pirate . . .

"You don't know how to fix a paper jam," I said.

"But I do know how to ask for help."

"You're clumsy. Since you've started working here you've dropped five cups of coffee, knocked over three soda cans, tripped over the doorsill to the conference room at least once a day, and stapled your tie to your notepad. Twice."

"But I am endearing," he countered.

Again, that smile.

"Yeah," I admitted, smiling now myself. "In an oafish sort of way."

"So, will you go out with me?"

I scrunched up my face as if seriously considering a life-altering decision. "Okay," I said. "What the hell. But I'm not getting into a car with you unless I do the driving."

"Deal."

"And don't make a big to-do out of it at work, okay?"

"Why does anyone have to know?"

"Saturday. Daytime."

"Fine. I'll meet you—?"

"On the corner of Tremont and Boylston. Ten o'clock. Don't be late."

"I won't," he said.

And so it began.

Clare

Wed Lock

It happened at the dry cleaner's, and at the corner bodega, and the next day, at the greenmarket in Copley Square.

Three women, all about my age, stopped to comment breathlessly on my engagement ring.

"It's so big!" the first woman exclaimed, eyes sparkling with envy. "Oh, my God, I'd kill for a ring that big! You are so lucky."

"Thanks," I murmured, grabbing the box of Win's shirts off the counter. Before she could kill me for the prize, I was gone, cheeks flaming.

Later that day, while preparing a casserole for dinner, I realized we were out of milk so I dashed to the nearest independent market. Just as I was reaching into one of the cold cases for a half gallon of 2%, someone screamed.

I jumped, the door to the cold case slammed shut, and I whirled around, ready to find myself at gunpoint.

But there was only a woman in workout gear, a yoga mat on her shoulder, her mouth hanging open and her finger pointing to my hand as if I were holding a snake.

"That is the most gorgeous ring I have ever seen, ever," she whispered.

I wanted to slap her for scaring me so, but all I said was, "Thanks," and hurried past her, milk forgotten.

I knew that newly engaged women were supposed to be just dying to show off their ring.

They got weekly manicures with O.P.I. or Essie sheer colors to assure their hands were in perfect shape.

Kiss the Bride, Ballet Slipper, Rosy Future.

They frequently touched their hair and adjusted their necklaces with their left hand.

Occasionally they stopped dead in the lingerie section of Express or the handbag section of Lord & Taylor to admire their new possession.

I didn't do any of those things. I didn't want to show off the fact that I was now, more than ever, committed to Win.

I didn't own that ring. That ring—that monstrous ring!— owned me.

So why didn't I put it in a drawer and wear it only when Win was around? Why didn't I tell him it was too big and fancy for me, even though that wasn't really the main issue?

Because I was possessed of absolutely no courage.

I was selecting tomatoes from my favorite farm stand the following afternoon when suddenly I became aware of a sleek, ultra-sophisticated, super-tan, professional blonde staring at me.

I looked back at her, wondering if I knew her from someplace.

"You have it insured, don't you?" she said, by way of a greeting. "Because that ring's got to be worth fifteen, twenty thousand, easy. You should probably have a copy made up in cubic zirconia to wear just around, you know? Like to this market. Or on vacation to the Islands. You know how the locals can be. You don't want to take any chances on losing it or having it stolen. On the T? Turn it around so no one can see the center stones. Do yourself a favor."

I opened my mouth to mumble something incoherent but the woman went on.

"And don't wear it to the beach," she said, "because your finger will shrink in the water and the ring will fly right off. I've seen it happen, trust me. Well, I haven't actually seen it but a friend of a friend lost her engagement ring that way. Or was it at a pool? Either way, avoid water."

Dumbly, I nodded. The oh-so-helpful woman sauntered off, and as she went, I caught a massive flash from her left hand.

I was petrified.

There was a time bomb on my finger. Something too big, too outrageously noticeable, too expensive for comfort.

I considered taking the ring off right there and putting it in the front pocket of my chinos. But it would be too easy for it to fall out. And Win would have spent twenty thousand dollars for nothing.

Twenty thousand dollars? For a ring?

I felt sick and stunned.

Then I considered slipping the ring into my purse, but what if my purse were snatched?

What if I just left the ring on and I was snatched? What if the thief cut off my finger to get the ring?

Twenty thousand dollars could feed a lot of poor kids for years. Or one very devoted drug addict for a week or two.

"You ready?" the farm-stand guy asked.

I nodded and handed him the plastic bag filled with toma-toes. He weighed them and I gave him a five-dollar bill. As he took it, he put his other hand over his eyes as if to shield them.

"Whoa," he said, laughing. "You almost blinded me!"

I just wanted to cry.

Gincy

Just Full of Surprises

*C*ancel the date.

*C*That was my first thought upon waking at six-thirty that Saturday morning.

If I called Rick right then, sure, I might wake him up, but on the other hand, I'd be giving him plenty of notice to replan his day.

Right?

And then I had to ask myself: *Why do you want to cancel?*

You like Rick. You've got nothing else to do now that you bagged out of the Vineyard for the weekend. Except go to the office and get a jump-start on next month's issue.

So what's the problem?

With a loud, old man groan I got out of bed and flipped on the drip coffeemaker.

And while I waited for the mud to brew, I tried to figure it all out.

The problem was this:

My track record with guys sucked. I mean, in spite of my lack of fashion sense—reading the September issue of *Vogue* didn't mean you had the skills to tranlsate what you'd learned to your own life—or maybe *because* of my lack of fashion sense, who knew, I'd never had a problem getting guys.

All guys always want to have sex. Always. So if a girl's got a good sense of fun and is willing to play the game, hey, guys are gonna like her.

Which is not to say I was a sleep-around or that I let guys walk all over me.

No way. I called the shots. I was tough.

I dumped them way before they could get around to dumping me for the girl they'd marry, someone all cute and cuddly. Blah.

Gincy Gannon was not a stupid person.

The mud was ready. I poured a cup and took a first trembling sip. Ah, scalding! Just the way I liked it. A few more sips and maybe I'd feel all better.

All calm.

No more butterflies in my stomach.

No such luck. I drank two cups and still I felt no more courageous than I had upon waking.

There was something about Rick . . .

I don't know. Maybe, I thought, *it's my age. Maybe I'm hitting some major hormonal peak or valley that's making me . . .*

Afraid. I felt afraid. Almost afraid.

Not of Rick, exactly. Jeez, it was pretty clear I could totally take him in anything from arm wrestling to kick-boxing. If I kickboxed. Which I didn't, but with Rick's native clumsiness, I was pretty damn sure he'd be no challenge at all.

Was it because he was older than me by about six years? (The receptionist had told me his age.) Was it because he wore adult, dress-up clothes to work? Even if they weren't the height of fashion—like I would really know that—they were clearly adult clothes.

Or was it simply because, unlike virtually every other datable guy I'd ever met, Rick was just—himself. No posturing, no blustering.

He was unself-conscious in a way that made me take notice and approve.

And that made me wonder if by being with him I'd have to learn how to be self-truthful, too.

I dropped the empty coffee cup into the sink. It made, of course, an annoying clatter and I asked myself why I never learned from my annoying habits.

You're getting ahead of yourself, Gincy, I scolded. *Sure, Rick seems nice and genuine and all down-to-earth. But is he, really?*

For all you really know he's a self-serving slime just like every other guy you've met and had to toss aside.

So, relax. Calm down. Just go on the freakin' date and see what happens.

But keep your wits about you, your eyes open, your senses tuned.

At exactly ten o'clock, Rick and I met at the assigned corner.

"You're on time," I noted.

Rick shrugged. "I'm always on time. It just happens."

Rick looked different. In a good way.

I'd never seen him out of the office, in daylight, not in a tie—even if the tie was stained with jelly. He wore slouchy chinos and a navy T-shirt that revealed he had muscles. Big ones. And a pretty flat stomach. Hard to tell the truth in his work attire.

Note to self: Reconsider the ease of the arm-wrestling victory.

I was scrappy but no one had ever called me muscular.

"Hey," he said, then. "I thought you had a house on the Vineyard?"

"Who told you that?"

"Kell mentioned it. So why are you in town on a Saturday?"

The question was delivered in an innocent way, but I sure as hell wasn't going to tell him I'd rearranged my schedule to go on this date.

"I've got a prior commitment tomorrow," I lied. "A distant family thing. So my being in town has nothing to do with you. Just so you know that."

"I wouldn't think anything of the kind," he said without a trace of sarcasm.

And I believed him.

"So, I had a couple of ideas," he said, sticking his hands in the front pockets of his pants. The gesture struck me as very youthful. And it made a tendon or something in his forearm flex. "About what we could do."

"What?" I said, momentarily distracted by lust. "Oh. Right. Shoot."

"We could go to the Science Museum."

"The Science Museum? Isn't that really for kids?"

Rick smiled. Again, I noted big strong sexy teeth. "Yeah. Or we could go to the Aquarium. Afterwards, I thought we could walk to the North End, get some pizza. What do you think?"

I grinned. "Sounds great. Let's do the Aquarium. I love the seahorses."

We headed through downtown towards the waterfront.

I watched him walk from the corner of my eye.

Nice gait.

Tendons. Teeth. Gait.

I gave myself a mental boot to the head.

What is he a horse, Gincy? Snap out of it!

"Hey," I said, utterly casually. "What do you like on your pizza?"

Rick shrugged. "Everything. Except anchovies. They make me burp. I don't know why."

Excellent.

"They give me the skeeves," I told him. "No anchovies."

Rick and I had the best day. Totally easy and fun. I paid for the Aquarium and he paid for the pepperoni pizza. And the cannolis afterwards.

We discovered we both liked walking and hardly ever took the T unless it was absolutely necessary.

He admitted to being a reality TV addict.

I mocked him, then admitted to sucking at all sports.

We both admitted to being Hunter S. Thompson fans.

We were sitting on the steps of City Hall when Rick looked at his watch and sighed. "I wish we could hang out more. But I've got to get home."

"Why?" I asked. "What's the rush? It's only—" I looked at his watch as the battery in mine had been dead for weeks, though I continued to wear it. "It's only five-fifteen."

"Yeah, I know, but Justin's sitter is only available until six, so—"

"The what now?" I interrupted. "Who's Justin?"

Rick looked thoroughly perplexed. "Justin. My son. You know about him."

I'd known it was too good to be true! I scooted away from Rick a bit so I could look straight at him.

"Uh, no," I said. "I don't. When were you planning on telling me you have a kid? When you got around to telling me you have a wife, too?"

Rick looked truly stricken. "Gincy, I'm sorry. I thought you knew. It's common knowledge around the office. At least, I thought it was. The receptionist knows. Don knows. Sally knows. Even Kell knows, and he's kind of oblivious to . . . Sorry. I didn't mean to say that you're oblivious . . ."

"Sally? Sally knows?"

And she'd never mentioned it to me? Okay, I hadn't told her I was going out with Rick. But still.

"Yeah. I've even got a picture of Justin on my desk."

"I've never actually been in your office."

"Oh."

I took a deep breath. "So—about the wife?"

Divorced creep. Probably dumped her for a newer model.

Cheated on her. With her best friend. Or her younger sister!

Stiffed her in the settlement so now she was raising a kid on her own—except for Saturdays when her slime of an ex-husband had him but tossed him off on a baby-sitter—and working two jobs and—

"I'm a widower, Gincy. My wife died about four years ago, a few months after Justin was born. Breast cancer."

Oh crap, crap, crap.

I put my head in my hands. "Jeez. I'm sorry, Rick. Jeez. So, uh, that makes Justin how old?"

"He's five. His birthday was in February."

The poor kid probably didn't even remember his mother.

"Oh," I said lamely. "Happy birthday. Belated."

"Thanks. From Justin."

What now?

"So, he's in kindergarten?" I asked. "Do they have kindergarten anymore? I don't really know anyone with kids. Little kids. My sixteen-year-old cousin is pregnant, though."

Now that would impress my date . . .

"Oh. Congratulations. I guess."

"Well, she is marrying the father," I said inanely.

We ended our date awkwardly, both visibly upset.

Rick didn't try to kiss me. I still kind of wished he had, even though I knew our relationship was over before it had ever really begun.

I sat on the cooling steps and watched Rick walk off, on his long way back to Charlestown. I felt queasy. Suddenly, the pepperoni pizza we'd shared didn't seem like such a good idea.

I liked Rick. A lot. Man, I'd had a great time with him, just hanging out.

But a kid?

No. It wasn't in my plan.

It just wasn't.

Clare
Personal Space

Having summers off is a mixed blessing.

On the one hand, the free months stretch out like a wonderful promise. Plenty of time to catch up on all the things you just didn't have time to do during the school year.

Like sleep.

One the other hand, the free months come as a shock to the system. From September through June you had virtually no downtime and suddenly, there you were, cut loose and swinging in the wind.

Lost and alone, while most other people you knew were still heading to the office every Monday through Friday morning.

I often felt out of sync with the average adult world.

That summer, as always, I vowed to fill my "time off" constructively.

Back in high school and the early days of college I'd kept a journal. Journaling gave my daily life a structure and a sense of importance.

It gave me time to be alone with my thoughts, and it allowed me to create a sense of relative peace.

Shortly after I met Win I stopped keeping a journal. I don't know why, exactly. It was like Win took up so much space there was no longer room for my private self.

Back then, it felt like a relief.

But now, eleven years later? It was time, I felt, to start looking for my private self, wherever I'd misplaced her.

I would start another journal. But where could I keep a journal that would be truly private?

And then I began to wonder if I had a right to total privacy. Weren't couples supposed to share everything—every thought and dream, every success and failure?

Maybe in romance novels and chick flicks couples shared such intimacy. But my reality was different.

Win and I hadn't had a truly meaningful conversation in years. We never talked about spirituality or ethics or philosophy. We never really had, not even in the beginning.

The myth of the Start of the Romance: During those heady times the two lovers sit up all night talking; they ask penetrating questions and share intimate longings, they laugh and they cry, they voice deep desires and exchange fanciful hopes.

To be fair, in those early days of our relationship Win and I had shared a few amusing family stories, a few childhood memories, our tastes in music and film. Shorthand for our personalities.

But as for our souls?

I couldn't speak for Win but my soul had never been touched. A virgin soul.

Maybe, I thought, *it's asking too much to have your spouse touch your soul.*

Maybe it's enough that he be generally pleasant and hardworking and tolerant of your parents as they age.

Maybe it's just fine if your heart doesn't swell with affection when you run into him on the street, all unexpected.

Maybe.

And maybe it wasn't.

I'd done nothing more than consider keeping a journal, and yet I felt guilty.

Was it cheating somehow to pursue a completely private, separate venture without telling Win that I was embarking on such a course?

But if I told him, the venture would no longer be truly private and separate, would it?

Oh, Clare, I thought. *Why is everything so complicated with you?*

With some effort, I put aside my reservations and bought a five-by-seven spiral bound notebook with a floral cover. Lined, cream-colored pages.

My journal.

One afternoon while Win was at work, I determined to begin. For a long moment I stared at the blank page. And then, the words flowed.

I think it's all over for me, sexually. In spite of Win, sometimes I feel sure I'll never have sex again. I know I'll never be kissed—really kissed—again. It's horrible to contemplate. I want to be wanted. I want that very badly.

I dream all the time about being kissed. Not by Win. I dream about being with a man who's so, so beautiful. His body is beautiful. I crave him in a way I've never craved anyone in real life. When I'm awake. I— it's like I'm in love but also—the feeling in the dream is like—adoration. The man almost isn't a person. An individual, you know, with a particular past and particular flaws and . . . He's not real. I think he's supposed to mean something or represent something beyond any one man. I never see his face clearly, but he kisses me and I rub my cheek against his. He's tan but not like from the sun. His skin is a color I don't think I've ever seen in real life. His shirt is often off. I cling to him, mostly.

Sometimes, he's someone I know from the past, from early years, oddly enough, from grammar school. He's someone who's mysterious, has a life I know nothing about. He just seems to appear. He comes back into town unannounced. He leaves again without warning. He's not unkind. We're friends. He's never shown any interest in me, romantically. Or, sometimes, we've kissed but it's never gone far. He's drawn to me but—but he's always chosen someone far more glamorous to be with. Often I don't know where he lives or what he does for a living or if he's married. Sometimes I wonder if he's gay. Sometimes I wonder if he's dying.

He's somehow—popular. Other people wait for him to come back home, not only me. He's part of a group but he can't be expected to act like it. He's a member of a graduating class but no one expects him to come to graduation exercises. And he doesn't. And I'm waiting for him, desperately waiting. Wanting some small bit of affection. When he does appear later, unexpected, he's always glad to see me but loses interest before long. And he's never come back for me. He's got his own reasons for showing up. And I never know those reasons. I'm too afraid to ask and he doesn't volunteer.

I care for him like no one else does, I just know that. I feel almost like his mother, or a big sister. I want to be his lover. I want to be an integral part of his mysterious world. I want to be indispensable. But I'm not. I'm highly dispensable.

He goes away, and by the time he does, I'm almost forgotten. And I wait, desperate for his next return.

These dreams are plaguing me. I yearn for them—for the intensity of emotion I feel in them, for his beauty. The days after the dreams, I try to hold on to them. I look forward to the next dream. And I want to find this man in the real world.

Even for a moment.

Does this mean I shouldn't marry Win? Of course not. This man of my dreams is no rival to Win. Of course not. Win has nothing to worry about. I'm not cheating on him by dreaming. I'm not.

Gincy
Fashion Victimista

O ur weekend on the Vineyard was off to a lousy start.
See, I was learning that you couldn't always ignore your
roommates, much as you might want to. When someone was in
trouble and you were looking right at them, you pretty much
had to help out.

Unless you were okay with being a horrible person.

It sucked, but what were you going to do?

Saturday morning, Danielle came hobbling out of the bathroom and sat at the kitchen table with a grunt.

"What's wrong with you?" I asked, not so graciously.

She pointed at her left foot.

The entire side of her foot was swollen and red. Where it wasn't
full of pus under the stretched skin.

"That is hideous."

"Thanks," Danielle said, gingerly poking at her foot. "Your remarks are so helpful."

Clare squinted at the abomination that was Danielle's foot. "I
think you should see a doctor," she said. "But I'm not sure you
should wait until you get back to Boston. See those red streaks
forming? That's bad. You could go septic and die."

Danielle put her hand to her head. "Oh, my God. I think I'm going to faint."

"Don't faint," I ordered. "We'll take you to the emergency room. You can faint there if you want."

"Do I have to go?" she wailed.

"I'm no doctor," I told her, "but I'd say, yeah. You need to get that drained or something. Get some antibiotics."

"Why do you wear shoes that like, anyway?" Clare asked, pointing to the skinny purple sandals that had cut Danielle's foot so badly.

The night before she'd been bragging about finding them on sale, but I'd noticed that the moment we got home from the bar she'd wrenched them off and left them by the back door.

"They're sexy. They make my legs look fabulous."

"They're sending you to the emergency room, Danielle."

Danielle glared.

"You know," Clare went on, "wearing high heels can cause back problems later in life. You might want to try more practical shoes. There are plenty of fashionable flats these days, and sneakers—"

"My legs," Danielle said, between gritted teeth, "look stumpy in flats. Now, get me my makeup bag!"

Clare jumped and I grabbed a shiny zippered bag from beside the sink.

"No, no, no!" Danielle cried. "Not the black one. That's my resource bag. Get me the red makeup bag!"

"Well, why didn't you say so in the first place? Jeez. I'm not a mind reader. Who has two makeup bags anyway?" I mumbled, searching the room for the red bag. "What's so special about the red one?"

"The red one contains the palate I'm currently using on a daily basis. The black resource bag contains the colors I'm not currently using on a daily basis."

"The special colors?" Clare asked.

"Not necessarily. It's just that . . ."

I spotted the red bag on the small coffee table in the living room and grabbed it. "Uh, kids? Could we get moving here? We're not going out to a club. We're going to the hospital, remember?"

"I still want to look my best," Danielle said with a pout.

"You're already wearing makeup," I shot back.

"I might need to touch up."

"You're not going to meet anyone in the ER."

"Uh, hello? Doctors work in the ER. Jewish doctors."

"My father thinks the doctors who work in the ER are failures," Clare said.

"What?" I said, checking my wallet for cab money. Three lousy singles. "What are you talking about?"

Clare shrugged. "That's what he says. He says the successful doctors work in specialties and private practice."

"What about at a teaching hospital?" I shot back. "Every young doctor has to rotate through every department, right? You know, as in rotations."

Danielle nodded. I noticed her color was bad, and grabbed a plastic shopping bag in case she needed to hurl in the cab.

"Gincy's right," she said, a bit weakly. "I could very easily meet a gorgeous, brilliant, and potentially highly successful—i.e., rich—doctor today. Besides, it never hurts to look your best."

I laughed. The girl was amazing. "Yeah, in case the druggies and poor folk who hang at the ER give a shit about the little rich girl in for an infected blister."

"I'm not rich," she protested, wiping sweat from her brow with the back of her hand. "Exactly. Though I'd like to be. I aspire to be. In fact, I think I was born to be."

"That's nice for you," I said, squatting and wrapping her right arm around my shoulders. "Now, heave ho! We're out of here before you're sprawled on the floor."

Danielle
Cruel and Unusual

Gincy and Clare got me to the emergency room—though Gincy stepped on my good foot twice on the way to the cab—and after a lengthy process called triage, I found myself alone in a curtained-off section of the room, sitting on a hospital bed without even a pillow for comfort, wearing nothing but a flimsy wraparound gown called a johnny.

The johnny was a pallid pale blue. It did absolutely nothing for me.

I felt cold and scared and lonely. Some evil nurse told Gincy and Clare they couldn't stay with me. Something about their not being family.

Stupid.

"BLLLAAAAAGGGHHH!"

And behind curtain number two, Mr. Retchie McRetcher.

I put my hands over my ears and hummed loudly. Couldn't they have put the guy in, like, a soundproof room or something?

After almost an hour a doctor came in through the ugly pale blue curtains. She was barely five feet tall and had a massive amount of shiny black hair gathered in a bun at the nape of her neck. She introduced herself as Dr. Alotofsyllablesinverystrangeorder.

And then she said a lot of words I couldn't understand at all.

"Excuse me?" I said, trying to look all apologetic. I'd never been very good at catching foreign accents.

Without changing her no-nonsense expression, Dr. Alotofsyllablesinverystrangeorder said more words. Maybe she repeated what she'd said earlier. I don't know.

"I'm sorry," I said. "I don't know what you're saying. Maybe you could get a translator?"

Dr. Alotofsyllablesinverystrangeorder ignored my suggestion and babbled on while poking vigorously at my injured foot with a gloved finger.

Maybe, I thought, *if I just blank my mind and then start listening all over again, I'll catch the cadence and the meaning will follow.*

"Verystupidyouareagirlsotobesostupidthatyoudothistoyouastowearthestupidshoes.Very."

Darn. I got nothing.

"I'm sorry." I shook my head, grimaced, raised my palms in questioning defeat. *Please, could a nice Jewish doctor—without any accent—please, please just come through that flimsy curtain right . . .*

"Blaahhhhrrrrggghhhhh!"

I clapped my hands to my ears and hunched my shoulders while Mr. Hurly McVomit in the next "room" retched his brains out for the tenth time and Dr. Alotofsyllablesinverystrangeorder babbled on incomprehensibly, obviously to further torture me.

And then the real torture began. Dr. Incomprehensible—as I'd come to call her in my head—tore open a cellophane packet and pulled out a needle.

The needle was long. And fat.

Dr. Incomprehensible smiled. I swear, she smiled.

And then she stabbed me.

"Ow! Ow, ow, ow!" I wailed.

Nothing, I thought, *could ever be more painful than what Dr. Incomprehensible has just done to me. Nothing! Bring on childbirth! It will be a breeze after this!*

My shrieks brought a nurse running. Tears streaming down my face, I pointed to my poor foot.

Nurse Mary spoke English with a Southie accent. Fine. That, I could understand. She peeked at Dr. Incomprehensible's notes and explained that I'd just been given a shot of something to numb the infected area. And what would happen next would be an "unroofing" of the blister. To allow it to drain.

Nurse Mary winked, patted my knee, and promised she'd be back with antibiotics; I'd need to take them for the next five days.

"Thank you, Nurse Mary," I gulped.

Dr. Incomprehensible glared at me and, with a fierce move, stabbed my poor foot again, this time with a knife.

I think I passed out. When my head cleared I was flat on my back. Dr. Incomprehensible was gone. I took a few deep breaths and sat up.

My foot was loosely bandaged. Okay. Now all I had to do was wait patiently for good, sweet Nurse Mary to bring me my drugs.

I reached for my makeup bag. A fresh coat of lip gloss would definitely help my spirits. Plus, I reasoned, the super-sweet raspberry smell might help distract my nose from the icky smell of throw-up.

But the bag was gone. At least, it wasn't on the little table where I'd put it. I leaned over the side of the bed and checked the floor.

Nothing.

I checked the other side of the bed.

Still nothing.

And then the ugly truth dawned. While I was unconscious, someone had stolen my makeup bag!

What was the world coming to when you couldn't go to the emergency room without being robbed! Quickly, I checked my jewelry and was relieved to find it all still intact.

Still, I started to cry. I'd never felt more miserable. Right then I made a bold-typed mental note to cross hospitals off the list of potential husband-meeting places.

Forever.

Gincy
The Marriage Game

Danielle lay propped up on the couch, surrounded by magazines, the TV remote, a pitcher of some fluorescent low-calorie drink, and a box of low-fat cookies. She was making a list of makeup she needed to replace.

"Did you take your antibiotic?" Clare asked her.

Danielle nodded. "They're so disgusting. Did you see the size of them?"

"Just take them," Clare said, dropping into an armchair. "Infections are no laughing matter."

"Is there any beer or do I need to go out for more?" I said.

"There's a six-pack in the fridge. Bring me one, please?" she asked. "Only if you're going to the kitchen."

Yeah, I thought. *The extra ten feet will kill me.*

I brought us each a beer and a big bag of pork rinds.

Clare refused the pork rinds with a grimace. I offered some to Danielle, but she gave me the "oh, please" look.

I shrugged. "More for me. Hey, Danielle," I said, plopping into a rickety wooden chair that was going to fall completely apart before long if I kept plopping into it. "I don't get it. If you want so badly to marry a doctor, why don't you just ask your brother to introduce you to one of his colleagues?"

Danielle sighed. "It's not that I want to marry a doctor, as opposed, say, to a lawyer. He doesn't have to be a doctor. Besides, I've already dated David's eligible colleagues. Let's just say that none of them were in my league."

"Doctors are under so much stress," Clare added. "It can be hard to be married to one."

"Your mother's married to a doctor," I pointed out. "Are you saying she's had a rough time of it?"

Clare looked uncomfortable. "No. I'm not saying anything about my parents. Their marriage is just fine."

Clare was a lousy liar but I let the subject go.

"Hey," Danielle said from her throne. "Here's an article about friendships among couples. It says it's hard for a couple to find another couple to hang out with. Where all four people get along. I can see that."

"I have no opinion," I said. "I've never been in a couple long enough to have to deal with that situation."

Danielle tossed the magazine to the floor. "I'd settle for my husband liking my girlfriends. I don't care if he likes their boyfriends or husbands."

"But then you might not see your girlfriends so much," Clare said.

"Why?" I asked through a mouthful of grease.

"You aren't supposed to see your girlfriends a lot once you're married," Clare said.

I swear it sounded as if she were reciting from a manual.

"At least, not as much as before you were married. You're supposed to spend most of your time with your husband. And if he doesn't like your girlfriends' husbands, well then—"

"That's just fucked up!" I said. "I am so never getting married."

Danielle grimaced. "With a mouth like that, I doubt you'll ever have to deal with the issue."

"And if you keep making those ugly faces, neither will you."

"I am in pain. I just endured a terrible medical trial. I think I'm allowed to make faces if I want to."

I shrugged.

After a moment Danielle announced: "I was thinking."

"Call the papers!"

"I was thinking," Danielle went on, "that it wouldn't be wise to marry a guy with more than two siblings. Too many gifts. Birthdays, anniversaries, nieces and nephews graduating from high school. And too much travel at the holidays. And it totally wouldn't be wise to marry a guy whose mother lives within a fifty-mile radius. You'd be pressured to spend every Sunday afternoon eating dried-out pot roast and listening to stories about how perfect your husband was."

"Oh, come on," Clare said, with a small, worried little laugh. "You're overreacting, Danielle. You don't marry a family. You marry a man. One person."

"Are you high?" I asked. Rhetorically, because I so knew she'd never done drugs. Not that I had, either, but I seemed the one more likely to have dabbled.

"Marriage is a social institution," I announced, with all my years of wisdom. "Forget about what goes on in the privacy of your own home. When you marry a guy you marry his family, believe it. You marry his past and his present and his future.

"You marry the detergent his mother used to wash his diapers and the teacher who crushed his youthful spirit and the first time he got laid.

"You marry his health insurance and his retirement account.

"You marry his midlife crisis. You marry his parents' aging and getting Alzheimer's and you marry the nieces and nephews you'll be buying birthday presents for.

"Because we know men don't buy the presents and send the cards. That's women's work."

Danielle sighed. "It all sounds so exhausting, doesn't it? When I'm married I'm hiring a personal assistant to handle my correspondence and gift shopping. Like I'll have the time? Supervising the nanny and organizing dinner parties and hosting fund-raising events? Please."

Clare got up and headed for the kitchen. "Another beer?" she asked as she passed me.

Poor thing. She looked sad.

Could it be that Clare wasn't entirely thrilled with her impending fate?

Danielle
The Right Moves

I'm still not sure why I accepted a date with Chris Childs in the first place. He so clearly didn't meet several of my criteria for a husband.

He wasn't Jewish.

He didn't wear a suit to work, which meant he probably didn't have things like investments and stocks and a four-week paid vacation during which he could take me to Europe while our kids spent the month in sleepaway tennis camp.

And something told me he wouldn't necessarily appreciate the new Missoni skirt I'd picked up at Filene's Basement for only three hundred dollars.

Also, at that moment in my life, I wasn't particularly interested in casual sex, a fling, an affair. I viewed a quickie as a waste of precious time. Why be rolling around in some hottie's rumpled bed when I could be out scouting for a lifelong relationship?

A woman on the verge of thirty had to carefully budget her time.

Still, when Chris called the house and suggested a sunset picnic, I readily accepted. I mean, I didn't have a date scheduled for that evening, so why sit at home?

He came for me in the black pickup. Thankfully, neither

Gincy nor Clare was home. I could all too easily imagine Gincy's smirk and Clare's frown of concern.

God, I thought, as Chris smiled and opened the passenger-side door, *I hope the seats are clean because I'm not sure even a dry cleaner can get grease out of taupe linen pants!*

Frankly, I knew nothing about truck attire.

Chris wore a gray, long-sleeved T-shirt and his standard jeans. Everything was clean. Honestly, I'd never seen him look anything but spick-and-span. *Maybe,* I thought, *he pays a mechanic to do all the work on the truck.*

"By the way," I said as we drove off, "how did you get my number?"

Chris blushed. Through his tan I actually saw a blush!

"Don't freak, okay?" he said. "I was driving through town the other day and I saw you come out of a house. I took a chance that you were staying there and not just visiting. So I looked up the number in the phone book. Everyone here knows the people who own the house are the Simpsons, so . . ."

Huh. Determination. That was good.

And honesty. Also good.

And the blushing was unexpectedly sexy.

I watched him drive—his hands firm on the wheel and shift knob, his thigh muscles bulging when he put in the clutch.

Watch yourself, Danielle, a voice in my head warned. *This guy could be big trouble. He could divert you from your chosen path. He could delay your process.*

Stick to the program, Danielle, the voice said before I closed my ears to it.

For our picnic Chris had chosen a totally unoccupied stretch of Lucy Vincent Beach. Unoccupied by humans, that is.

"Do we have to sit here?" I asked nervously, as Chris spread a large plaid blanket on a flat, dry area of sand.

"What's wrong with here?" he asked, oblivious to the threat.

I pointed to the herd or flock or gang or whatever it was of seagulls a few yards away.

"The gulls?" Chris looked confused. "They won't hurt us. Come on, have a seat."

I did, but I never took my eyes off the gang of feathered hoodlums.

"That one's looking at me!" I cried, clutching Chris's arm.

Let him sit with his back to the enemy! Not me.

"Which one? The little brown one? I don't think he's looking at you, Danielle. I think he's got a lazy eye or something."

"No, no, no! Not the little brown one. That one! The big one! Oh, my God, it's as big as a car!"

Chris laughed. "They're kind of cool, don't you think? Their breast feathers are so amazingly white."

I shuddered. What was wrong with him? "They're disgusting. They're scavengers. They eat garbage. I think they know I don't like them. Chris, I'm scared. Let's get out of here."

"You sure you don't want to have our picnic first?"

I considered. I was awfully hungry. "Okay. As long as you promise to keep those—things—away from our food. If even one comes within twenty feet of us I know I'll have an attack."

"Are you subject to, er, attacks?" he asked.

I thought I saw a smile playing around his lips.

"No," I admitted. "But a seagull snatching my dinner could definitely start a bad habit. They're just rats with wings, you know."

"Pigeons. Pigeons are rats with wings."

"You have your rat and I'll have mine."

Leather and lace, I thought. *Town and country. Jew and Christian.* It would never work. In the long run.

But tonight?

I was sure it would work just fine. Especially after I saw the contents of the big picnic basket Chris had brought.

He'd brought wine—it wasn't very expensive, but it was tasty—and a baguette and a piece of brie and grapes. Standard picnic-date fare. It was very nice. He'd even thought to bring napkins! Not a lot of guys remember napkins. And a corkscrew. And plastic cups.

Chris had thought through the details.

That was a good thing. In my experience, most guys were not detail-oriented about anything other than cars and computers.

We ate and talked, and though the conversation wasn't about politics or art, it flowed easily.

And the sunset was spectacular. I mean, I'd seen my share of sunsets, but this one was really something.

"I'd love a wraparound dress in those shades of orange," I said, pointing to a band of fire along the horizon. "See?"

"You'd look beautiful in those colors."

I sighed. "I know. I wish I'd brought my camera tonight. I could take a photo with me when I go shopping . . ."

Chris touched my chin with a finger and turned my face to his. His eyes were brilliant in the light of the setting sun.

"Danielle, I've never met anyone like you. You're so . . . I don't know, just so alive. And fun. And you just seem so yourself."

Well, of course, I thought. *Myself is an excellent person to be.*

"Thank you," I said.

I didn't compliment him in return. It wasn't smart to be too free with compliments. A man might think he could stop trying.

And even though I had no intention of seeing Chris after that night, I did still want him to try for the duration of the evening.

Just as the sun was touching the horizon, Chris kissed me. It was a long, deep kiss, not all slobbery though. The man was an artist, a master of the kiss.

But I didn't tell him I thought so.

Forehead to forehead, Chris's sweater draped around my shoulders, fingers entwined, we sat there in the growing dark.

I wish a professional photographer would stroll by right now, I thought. *We'd make a wonderful cover shot.*

Gincy
You Scratch My Back

The things we do for friends.
Or acquaintances.
Or roommates.
Basically, for people we hardly freakin' know.

Clare called me at home one night—a first—and asked if I'd go with her to a baby shower the following afternoon for one of her colleagues.

"Since when do you take a date to a baby shower?" I asked, stomping a roach with my bare toe. "I don't even know this chick. And do I have to bring a present?"

Clare was silent, as if trying to come up with a reasonable explanation for her request.

She should have thought of one before picking up the phone and wasting my time.

"Well?" I prompted.

"Can you please just come with me? You don't need to bring a present. And I'll say you're a friend visiting from out of town. We won't have to stay long. Please, Gincy?"

How lonely is this girl, I thought, *when she has to ask me, a virtual stranger and someone who's always poking fun at her, for such a big favor?*

"Yeah, all right, I'll go," I said. What a softie I was becoming. "I have lots of sick days built up. Just tell me where to be and when. And what to wear."

Clare sighed. "Thanks, Gincy. I mean it. I owe you one."

The shower, it turned out, was afternoon tea at the Four Seasons. The freakin' Four Seasons!

I pictured the baby showers my mother and aunt had given—Jell-O mold, ambrosia, cake from a Duncan Hines mix. Soda. Not a vegetable in sight. Certainly not finger sandwiches. Unless you counted squeeze cheese between two Ritz crackers as finger sandwiches.

Sitting there next to Clare, all dressed up in my one good black suit, a snowy white napkin on my lap, I had a sudden, serious craving for sliced bananas suspended in red goo.

But alcohol would do.

Clare
Baby-o-Rama

"Isn't there booze? Can't I get a drink?" Gincy asked.

I sighed. Maybe it hadn't been such a good idea to ask Gincy along. She was the only one at the table wearing black. She was a beetle among pastel butterflies.

"It's tea, Gincy," I whispered. "Not cocktail hour."

"I know but I'm having a few problems with this," she hissed. "First: I don't like tea."

"You could order coffee," I suggested reasonably.

"Second: I hate hotel coffee. It's just flavored water."

"Seltzer? Iced tea? Everyone likes iced tea."

"Third: No iced tea. Fourth: I am bored out of my mind. I don't know Ms. BabyMaker. Why am I here, Clare? Do I care about receiving blankets? No, I don't care about receiving blankets. What the hell is a receiving blanket anyway? The least they could do is provide alcohol for the single women."

Why, oh, why hadn't I asked Danielle to come with me?

I shot a look around the table of twelve smiling women. My colleagues: Tara, the mom-to-be; Rita, a third-grade teacher; and Alana, an art teacher, only fifty-eight and grandmother of three. The other women were Tara's family and friends.

Thankfully, no one seemed to be paying any attention to my grumpy, out-of-town visitor.

"Well," I whispered, "I suppose you could ask the waiter . . ."

Gincy rolled her eyes. "For a Manhattan? And have everyone look at me like I'm an alcoholic? No thanks. I'll just grin and bear it and nibble this—what is this, anyway?"

"It's a tea biscuit," I pointed out. Really, sometimes I wondered if Gincy had been raised in a cave.

"Figures. Not even a bagel on the table. And no cream cheese. Do you see any cream cheese?"

"It isn't breakfast. It's tea."

"More petits fours?" Tara's mother asked, offering me the doily-covered plate of pastel sweets.

I smiled politely, put one on my plate, and passed it to Gincy. She frowned and practically tossed the plate to the woman on her right.

"All I'm saying," she hissed in my ear, "is that this is America, not bloody old England. I should be able to have bagels and cream cheese when I want them. And Sno Balls. Not these little square things."

It was time to put an end to our mutual agony. *Besides,* I thought, *the semester has just ended. I won't have to face my colleagues again until September. Maybe by then they will have forgotten about my odd little friend.*

"Look," I said, pretending to dab my lips with a napkin, really trying to hide from any lip-readers at the table. "How about we cut out now? We'll tell everyone one of us suddenly feels sick, and go, I don't know, go someplace with other single people. And have a drink. Okay?"

Gincy looked at me with dawning amusement. "You're bored, too, aren't you?" She chuckled. "Oh, my God, you had me totally fooled but you're bored, too!"

"Gincy," I admitted, "I am about to stick a fork in my own eye. And twist it sharply."

"Then why did you want to come in the first place? Why did you drag me along with you?"

Why, indeed.

I stood and excused the two of us, indicating that we were paying a visit to the ladies' room. And once outside the dining room we made a dash for the lobby.

Clare

Let Me Get What I Want

Gincy called Danielle on her cell phone as we walked toward Joe's American.

"She'll be there." Gincy snapped shut her phone and laughed. "She says she's been dying for an excuse to wear her new sandals. She's such an airhead."

"She's more than an airhead," I countered.

"Whatever. I just don't want to have to pay another visit to the emergency room. It took three showers before I got the smell of wet gauze off my hands. And I hadn't even touched any gauze."

When we were settled at the upstairs bar and Danielle had come rushing in, cheeks red with heat, Gincy said: "Okay. I know why that little society event freaked me out. But why did it make you so wiggly, Clare?"

Good question.

It couldn't be jealousy. I was engaged. My ring was massive, a good thing in a world in which size seemed to matter. I'd soon be on the mommy track and living in a sprawling suburban house, complete with deck and in-ground pool.

So, what then?

Fear.

Of motherhood? Delivery? Pregnancy?

Or of that first step.

Marriage.

And if not fear, then—reluctance?

Maybe I just wasn't ready for marriage.

Maybe I wasn't ready for marriage with Win.

But I'd accepted his proposal. Reluctantly, but I'd accepted.

How could I explain how I felt to Gincy and Danielle when I couldn't really explain my feelings to myself?

And then words were pouring out of my mouth. "I don't know," I said, twisting a napkin to shreds. "Today I'm single and dancing till dawn at a club in downtown Boston . . . Not that I'm into the club scene—all right, I've never even been to a Boston club—but you know what I mean. And tomorrow I'm nine months pregnant and soaking my grotesquely swollen feet. It just—"

"I thought you wanted children," Gincy said, eyeing me keenly.

"I do! Just not . . ."

"Now?" Danielle, too, speared me with her eyes.

Their intensity pinned me. "I don't know," I admitted, unable to lie or prevaricate. "I don't know if I was going to say not now or not with Win. Maybe that's the same thing."

Gincy and Danielle continued to stare at me, waiting.

I took a deep breath and prepared to admit something I'd never told anyone. "Look," I said, lowering my eyes, "Win's my first real boyfriend. I mean, I've never slept with anyone else. Okay? I know, it sounds so old-fashioned . . ."

"It sounds pathetic," Gincy snapped. "Sorry."

What was she sorry for? It was pathetic. At least, I'd come to think so.

"I know," I said, looking back up. "And now I can't help but wonder what I'm missing. And if it matters that I'm missing it."

Danielle shook her head. "Honey, only you can answer that. Personally, I can't imagine never having had sex with other men before marrying a guy. But then again, I've never been in a long-term relationship like you. I mean, my record is three, no, four months. Once, with a much older man. We've had totally different romantic lives, you and me."

"I just don't know what to do," I admitted again, continuing to surprise myself with every word. I'd never, ever given voice to my doubts and fears.

"Is Win the right one? Or am I marrying him because I'm turning thirty and it's the thing to do? I didn't ask him to propose," I said, almost pleadingly. "I never even mentioned a wedding. But now that I'm engaged . . . I mean, there are so many horrible guys out there and I've been with Win for so long. We really know each other. In some ways. Would I be stupid to walk away from this? It's a sure thing with Win. Right?"

Please, I prayed. *Someone say I'm right.*

Gincy excused herself to go to the ladies' room.

Danielle cleared her throat and took a compact from her purse.

"Another round?" the bartender asked.

That question I could answer all on my own.

Gincy
Missing Socks and Shining Armor

It had been one of those typically crappy evenings.

The Chinese food delivery guy brought the wrong order, which I didn't discover until he'd gone off with my money.

The water from the kitchen faucet was running rusty so I had to settle for flat Dr Pepper.

The water in my tiny Allston apartment often ran rusty. When it ran at all.

And then there was the phone call that came while I was in the bathroom.

The phone rang. And rang. And rang. Clearly, the answering machine was on the fritz. Again.

When I was free, I dashed into the mini-kitchen, grabbed the receiver from its cradle, and barked, "Hello?"

A highly chipper female voice said, "Hi! May I please speak to the lady of the house?"

"The what?" I hadn't meant to be rude. The words just shot out of my mouth.

The owner of the highly chipper voice wasn't in the least fazed. "Is the lady of the house at home?" she repeated.

"Excuse me," I shot back. "Are you calling from the nineteenth century?"

Now there was silence. Clearly the telemarketer's script had not anticipated this particular remark. I took advantage of the silence.

"What are you selling, anyway?" I asked. "Corsets? Smelling salts? Chastity belts?"

The telemarketer disconnected the call without further remark. I suspect she thought she'd dialed the home of a lunatic lady, someone better suited to a life in a musty attic than to domestic bliss in a well-appointed kitchen.

I shrugged and replaced the receiver. No one had ever called me a lady and gotten away with it.

I ate what I could stomach of the cashew-and-bean-sprout mush and flopped into bed. But sleep didn't come easily. I tossed and turned for almost an hour before I fell into a deep sleep and dreamed of a parade with a big balloon of a naked, hairless man. I was one of the handlers, or whatever you call the people who hold the strings beneath those balloons, and I kept looking up to check on the balloon's genitals.

Yup. They were there and they were dangling.

I was wakened from this odd but oddly enjoyable dream by a sound I couldn't at first identify.

A wrong sound.

A sound that should not have been.

I sat up as if that might allow my ears to better detect the origin of the sound.

No doubt. Someone was at the door. And there was no way out except down the rusty old fire escape which, if I was any judge of anything, would crumble to dust the moment I put a foot on the first rung.

"Oh, shit, oh, shit!" I muttered.

As quietly as I could, I slipped from bed and scurried over to the phone.

Don't turn on the lights, Gince! The burglar—rapist!—would know I'd heard him and that would infuriate him and he'd hack down the door with the axe he was sure to have in his utility belt and I'd be in bloody shreds before I could dial 911.

An easy number to dial, Gince. You don't need a light to dial 911. Carefully, I lifted the receiver of the portable phone and dialed.

And prayed. *Oh, please, please pick up!*

After three rings, an emergency operator!

"Someone's trying to break into my apartment," I whispered.

"Are you sure, ma'am?" she asked. I swear she sounded bored.

"What! Yes, I'm sure. Someone's at my door!"

"Ma'am, what is your address?"

I told her. "Hurry, please! I'm too young to die!"

"Ma'am," the voice droned, "we have no cars in the vicinity at this time. We'll send one as soon as possible. In the meantime, don't let the person in."

Don't let the person in?

"Ma'am?"

"What does that mean?" I hissed, shooting a look at the now rattling door. "Do you really think I'm going to invite a murderer in for coffee? Are you crazy!"

"Ma'am, there's no need for—"

I hung up on the bitch. *Who to call? Who to call!*

Rick. I'd call Rick!

I grabbed my backpack and dumped the contents on the table. Who cared if the killer heard me!

There, my address book! I hit the table lamp and made the call. "Rick!"

"Gincy?" he mumbled. "What's wrong. It's—it's two o'clock in the morning."

"Someone's trying to break in to my apartment!" I wailed.

God, I was getting hysterical.

I thought: *How will I ever live this down?*

And then I thought: *You won't have to if you're dead.*

"Did you call 911?" he snapped.

"Yes, yes, and they said they had no one to send and—"

"I'll be right there. Barricade the door. No, stay away from the door in case—in case he has a gun. Lock yourself in a back room or a closet or something. I'll call the police again on the way. Gincy?"

"Yes?" I sobbed.

"It'll be okay. Now, go!"

I did. Directly under the bed. There are benefits to being

scrawny. I scooted back against the wall and covered my mouth with my trembling hand. The dust under there was awful.

And I waited. The rattling and fumbling continued, and slowly I began to wonder what kind of thief this guy was.

New to the game? Drunk? Oh, God, or high on crack!

People got very violent when they were high on crack. I'd seen it on HBO.

I don't know how much time had passed when I finally heard the siren. And then, the heavy tramping of feet up the hall stairs, male voices shouting, and then, a brief confused silence.

"Gincy!"

Rick! I scrambled from under the bed and cried out. "Rick!"

"It's okay," he called back. "The police are here. You can open the door."

All dressed up in sweats and a ratty old T-shirt I tore open the door and flung myself into Rick's arms. He held me and stroked my back and I cried and kissed his neck.

It was a moment before I was aware that we had an audience. I pulled away, wiping my tears with the back of my hand.

"Did you get him?" I asked the policeman watching us too closely. Pervert.

Officer Beefy McBeefster grinned. "There was no burglar, ma'am."

Why did everyone keep calling me ma'am?

I turned back to Rick. "Yes, there was! Someone was trying to break in!"

"Uh, Gincy." Rick pointed to the far end of the dim hallway. Another policeman was talking quietly to a frail, stooped old lady in a housecoat.

"What's Mrs. Norton doing out here?" I said. "Oh, my God, did the burglar try to get into her apartment, too!"

Rick cleared his throat. "Gincy, Mrs. Norton is your burglar. I mean, she left her apartment for whatever reason—you do know she has Alzheimer's? We called her son, he's coming right over—and then she thought your door was hers and—"

I looked again at Mrs. Norton. The poor thing seemed very frightened.

"Oh," I said. "I—I'm sorry—"

The big policeman continued to grin annoyingly. "Better safe than sorry, ma'am," he said.

"You did the right thing, Gincy." Rick turned to the Beefster. "Can she go inside now?"

He shrugged. "Yeah. There's been no crime."

As I walked back into my apartment I heard him add, "Except a waste of police time."

Rick heard him, too, because he shoved me ahead of him and closed the door. "You don't want to pick a fight with the police," he warned.

Now I was angry and mortified. Not a great combination.

I mean, I hadn't even thought about finding a household item I could use as a weapon! No. I'd called for help and hid under the bed.

And now, everybody was laughing at me. "You'd better not be laughing at me," I warned.

"Does it look like I'm laughing?

"Well, inside. You'd better not be laughing inside."

Rick sighed. "Gincy, let's sit down. I'm going to call my neighbor and ask her if Justin can stay with her until morning. Then we're going to have a drink and toast to your being alive. Okay?"

"You don't have to be all hero, you know."

I wrapped my arms around my chest and shivered.

Residual fear. Cold.

"Put on a sweater," he instructed. "And deal with it. Tonight, I am the hero. Next time, no doubt you'll be the hero."

I looked at Rick, at his sleep-rumpled hair, at his sockless feet shoved into mismatched sneakers, at the dark circles around his eyes.

My hero.

I burst out crying.

Clare

Communication Breakdown

The television was on but I wasn't paying much attention to
the show.

Something on the History Channel. Something about the
French Revolution.

Daddy was right. It should really be called the War Channel.
Or the Warmongers Channel.

Or the How Bloodthirsty, Power-Hungry Men Have Made a
Mess of Things Channel.

I scooped another spoonful of ice cream from the pint on my
lap and let my mind drift along.

Random thoughts.

My third-grade teacher, Mrs. Healy, in her baggy orange cardi-
gan.

My grandfather's grumbly voice, silent now for ten years.

The first day of college, the temperature almost ninety.

The night I met Win, the first chill wind of the fall.

At almost eleven P.M. I heard a key in the door. A minute later,
Win came into the living room and tossed his suit jacket on the
back of a chair.

I, of course, would hang it up later.

"So, who did you have dinner with?" I asked.

Win slipped off his tie and tossed that, too. "Hello. And, no one you would know."

I lowered the volume of the TV and sat up. "I guessed as much. But I want to know anyway, okay? I'm curious. About your work."

Win looked at me strangely. "I know. I just don't want to bother you. You've got enough on your mind right now."

"How do you know what I have on my mind?" I snapped. "You're always—you're always—"

Win sighed. "I'm always what?"

I sat back again. "Nothing."

Win left the living room. I heard him rattling around in the bathroom for a few minutes. When he returned he was in his pajamas and glasses.

"I'm going to bed," he announced.

I shrugged and turned the volume back up.

Win stood there. I waited for it.

"Hey, sweetie?" he said. "Why don't you put down that ice cream, okay? I think you've had enough. You don't want to be putting on weight with the wedding coming up, do you?"

I said nothing and continued to stare at the TV. At the portrait of King Louis the Something-or-Other.

Finally, Win left the room.

Deliberately, I ate my way to the bottom of the pint.

Win didn't see me anymore. Not really.

If he did, he'd have noted that I'd lost seven pounds since our engagement.

When Win looked at me he saw what he wanted to see.

I wondered: *What was that, anyway?*

Danielle

If This Is Love

I'd always prided myself on my ability to self-entertain.
And I'm not talking about anything sexual, thank you very
much.

See, as far back as I can remember I was a bit of a loner. Not
antisocial or anything, just perfectly fine on my own.

But loners and individuals make the average person uncomfortable. Especially when the loners and individuals are children.

For years adults tried to get me to join things. The average
adult just doesn't understand kids who aren't joiners.

In grammar school, my mother took up the cause.

"But every little girl wants to join the Girl Scouts," my mother
said, pleading.

"Not me," I answered simply.

"But why, Danielle? It will be so much fun."

I considered this for about thirty seconds.

"No thanks," I said, smoothing my new pink skirt, a recent gift
from my grandmother. "Besides, those uniforms are ugly. The
greens and browns are so muddy."

In high school, the administration took up where my mother
had left off.

In my junior year the guidance counselor warned me I wouldn't get accepted into a good college unless I joined an athletic club or got involved with some other kind of after-school activity.

"Like what?" I'd asked.

"Like cheerleading," he suggested. "Or, I don't know, the school newspaper. What are your interests, Danielle?"

"Clothes and jewelry."

"Well, we don't have a sewing club, but maybe you could start one! Now that would show initiative and—"

I suppose it was the look of incredulity on my face that stopped Mr. Burns in midsentence.

"Well," he finished lamely. "Just think about it, okay?"

"Okay," I said, getting up to leave his stuffy little office. "But I wouldn't get your hopes up."

Thankfully, by the time I started college most adults had decided to let me live my own life. Maybe because I was almost one of them.

Whatever the reason, no one protested when I declared my intention to live on my own. I juggled several jobs each summer—not an easy thing when you're also trying to have a social life—in order to pay for a single dorm room.

I mean, the possibility of getting stuck with some horror show of a roommate who wanted to chat 24/7 was not one I was willing to chance.

Truly, I'd never, ever been bored by my own company. And I'd never once felt dissatisfied just spending an evening alone at home.

Until that particular night in June, six weeks or so before my thirtieth birthday.

My very adequate Back Bay apartment was newly cleaned.

The air-conditioning was gently humming.

The fridge was stocked with all the essentials: champagne, diet soda, yogurt.

I'd just been to my favorite nail salon for a manicure and pedicure.

Everything was perfect and in place.

Except for me.

I found myself standing in the center of the living room.

Just standing.

See, ordinarily, I don't just stand. Or sit.

Sure, I lounge. But that's an activity, some might say an art. This was different. This was new.

I'm restless, I realized. *This might be what people call being at your wits' end.*

I had absolutely no clue as to what to do with myself.

I didn't want to do anything in particular, yet I wanted to do something special, something meaningful, something . . .

That's it, I thought. *I'll call my mother. When all else fails, make a phone call.*

But halfway to the phone I rejected the notion. She'd ask how the husband-hunting was going, and suddenly, I wasn't in the mood to review my progress.

Especially when my progress had been interrupted by a hunky Christian guy who was occupying far too much of my time.

My mental space.

My heart?

TV, I decided. *That's what I'll do, watch TV. Then I won't have to think. About anything or anybody.*

But a quick flip through the channels I received proved that none of my favorite shows were on. *Danielle,* I scolded, *you really must get TIVO.*

I looked around the living room as if expecting a brilliant idea to be sitting on a shelf or side table, just waiting to be noticed.

But there was nothing.

Danielle, I scolded again, *you really should develop some hobbies. Maybe knitting. Or beadwork. Or sewing. You could make your own clothes . . .*

Like that was ever going to happen.

I flopped down on the couch and sighed.

I considered reading. Reading was something.

But I owned only two books. A dictionary from college days. And a Bible, a gift from many years before that.

The truth was that I hardly ever read. Except magazines, and I'd gone through each one in the house at least twice.

A third flip-through wouldn't be too bad, though. I grabbed the latest issue of *Vacation.*

About halfway through I came across a photo of a couple on the beach at sunset. They were gazing into the distance, the remains of a picnic around them. No nasty gulls fouled the scene.

Great. Now I was thinking about Chris again.

In my experience, Christians and Jews just didn't work out as couples, with the rare exception of Charlotte and Harry on *Sex and the City*. And for a while, it had looked like a total disaster. She'd even converted for him, and poof!

Instead of a marriage, a breakup. Instead of a ring, a slammed door.

Okay, so it had worked out in the end, and Charlotte had gotten a huge diamond from her future husband the lawyer, but Charlotte and Harry were a fictional couple.

Cute, but fictional.

Maybe, I thought, *I should get out of the apartment. Maybe go out for a drink.* But when I started to consider what I'd wear and where I'd go and how I'd get there, the whole thing just seemed too complicated.

I went into my bedroom, thinking maybe I'd just go to bed, try to sleep. And then I spied the computer. I could, I thought, e-mail my old Long Island friends. They just might be at their computers and ready to chat.

And then I realized how unlikely that was.

Michelle had a three-month-old baby and Amy had a manic toddler and, God knows, Rachel and her new—second—husband wouldn't want to be disturbed at nine o'clock at night.

Besides, what did I have to chat about? The weather, who had just bought a new house, whose grandmother had gone into a nursing home.

I doubted the girls would be interested in the dating exploits of their remaining single friend. About the totally ineligible guy who was worming his way into her life.

And honestly, without a family of my own, I wasn't really interested in stories of diaper rash, breast-feeding, and baby-sitters.

I sat on the edge of the crisply made bed—Ralph Lauren sheets and comforter—dejected. On the dresser were framed photographs of my parents, grandparents, and David.

David alone.

David and me.

David and Roberta in their official engagement photograph, David's hair all neatly combed and glossed.

It was too late to call David. He was religious about getting to bed and rising early. Healthy, wealthy, and wise, that was my brother.

What about my new friends, I wondered. Gincy and Clare. *I could call one of them.*

Maybe.

The idea was both appealing and disconcerting.

I'd never called either of them just to chat. I wasn't sure we were close enough for that. I wasn't sure I'd ever been close enough to anybody outside my family to call just to chat.

Besides, Clare was likely to be out with Win, and Gincy was sure to be out partying at some club. Or working late on some project for work. She was a bit of a workaholic. An unlikely one, but definitely more devoted to her job than I was to mine.

Are you devoted to anything, Danielle, a strange new voice in my head asked. *Besides your family? Or your notion of who they are and what they want from you?*

Nasty, meddling voice. I tuned it out.

What to do, what to do!

Activity. Action.

I went to my desk and reached for my account book. I reasoned it would boost my spirits to note all the men who had shown interest in me recently, the men I'd dated, the ones who'd given me their numbers.

The eligible men.

The ineligible, that strange new voice whispered.

Chris. Again.

And then I was flooded by sense-memories. His touch. The salty-sweet smell of his neck. How beautiful he had looked in the light of the setting sun.

I put my face in my hands.

Oh, Danielle, I cried. *Don't let this happen.*

July

Danielle
The Ties that Bind

I loved my brother.

David was probably the person I felt closest to in the whole wide world.

Sometimes he could be bossy, but that was just a function of his being the older sibling.

Maybe it also had something to do with his being a doctor, someone in a position of authority, someone on the front line of life and death.

Whatever. It didn't matter. David was king. King David.

I loved and admired him.

And part of me wanted to introduce him to Chris. I wanted to share with David this sweet guy in my life.

Another part of me wanted to keep Chris far, far away from my brother.

The latter feeling was so strong that when David agreed to spend a weekend on the Vineyard, I skillfully arranged to keep the two men apart.

Besides, the visit would be difficult enough with Roberta in tow. My brother's twenty-five-year-old fiancée.

I didn't like the fact that I was losing my brother to Roberta, but I had to accept the reality.

When a man married, he joined the woman's family. It was just the way it went. Forever after, his parents and siblings would come second.

In the beginning years of marriage, though, there was a constant tug-of-war for the son/brother/husband. A new wife tended to be suspicious of her husband's relationship with his mother and sister; even a casual reference to his old girlfriends could wreak domestic havoc.

All of it was normal. Wives most often won the prize and that was the way it should be. Even the Bible said so. A man shall leave his mother and a woman leave her home and all.

So, when I first met Roberta I was wary, naturally. But I came to tolerate her. Even sort of like her. She seemed to want to be friends.

Maybe that was just her tactic, to befriend the sister instead of to antagonize. Whatever. Her pleasant behavior made David's moving on easier for me. And for that I was grateful.

Also, Roberta and I shared an interest in clothes and jewelry. For example, she had this gold-and-ruby pendant I would have died to own. She told me it was one of a kind, but I made a mental sketch at that very moment and, later, put it down on paper.

My future husband, I thought, would appreciate my input on his gift choices.

Anyway, I was thrilled that David had agreed to come to the Vineyard for a long weekend. I didn't see him as often as I would have liked and I knew it cost him to leave the practice.

David, unlike me, had chosen a career he was passionate about. Maybe it had chosen him. I'd heard passions often chose their people.

My brother arrived at the house that Friday in the late morning, lugging four large overnight bags. His fiancée, trotting behind, carried a small Kate Spade summer plaid tote. I showed them to the second bedroom and waited in the kitchen with Gincy and Clare for them to get settled.

"David seems sweet," Clare said earnestly.

"The poor guy looked like a pack mule," Gincy said. "A sweet pack mule," she added when she saw my glare. "But I guess he's used to carrying bags, what with having you as a sister."

"Ha. David's a gentleman," I retorted. "Maybe you're unfamiliar with the type."

About half an hour later David and Roberta reappeared in the tiny kitchen. I thought I sensed a strain between them, but David's sudden bright smile set me at ease.

"My little sister gets more beautiful by the minute," he said, throwing his arms around me.

"Thank you," I told his chest. "I know. And you get more handsome!"

David pulled away and sighed dramatically. "It's a family burden, what can I tell you."

"Oh, you silly!" Roberta squealed, pulling on David's arm so that he was forced to turn to her.

My smile changed from natural to forced but I said nothing.

Roberta announced that she and David were going off right then to see the beachfront. Before I could suggest we all go, they were gone, Roberta tugging David along behind her.

Gincy gave me a funny look.

"What?" I demanded.

"I wouldn't let my brother touch me with a ten-foot pole," she said.

"You've told us your brother is scum."

"True."

"Neither of my brothers ever hugs me," Clare said. "Not really. Not like you and David. I wish my brothers and I were closer. But I guess it's too late for that."

"I don't know," I admitted. "David and I were always close. My mother says that from the moment I was born he was totally a protective big brother. And naturally, I adored him."

"Yeah, well, lucky you," Gincy said. "Personally, I've done just fine on my own. If Tommy fell off the face of the Earth tomorrow I doubt I'd give a—"

"Don't say that!" Clare scolded. "Family is precious. Even if it's not perfect."

"She's right," I said. "Maybe Tommy deserves another chance."

Gincy grinned menacingly. "Maybe," she said, "you both should just butt out of my business."

Danielle
Girl on the High Seas

The next morning I tiptoed out of the house so as not to wake the others.

Who was I kidding? The next morning? It was the middle of the night!

Four A.M. might technically be morning, as in not P.M., but no sane person really thinks it's morning.

Except fishermen. But maybe they're not sane by nature. I don't know. All I know is that Chris was waiting for me just outside the house, pickup truck engine rumbling.

"It's still dark," I whispered, climbing into the front seat.

"You don't have to whisper," he answered with a grin. "It's only me and I'm already awake."

"Well, that makes one of us."

Chris leaned over and kissed me.

"I'm awake!" I said brightly. "That was quite a trick, Mr. Childs."

"No trick. It just comes naturally."

"You!" I swatted him playfully and we drove off to the dock or pier, or wherever he parked his boat.

But the rocking of the truck lulled me back to sleep. When

Chris cut the engine, I startled awake. I tried to stop a huge yawn, but no luck.

"This hour is ungodly," I pointed out, drawing the rain slicker I'd borrowed from Clare more closely around me. "No sane person should be awake at four in the morning, let alone heading out to sea. You know that, right?"

"Do you want to forget the fishing?" Chris said, all serious. "I could take you home—"

I touched his arm. "No. No, I want to do this. Really. Look, I brought this tote full of stuff we might need. Like tissues and Band-Aids and juice. And a camera. I'm all set. All prepared. Ready to go."

On a boat.

I stared at the thing bobbing in the water. In the big, cold expanse of water.

"Danielle," Chris said carefully, "are you afraid of the water?"

"Of course not!" I lied, as he helped me board the boat. "I did grow up on Long Island, you know. We have beaches. And backyard pools. My uncle had a pool. My cousins and I played in it all the time when we were kids."

"Oh, so you can swim."

"Well, no," I admitted. "But I can do the doggie paddle."

Chris frowned and reached into a compartment for something big, bulky, and an ugly shade of green. "Here. Wear this life vest. It's the best one I have."

As long as no one sees me, I thought, shrugging into the vest.

We set sail or whatever you do in a motor-powered boat. Chris waved to some guy in another boat. Other than him, we were all alone in the world.

The water was choppy and gray; the sky, gray and silver. Drops of water shot up onto exposed areas of skin and made me shiver.

Suddenly, I was aware that I couldn't see the shore. "Chris," I said, voice quivering, "I don't feel so good."

"Keep your eye on the horizon," he said. "Try not to blink. There you go—"

"Blllaaaaggghhhhh!"

I felt someone's hand on my back. Who . . . The world was spinning, my head was pounding . . .

"It's okay, Danielle." Chris. It was Chris. "It happens to everyone. Well, a lot of people. Next time you go out on the water you'll know to take a Dramamine beforehand."

Next time? Was he kidding?

I crumpled to the floor of the boat, too dizzy to be mortified. But in another minute, I was back at the rail.

The one thing I'd neglected to stuff into the tote was a barf bag. Throwing up into the sea was simply terrifying. Even through the nightmare of nausea I was beset by a horrifying vision of hurtling headfirst into the briny deep.

And I almost didn't care. Drowning was sure to solve the vomiting problem.

"Good thing I didn't eat breakfast this morning," I mumbled after some time.

"Well, if you feel better soon, I did pack some muffins," Chris offered.

When I'd emptied my poor stomach again, I gasped, "People actually eat on these things?"

"People actually drink beer," he said.

Well, you know what happened next.

Oddly, after a long half hour or so, the nausea passed and I was able to enjoy the experience of being out to sea with Chris.

Or so I let him think. It was one of my best performances, ever. I oohed over the sunrise and ahhed over the sparkling waves . . .

"Danielle," Chris asked suddenly, "is this the first time you've ever been on a boat? I mean, aside from the ferry?"

"Of course not! I went on a dinner cruise once."

"Did the boat actually leave the harbor?"

"Uh, yeah. That's why it was called a cruise, silly."

"Just checking. I'm going to cut the motor here and drop a line. If we're lucky, we'll catch some fish."

Actually, he didn't say fish. He said what I think must have been the name of some type of fish. But the moment he said whatever it was he said, I forgot the word.

Chris busily tied a brightly colored lure to the line. There was a big, barbed hook hidden among some feathers at one end of the lure.

"So, the hook actually goes in the fish's mouth?" I asked, trying to imagine just what that meant, and failing.

So I'd never watched a nature show or a *National Geographic* special in my life. Big deal.

"Right. Now, stand back while I cast."

I did. And only moments later I discovered exactly what happened to the hook and the fish's mouth.

"Bingo!" Chris cried. "I think."

I watched him work to haul in whatever it was he'd caught.

Finally, Chris pulled a big, wet, flapping fish over the rail and I leapt back and stumbled into a bucket.

Chris laid the fish on the deck and started to yank the hook from its poor mouth.

"Ew, ew, ew!" I shrieked. "How can you do that to the poor thing? Doesn't the hook hurt the poor fishies? Oh, I can't watch!"

"I thought you liked fish." Chris's lips twitched.

"Cooked and seasoned, yes," I replied haughtily. "Not alive and squirming and suffering. Ew."

"So, I'm guessing you won't stop by the house later and help me wring the necks of some chickens I had my eye on for dinner."

I feigned horror and we kissed. And then we kissed some more.

I hasten to add that first I'd thoroughly rinsed my mouth with Scope. I always carry a travel-size bottle in my bag.

I was home by nine o'clock, little worse for the wear.

Truthfully, I'd surprised myself. I'd been quite the sport. Quite the trouper.

Maybe this outdoor life isn't all bad, I thought, unlocking the front door of our little house.

Not that I wanted to do anything drastic like run off to sea.

But if I was going to spend more time in nature, I was going to need an appropriate wardrobe.

I made a mental note to borrow one of Clare's L.L. Bean catalogues.

The thought of shopping made me smile.

Clare
Gabfest 2004

"So, how was your fishing date with Nature Boy?" Gincy asked, pouring a third cup of coffee.

Not that it mattered to me how much coffee she drank, though I didn't want to imagine the state of her stomach lining. It was just that she had a habit of finishing a pot and neglecting to make another.

I know Gincy wasn't inconsiderate on purpose. But still . . .

"I wouldn't call him that," Danielle protested. She was fresh from the shower and dressed in a white shorts-and-halter set. "And it was a lovely date. Chris caught a few fish. I can't remember what he called them. Anyway—sshhh, here comes David."

"Why—" I began, but Danielle cut me off with an impatient wave of her hand.

"I'll explain later," Gincy whispered. "Basically, she doesn't want her ideal brother to know she's dating a mere fisherman."

David was a friendly sort. He and Danielle shared olive coloring and dark hair and eyes. But where Danielle was voluptuous, David was lanky. He had the look of a runner, though Danielle told us he'd never been much of an athlete. He preferred to spend his time at the library or at his computer.

THE SUMMER OF US 149

David, she said fondly, was kind of a nerd. It was, she claimed, what made him such a good doctor, technically speaking.

That morning he was dressed like most other casually dressed professional men, in a pair of chinos, a navy polo shirt neatly tucked in, and dress-style moccasins.

Win had a similar pair.

"Well, we're off," he announced, after greetings all around. "Seems we have to do a little shopping this morning."

Roberta smiled hugely. She seemed pleasant enough but also struck me as terribly spoiled.

But that was just my impression, based on nothing more than her appearance and the fact that the night before I'd overheard her complaining to David that our house was awful and that he should have booked them into a hotel.

They were staying in the second bedroom, which meant that I was bunking with Danielle in the first bedroom. Gincy had offered to take the couch for the duration of their visit.

As I had closed the bedroom door behind me, mostly to block out Roberta's whining, I heard David mumble something about not hurting his sister's feelings.

David, I had thought, was henpecked.

But this morning, there was no sign of trouble in paradise.

"Isn't he sweet?" Roberta asked rhetorically, petting David's arm. "He buys me a present from every place we go. Of course, I wouldn't be marrying him if he didn't! Right?"

Gincy's mouth opened, but a stern look from me kept her quiet. Amazingly.

Maybe she was trainable after all.

When David and Roberta had gone off, Danielle suggested we go out for breakfast.

We strolled into town and settled at a tiny table at Bessie's Breakfast Bests, a place dubbed "Triple Bs."

"I was thinking about that article," Danielle said, "you know, the one on couples having trouble finding other couples to hang out with. So that everyone gets along. Do you think it's, like, a duty for the wives of male friends to like each other?"

Gincy took a gulp of her fifth cup of coffee that day.

"I think most men expect that when they get married they'll never see their buddies again," she said. "Or only when their wives allow them to. Take my family. My mother was ironfisted about my dad seeing his buddies. Once she caught him sneaking out to catch a beer with this guy Bill and she freaked. At the time I was too young to know what was going on but I found out later.

"I kinda had a thing with one of Bill's sons. A minor thing; it lasted about ten minutes. Anyway, I never saw my mother hanging out with Bill's wife. Come to think of it, I never saw my mother hanging out with any women friends. She's not very likable, my mother."

I didn't share my thoughts just then for fear of insulting my housemates needlessly. But the truth was that Win would have far preferred me to have taken a summer rental with two wives or fiancées of his colleagues than with two strangers, neither of whom was seriously involved with a professional man.

He'd told me so.

And then I'd pointed out that none of the wives or fiancées ever went off without their men. And that I wasn't particularly close to any of the women, anyway.

And then Win had said, "Maybe that's your fault, Clare. Maybe you should try harder, learn to be a better hostess. Entertaining is important in my profession. I need to know I can rely on you.

"A man needs to know he can rely on his wife."

"You can rely on me," I'd answered automatically.

"I hope so," he'd responded before going back to the computer.

"I think lots of guys are like Gincy's dad," Danielle was saying, when next I tuned in. "I bet the last thing Mr. Gannon wanted was his wife and Bill's wife banding together and forcing them to stop smoking cigars or eating Cheez Doodles."

"I love Cheez Doodles," Gincy said. "Why is it that TV commercials always portray the wife as the one who knows best? Why is she the one who eats low-fat food and the hubby the one who scarfs donuts? Plenty of women scarf donuts. I scarf donuts."

"The contemporary myth of American domesticity," I replied,

poking at my own healthy fruit salad, thinking of how I routinely nagged Win to eat properly. "Why do you even pay attention to commercials?"

"Because half the time they're more interesting than the shows. You can't tell me that *Big Brother XXV* is more interesting than the latest round of Nike ads."

"I wouldn't know," I admitted. "I've never watched any reality TV show."

"Women," Danielle proclaimed, "don't want their men picking friends for them. Women have their own selection process."

Yes, I agreed silently, *we do. But tell that to Win.*

The waitress cleared our table then, though we lingered over final cups of coffee and for me, another glass of water.

"Wouldn't it be nice if our guys got along?" Danielle said. "I mean, assuming we each had a steady guy. Then we could hang out as couples."

Gincy laughed. "We three barely get along! What are the chances of us finding three compatible men to add to the mix?"

"I hate that cliquish couple thing," I blurted, surprising myself with my boldness.

Maybe it was due to the fresh, invigorating breeze coming off the water.

"It's like there's a law," I went on, "a law that dictates that once you're in a couple it's only valid to socialize with other couples. Anyway, that's what Win likes to do. Socialize only in couples. Only with people he knows from work."

"Sleazy corporate lawyers," Gincy mocked.

Boring corporate lawyers, I amended silently. *At least the people Win chooses to spend his time with.*

"You know," Gincy said, fiercely.

She often spoke fiercely and with conviction, even on topics that couldn't possibly matter in the long run. Like people who spelled Stephen with a "ph" versus those who spelled it with a "v."

"I hate those women who stop saying "I" once they're part of a couple. It's like they can only say "we." Like, 'Oh, we just hung around on Saturday afternoon' instead of telling the truth, which might be, 'Bob simonized the car and I read a book.' "

"Well, isn't the point of being a couple spending time together?" Danielle countered.

"Yeah, but you're not a couple first," Gincy argued. "You're an individual who's 'in' or 'part of' a couple. See the difference?"

"I don't know about that," I admitted. "Lately, it doesn't feel like I'm me first, then part of a couple. Mostly it feels like . . . it feels like I'm just part of Win. I don't know if there's even a couple anymore. I don't know if we have a partnership."

Did we ever have a true partnership, I wondered. A blasphemous thought.

"Win and sub-Win." Gincy considered. "I think that stinks."

"Why don't you tell us what you really think?" Danielle commented dryly.

Gincy grinned. "I think I just did."

The morning breeze was suddenly gone, sucked away by a heavy, early-afternoon heat.

I decided I'd said quite enough about my personal life for the moment.

Gincy
And Another Thing

Stupid Rick Luongo.

There I was, strolling along the shore at the Edgartown-Oak Bluffs State Beach, water gently lapping at my ankles, the sun toasting my skin, and all I could think about was that stupid Rick Luongo.

Since he'd come to save me from the burglar-that-wasn't, he'd risen yet another notch in my estimation. Make that two notches. Because not once had he lorded over me his middle-of-the-night ride to the rescue.

Believe me, I watched and listened for any signs of mockery or derision from our colleagues. And when I could find none, I confronted Rick.

I walked into his office and closed the door behind me. Rick looked up from his computer and, in doing so, somehow managed to knock several fat files off his desk.

"Hi," he said, looking momentarily at the new mess on the floor. "What's up?"

"So, who did you tell?" I demanded. "Everyone's acting all oblivious. How much are you paying them to keep quiet?"

Rick eyed me carefully. "You're a bit insane, do you know that?"

"That's beside the point," I said, though of course, it was exactly the point.

Rick stood and came around the front of his desk. I moved aside as he perched on the edge, nearly impaling his butt on a pair of open scissors.

"Gincy, I didn't tell anyone about the other night. Assuming that's what you're referring to. The alleged break-in?"

"Alleged? What are you now, a cop? Mr. Law Enforcement with the lingo. And yes, that's what I'm referring to. The incident to which I am referring."

"I didn't tell anyone," Rick said, matter-of-factly. "Except Justin. I wanted to explain why I dragged him out of bed in the middle of the night and left him with Mrs. Murphy. I told him a friend needed help. Which was the case. End of story. Why?"

Rick had called me a friend. At least, he'd referred to me as a friend.

Oh, boy, Gincy, I told myself, looking stupidly at him sitting on his desk, noting how the muscles of his thighs were outlined through his pants. *You really want to be something more, don't you?*

Oh, yes.

Still, I said nothing.

Rick crossed his arms across his chest. His sleeves were rolled halfway up his forearms. Which were strong. His wrists were broad.

"Do you think there was something funny in it all?" he asked.

The question took me totally by surprise.

"No! Absolutely not! I mean, I was scared out of my mind, and poor Mrs. Norton, I don't know how long she'll be able to live on her own—"

"Then why," he interrupted, "should I find something funny in it all?"

I shrugged. *Gincy,* I thought, *you are a big fat idiot.* "I can be a bit defensive," I admitted. "Sometimes."

"We all have our things," Rick said, grinning.

"Like you're klutzy?"

"Among other things."

"What other things?" I asked, wondering if we were flirting.

"How stupid would I be to tell you all my faults?" he replied.

Oh, yeah. Flirting.

"That bad, huh?" I said.

There was a beat of silence during which we looked at each other eye to eye and, unless I was imagining it, the sexual tension was running rampant.

I'd never been prone to misreading sexual signs. At least the ones I'd been interested in following.

Finally, Rick opened his mouth to reply and just at that moment Kell was at my shoulder.

"There you are!" he cried, breathing garlic fries all over my neck. "I need you, now."

Kell grabbed my arm and half dragged me from Rick's office. I shot a look back at Rick as I went. His eyes were still smoldering.

Smoldering?

Watch it, I warned myself. *Danielle is rubbing off on you.*

I dodged a gang of delinquent ten-year-olds charging toward the water. Kids. Whose idea were they, anyway?

Rick had a kid.

Damn! In spite of the dazzling sun and sparkling water, I just couldn't get the feel of Rick out of my head. That hug when I'd flung open the door. My kisses on his neck. God, how embarrassing!

I reached the end of the two-mile stretch of shoreline and turned back for home.

A few strides later I spotted David and Roberta, up toward the road, away from the rolling water.

David was wearing what seemed to be his standard vacation garb, chinos and a polo shirt neatly tucked in. Roberta wore a hot-pink midriff-baring top and super-low-rise white pants.

It looked as if they were having an argument. Rather, it looked as if Roberta was having the argument all by herself. She was shouting and waving her arms wildly at David who stood stock-still, arms at his sides.

I looked away and walked on.

It had to be as embarrassing for the onlookers of an argument between a couple as it was for the member or members of the couple who were aware of the onlookers. No one liked their dirty laundry to be aired in public. And no one wanted to witness anyone else's dirty laundry flapping in the breeze.

At least, I didn't. I knew that some—most?—people derived a rabid, hand-rubbing pleasure from watching other people's civilized facades crumble. I mean, isn't that what *E!* was all about? *People* magazine? Katie Couric interviews?

After another minute, I snuck a peek over my shoulder. David and Roberta were gone.

I wasn't sure if David had seen me. I hoped he hadn't. He was okay. A bit spineless if his choice of fiancée was an indication of his larger personality, but okay.

Roberta must be dynamite in bed, I thought. Because it wasn't like she had a lot else going for her. The scene I'd just witnessed simply confirmed the impression I'd already formed of Danielle's future sister-in-law.

Roberta was your classic spoiled bitch. And I was sorry a good kid like Danielle was going to be stuck with her.

Not that Danielle was suddenly my best friend or anything. I wasn't ready to attest before a jury that she was of the highest moral character or that if we were stranded on an island she'd willingly sacrifice herself for me by feeding herself to a tiger. Or whatever wild beast had attacked us. A boar, I imagine.

Still, I wasn't a terrible judge of character and it was pretty clear that under Danielle's bright and sparkly airhead exterior was a good person. Someone of some depth.

Maybe she was a bit confused, maybe a bit in denial, but hey? Who wasn't confused and in denial?

Roberta. That's who. And people like her.

I swear she was as transparent as a pane of glass, as insubstantial as a sliver of styrofoam, as shallow as a wading pool. I wouldn't trust her as far as I could throw her, which wouldn't be far, what with all the hairspray and jewelry she wore.

Nice, Gincy, I scolded. *It's so easy to slam other people, isn't it? Keeps you from getting your own life in order. How can you work through this Rick infatuation if you're spending all your time mocking some bubblehead from Long Island?*

I continued home along State Road, feeling a bit too much like the rabid, hand-rubbing voyeurs I claimed to loathe.

Clare
The Calm and the Storm

The skies opened up around one o'clock that afternoon.

I'd always found rainy days so terribly depressing. They brought back memories of the summer vacations when my mother wouldn't let my brothers and me into the lake during the slightest bit of rain.

There was the big beautiful lake, only feet away, and yet it was forbidden territory. My mother's rule seemed so horribly unfair.

What could happen that would be so bad?

Lightning might strike and burn you alive. A wave might rise and drown you. A wayward boat might knock you on the head and force your body down, down into the muddy deep.

The rain itself and my mother's extreme caution seemed to cut short the vacation. They forced me to think of summer's end. Of going back to school. Of returning to the daily sameness of ordinary life.

When I was a child I felt there was real magic in difference. Change of place meant changes of thought, perceptions, feelings. Different clothes, different food, different people. Change meant excitement.

When I was a child. Children are brave.

Starting at about the age of twelve, I began to feel differently.

I began to feel that change was messy and frightening. Difference was just too challenging. Sameness meant safety and security.

For most people, I guess, adolescence is a time of rebellion, testing limits, sexual exploration. For me, it was a time of fear, a time of closing up and shutting down.

Of course, I didn't realize all that until years later when it was far too late to recapture my youth. Until I'd been with Win for close to a decade.

I could hear Gincy quoting her father: "Hindsight is twenty-twenty. Youth is wasted on the young."

I could hear Danielle chiming in with her grandmother's words of wisdom: "You're dead a long time. Seize the day."

Carpe diem.

Well, I wasn't sure I'd ever seized anything, let alone the entire day.

I mean, what kind of person was I that at the age of twenty-nine I was still haunted by those dark, depressing days at the lake?

The rain worsened and by two o'clock all thoughts of salvaging the day had disappeared. We settled in the living room with books, magazines, and the TV.

Gincy groaned. "I can't believe the only thing on is *Antique Roadshow!* This has got to be the most boring show ever produced."

"Are you crazy?" Danielle cried. "It's great! Though I will admit it bothers me when some semi-illiterate, toothless, three-hundred-pound woman in a caftan finds out she's got a bedpan worth three hundred thousand dollars or something. I mean, someone like that doesn't deserve a lot of money. She obviously has no idea what to do with it!"

"And you do," Gincy shot back. "Wait. You probably do know what to do with money."

Danielle nodded. She had a very queenly sort of nod. It seemed completely natural to her. "I was born with a dominant taste gene and I've honed my talent over the years. You know, it says in the Bible that you shouldn't hide your light under a bushel. Meaning if you have a God-given talent, you should use it."

"I thought you attributed your taste to genetics," Gincy said slyly, "not God."

Danielle gave Gincy one of her now-famous looks. The one that said, "Okay, we all know you're smart, so why don't you just shut up now?"

"Clare, don't take this the wrong way," she said, turning her attention to me, "but honey, you're looking a little dragged out these days. A little peaked. A little undernourished. I'm not seeing that glow in your cheeks. I'm seeing dark circles around your eyes and tiny lines around your mouth."

"What Danielle is trying to say is that it looks like you've lost weight," Gincy said.

"Oh, I'm okay," I said dismissively. "I guess I've just been running around a lot lately. I guess I've skipped lunch a few times."

"Honey, again, with all due respect, but you don't want to be a skinny bride. You want to be a healthy, glowing bride. Am I right? You don't want the dress to hang off you on your big day. You want it to fit."

"It will fit," I said, without any conviction at all. I hadn't even thought about a dress, though of course I'd lied about that to Danielle.

Danielle leaned forward in her chair and clasped her hands on her knees. "Clare, be honest with us. You're not having an attack of anorexia, are you?"

"What!" I cried. "No! Besides, I don't think anorexia comes in attacks, like cluster headaches. Anyway, no, I'm not anorexic. God, Danielle."

Danielle shrugged. "All I'm saying is that if you are having an attack of anorexia, there are people who can help you. There are places you can go. Just keep in mind you don't have to suffer."

I bit my tongue. Literally.

Gincy seemed to sense my outrage. "I'd offer you a Sno Ball," she said, smiling coyly, "but I know you'd just throw it up."

I laughed. "No, I'd toss it right back at you! Ugh! You know there's absolutely no nutritional value in those packaged desserts."

"Yeah, well, at least I don't smoke. Much. Everyone's got her bad habits."

"What are your bad habits, Clare?" Danielle's voice betrayed some annoyance. I suspected she didn't appreciate being teased or ignored by both housemates in the same sitting.

"I'm afraid of change," I blurted. "I don't take risks. At least, I haven't for a long time."

Danielle waved her hand dismissively. "Everybody is a bit afraid of change. It can be very exhausting. And sometimes it's not worth the effort and things don't work out to be better than before."

"I'm not talking about change that just happens, like accidents you can't control," I explained. "I'm talking about change that you choose. I never choose to change. Almost never."

"Fear of change isn't exactly a vice," Gincy pointed out.

"It's harmful enough," I shot back.

Gincy got up and went to the kitchen. Danielle raised the volume on the TV.

I stared at the screen and thought.

Oak Bluffs is a new venue.

Gincy and Danielle are new people. New friends?

Maybe. If we didn't kill each other by the rainy day's end.

And I was . . .

Well, that was still to be determined.

On TV, a tiny woman in a flowered dress was crying tears of joy. She'd just learned her grandmother's teapot, a piece she'd always thought worthless in terms of price, was, in fact, quite valuable.

"This changes everything," she sputtered.

Maybe change isn't all bad, I thought. *I'll just have to wait and see.*

Gincy
She Doth Protest

The TV show droned on.

Antiques. I just didn't get the appeal.

I mean, I enjoyed reading about historical events. I just didn't want to live with history's musty, bloodstained relics.

Hair jewelry? Can you get more disgusting?

"I don't know one man who would choose to go antiquing in Vermont," Clare said musingly. "Win certainly wouldn't. He'd suggest I go with my mother."

I laughed. "Have you ever asked him? A man who wants to get laid will do anything the woman asks."

"That's not about choice," Danielle corrected with that "Let me tell you how it really is" voice of hers. Which pissed me off, even when what she had to say was right.

When someone declared she was right, she was also declaring you were wrong.

"A man who wants to have sex has no choices," Danielle said. "He is a slave to the sexual imperative. He does what needs to be done, and if he's really smart, he keeps his mouth shut about things like going antiquing in Vermont. And if he's supersmart and wants to get lucky more than once, he buys the woman a fantastic meal and maybe even a nice piece of jewelry."

"How much jewelry do you have, anyway?" I asked, surveying the quantity of heavy gold adorning Danielle. She and Roberta could open their own jewelry mall. "How much jewelry do you need?"

My own collection of jewelry—if it even deserved the title of "collection"—consisted of a five-year-old Swatch I'd paid twelve dollars for; a 14-carat gold Claddagh ring I'd gotten for my grammar school graduation and which now didn't even fit on my pinky—where was that ring, anyway; and a pair of tiny silver studs I'd put in my pierced ears a year earlier and had never bothered to remove.

Danielle smiled smugly. "It's not about need. And, would you like to see my catalogue? Detailed written descriptions. And photos. For insurance purposes."

"A gay man might want to go antiquing in Vermont," Clare mused.

"Only if he's genuinely interested in antiques," Danielle said. "Or if he's trying to have sex with a much younger, supercute guy."

"Well, I'd never go antiquing in Vermont," I said. "Even to get laid. It sounds colossally boring."

Clare looked genuinely surprised. "Not even if you could stay in a charming B&B?"

"Huh. Especially if I had to stay in a B&B! You have to talk all hushed and smile a lot and oooh and aaah over chintz-covered couches and needlepoint pillows. And you can't even get seconds for breakfast like in a hotel with a buffet. And you can't scream during sex. And forget about the bathroom situation. Have you ever tried to take a crap and make no sound at all?"

Danielle looked at me disapprovingly so I went on. "Or leave no smell? That's a vacation, a shared bathroom? That's visiting my father's family at the trailer park."

"So," Danielle said sharply, as if she were talking to a naughty, antisocial child, "I gather you've stayed in a B&B before."

I smiled blandly. "Oh, no. I've only heard about them. Where would a lowlife New Hampshire kid like me get the bucks for a charming Vermont B&B?"

"While we're on the subject of charming," Danielle said with mock weariness, "I think I'm going to enroll you in charm school, Ms. Gannon. Your lack of it is wearing on my nerves."

Ah, mission accomplished!

Danielle
In a Mirror

Poor David had one of his migraines, a condition he'd suffered since childhood, so just we girls went out for dinner the last night of David and Roberta's long weekend.

I'd hardly spent any time alone with my brother during his visit. I wasn't happy about that. I offered to stay home with him that last night, but he urged me to go out and have a good time.

Maybe he just needs to be alone, I thought. *Totally alone.*

Sometimes I forgot how much of a loner David had been as a child. Even more of a loner than I had been.

Reluctantly, I agreed and left David to the peace of his own company.

Over our lengthy meal at Lucca's, I listened to Roberta chatter on about the cute instructors at her tennis club and the bitchy Korean girls at her nail salon and the Saks Fifth Avenue charge card her daddy had just given her, and how she planned to have her first plastic surgery by the age of thirty, and something hit me.

Just hit me smack in the face.

Roberta was boring. So awfully boring.

And she was shallow. Terribly shallow. Like a puddle.

I mean, I'd never found her to be fascinatingly interesting or a careful, deep thinker.

But this vapid?

God, I thought, *what had David been thinking when he proposed?*

I looked across the table at my future sister-in-law. She was still rattling on. Not once had she asked any of us a question about our own lives.

A vision of Roberta having an affair with one of the tanned tennis instructors she so admired flashed across my brain.

Poor David! So intelligent and caring and sensitive. This woman would eat him alive!

Why hadn't my brother seen the real Roberta yet? Why hadn't he seen past the pretty face, artful hair, and toned limbs?

Because he was only a man.

I wondered. David had an excuse for being blinded by Roberta's flash—testosterone—but what was mine? Women were supposed to be more sensitive to nuances, to reading character clues.

And then, right there over glasses of Merlot and plates of pasta, I was hit by another disturbing thought.

There was something oddly familiar about Roberta.

Roberta reminded me of—me.

At least, on the surface. Who knew what went on in Roberta's mind, in her heart of hearts. Who knew if she even had an under-surface.

I have a mind, I protested silently, noting an unfamiliar—new?—sparkly bracelet on Roberta's wrist. It had to have set David back at least five hundred dollars.

If it was from David and not from some tennis club gigolo.

I have a heart.

I don't know how spiritual things work but I think I might even have a soul.

But had I ever let anyone see those real valuables?

The answer was no. It was a startling, uncomfortable answer.

I shot a look at my housemates.

Gincy was rolling straw paper into little balls, mini-bullets I just knew she'd love to aim at Roberta's head.

Clare seemed inordinately interested in her fettucine alfredo.

Every so often she mumbled, "Oh?" or "Ah," but it didn't fool me.

Clare was bored. Gincy was disgusted.

Suddenly, I felt strangely embarrassed. It was clear what my housemates thought of Roberta.

But what did they think of me, really?

Did Gincy and Clare see a resemblance between me and my brother's fiancée?

And if so, did they even like me? Or were they simply tolerating me for the duration of our house rental?

By the fall, would I be just an unpleasant memory, the typical spoiled JAP, a figure of fun?

I stuffed a garlic bread stick in my mouth and fervently hoped not.

Gincy

You Never Know Unless You Try

O kay. So I went out with Rick again.
Maybe I thought that as long as I didn't actually see his kid, live and in person, the kid—Justin—didn't exist.

Honestly, I don't know what I thought. But after that heated moment in Rick's office, the moment interrupted by Kell, I was a goner.

In fact, I asked Rick for our second date.

"You beat me to it," he said. "And, yeah."

We went out another time after that. First to the movies, then for burgers, beer, and pool at Jillian's.

Things progressed. There was no choice about it. I was too powerfully attracted to be all cautious and wary.

Rick had the physical attributes I found most appealing: wavy dark hair, dark brown eyes, olive skin, a compact body. It was a body built for power.

Where the clumsiness came from, I had no idea.

He was also really smart and keenly interested in everything from food to music to the history of European cinema. We belonged to the same political party and our stand on the big ethi-

cal issues of the day, from war in the Middle East to the potentially explosive issue of stem-cell research, were utterly compatible.

Finally, I was drawn to Rick by his total lack of guile. The
guy just didn't seem capable of telling a lie, even a social,
white lie.

He was the original foot-in-mouth fellow, infuriating at times,
but a huge relief after years of wasting time with cheats and guys
so full of crap you could smell it a mile away.

"How do I look in this blouse?" I asked him once.

He frowned and said, "Not good."

"How do you mean?" I asked, blood simmering. I'd paid a
whole ten dollars for the thing!

He shrugged. "I don't know. It just doesn't look good."

Well, I'd asked.

When I got home later that night I took a good look at myself
in the mirror.

Rick was right. The blouse sucked on me. I looked like a starving nineteenth-century peasant.

Score one for the guy in my life.

So, we went out a fourth time, to a movie and then for Indian
food.

And after dinner we went back to my place. It was the first
time Rick had visited—not counting his rescue mission—so I
gave him the tour. That took a whopping two minutes.

There we were, standing face-to-face in my minuscule living
area. Rick's hair was tousled from the evening's unusually cool
wind. I wanted very badly to climb all over him.

"So, uh, we're going to do this, right?" I blurted.

"Yeah," he said. "If you want to. I want to."

"I want to, too."

"You know I can't stay over. Justin. I have to drive the sitter
home."

"Who said I want you to stay over, Mr. Presumptuous?"

"Sorry. It's been a while since I was last single. And then I didn't

have a five-year-old. I know far more about *Nickelodeon* than I do
about current dating etiquette."

"Forgiven," I said, putting my arms around his neck. "Now
shut up and let's get busy."

And we did. And it was great.

Totally freakin' great.

Gincy
Venus and Mars Collide

Life can suck, but sometimes it's just incredibly good. Like when you're blessed with yet another weekend of perfect weather.

Danielle chose to spend the gorgeous day shopping. When she returned later that afternoon she was lugging three large and overflowing shopping bags. Her purchases included a gold and enamel charm in the shape of the popular Nantucket basket (for her mother), a bright red Martha's Vineyard sweatshirt (for her father), and several pairs of sandals. They were for Danielle.

I'm not sure where Clare disappeared to exactly but she returned all glowy and energized, babbling something about five miles and running and needing new a heart-rate monitor and about how kayaking was her new favorite sport.

Me? I'd spent the day popping in and out of art galleries and paying my first visit to the Vineyard Museum in Edgartown.

At about five, Danielle, Clare, and I met for drinks and appetizers at a popular place called Keith's. It overlooked the water with a large deck and both indoor and outdoor bars. We were lucky to get a table with a good ocean view.

I suspected our luck had something to do with whatever it was Danielle had slipped the hostess.

Funny.

At the start of the summer I hadn't expected to be spending much time at all with my roommates, outside of the house, that is. But somehow, without effort, we'd begun to bond.

Sometimes, it weirded me out. Other times, it was okay.

Okay, a little more than okay.

"Hey there!" Danielle waved to someone and then turned to us. "I hope you girls don't mind. I told him we'd be here. He's only stopping by. He's got to work."

"Who?" Clare asked.

"Chris."

"Wait, David's too lofty to meet him but we're low-class enough?"

"Oh, Gincy, it's not like that at all! Now, sshhh. Hello!"

We were joined by Danielle's Man of the Sea. He was extremely cute in a very outdoorsy way. Far more Clare's type, I thought.

And he was very charming. Truly charming, not smarmy and sly.

After introductions, I asked him if he wanted to join us for a drink. I figured Danielle wouldn't mind.

"Oh, no thanks," he said. "I never touch alcohol when I'm going to work."

"That's wise," Clare commented.

Chris grinned. "Let's just say I learned wisdom the hard way. The way most of us do."

"Ain't that the truth!" I said.

Danielle got up from her chair and took Chris's arm. "Don't you have to be going, Chris?" she cooed. "You don't want to be late for work."

Chris looked at his watch. "Yeah, you're right. My boss is a real jerk when I'm late by even a minute."

"Don't you work for yourself?" Clare asked.

"Yup. And I meant just what I said, the boss is a real jerk."

Everybody but Danielle laughed, and Chris loped off to his truck.

"You practically threw him out," I commented as soon as he was gone.

Danielle frowned. "I did not. I just didn't want him to be late for work."

"What do you care if he's late for work? If his business goes bust? You're not going to marry him, right?"

"He's so nice," Clare said quickly, before Danielle could reply. "He seems so genuine."

"Yeah," I agreed. "But personally, I'm more interested in his body. When you're done with Chris, pass him on to me, okay?"

"What about Rick?" Danielle shot back, clearly angry at me.

"What about him?" I replied, pretending nonchalance. "I'm not the one who wants to get married. I'm not the one with a system and a checklist."

"But—"

"But nothing. Don't put words in my mouth."

"Okay," she said, "the Rick question aside, let me just say that a guy who dates Danielle Leers is not going to be interested in dating Gincy Gannon."

"Is that an insult?"

"No, just a reality check. Gincy, we are, like, total opposites. We're barely the same species, let alone the same sex."

"You *are* insulting me!" I cried.

Danielle remained calm in the face of my growing rage. "No," she corrected, "I'm just pointing out the visible truth. Look at what you're wearing. Look at your hair. When was the last time you got it cut? Have you ever used a blow-dryer? What about gel? When was the last time you wore a skirt? Have you ever had a professional manicure?"

"Of course I've used a blow-dryer!" I spat back. "Where do you think I grew up, in a swamp?"

"Well," she drawled, "the way you talk about your hometown, I have wondered."

"Oh, Danielle," Clare said now, shooting me a look that said, please don't throw that punch. "You're making too big a deal about silly little differences. Things that mean absolutely nothing in the long run. You and Gincy are each hardworking, intelligent, kind women. That's all that matters. Any man worth his salt would be happy to be with either of you."

Danielle and I stared at each other until, finally, she shrugged and looked away.

Good ole Clare. Ever the peacemaker.

And I had my own way of conceding to peace. I ordered us another round, in spite of Clare's protests that one margarita was her limit.

"Eat more chips," I told her. "You'll be fine."

Halfway through our second margaritas, a couple was seated at the next table, close enough for observation but at an odd enough angle that they couldn't be sure if we were sneaking glances at them or the cute bartender just beyond.

She was straight out of the Young Female catalogue; he, straight out of the Young Male.

She had long blond hair, which she tossed with frequency, a flawless figure, and a pert and pretty face. She wore a mini-sundress and strappy high-heeled sandals.

He was muscled from regular workouts at the gym. His hair was not quite, but almost, cut in a buzz; on his left wrist was a heavy, round-faced, gold-tone Rolex. His crisp white cotton shirt was open to mid-hairy chest; his front-pleated black cotton pants flared just so.

Danielle, of course, helped refine my observations. I wouldn't have recognized a Rolex in a Rolex display case.

The woman's expression was alternately studiously bored and eyes-half-closed seductive.

The man's expression was alternately low-browed defensive and I'm-gonna-do-right-by-you-baby.

"Here's the difference between men and women, as I see it," Danielle suddenly announced.

"You really need to point out the differences?" I asked, incredulous. "The stereotypical male and female are on display right in front of us. You can extrapolate every detail just from the appearance and mannerisms of those two specimens! What more is there to say?"

"The difference is," she replied, "that with women there's always more to say. Men do; women talk. Guys go golfing and women get together for lunch."

"That's stupid," I said. "Eating lunch is doing something. You're biting, chewing, swallowing, digesting."

"Yes, but lunch is not really about the food, is it? It's about the conversation. It's about the juicy gossip and unwanted advice. It's about setting up your slightly overweight single girlfriend with your forty-five-year-old bachelor cousin."

"I think you're splitting hairs," Clare protested, "making a big distinction about talking and doing. You always—"

"Go on," Danielle urged, nonplussed. "I always what?"

Clare blushed. "I shouldn't have said 'always.' What I meant to say was that you try to categorize the world. A lot. Often."

Danielle shrugged. "So? A lot of things are just obvious. Categorizable. If that's even a word."

"But nothing is black-and-white," Clare argued. "Especially not people. Not behavior. Not—"

"Pardon me if I'm generalizing again," Danielle drawled. "But I've been thinking. See, my brother just asked his friend Jake, a guy he's known since kindergarten, to be his best man. David and Jake have had absolutely nothing in common since the age of, well, let's say five. I mean, Jake's a personal trainer. Nice, but dumb as a doornail. And David, well, he's a brilliant doctor. Still, they're like, best friends. And I've seen this kind of thing before."

"Your point?" I asked, bored enough to be fascinated by Young Male feeding Young Female fried calamari with his thick fingers.

"My point is that guys tend to find a few friends when they're like, toddlers, and keep them forever, even if they grow up to be totally different and have nothing in common but a penis."

"Well, I don't know," Clare said. Predictably. "Women keep some friends throughout their lives. My mother is still best friends with her best friend from high school. But it is true that women change so much. We move on, we shed friends and acquire new ones and . . ."

I pretended to shudder. "We sound like freakin' snakes with all the shedding. I don't like snakes."

"Of course," Danielle confirmed, ignoring my remark. "Women are about flowering and flux and flow."

"And so men are about stasis and stability and . . ." I hesitated. "I need another 's' word."

"You're still stereotyping," Clare said now to Danielle. "If that's all true, how do you explain the observable reality that women nest and men roam? Nesting is about stability. Roaming is about, well, chance. Instability. And if women are about change and flux, how do you explain the fact that they love boxes?"

I frowned. "They what now?"

"I've thought about this," Clare said earnestly. "Every little girl has a box for her secret treasures. Purses are just an extension of the treasure box. Think about it. What does it mean that a woman has a jewelry box for her watch and a pretty little dish for her change, while a guy throws his watch and change on the counter, all mixed up, right out there in the open?"

"Maybe it's about order versus chaos?" Danielle suggested.

"No, I don't think so," I said. "At least not in my case. I'm a slob and Rick is anally neat despite his clumsiness. I'm the one throwing quarters. Rick's the one collecting and rolling my spare change. Of course, he usually drops the roll on my foot, but . . ."

"Well then: Enclosure versus exposure?" Danielle asked.

"Safety versus risk?" Clare offered.

My turn. "It's about the fact that men are urged to spread their seed across the land and women are urged to hold themselves close."

"Good point," Danielle said. "And think about this: Women have a womb."

"Do I have to think about it?" I said. " 'Cause I'm not planning on using it for a while. Why does everything come back to the womb?"

But Danielle was warming to her train of thought. "A womb is a secret space for growing things. On the other hand, men have no secrets. They have a penis. And testicles. Just all hanging out there, shameless . . ."

"Ah, now we're onto something!" Clare cried.

She was more than a little tipsy. It was the first time I'd seen her that way.

She'd feel like crap in the morning, but right then, it was cute. I'd take happy drunk over belligerent drunk any time.

"Shame," Clare mused. "Women have always been taught to feel shame about their bodies, their feelings, their thoughts. Exposing any part of a woman's self is shameful. So women have learned to keep everything inside. Hidden. In a box. I am so smart."

"Yes, you are, honey," Danielle assured her. "And consider this: Women are urged not to go topless. I mean, in public. A woman without a shirt is a slut. Except on a nude beach. But it's okay for men to go shirtless. Tacky but not illegal."

"Yeah," I said, "and tell me who enjoys some stranger's nipples in their face. Or some stranger's big fat gut."

"I wouldn't mind seeing Ashton Kutcher's nipples," Danielle said.

"Ashton Kutcher isn't a stranger," Clare corrected. "He's a celebrity. There's a big difference between a stranger and a celebrity."

"While we're on this strange topic," I said, "let me just say that I don't particularly want to see any part of a stranger's naked body. Even his stomach. Or her stomach. Even if it's flat. I mean, I respect a person's right to put it out there, but why can't that person respect my right not to have to look at it put out there?"

"Secrecy versus frankness," Clare piped.

"Shame," Danielle said.

"Oh, no," I groaned. "The dreaded circular conversation."

"Polly Pocket! toys!" Danielle looked very pleased with herself. "Those teeny little dolls. Very easy to hide."

"Miniatures. Tiny little statues. And dollhouses. A little girl is given a dollhouse," Clare said. "An enclosure. A place that she can lock up tight. While a little boy is given a racetrack. How different is a dollhouse from a racetrack? Very different."

"Things are changing," I pointed out. "Things have changed. Look at all the little girls on soccer teams and, I don't know, doing amazing computer stuff. It's not like they're all skipping around in frilly dresses anymore."

"True," Clare admitted. "About the dresses, anyway. But have you seen the Barbie section at FAO Schwarz? Have you? And the baby-doll section? Pink still rules. There are still plenty of traditional girly things being pushed on kids."

"Well," Danielle said, "I, for one, don't see anything so wrong in that. I grew up with plenty of pink and I turned out just fine. And shut up, Gincy."

"Me! I didn't say anything!"

"You were going to."

"You really think you know me that well?"

"Yes, I do."

"There's a rock star named Pink," Clare said.

Danielle sniffed. "She's not the kind of pink I like."

"Russian stacking dolls," Clare said, suddenly. "A series of dolls within dolls."

"Who plays with them?" I asked. "I always thought they were, like, ornaments. Stuff you find in old lady houses. Old lady houses in Brighton Beach."

"Diaries that lock," Danielle said. "Electronic diaries that have, like, sirens if your little brother tries to open them without the password. I've seen them on TV."

"Do you remember your first suitcase?" Clare said suddenly, with the genius of someone gearing up for a major hangover.

I snorted.

"Suitcase? You mean, like, duffel bag? Backpack? We didn't really travel in my family. We piled in the rat-ass car and drove for an hour to AntLeg, New Hampshire. You don't need an actual suitcase to go to AntLeg, New Hampshire."

"Oh. Well, we used to go to Chicago. We have some relatives there. And the Upper Peninsula. I suppose you didn't need actual luggage for going to the lake house but . . ."

"Excuse me," I interrupted. "The lake house? You had a second house?"

Clare had the decency to blush. "It was no big deal," she protested. "Really. I mean, everyone we knew had a house on a lake. I mean . . ."

"Spare me."

"What color was it, anyway?" Danielle asked. "Your first suitcase."

"Blue. Kind of a dark baby blue. My parents had matching navy bags. I think it was an American Tourister set."

"I had a hatbox," Danielle said. "It was very impractical. Very chic but very impractical. Not that I cared about practicality."

"You still don't," I pointed out.

"My grandmother gave it to me. I loved it. It was pink patent leather. God, I wish I still had that hatbox. It would be perfect for storing some hair pieces."

"First makeup kits, first dress-up pocketbook . . ."

"So, what it's really about is stuff," I said with some distaste. "Girls have a lot of stuff. And they need places to put all their stuff."

Danielle considered. "Boys have a lot of stuff, too," she pointed out. "And men. Like tools and toolboxes and tool belts."

"I have a toolbox," Clare said brightly. "A shiny black one. The screwdriver's handle is fluorescent purple."

"I never thought I'd say this," I muttered, "but thank God for Win. He can use a screwdriver, right? Fix a broken toilet? Change a light bulb?"

"Briefcases," Clare went on, ignoring my rhetorical questions. "Both men and women have briefcases."

"And lunch boxes," Danielle said.

"Not my family. Tommy and I took our lunch to school in brown paper bags. They leaked. Especially, for some reason, when we had cream cheese and jelly. It didn't happen with peanut butter and jelly. Something about consistency, I suppose."

"Remember how exciting it was to open your lunch box even if you already knew what was inside?" Danielle sighed. "I miss being a kid. I just loved eating Twinkies."

"Twinkies?" I cried. "Gack. I preferred Suzy Qs. And, of course, Sno Balls."

"How could you?" Clare said with what sounded like genuine horror.

"What, like Suzy Qs are any worse than Twinkies? What did you eat for dessert?"

"Mostly, my mother baked. Sometimes she bought Little Debbies. It's a brand."

"What have you got against Hostess?"

"Nothing! I'm just telling you what we ate for dessert. We just ate what my mother told us to eat. I remember a little cake with caramel icing. Or maybe it was butterscotch. I remember the color distinctly. Whatever it was, I loved it."

"It's amazing what sticks with us, isn't it?" I remarked. "I mean, I can't remember major events, like grammar school graduation, but I can totally remember what the nerdiest kid in class wore every single day of school."

"Which was?" Danielle asked.

"A gray clip-on tie. Every single day, the same tie. Maybe he had an entire drawer full of them, I don't know. I can't remember my grandmother's face, and I loved my grandmother, but I can remember that tie. It was kind of shiny after a while. And it had a perfectly circular stain on the bottom left corner. Why do I remember that and not important stuff? What does that say about me?"

"What does it say about memory in general?" Clare wondered. "About history, about biography, about autobiography."

"What was the kid's name?" Danielle asked.

"I don't remember." I shrugged. "Tie Boy."

"I remember a boy who sat across from me in class, maybe in second or third grade," Clare said. "I don't remember his name or even what he looked like. But I remember there was always a huge plug of wax sticking out of his ear . . . ."

"Oh, God," Danielle cried. "I'm going to be sick! Clare, how could you!"

"I know," she said, draining the last of her glass and smacking her lips. "It's a horrifying little detail to remember. I can still see, so clearly, the side of the boy's head and that dirty ear. Didn't his mother ever check him before he left for school in the morning? Didn't she ever make him bathe?"

"I wonder why the teacher didn't send a note home to his mother asking her to wash her kid!" I cried, remembering in a flash my own mother wielding a Q-tip with more determination than caution.

More lovely memories.

"Why is that awful memory still with me?" Clare went on. "What can it possibly mean to me now? I guess at the time it was kind of fascinating, in a gross sort of way. But why does my mind waste brain cells storing that bit of memory? Why can't I remember the French word for, say, shelf, but I can remember Ear Wax Boy?"

"It's only one of God's many sick jokes," I said.

"To remember things that horrify us and not edifying bits of information we learned in language class?"

Clare looked seriously distressed.

"Or pleasant memories," I continued. "Like a great afternoon of sleigh riding. Or the details of one of the books I loved as a kid. I remember certain titles and I know I loved the stories, but I can't remember exactly why I loved them. What kind of memory is that? It's like a black-and-white memory. Why can't we have memory in full color? Like the sunset? Look, isn't it amazing. And I guarantee that by tomorrow's sunset I won't remember the details of this one at all."

That melancholy observation put a temporary damper on our festivities. The damper was relieved when Young Male and Young Female got up to leave. Male put his massive arm around Female's teeny waist and unnecessarily guided her off the deck.

Danielle nodded in a manner she no doubt thought indicated wisdom. How many margaritas had she had?

"That guy? He's just like all the rest. All men are the same. And they're just completely the opposite of women. Venus and Mars. You just don't understand. Opposite ends of the pole. Men are idiots."

"There you go again," Clare scolded. "Generalizing. I don't think you should talk like that."

"Why not?" I challenged, as Danielle seemed inordinately interested in the bottom of her glass at the moment. "What Danielle's saying isn't hurting anyone. It's not like she's dictating behavior. She's just observing and commenting, that's all. That's her right as an American citizen."

"Things are never really opposites, you know," Clare went on, ever so patiently. "So-called opposites exist because of each other. Opposites define each other. Light is the opposite of dark because it's not dark . . ."

Danielle looked up from her glass, befuddled. "So everything is part of everything else? What?"

"God, we're boring!" I cried. Or seriously loaded. "How old are we anyway? Like, fifty?"

"Intelligence doesn't have anything to do with age," Clare said. "Necessarily."

"This conversation is about intelligence? What we're doing here while guzzling margaritas is being intelligent? Huh. I never would have known."

Danielle grinned. "You mean, you wouldn't recognize intelligence if it bit you in the ass."

"Of course not. Do I have eyes in back of my head? Now, if it bit me on the belly, I might have a chance. And I can't believe you said the word 'ass.' Ha! I'm rubbing off on you!"

"God forbid. Men don't like a woman with a foul mouth."

"That's absurd!"

Danielle preened. "Well, the kind of men I want to associate with don't like a woman with a foul mouth. Okay?"

I stuck out my tongue and ordered a final round. An hour later we stumbled back to the house and within minutes, though it was barely nine o'clock, the lights were off, Danielle was snoring, and Clare had disappeared into the second bedroom, mumbling something about Barbies and boobies.

It occurred to me later that night, as I lay on the couch, eyes wide, waiting for the room to stop spinning, that I'd never heard Rick use a four-letter word, much less a foul or rough or dirty word. I wondered if that was because of having a kid; maybe he'd just gotten out of the habit of cursing since Justin was born. Or maybe he never had been in the habit of using "bad" language.

Huh. Now that I thought about it, I'd never heard my father use a nasty word, either. That didn't mean he didn't curse with his buddies from work, but in the house, in front of the family, never.

Unlike my piggy brother, Tommy.

Unlike me.

Maybe you should work on the language thing, Gincy, I thought, just as the room stilled and I began to drift off to sleep. *Maybe guys like Rick don't marry gutter-mouths like you . . .*

I shot up and clutched my head.

Marry?

"Holy crap, Gincy," I whispered to the room. "You really have to watch those margaritas."

Clare

Mothers and the Daughters Who . . .

Mother called to announce that she was coming to Boston. Ordinarily, I enjoyed her visits. We'd shop and have lunch at fancy restaurants. Sometimes we'd just stay at the apartment, reading, sipping tea, and chatting about nothing in particular.

Our time together was always very pleasant.

But I knew this visit would be different. Now that I was about to become a married woman, Mother would be all business.

The lazy afternoons of fun were over. Now, there was work to be done.

As a precaution, I tucked my journal under the mattress where it would be safe from Mother's keen eyes. The only room Mother didn't enter, out of delicacy, she said, was our bedroom. I don't know what she expected to find going on in there.

And Win never did a bit of housework; he didn't need to tell me he thought it was woman's work. There was no chance he'd be changing the sheets any time soon.

After Mother had unpacked her bag and inspected the guest room for all amenities, she emerged with a look of determination I hadn't seen on her face since she chaired a big fund-raiser at Daddy's university.

"Clare," she said, "have you considered the vows?"

Her question startled me. Since the time I was a little girl first dreaming of her wedding day, I'd thought it would be nice to write my own vows. For my husband to write his.

But now, faced with the actual event, I wasn't so sure.

What, exactly, would I say about my feelings for Win? About why I was marrying him and no other?

My own words, spoken aloud to Win, in the hearing of friends and family. It seemed frighteningly intimate. Suddenly, I wasn't sure I wanted to do it. I wasn't sure I could.

"Uh—" I said.

"Well, I hope you'll be more eloquent than that," Mother replied, frowning.

Then she turned to Win. "Win, dear, what do you think about the vows?"

Win looked surprised. "Me? I don't care. Whatever Clare wants is fine by me."

And then he grinned his oh-so-charming grin. "But I have to warn you ladies. I didn't major in English."

"I think the standard vows of the Church are perfectly lovely," I said firmly, decision made. "We'll go with them."

Mother wasn't ready to let the subject rest. "Clare, honey, are you sure? Even as a little girl you used to talk about how romantic it would be to write your own wedding vows—"

"We'll go with the standard," I said hurriedly, scared I'd lose my nerve. "It'll be easier for Win."

Win chuckled. "Thanks, sweetie. I owe you one."

Mother gave me a searching look but moved on. "Clare, have you thought yet about music for the ceremony? You might want to work with the church's music director and meet with the choirmaster—"

"Win," I blurted. "Do you have a favorite hymn you want sung at the ceremony?"

Win looked up again from the computer screen and sighed good-naturedly.

"Look, sweetie, just tell me where to be and when to be there, okay? This shindig is yours. I'm just the guy in the black suit."

Mother seemed pleased by his answer and began to rattle off a list of musical pieces she considered suitable.

I nodded on cue but tuned out her words.

Danielle said it was wonderful, every bride's dream, for the groom to back off and let the bride have her way with the planning. I guess she had a point. I mean, I wouldn't want Win taking charge, which he tended to do with everything.

Still, his total lack of interest in the "project" made me feel alone. Like he thought the wedding was all for me when really, it hadn't even been my idea in the first place.

I watched Win squinting at the online news. I noted the perfect line of his hair against his neck. It struck me that I knew every inch of Win's body as well as I knew my own.

Of course Win thought I wanted a wedding.

Of course he thought I wanted to get married.

Because I hadn't told him otherwise.

Gincy

Who's Lying Now?

Danielle was decked out for the holiday. I mean, she was actually wearing a red, white, and blue outfit.

"You look like Shirley Temple in some World War Two propaganda film," I said as the ferry made its approach to the Vineyard.

It was a gorgeous day, boding well for a sun-filled weekend.

"Or whoever starred in those things. Don't you think you're being a little obvious?"

Danielle looked at me with disappointment. "That's the point, Virginia," she said. "And it's not like I'm wearing a cheesy T-shirt with a silkscreened flag across the back. I'm wearing a classic red, white, and navy ensemble. It's all Ralph Lauren, you know. Even the sandals. I think I look quite spiffy. Very nautical. Very appropriate for the ferry."

I shrugged. I didn't really care what Danielle wore. I just liked to pick on her. She was generally pretty unflappable.

"I can't believe Clare's staying in Boston this weekend," Danielle said suddenly. "It's, like, the official start of summer on the Vineyard! What is she thinking?"

Why did I feel the need to play devil's advocate?

I shrugged. "She's thinking she has a fiancé and they need to spend time together. It's perfectly normal."

"Well, she could have brought him out to the house. I wouldn't have minded."

"I'd have minded," I admitted. "It would have been weird having Win around. I think it would have put a cramp in my style."

Danielle lowered her aviator sunglasses and looked me up and down. From worn black T-shirt to torn jeans to ratty old Keds.

"I wasn't aware you had a style," she drawled. "Of any sort."

"Very funny. Come on. We're about to dock."

We gathered our bags and watched as the shore grew closer. And then, I spotted him. A guy on the dock, carrying an armload of wildflowers, and waving at us. Or . . .

"Danielle? Why is that guy waving at you? Wait. Is that Chris?"

"Oh, my God, it is!" she squealed, waving merrily back at him.

"Damn, he looks even hotter than the first time I saw him. I hope you appreciate what you have," I said to my preening companion.

"What?" Danielle was now studying her face in her compact mirror. "Oh, right. Yeah."

A few minutes later we stood with Chris by his truck.

"To what do I owe this pleasure?" Danielle cooed, clutching her bouquet.

Chris shrugged. "Well, I'm going to be tied up a lot this weekend but I wanted to see you, so . . . here I am."

I feigned a need for a pack of gum and left the two lovebirds alone. At the door of a tiny gift shop I turned and saw them embrace.

That's so not going to work, I thought. *Too bad.* They were both good people, just seriously mismatched.

Yeah, and I was a such a freakin' expert at love.

That evening before Danielle and I left for separate adventures, we spent some time hanging out in the tiny living room. She had put on a CD of some techno dance music stuff, which I loathed and despised but some counterimpulse made me keep my mouth shut about it.

I flipped through the latest issue of the *New Yorker* but not much more than the cartoons registered. I was thinking about the plans I'd made for the evening.

I'd arranged to meet a guy I'd spent some time with over the past visits to Oak Bluffs. He was a few years younger than me, African-American, and very good-looking. Better, he didn't seem to know about the good-looking part.

We'd have sex—of that I was sure—but we'd never make it as a couple. He was too sweet. Which was fine by me because I wasn't looking for a relationship.

I had a relationship back in Boston.

So, what the hell . . .

You might not want to overthink this, Gincy, I told myself, suddenly all uncomfortable.

Damn Rick! He was ruining my good time!

In a mood of defiance, I announced my plans for the night to Danielle.

"Hmmm," she said.

"Hmmm, what?"

"Nothing. Have a good time. Be careful."

"You're dying to say something else," I pressed.

Why? Did I really want to hear from Danielle what I'd already been telling myself?

Danielle sighed. "Fine. I think the only reason you're going out with Jason tonight is because you're afraid of commitment. You say that everything's good with Rick, so why are you bothering with a boy toy?"

And there it was.

"Me, afraid of commitment?" I cried. "What about you! Why are you going out with that Eurotrash guy tonight when you've got Chris, huh? He's gorgeous. He's sweet. What's not to like?"

"Mario is not Eurotrash," Danielle said. "He just dresses like Eurotrash. Besides, my situation with Chris is totally different from your situation with Rick."

"No it isn't! What's different about it?"

"For one, I haven't slept with Chris and you've slept with Rick."

"Well, jeez, what are you waiting for!"

"Excuse me if I don't just jump into bed with every guy I meet," Danielle said loftily.

"Are you implying that I do? Are you saying I'm a slut?"

"I'm not implying anything. Why would I imply? Besides, a guilty conscience needs no accuser."

"I don't have a guilty conscience!" I cried. "About anything. Rick and I never said we wouldn't date other people."

Danielle pinned me with her eyes. "I bet he isn't seeing anyone else. And not just because he has a child to care for."

Huh. I didn't think Rick was seeing anyone else.

I hoped he wasn't.

He had better not be!

"Well," I said weakly, "that's his problem."

"Besides," Danielle said, "Chris isn't a contender. He's not in the running."

"For what? Being chosen as one of your hapless male victims?"

Danielle looked daggers at me. She really was an incredible actress with her eyes.

Bravely, I persisted. "So you don't care if Chris is seeing someone else?"

"No."

"And you don't care if he knows you're seeing other people?"

Danielle's mouth opened and closed and opened. "I'm not talking to you anymore," she said finally.

"Fine, because I'm not talking to you, either. You know, I'm beginning to wish Clare were here, even if she had to drag Win along. She's like a buffer. You and I, we're just way too different to get along without that soft center. Our personalities are way too strong. And you can't bend."

"Why should I! Anyway, like you can bend?"

"I can bend. I just choose not to. About most things. And look! We're talking again!"

Danielle grinned. "Well, what can you expect from two big-mouths?"

She really was a good sport. Annoying, but a good sport.

"Well," she said then, "the truth is I really do wish Chris were around this weekend. Mario's insanely rich but he's just too oily to make it past this next date. Maybe one more after that."

"Bring the blotting paper."

"On another topic, I wonder when we're going to meet the elusive Win Carrington?"

"I don't know. And I don't care," I added truthfully.

"Doesn't it strike you as odd that Clare's never suggested we get together with them?"

"No. Anyway, he sounds like a drip."

"Why?" Danielle said. "Just because he's a corporate lawyer?"

"No. Do you think I'm an idiot? I'm not that addicted to stereotypes. It's just that Clare's marrying this guy, right? And she never lights up when she talks about him. Come to think of it, she never even smiles. And have you ever heard her go, 'Win's so great' or 'Win's so cute. Guess what Win did for me'? Have you?"

"Well, no," Danielle admitted. "But Clare's kind of shy."

"Uptight."

"Whatever. I don't think she's the type to gush. That doesn't mean Win's not worth gushing over."

"Speaking of gushing," I said, noting the dusty clock that hung over the stove, "it's almost seven o'clock. Shouldn't you be getting ready for your date with the oil slick?"

Gincy

Interruptus

Jason Davis was the kind of guy who probably had a good relationship with his mother.

The kind of guy who usually avoided sharp-mouthed types like me like the plague.

I'd met Jason a few weeks earlier at one of my favorite dives. His family owned a summer house in Oak Bluffs and a primary residence back in Newton. Jason worked in Boston as a financial analyst, so he didn't make it out to the Vineyard all that often. Apparently, crunching twenty-digit numbers requires far more than a forty-hour week.

Anyway, that night I joined him at a bar distinctly nicer than the dive at which we'd met, and after a few beers we headed for his family's house. He assured me that he was there alone that weekend. There'd be no awkward moments of our running into Mom and Dad in their bathrobes and slippers.

"Seriously nice house," I said, practically choking on my first-ever case of house envy.

"We've had it for years," Jason explained. "My dad's architecture firm did some major renovations recently. The back deck is new and the kitchen's been totally redone."

He showed me the kitchen. My mother, I thought, would pass

out if she saw this. A double oven. An indoor grill. A Sub-Zero refrigerator.

Oh, yeah. Mom would be on the floor. Drooling. And then condemning it all as wasteful. Sour grapes were my mother's favorite fruit.

There was no romance about the evening's tryst; just two consenting adults, two basically nice people out for some fun. We had another beer and Jason put on some CDs and before long, we were in his bed.

There were the usual preliminaries. And then the clothes all came off and I froze.

What the hell am I doing? I wondered, catching a glimpse of an unopened box of condoms on the massive antique dresser.

Damn. I just couldn't go through with it.

It was all Danielle's fault.

It was all Rick's fault.

It was all my fault that I was naked in Jason's bed.

"I can't do this," I muttered, extricating myself from his embrace. Jason was too deep into the moment to realize at first what was going on.

"Mmmm," he said.

"No, Jason," I said, speaking more loudly. "I mean it. I can't do this. I have to go."

Oh, my God, I thought, getting to my feet on the Oriental carpet. *I'm a tease! A classic cocktease!*

The fog had cleared from Jason's eyes. "I can't believe you're leaving!" he cried. "What's wrong?" He leapt from bed and I turned away from the sight of his erection.

"Nothing's wrong," I said, hurriedly yanking on my clothes. "I mean, nothing's wrong with you. It's me. It's just—"

"I thought we were getting along," he protested. "Did I say anything weird or something?"

Poor guy. He was the innocent victim in this. The innocent, seriously disappointed victim.

"No, no, no! Look," I said, grabbing my bag and retreating to the door of his room, "it's only ten o'clock. You can still go out and maybe meet someone—"

Jason's erection flopped as if it had been shot down. He reached for his boxers and slipped them on.

"What kind of person do you think I am?" he said, his voice thin. "I'm not some sort of slut, you know. I thought we were connecting. But I guess I was wrong."

Guilt swarmed over me like a horde of flies. I felt sick to my stomach. "I'm sorry. Really, I'm so sorry. I'll go now."

"That's a good idea," Jason said quietly. "Pull the front door tight when you leave. It tends to swell in the heat."

"Okay," I mumbled. And I got out of there fast.

Danielle
In Flagrante Delicto

I wondered if Gincy was having a good time with her hottie. *Everyone,* I thought ruefully, *is probably having a better time than me.*

Even though I'd just had a fabulous meal and excellent wine, all paid for by my handsome date, who had picked me up in his fabulous car.

Mario wasn't as horrid as Gincy assumed he was. I'd never have agreed to go out with him if he didn't have some good qualities.

If I can tolerate him for a few more dates, I thought, noting again the rather large diamond in Mario's gold pinkie ring, I just might get some jewelry out of my efforts.

Mario wasn't unattractive. And he was very clean. He smelled crisp.

I could have sex with him, I determined. It could be done.

Mario and I and one of his European friends, a short, balding man named Vinikourov, were standing outside the restaurant, chatting, Mario's arm around my waist, when it happened.

A black pickup truck rolled down the street, slowly, as if the driver was looking for an address.

Or as if the driver had seen someone he thought he knew?

Chris! I tried not to look directly at the truck as it passed us though I was suddenly desperate to know if he was behind the wheel.

Though the night was warm I pulled my wrap closer around my shoulders. Mario removed his arm from my waist and his friend lapsed into animated French.

I was left with my own thoughts, which weren't very pleasant.

I felt horrible. I felt guilty.

Danielle, I scolded. *What's wrong with you? It's not as if you've been caught in a lie. You never promised anything to anyone!*

Oh, but I wanted to know!

Had it been Chris's truck? All trucks looked alike to me! And I hadn't bothered to learn Chris's license plate number. Why should I have?

Mario and his friend were deep in heated conversation now, about what I had no idea. Mario liked the sound of his own voice; I assumed we'd be standing on that sidewalk for some time.

Maybe, I thought, that truck will come around the block again. Maybe this time I'll see the driver. And maybe he'll really see me. Out on a Saturday night with another man.

And did I really, truly care?

I wondered.

Would I feel any more comfortable if my date were an average American guy and not a wealthy European visitor with his silk jacket and diamond pinkie ring and one hundred and fifty thousand dollar Ferrari?

And then I had a horrible realization.

I was actually ashamed of myself.

Not a lot, just a little bit, but even a little bit of shame was bad news.

I was ashamed of myself for going out with Chris.

I was ashamed of myself for hiding him from David.

For pushing him off when my friends wanted to chat that evening at Keith's.

I was ashamed of myself for choosing Mario.

For wanting to hide him from Chris.

I took a deep breath and tried to calm my thoughts. Get some perspective, Danielle, I urged. Forget this shame nonsense and let's look at things logically.

Fact: Chris and I had never talked about an exclusivity agreement.

Oh, but did that mean I could assume we had no responsibility toward one another?

Didn't the terms of decency dictate that I tell Chris I was dating other men?

Maybe Chris just assumed that I was seeing only him.

You know what they say about people who assume? They make an "ass" out of "u" and "me."

That was one of my father's standard lines. He said he got it from an episode of the old TV sitcom *The Odd Couple*.

While my wealthy date gesticulated and debated with his cohort, and couples strolled by enjoying the warm summer night, I thought about assumptions.

The act of making an ass of everyone around you.

Everybody assumed. Nobdy was immune from assuming.

Men assumed. They assumed that women dated only one man at a time.

And they assumed that men were free to date several women at a time.

At least until one of their buddies decided that it was time for everyone to settle down. Then each man weeded out the "women you had sex with" from "the women you married"—the assumed madonnas from the assumed whores—until finally, only one woman remained for each guy.

Assumed wife material.

The blare of a car horn roused me from my thoughts and I shot a look up and down the street. No black pickup truck.

Relief.

Because something told me that Chris wasn't a guy who dated several women at once. And the same something told me that he absolutely would not appreciate my seeing other men.

Especially men like Mario.

Of course, Danielle, I thought, *that's an assumption on your part.*

So there I was, making an ass out of us all, Chris, Mario, and myself.

But what did I really care about any of it? Mario was a passing fancy. And Chris was only a diversion.

He couldn't be anything but a diversion.

No matter how special he was.

"You want now to go to the club?" Mario asked, nuzzling my neck with his artfully stubbled face. I noticed that his chatty friend had gone.

"Sure," I answered distractedly. "Whatever."

Clare
Do As I Say

Mother left for Michigan after imparting several tidbits of unasked-for advice.

One concerned the July 4th holiday. I'd told her that I'd be spending it on the Vineyard with my new friends.

With a stern voice and a look to match, she argued that I should stay in Boston for the Fourth of July holiday and spend quality time with Win.

I thought of all the nice things I'd be missing—the beach, a parade, fireworks—and reluctantly agreed. Win worked hard for us. He deserved to spend the holiday with his future wife. Besides, there were plenty of events in the city we could enjoy.

So why did it feel as if I were making a huge sacrifice?

After dinner one evening, when Win had retired to his favorite armchair to enjoy a half hour of CNN before bed, I told him that I'd decided to stay with him in Boston for the holiday weekend.

I knelt by the chair and smiled up at my fiancé. I expected him to be thrilled. At least, grateful.

Did I expect to be rewarded, a dog at his knee?

"Oh, sweetie, that's so nice of you," he said, in that you-poor-thing, I-feel-so-sorry-for-you voice. "But I just assumed you were going off to the Vineyard. I've already made plans with some of the guys from the firm. We're going fly-fishing in upstate New York."

I was stunned. Win had never gone anywhere without me, except home to visit his family when his grandmother died and I was too sick with the flu to accompany him.

All I could say was, "Oh."

"I'm sorry, sweetie. But I really can't back out of these plans. We've already booked and I'd lose a good chunk of change. You understand, don't you?"

"Of course I understand," I told him. "You go and have a good time. I'll be fine."

"After all," he went on, his manner very earnest, "you do have the Oak Bluffs house and I haven't been able to get away at all since—"

"It's fine," I said, a bit sharply. "It's no problem. Really."

Win bent down and kissed my head. When he'd gone off to the bathroom, I wiped my hair where his lips had touched. And then was shocked at what I'd done.

I went directly to bed though I couldn't sleep for what seemed like an eternity. While I lay there next to Win, wide-eyed, it occurred that Win might be punishing me with this trip.

Or by telling me about it at the very last minute.

Or maybe Win was innocent of nasty intent and it was my own guilty conscience that made me feel as if I were being slapped for daring to carve out some personal space.

Win left the next morning at dawn. I pretended to be asleep so I wouldn't have to face the possibility of sex.

Or, maybe worse, of helping him pack, making him coffee, wishing him bon voyage with a sweet kiss.

Because every woman knows that a kiss is far more intimate than sex.

Clare

Declaration of Independence

As soon as Win was gone I got up and walked through the entire apartment as if it were a completely unfamiliar space.

Which in a way it was, without Win. Sure, he was gone every day for hours, but knowing that this time he'd be gone for days changed things.

It changed the way I saw everything.

In spite of spending so much time alone because of Win's devotion to work, I wasn't used to doing much on my own. Chores were one thing. But social activities—well, I usually opted to stay home rather than go to the movies or lunch by myself.

I don't know. Maybe spending time with Gincy and Danielle was changing me. Helping me to be more independent.

Because right there and then, alone in the vast apartment, I decided to spend the weekend in Boston instead of changing plans and joining my friends on the Vineyard.

And I would do fun things.

Like go to hear the Boston Pops's Fourth of July concert at the Hatch Shell on the Esplanade, even if going alone would be a bit scary.

The forecast told of heavy showers later in the afternoon so I loaded my backpack with an umbrella, a baseball cap, and a slicker.

I poured a bottle of white wine into a thermos and slid it down next to a turkey sandwich and an apple. Alcohol is illegal in the parks but this was a new Clare.

This was a Clare who took chances.

Besides, if I spotted a policeman I could discreetly pour the contents of the thermos into the grass.

The Pops were very popular. People staked out space early in the day for an early evening concert. People in need of lots of space, people with friends and family in tow.

Since I was going alone, I left the apartment around three and walked over to the Charles.

It was very hot and very humid and by the time I reached the Esplanade I was soaked through with sweat and very much in need of a cool glass of water.

Pushing my sunglasses up on my nose I looked around for a free inch of grass. There weren't many options. Finally, I thought I saw a small space near the middle of the field between a group of young married couples with babies and a group of middle-aged gay men.

Gingerly I made my way through the crowd, apologizing each time I stepped on an edge of blanket though no one seemed to care. When I reached the teeny square of grass, I spread out the old picnic sheet and got settled.

You're on an adventure, Clare, I thought, noting a black bank of thunderclouds over the water to my left. It might not be a long-lived adventure but at least you're on one.

"Hey."

I looked up and around. "Oh, hi," I said when I caught sight of a young guy standing almost directly over me to my left. He was smiling as if we were old friends.

"Crowded, huh?" he said.

I smiled back. "Yeah."

"Um, do you mind—I mean, do you think I could—"

The guy pointed to a beach towel folded under his other arm.

"Oh. Sure." I gathered up one side of my sheet to make room for him.

"Thanks," he said when he was settled. "I was beginning to think I'd have to stand all the way in the back."

"You like the Pops?" I asked politely.

He was younger than me. Unruly dark hair. Big dark eyes. Slim. His T-shirt read "Life is good"; he wore a pair of baggy cargo shorts.

The guy shrugged. "They're okay. Not really my kind of music. But I love the crowds, all mellowing, having a good time. And I love being outdoors. Nothing better."

"Me, too," I said. "Love the outdoors, I mean. I'm from Michigan. I kind of grew up outdoors."

The guy extended his hand. I noted he wore a silver ring with some scrolling I couldn't interpret. "My name is Finn, by the way."

I took his offered hand. "Clare."

"Hey, Clare. So what are you doing in the city. Visiting?"

"No. No I live here. I moved here with—"

I stopped cold. An adventure. I could have an adventure.

I could be a completely different person, even if only for an afternoon.

Clare the Wild and Uninhibited.

Wearing an engagement ring.

Had he noticed? Did it matter?

"I came here with my college roommate after graduation," I lied. "I guess I just stayed. I don't know."

Finn laughed. "Yeah, sometimes it feels like life just happens. I'm here for a reason, though. I'm at Berklee, studying jazz."

A musician! I'd never met a real musician before. I mean, except for the music director at York, Braddock and Roget.

"What do you play?" I asked.

Finn shrugged. "A little guitar, a little bass, and a lot of sax."

I jumped as a crack of thunder exploded and the crowd around us ooohed and shrieked with anticipation.

"Here she comes!" a woman near us cried.

"Look!" Finn said. "The hair on my arms always stands up in a storm. Cool, isn't it? It's like, every nerve goes live."

"Oh," I said eloquently. "Yeah. But shouldn't we, I don't know, leave? It might be dangerous, especially if there's lightning."

Finn grinned. "No way. We're safe enough here. Hey, I'll move onto your sheet and we'll use this towel as cover. We'll watch the show! Celebrate our independence from the tyranny of Mother Nature!"

And we did. Keith Lockhart and his orchestra played valiantly through the short-lived storm and the lingering drizzle afterward. The crows had thinned but only slightly. The mood was joyous.

Everyone is on an adventure today, I told myself, sitting close enough to Finn to brush arms when one of us lifted a cup of wine or shifted for comfort.

Finally came the 1812 Overture and fireworks display. It was moving in the way that spectacle always is. For some.

My father scoffed at spectacle and called it just another opiate of the people.

When the show was over I felt the inevitable letdown, the adrenaline hangover, that awful deflation of spirits that makes you wonder if the excitement was worth it all in the first place.

"So," I said, suddenly unwilling to let my adventure end.

Finn rocked on his heels. "So."

"Do you have to be anywhere?" I blurted, standing up to face him.

Back to the ordinary world tomorrow. Back to the daily sameness.

The calm after the storm.

"No," he said.

With my thumb I twisted my engagement ring so that the massive stones were hidden in my palm.

"Do you want to get a drink or something?" I asked.

Clare the Bold and Free.

Finn's eyes burned into mine. I hadn't seen that look since the very early days with Win.

It was the look of desire.

"A drink sounds good," he said. "But the 'or something' sounds better."

"Or something," I mumbled inanely.

Finn took my face in his hands and we kissed. He was the one who finally pulled away. I felt dizzy.

"Do you want to go back to my place?" he said, wiping stray raindrops from my cheek with his thumb.

He smelled so good, his hands were slim and beautiful, his stomach hard and flat.

"I'm alone for a few days. My roommate went home for the holiday."

I wondered if my nerve would hold out on the way to Finn's apartment.

There was only one way to find out.

"Okay," I said. "Yes."

Gincy

Last-Ditch Effort

Don't ask me why I answered a personal ad.

Okay. I'll tell you why.

I was a glutton for punishment. That was one of my father's favorite phrases.

The older I got the more I found myself ordering the world in terms of my father. Or ordering the world in my father's terms?

It was both amusing and slightly disturbing. Was I more of a Gannon than I'd realized?

Anyway, after the disaster that was the night with Jason I should simply have given up other men and concentrated on my relationship with Rick.

I should have done the right thing.

But no. That would have been too mature.

And I was so not ready to be mature.

I didn't tell Sally or Danielle or Clare what I had in mind, which was probably a clue that I shouldn't have been doing it in the first place.

I'd learned early on that, generally speaking, secrecy was not a healthy thing.

Another confession: I hadn't told Danielle the truth about the outcome of my rendezvous with Jason. I hadn't exactly lied about it either but I'd left the night open to interpretation.

Another not-so-mature decision on my part.

But back to me and the second disastrous date of the summer.

The basic idea wasn't all bad. I mean, I know lots of people have successfully hooked up through personals and dating services and sponsored singles events.

I just really should have known that I wasn't the type with that kind of luck. I really should have.

But in the words of my father, you live and learn.

Not that he seemed to have learned all that much in his fifty-eight years. Probably because he hadn't really lived all that much. I knew for a fact that he'd never traveled farther than two hundred miles from BadgerPellet, New Hampshire.

Unlike his utterly urban and urbane daughter.

The mature one. The one going on a blind date when she had a perfectly great guy already.

I'd suggested to Rob, the guy who'd placed the ad, that we meet at the bar at Joe's American. Witnesses and all.

Though on paper the guy sounded pretty harmless, you never could tell. He'd listed his occupation as assistant marketing director. Of what, he didn't say. He also claimed to be thirty-two and a graduate of Brown. Whatever.

Where a person went to college didn't impress me. It was what he'd done with his life since graduation that impressed or depressed me.

At five minutes after seven a tall, very thin, almost pretty guy came in and after a quick glance around the bar, made a beeline for me.

"Gincy?"

"Rob?"

You can't be Rob, I thought. *You're, like, twelve! Well,* I thought, *I'll give him the benefit of the doubt. Some people just don't show their age.*

"Yeah. Hi. Thanks for coming out."

What was I, his audience? But all I said was, "Yeah."

Rob settled on the barstool to my left and ordered a light beer. He seemed nervous. Was I that intimidating?

Okay, my nose was peeling from that sun-sun-sun–filled week-end on the beach, but what was a little flaking skin? It hadn't seemed to bother Jason.

My running out on him at the last minute had bothered him, but not my flaky skin.

"So," he said abruptly, "I have a confession to make."

Another one? Contrary to the information contained in his ad, I was now convinced this kid was no more than twenty-two.

"Yes?" I said sweetly.

"Well, you know how people can be, right?" he said earnestly. "Discriminating. Judgmental."

"Mmm."

Oh, I wasn't going to give this kid an inch.

"Well, okay, so in my ad I said I was an assistant marketing di-rector, right? Well, I'm not. Actually."

"Oh?" I said, taking a swig of my own beer. "And what are you? Actually?"

Besides a pathetic fool.

"Actually," Rob explained, leaning in toward me and lowering his voice, "I'm a Cher impersonator. I know it's not a traditional career choice, but I love what I do and it pays pretty well. Mostly. Well, the tips can be good."

What about health insurance, I wondered. *What if you fall off your stilettos and break your neck?*

I declined to ask.

Instead, I said, "So, are you gay?"

The kid blushed. Blushed! I hadn't blushed since I was—

Well, maybe I'd never blushed.

"No way," he protested. "I mean, a lot of impersonators are, so I can see why you'd ask, but I like girls."

"Enough to make a career out of lampooning them."

The kid looked utterly confused.

Ah. A new word for his vocabulary.

"And I'm missing a rerun of *Friends* for you," I muttered.

"Why are you so hostile?" Rob shot back. "I thought someone who looks like you would be more open."

Now who was being judgmental?

"Well," I responded, "let's see if I can put this so that you'll understand. You. Lied. To. Me. And I don't like liars."

"Hey, it's just—"

"It's just nothing." I grabbed the check off the bar. "You can go now. After you pay for your drink. Six dollars, with tip."

Rob tossed a five and a one onto the bar and, looking highly offended—and on the verge of tears—ran from the bar.

If I could turn back time . . .

What would the real Cher have done to this kid, I wondered.

I finished my beer in one long draw and gestured for another.

The bartender, a plump chick with a mop of red hair, served me with a scowl. "You were a little harsh with him," she said. "He seemed very sensitive."

Yeah. As sensitive as my alcoholic uncle's pickled liver.

"Oh, so you're paid to eavesdrop?"

"I'm just saying—"

"And I'm just saying it's none of your business. Besides," I added in a sudden burst of lunacy, "I only go out with men to mock them. I'm a mocker. It's what I do. And by the way, I guess you won't be needing your tip."

Miss Nosy took her chubby, interfering self off to the other end of the bar with a huff and I finished my drink in relative peace.

Once outside, I was hit with a big and despairing sense of loneliness. I felt like I'd been sucker punched in the gut. In my heart's gut.

It made sense at the time.

Anyway, it was only eight-thirty. I didn't want to go home yet, all alone.

Poor me.

Rick, I thought. *I'll call Rick!*

But as soon as the thought occurred, another one pushed it aside.

Rick can't come out to play at any old time, Gincy. He's got Justin.

And that was the thing.

Rick wouldn't—couldn't—always be there when I called. No matter how much he might like me.

That sort of thing—someone you could call on at any time—had never mattered to me before.

What the hell was happening?

Commitment was not something I'd ever pursued and it wasn't something I was supposed to be pursuing this summer.

The summer before I turned thirty.

The summer before I stepped over the hill.

Clare
Sex, Lies, and Observations

Gincy called at about eight forty-five and asked if I could meet her for a drink.

Win wasn't home yet—he'd called to say he was staying late to deal with some work that had piled up while he was on his fishing trip—and I didn't have anything in particular to do, so I said yes.

Besides, since the night with Finn, I'd felt oddly uncomfortable in my own home. Almost as if I had no right to be there.

And maybe I didn't.

I got to Flash's a half hour later and met Danielle in the vestibule, also just arriving.

"Did she tell you why she wants to see us?" she asked, a woman on a mission.

I shrugged. "No idea."

Together we went inside and found Gincy slumped in one of the comfy chairs by the window facing onto Stuart Street.

"Hey," she said, almost sheepishly. "Thanks for coming."

"It's no problem," I said, thinking of how I'd dragged her to that perfectly lovely, perfectly awful baby shower.

If Gincy needed help, I owed her.

We sat and gave our drink orders to the waiter. When he'd gone, Danielle folded her hands in her lap, all business.

"Spill," she commanded.

So Gincy told us about Rob, her blind date, the Cher impersonator.

"I can't believe you went on a blind date!" Danielle hissed. "I can't believe you didn't tell us what you were up to! Do you know how dangerous that could have been? What if the guy was a rapist or something!"

"I can't believe I told you even after the fact," Gincy muttered. "What's happening to me?"

"What's happening," Danielle went on, "is that you're learn-ing—slowly—to trust us. We're all becoming friends. Isn't it great?"

Gincy groaned but Danielle was undeterred.

"Well, I think it's great. And don't you feel better for confess-ing?"

"It wasn't a confession!" Gincy protested. "I didn't do any-thing wrong! If I'd committed a crime do you think I would have told you?"

Danielle shook her head. "I think maybe you would have. Say, if you cheated on a guy you were committed to. I think it would feel good to get such an awful burden off your chest. Get some perspective. You know."

"Uh," Gincy said, looking absolutely miserable, "speaking of awful burdens, there's something else. I didn't exactly tell the truth about what happened with that guy Jason."

Danielle gasped and quickly filled me in.

"So, what did happen that night?" Danielle then demanded.

"Nothing. I couldn't have sex with him. It felt too weird. I kept thinking about Rick and I felt all guilty. So I just left. You know, in the middle of things. I'm not such a horrible person after all, right? At least, in terms of Rick. I'm pretty sure Jason thinks I'm scum."

Danielle beamed. "I am so proud of you! Aren't you proud of Gincy, Clare? You kept your promise to Rick."

"We don't have a promise," Gincy protested, but weakly.

Danielle continued to chatter on about Gincy's moral courage. I feigned great interest in my colorful drink, hoping to hide the guilt I knew was all over my face.

Gincy might have been a heroine, but I'd done something terribly wrong. I'd cheated on the man I was bound to marry. A man who, as far as I knew, had never cheated on me.

Oh, how I wished that Win was having an affair! That he was staying late at the office three or four nights a week because he was cheating on me with his secretary or that sexy woman in the office down the hall from his. Macey something.

It would all be so easy then. I could break up with Win, call off the wedding, and feel justified in the process.

I'd be the injured woman, not the adulterous fiancée.

I wouldn't have to continue this excruciating examination of myself.

All by myself.

I knew friends were supposed to tell each other everything. I knew they weren't supposed to be afraid of being judged or ridiculed.

Still, I couldn't bring myself to tell Gincy or Danielle what had happened on July 4th. I was just too ashamed to reveal such moral weakness to people I'd known for so short a time.

Maybe if we'd been friends since childhood . . .

But I doubt even then I'd have had the courage to admit such frailty.

Wellmans weren't in the habit of revealing weakneses.

Better to live all alone with your wrongdoing, I told myself, than to confess it to anyone. Even to your journal. And especially to the one you hurt most.

Win.

Oh, I had cheated on him so casually!

What could Win ever do to me that would be as bad as what I had done to him?

God, a one-night stand. I deserved the awful burden of a secret infidelity.

Why, why had I gone home with Finn, a total stranger?

Temporary insanity.

Sexual frustration.

Boredom?

Whatever the reason, the reality was that what had happened between Finn and I was too wonderful to remember with blushing.

The abandon. The passion. My frenzied need for Finn's boyish body . . .

"Clare," Gincy said, and I startled. "You're just sitting there like a bump on a log. Are you okay?"

"Fine." I tried to smile. "I'm fine. Just a lot on my mind."

Danielle nodded wisely. "Of course. The wedding. Every bride-to-be gets totally distracted the closer she gets to the big day. By the night before, you won't even know who you are!"

My feeble smile died.

Great.

The last thing I needed was a more serious identity crisis than the one already plaguing me.

Gincy
If the Truth Were any Bigger

Y ou had a summer house, you had guests.
It was an unwritten rule but a rule all the same.

Interestingly, Clare had yet to bring Win to the Vineyard. The fiance remained a mystery, which was fine with me.

Danielle had brought her brother and his ditzy fiancée, Roberta. She'd been good for a sick sort of laugh but by the end of the weekend, even Danielle had seemed glad to see her go.

Now it was my turn. Danielle and Clare were spending the weekend in Boston running wedding-related chores, which left the Vineyard house all to me.

Briefly, I'd considered asking Rick to come out with me but I shied away from the idea. An entire weekend alone together was big.

Plus, there was the issue of Justin. Would Rick insist he come along? And if so, would Rick be sleeping in the second bedroom with his son and not with me?

Besides, I hadn't even met the kid yet.

And that was a potentially major trauma.

See, I'd never met a kid I really liked. Or maybe it was that any kid I'd ever met hadn't liked me, so I'd responded in kind.

Finally, it seemed much simpler to avoid the Rick and Justin issue and invite Sally to the Vineyard.

It's not that I was dying to spend the weekend alone with Sally. It was that she left me little choice. She was the queen of unsubtle hints.

Still, she feigned enormous surprise when I finally offered the invitation.

"Yeah, you can close your mouth now," I said dryly. "Just be on time and bring your own towels. Danielle will kill me if she finds out anyone's used hers. She's very sensitive about her stuff."

"Since when do you care about other people's feelings?" Sally shot back.

I wasn't quite sure how to answer.

Early that Friday afternoon we settled on the ferry's open deck. The sun was hot but the humidity was low. My mood was good.

"Look, just so you know," I told Sally, face turned up to the sun, "I'm not going to cramp your style. If you meet someone and you want to bring her back to the house, fine by me. Just keep the noise to a minimum."

"No," Sally said quickly, "that's okay. I'm in a celibate phase right now. I'm centering and cleansing."

I looked at her closely. "What, are you into yoga now? Some bizarre Eastern feel-good practice? Are you going to be eating seaweed all weekend? Drinking some brown mess?"

"It's nothing so formal," she replied, suddenly intent upon the star tattoo on the back of her left hand. "It's just something I'm going through."

"Yeah. Whatever. But just so you know, I'm scattering and getting dirty."

Okay. It wasn't exactly the truth but I enjoyed teasing Sally. "So I might meet someone and—"

Sally's face took on a greenish cast.

"You're not going to hurl, are you?" I said, scooting away.

"No!" she protested.

Warily, I scooted back.

"Then, what? I thought you'd be thrilled to learn I'm not get-ting serious with Mr. Corporate Scum."

Another lie.

By the way, Sally was the only one in our office I'd told about my dates with Rick. No details, just that we were dating.

"Of course I am," Sally shot back. "He's so not right for you. What I meant was . . . It's just, don't you think you should—"

"What? Be careful? Of course I'm careful. I'm not a moron."

Sally clutched her pink hair in frustration. "I didn't say you were a moron! God, Gincy—"

"Look, chill, okay? 'Cause if you don't I'm gonna toss you overboard and you can swim back to Boston."

I waited for it.

Finally, Sally laughed. "You wouldn't dare."

"Try me." I patted her leg as if to belie my threat. "Go get us some sodas? I'll save the seats."

"You're paying, right?" Sally asked. "You make more money than I do."

With a phony grumble I handed her a five-dollar bill. "Keep the change," I called as she walked off. "You might want to get yet another piercing. Like, in your brain."

Clare

Kicking and Screaming

Danielle met me at the loft that rainy Saturday morning. "It's a perfect day for the mall," she pronounced as she strode through the door in a shiny red slicker and matching boots. "We won't feel like we're missing anything on the Vineyard."

"Do I really need to do this?" I asked, wondering if it was too late to feign a debilitating headache.

Danielle put her well-manicured hands to her head. "For the last time, yes, you do need to do this. What is your big problem with registering, anyway?"

The real problem is that I don't want to get married.

"Well," I said, "I guess I'm embarrassed about asking people to buy me things. I mean, particular things. It seems so selfish."

Danielle sighed magnificently. "Honey," she said, "let me explain to you the joys and convenience of a wedding registry. One: Everyone expects you to register and you can't let everyone down can you?"

"I—"

Danielle went on. "And everyone expects you to register at some high-end shops, like Tiffany, for all sorts of outrageously expensive gifts you can't possibly afford. That's the fun part. You get to go on a fantasy shopping spree and someone else has to pay the bill. Are you following?"

Not really.

"Yes," I said.

"Good. Now, everyone also expects you to register at places like Williams-Sonoma and Crate and Barrel for everyday items. Once you're in their systems, relatives and friends all across the country—with all sorts of budgets—can go into any store location, call up your registry, see what hasn't yet been bought, and make a purchase. Do you see the beauty of this?"

I nodded. Did it really matter what I saw or didn't see?

"Believe it, Clare," Danielle went on. "In the long run, you're doing your guests a favor by registering. You're saving them the trouble of having to think. Nobody likes to think when they don't have to. Am I right?"

"I guess," I mumbled.

Just then I heard the bedroom door open. A moment later, Win shuffled through the hall to the bathroom. Thank God he was wearing his robe.

Danielle peered after him, then turned back to me with a grin. "So, can I meet him?"

"Uh, now's not a good time," I said. "Win's not a morning person and he hasn't had his coffee yet and—"

"I get it, I get it. Some other time." Suddenly, Danielle grabbed my arm. "Wait a minute. Win's not getting involved with the registry, is he?"

"No," I admitted. "I asked him to but he said it was girl stuff. I told him I've seen lots of couples registering together but he wouldn't budge."

"Well, thank God! Trust me, he'd only be in the way. Now, do you have the bottles of Evian I told you to pack? Good. Registering is thirsty work. And wear comfortable shoes. We'll be doing a lot of walking. Oh—have you thought about stationery? I'd suggest Crane's. We'll make that our first stop."

So, we set out. The reluctant bride and her super-wanna-be-a-bride assistant.

Crate and Barrel. Williams-Sonoma. Victoria's Secret. That was so Danielle could make suggestions about my wedding-night attire.

"I don't feel comfortable in this sort of thing," I whispered, embarrassed by the lacy white ensemble she'd chosen as sure to drive Win wild.

A wild Win was a person I had never met.

"It's not about feeling comfortable," she said. "Anyway, it will be off before you know it so—"

"I'll think about it," I lied. "Can we leave now?"

Next stop was Tiffany.

"Why here?" I asked when we were just inside and past the security guard. "I mean, exactly?"

Danielle regarded me like a mother short on patience might regard her deliberately slow four-year-old. "Because," she said evenly, "you need to consider crystal. Follow me. It's in the back."

"Why?" I asked, trotting after her.

The store made me uncomfortable. Everything was so hushed. And there was that guard at the door. His presence made me feel guilty in general.

"I don't really like crystal."

Danielle came to an abrupt halt and turned to me. Now her look was one of extreme exasperation.

"You have to have crystal," she said. "You're getting married. Doesn't your mother have crystal?"

"Yes," I said. "If you mean vases. She has a few crystal vases. And bowls."

"Well?" Danielle said, as if her point was self-evident.

It wasn't to me. But what did I know about anything?

"Okay. I'll think about crystal. Um—what am I supposed to think about it for?"

Danielle put her hand to her temple.

"Do you have a headache?" I asked innocently.

"All I'm saying is thank God I'm a patient person."

After storming the gift department—crystal, silver, and china— Danielle suggested we take a break. I readily agreed. We got two iced coffees and sat on one of the many wooden benches that line the halls of the mall.

"I guess it's dumb of me to think you've considered any of the details," she said after gulping half of her drink.

I looked at her blankly. Crystal wasn't a detail?

Danielle sighed, opened her ever-present notebook, and began to scribble.

"Bubbles, how many dispensers to a box; giveaways for the wedding guests, think seed packets or mini-picture frames, Lenox or silver plate; disposable cameras on each table. Maybe. I'm not a huge fan. Too many chances for unflattering photos of the bride. And speaking of photos, I'm assuming you never had a formal engagement picture taken but it's not too late you know. I'll just go ahead and make an appointment . . ."

Danielle worked on.

I let my mind drift to memories of that one incredible night with Finn.

I'd vowed never to see him again and I would keep that vow. But I couldn't promise myself not to remember.

Gincy
Rug Rat

The weekend on the Vineyard with Sally was pretty fun. We hung around on the beach and ate nachos and drank beer and made fun of people who looked even worse than we did in shorts.

One night I flirted with a jerk in a bar and then, just when he was sure he was going to score, I told him sweetly that I was hooked up with the massive bouncer. He stalked off, furiously thwarted.

I thought it was pretty amusing, if a little infantile of me. Sally didn't get as much of a kick out of the game as I did, but, whatever. I encouraged her to flirt a little, too, but she reminded me of her period of centering and cleansing.

By the time we were back on the ferry Sunday evening, both of us a few pounds heavier and very relaxed, I was kind of sorry to be heading home.

"We should do this again sometime," I told Sally as we watched the Vineyard fade from view.

"You mean it?" she asked.

"Yeah. I had a good time. Why, didn't you?"

Sally shrugged. "Yeah, it was okay. Just give me some advance notice. You know. So I can plan."

"Right. Because your social schedule is so full," I joked.

Sally just smiled.

The next morning, as I was checking e-mail at my desk, Kell popped in.

"What's up?" I asked, eyes still focused on the computer screen.

"Rick's got his little boy in the office today. He's a cute kid. If you have some time, maybe you could entertain him a bit. We're all going to take turns so Rick can get some work done."

"Sure, sure," I mumbled, typing madly. Kell left and I let the panic overtake me.

Jesus, I thought, *I can't meet the kid! Where can I hide—*

"Gincy!" And there was Rick, standing at the door to my office with a kid.

His kid.

Who looked like Rick's Mini-Me. Some odd little being who had sprouted from Rick's forehead without the benefit of another set of DNA.

"Er," he said, "I want you to meet Justin. His sitter is sick so he'll be spending the day with me. Here. In the office."

I came around to the front of the desk, every step an effort.

The kid stared up at me with a look of such intense concentration on his face I assumed a pimple the size of Seattle had just appeared on my chin.

"What?" I said.

"You look like my teacher."

"I do?"

"Yeah. His name is Mr. Randall. He's old."

You know what W.C. Fields said about kids? A lot. None of it good.

Here's my favorite: "I like children—fried."

Rick opened his mouth but nothing came out.

"Uh," I said, "that's nice. I guess."

Justin nodded. "Yeah. He's pretty cool. He has a pet rat."

"White or gray?"

"White. You should have seen when it almost got eaten by a snake."

"Yeah, that's great, kid. Great. Uh, Justin. How about we—"

What, Gincy? Go Xerox our butts? What did you do with a five-year-old, anyway?

I shot a panicked look at Rick. He looked blankly back. Did he expect me to baby-sit the kid all day? I had a job to do . . .

Then Rick's brain kicked in. "Justin, why don't we go back to my office. Gincy's got a lot of work to do."

"Dad," Justin said solemnly, "your office is kind of boring."

"Well, that's because it's an office. It's supposed to be boring."

"Why?"

"I don't know. It just is, I guess."

Justin looked up at his father with a look that said, "Come on, Dad. You can do better than that."

At least that's what I read the look to mean.

But Rick just looked puzzled.

"Gincy's got a rubber-band ball on her desk," Justin pointed out.

Observant kid. It was almost hidden behind a tilting pile of loose papers and industry magazines.

Rick shrugged. "What's not boring about a rubber-band ball?"

Oh, come on! Had Rick never been a kid? His poor son was doomed.

"Are you kidding?" I said. "Do you know what you can do with a rubber-band ball? Come on, Justin. You can hang with me while Rick—your dad goes back to his boring office."

From the look on Rick's face you'd think I'd just done something highly noble.

"Are you sure it's all right? I mean—"

"Yeah, yeah, it's fine. Now go. We'll be fine. Right, Justin?"

"Yeah, Dad. You can go now."

Rick hesitated. I made a shooing gesture with my hand and he turned to leave. At the doorway he tripped. Justin gave me a little smile that revealed genuine fondness for his goofy dad.

"So," I said when the other adult was gone.

"So," Justin repeated.

"So, I'm going to get back to work here. You can, you know, hang with the rubber-band ball. I've got some markers, too. And some paper. You know."

Justin reached for the ball and settled himself on the floor. "You can go back to work now," he said calmly.

I did. And I got a lot done. Every so often I'd remember there was a five-year-old on my floor and shoot a glance his way.

Each time, I found Justin absorbed in some task that involved his poking at the rubber-band ball with his forefinger, a deep frown of concentration on his face.

As long as he wasn't tearing apart any important documents he could spend the entire day with the silly thing for all I cared.

And then at one point I sensed someone else in the room. I looked up from the computer to find Sally standing in the doorway.

She was scowling but Sally was often scowling.

"Hey," I called. "Come in and—"

Sally shot a look of pure loathing at Justin and walked away.

Okay. Clearly, Sally still had something against Rick and now, not only against Rick but also against his son.

Was it all about their being male? Who knew.

Male was a good thing in my book. With a few notable exceptions, starting with my brother.

Men. Sex.

Thoughts of me and Rick in bed began to flash through my head as I watched Justin futilely try to count the top layer of rubber bands on the ball. I tried to stop the lascivious images but the harder I tried the more they bombarded.

What kind of lowlife was I to be thinking about sex with a little kid in the room?

Here's what I was thinking about most: How Rick's clumsiness totally vanished in bed. He was sure and strong and gentle in all the right ways and places. Amazing. Rick's sexual prowess was a well-kept secret.

Suddenly, I was aware that Justin was staring at me.

"What?" I said guiltily.

"You have a funny look on your face. Are you sick?"

"Uh, no. I'm fine. You okay?"

"Yeah. I lost count though."

"I have an idea," I said. "Why don't you start your own rubber band ball? Look, I've got a whole box of rubber bands here. Different colors, too."

"I don't know how to start," he said, taking the box from me.

"I'll show you. It's easy. Just watch and listen."

"Okay. But sometimes I'm not a very good listener. I'm smart but I don't listen."

I looked at the kid with a frown. "Who says you don't listen good? Well? Who says you aren't a good listener?"

Justin shrugged. "Mr. Randall. And my dad. It's okay. It's no big deal. My dad says he was the same way when he was my age."

I could see little Rick in my head as clearly as if he were sitting cross-legged on my office carpet. The image made me smile.

"My dad's pretty clumsy, isn't he?" Justin said suddenly, looking right up at me.

Was the kid testing me?

Had he been reading my mind?

"Uh," I said brilliantly, "I guess."

"He broke my dump truck the other day, on accident. He stepped on it."

"Oh."

I began to sweat. Like, serious wetness under my arms.

Justin shrugged. "That's okay. I love him, anyway."

"That's good," I breathed. "That you love your dad."

Justin spilled open the box of rubber bands I'd given him. "Yeah," he mumbled, already busy at work.

You know, I thought, noting the boy's hair was the exact same color as Rick's, *if Justin could retain his beguiling honesty, he'll be one hell of a catch someday.*

Like his father?

Clare
She Wants To Be Alone

I threw out my journal.

First, I ripped out all the pages, even the still-blank ones, and tore them into tiny pieces. I put the pieces in a paper bag and the paper bag in a plastic bag and put the entire mess into the kitchen trash, on top of which I added the morning's coffee grounds and orange peels.

I couldn't bear to see my pain and confusion in writing. Bad enough my mind was plagued by doubts and worries and random flashes of anger at no one.

At everyone.

And what if Win had found the journal? What if he'd read all those damning, revelatory words?

Words I wanted to say to him but couldn't.

Words like: "I'm so sad. You don't understand me."

Seven words—with contractions—seven simple words that told a story eleven years in the making.

Seven nonargumentative words.

Just words that stated an unhappy fact.

I am so sad. You don't understand me.

I am so sad because you don't understand me.

I am so sad because I have finally come to see that you don't understand me.

I was so sad. Angry, yes, and hurt, but mostly, just sad.

You can get over anger, direct it somewhere out of yourself; it can even be cathartic.

Hurt, too, can be mended; the pain can be ameliorated and time almost always aids in the healing process.

But sadness is different. It doesn't seem to ever go away; it rests deep inside.

Sadness is profound disappointment. Once you've been made sad by someone, once you've been disappointed by someone— say, by the failure of someone who claims to love you to truly understand you—that's it, hope is quite suddenly dead and the world an entirely new and puzzling place.

Everywhere I went the words were a mantra in my head. I walked to their beat, breathed to their rhythm, let their import color every person I passed. Their power was in the car horns honking and their finality was in the litter fluttering across the sidewalk and into the gutter.

I was so sad.

A city is not a good place in which to be sad.

I went home one afternoon midweek and packed. Then I called Win at the office and left a message on his voice mail telling him I was going to the Vineyard.

Clare
Static

It was nice being at the house alone.

It was peaceful.

No one stealing my yogurts. No TV blaring. No one hogging the bathroom.

For a day and a half I came and went as I pleased.

I had a bedroom all to myself, a luxury I hadn't experienced since high school. In college I'd had a roommate and when I wasn't sharing a bedroom with her, I was sharing a bed with Win.

I took long walks on the beach, collected pretty shells, and tossed them back in the ocean before heading home.

I read a novelization of the life of Eleanor of Aquitaine and counted my good fortune in having been born in the twentieth century.

I gazed at the stars. I thought. I was quiet.

In that day and a half I spoke to no one, not even a store clerk. The solitude was restorative.

But it wasn't to last.

When the phone rang one morning at eight-thirty, the last person I expected to hear on the other end of the line was Win's mother.

The formidable Mrs. Matilda Carrington.

"Hello, Clare," she chirped. "Did I wake you?"

"Oh, no," I said.

I'd been up since six. Sleep hadn't come easily since the engagement.

"How are you, Mrs. Carrington?"

"Well, I'm just fine dear. But what about you? Win told me you're all alone out there and suggested I call to make sure you aren't too lonely."

If I was lonely, I thought, I'd—I'd what?

Go home to Win? That wouldn't exactly solve the problem.

"Oh, I'm fine," I said brightly. "It's very pleasant by the beach."

"Well, now that I have you on the phone, there are a few matters I'd like to discuss with you, concerning the wedding."

I thought of telling her it wasn't a good time, that I was meeting someone for breakfast, but I knew she'd ignore me.

Win hadn't fallen far from his mother's tree.

"All right, Mrs. Carrington," I said, settling heavily into a chair. "What would you like to talk about?"

"Clare, dear, you are taking my son's name, aren't you? I can't really see you as being part of the family if you're not a Carrington."

My grip on the receiver tightened. What in the world could I say to that?

I'd talked about the name issue with Gincy and Danielle.

"Of course I'm taking Win's name," I'd said.

Gincy had just rolled her eyes, as if I was a lost cause.

Danielle had suggested another option.

"Why don't you use both last names? Wellman-Carrington. It's a bit long but it's a good compromise."

"But I don't want a compromise," I'd insisted. "I'm fine with taking Win's name. Really. I know who I am. I don't need to keep Wellman to keep my identity as an individual."

Gincy had challenged me, of course. "Do you really know who you are, Clare? And by the way, Wellman is your father's name, after all. Do you really know who you are apart from the men in your life?"

"Does anyone?" Danielle had said, before I could open my

mouth to gape. "No person's an island, Gincy. We all exist in relation to everyone else we know, especially our families."

"Miss Philosophy 101 over here," Gincy snapped.

"Ms. Feminist Bullshit," Danielle snapped back. "Oooh, it's all the patriarchy's fault!"

Now, on the phone with my future mother-in-law, I suddenly knew I didn't want to be a Carrington or a Wellman.

I wanted to be me. Clare.

I wanted to be myself!

"Of course I'm taking Win's name," I said.

Mrs. Carrington sighed audibly. "Good. That's settled. Now, about your dress."

"Oh. What about it?" I asked.

Was she going to offer to pay for it? Of course, I'd graciously decline the offer.

"I would be honored if you would wear my dress at your wedding, Clare. As you know, I have no daughters and, well, now that you and Win are marrying, it's as if I do finally have a daughter. Someone I can advise. Someone I can . . ."

Mrs. Carrington rambled on but I no longer heard her words.

I'd seen photos of the dress—and Mrs. Carrington in it—at Win's house back in Ann Arbor. The dress was classically simple and probably would look beautiful on me.

But . . .

I was overcome with conflicting feelings of resentment and appreciation.

How dare Mrs. Carrington present me with such a loaded offer!

And yet, how nice it was of her to consider me her own flesh and blood.

Offering her dress is a gesture of love, Clare, one compelling voice pointed out. *Of family solidarity. One generation passing on its prized possessions to the next.*

And then, another compelling voice argued its case.

Be real, Clare, it said. *Trying to guilt you into wearing her wedding gown is only the first of many acts of an overbearing mother-in-law.*

She wants to advise you? On what? How to please her son?

Danielle was right, I realized. I wasn't only marrying Win. I was marrying his mother, too.

But what about my own mother? How would she feel about my wearing Mrs. Carrington's wedding dress?

She'd feel bad. Left out. Not that her dress was an option. Mother was four inches shorter than me and very tiny. Still.

The second voice in my head won out.

I'd take Win's name. But I would not wear his mother's dress. I just wouldn't tell her that yet.

"Thank you, Mrs. Carrington," I said as firmly as I could. "I— I'll certainly consider your kind offer. See, I've been working with a small bridal shop on Newbury Street. They have some nice ideas. But I'll certainly think about . . ."

"Excellent, dear!" she interrupted. "I'll have copies made of the best of my wedding photos and send them along to refresh your memory, all right?"

We chatted about nothing for another moment or two and then ended the call.

I'd gone out to the Vineyard to be alone for a while, to think, to hide.

To rest.

But they had pursued me. They always pursued me.

Gincy
Good, Bad, Ugly

When Clare returned from her alone time at the Vineyard she called me at the office one afternoon and invited both me and Danielle to a cocktail party at the Ritz hotel on Tremont Street.

It was to be sponsored by Win's firm.

"I know Danielle's been wanting to meet Win," she explained, with an odd laugh. "Well, here's her big chance."

"Do I want to meet him?" I asked, surprising myself with the odd way I'd put the question.

Clare was silent a moment before answering. "Probably not," she said. "But you're invited."

Okay, I noted. This was a newer Clare. One who was speaking her mind right up front.

Maybe I'd been a good influence on my formerly uptight roommate.

It would definitely be the first time I'd been a good influence on anyone.

"Win's older brother Trey will be there," she went on. "He's visiting from San Francisco. He used to be a high school history teacher but he's changing careers. He works in the public defender's office during the day and goes to law school at night.

He's really bright. He just won some big award, I don't know, Win didn't really explain it to me. He's still getting over the shock of an illustrious Carrington wanting to become a public defender."

"So, are you trying to fix me up with this moral paragon?" I asked, half-jokingly.

"Oh, no! Trey's gay. I was just telling you about him because . . . Well, I think you'll like him."

"And you think I won't like Win."

Silence, for long seconds.

"Yes," she said, finally. "I think you won't like Win. But he probably won't like you, either, so what does it matter."

"Oh," I said. "Okay."

I wondered: Would this newer Clare become as annoyingly blunt as I was? Had I created a monster?

Either way, Danielle and I showed up in our finest. Which for Danielle meant a belted dress which, she told me, was an update of an old Diane von Furstenburg style. Whoever she was.

For me, it meant a French blue blouse—Danielle couldn't believe I actually knew the color—and black pants from the Gap. I'd gotten them on sale and sale pants were the best kind of pants.

And who cared if there was a Monsieur or Lady von Gap?

"I'm so glad we're finally getting to meet Win," Danielle said, popping a mini-quiche into her mouth and chewing with gusto.

"I think you're more excited about the free food," I commented.

"Free food is a good thing," she admitted, "especially when it's good quality. Have you tried the champagne? Veuve Clicquot. Very fine."

"I'm not a champagne person."

"Oh, please, Gincy. You're always trying to pretend you're so lowbrow when you've got as much sophistication as the next girl. Why you insist on hiding it is beyond me."

There was no point in arguing with Danielle. If she wanted to think I was Miss Emily Post, fine, let her think it.

Clare soon introduced us to Win. He looked like thousands of other guys. Medium height, brown hair neatly cut, brown eyes, navy suit, wingtip shoes.

There was nothing remarkable about him that I could see; even his affect was medium.

Maybe that's what had attracted Clare to Win.

Better her than me, I thought, thinking of Rick and his brutal honesty, rumpled clothes, and affinity for bluegrass music.

The four of us made very tiny talk for an interminable few minutes. And then a tall, handsome guy waved to Clare from across the room and she excused herself to join him.

"My brother," Win said. "He and Clare have always hit it off." Win hung his wrist in the age-old gesture.

Suddenly, the guy with no personality was obnoxiously loud and ragingly clear.

"What?" I said sharply. "What's that supposed to mean?"

"You know. Trey. He's queer. He's a homo. I don't know where he came from, boy. No one in our family has ever been a homo."

As far as you know, dickwad.

"Is that right?" I said, straining not to spit.

"Yeah. It's not something we're proud of. Trey being gay, I mean."

"I understand Trey was a teacher," Danielle said, her voice perfectly modulated.

I should have known she was an expert at polite conversation, even with jerks.

"And that he's getting his law degree," she went on. "And I believe Clare also mentioned that Trey recently won some prestigious award . . ."

"Oh, sure," Win said, as if the admission was a magnanimous act. "No Carrington is dumb."

Danielle pinched my arm in warning. I kept my mouth shut. For the moment.

Win continued to blab. "When Trey came out," he said, in a tone of confidentiality, "I had to seriously consider if I could maintain a relationship with him. Mother almost had a heart attack. She was rushed to the hospital . . . Mother can be a bit dramatic, but can you imagine the shock? Dad thought about cutting him out of the will. We had to wonder if it was worth including Trey in our lives. Well, you know how it is."

"Not really," I said with a big innocent smile. "See, I'm not—OW!"

Danielle had stomped on my foot with her stiletto.

"For Clare," she whispered through a fixed smile.

Win was so absorbed in his own idiotic pontifications and asinine ponderings he hadn't noticed our tussle.

"Frankly," he was saying now, holding aloft his martini, "I don't get this whole gay thing. I mean, suddenly there are all these people claiming to be gay. What's up with that? What's their point?"

"What's your point?" I said brightly, ignoring Danielle's frantic hand signals. "Being such a condescending—"

Before I could finish my tirade, Danielle grabbed my arm and with a false wave at nobody across the room, she dragged us both away from Mr. Winchester Carrington III.

We found the much-maligned Trey standing alone by the bar, sipping a glass of the fancy champagne.

"Your brother's an asshole," I said without preamble. "Shrimp?" I offered my heaped plate.

"Thanks." Trey popped an entire jumbo shrimp in his mouth. "I know," he mumbled.

"I'm Gincy by the way. Clare's friend. This is Danielle."

Trey introduced himself and took another shrimp from my plate.

"I don't know how Clare can stand talking to him," I went on, blood still seething, "let alone marrying him. Jesus Christ. He makes me want to spit."

Trey swallowed and grinned. "I'm glad Clare finally has a friend like you. She needs an advocate. She needs to learn to say, 'screw you.' She's not a bad person. She's just been pushed around a lot."

"Yeah, yeah," I said. "Clare's great and all. But what I want to know is how you can stand to be here. I mean, what are you, a

saint? How can you stand to be in the same room with Win? He's
despicable."

"He's an asshole and despicable and pathetic. But," Trey said,
with a wry grin, "he's also my little brother. Family owes something to family. Even if it's just pretending to get along."

"You're a far better person than I am," I said.

"I doubt that."

"You don't know me very well."

"You don't have the look of a creep. Trust me, I've seen my
fair share."

"Looks can be deceiving."

"Not to me. I have super-laser vision."

"Okay, you win," I said, laughing. "I don't suck. Totally."

"I can't imagine David ever turning his back on me," Danielle
said, more to herself than to us. "And nothing he could ever do
would make me turn my back on him."

"David's her big brother," I explained, and Trey nodded
wisely.

I neglected to mention my own brother. I was sure Tommy
would rat me out to the enemy for a quart of lighter fluid.

As for my loyalty to him, well, that was still up for debate.

Hours later, Danielle and I were hunched at the bar at Silver-
tone. Well, I was hunched; Danielle sat straight as she always did,
except when lounging. More than once she'd reminded me of
the importance of good posture.

"I don't think I can help Clare with the wedding any longer."
Danielle looked genuinely pained. It cost her to abandon such a
project. "How can I encourage such a sweet kid to marry such a
horrible jerk?"

"You can't," I replied shortly.

"But I just can't walk out on the planning, can I? Clare's relying on me. There's so much still to do . . . And what excuse
would I give? I can't tell her that I loathe her fiancé!"

We sat in silence for a few moments, until Danielle said, softly,
"You know, I can't help but compare Win to Chris. Can you
imagine Chris ever being such a jerk?"

"No," I said readily. "That's not what he's about. I mean, I hardly know him but I can just tell. Maybe I'm like Trey. I can spot a creep a mile away."

"And it's not what Rick's about, either," Danielle said. "If I can believe everything you've told me about him. And I don't see why you'd lie."

"You can believe me," I said. "Rick's one of the good ones. He's a man. Like the kind they used to grow. Like Gary Cooper or someone. He's always thinking of other people before himself. Not macho but manly. Women and children first but without all the condescending crap that goes with that."

"He sounds like my father," Danielle said. "He's a real caretaker. My father is very kind."

And so is mine, I thought, suddenly remembering how he'd go grocery shopping for the ancient Mrs. Kennedy down the street, and shovel the paths outside the church early every snowy Sunday morning, and bring my mother flowers just for the hell of it.

Not that she ever appreciated the flowers. Ellen Gannon had swallowed a bitterness pill some time in the early seventies— about the time I was born—and it had taken rapid and permanent effect.

But back to my father. I hadn't thought about any of those nice things for years. The memories hit hard.

"My dad's pretty okay, too," I said, feeling a bothersome tickle in my throat. "I guess we're both lucky daughters."

Clare
Girls on Film

When I first met Gincy I noticed she never looked fully at ease on the beach unless she was flinging rocks back into the ocean, as if she had some point to prove to the never-ceasing waves.

But for some reason, as the summer wore on, she spent more and more time sprawled with me and Danielle on our towels, chatting, reading, and sipping cold drinks.

And she'd even bought a bathing suit. It was a one-piece black racing suit. Gincy actually had a nice figure. It looked as if she might have gained a little bit of weight in the past weeks. It was attractive.

I wondered if her slow and partial transformation had anything to do with Rick. Was Gincy actually happy?

"I'm sorry I didn't get to talk to you after the cocktail party," I said, laying aside my novel. "We had a dinner reservation at eight."

"That's okay," Gincy said. "We understand. I'm sorry we didn't have more time to hang with Trey, though."

I smiled. "Trey is wonderful. He just started seeing someone new. A professor of urban studies, I think. Or urban design. Anyway, Trey seems to think this could be it."

"Is he cute?" Danielle asked. "This professor?"

"Why is that important?" Gincy demanded.

Danielle threw her hands in the air. "I'm not getting into this with you again. Go ahead and marry the Creature from the Black Lagoon if you want. No one's stopping you. Maybe the Elephant Man is free this evening. Here, you can use my cell phone."

"So, what did you think of Win?" I asked, interrupting the familiar wrangle.

A trick question? I don't know what I was hoping to hear.

"Well, he's very nice looking," Danielle said promptly. "Very neat. And his suit was impeccable. Do you help him pick out his clothes?"

"No. Win's mother visits once a year and they go shopping together."

Danielle opened her mouth but had nothing to say to that. Nervously, she cleared her throat and took a drink of iced tea.

"Gincy?" I said. "What about you?"

She scratched her head and frowned, as if debating her answer. "I insulted him right to his face," she said finally, "and he didn't seem to pick up on it. I'm not saying he's an idiot or anything . . ."

"Win's not stupid," I explained. "He just hears what he wants to hear. He scans for criticism or ridicule and converts it to compliments or neutralizes it somehow. It's rather amazing."

"It must be hard to have a real argument with him," Danielle noted. "I mean, a productive one."

"It's impossible," I said flatly. "The only time he listens is when I start a sentence with, 'I'm sorry, I know it's my fault, but.'"

Gincy frowned. "I just have to ask this question, Clare. It's a tough one."

"Go ahead."

"Do you know how Win talks about his brother? I mean, I won't speak for Danielle—"

"You can," she interrupted.

"Okay then, Danielle and I were really—"

"Shocked."

"Disgusted by his behavior. It was so offensive. And he just as-sumed we'd be right on board his gay-bashing train. I swear, Clare, I almost hit him."

"She did," Danielle said, nodding. "I stopped her."

"Yeah, by stomping on my foot!"

I was silent for a moment. I could feel Gincy and Danielle tensing, worried they'd upset me.

I looked out at the water sparkling with sunlight. It was so pretty. It posed no awkward dilemmas.

Yes, I knew how Win spoke about his brother. About all ho-mosexuals. I'd tried to argue him into tolerance and under-standing. I'd tried to cajole him into generosity of spirit, into kindness.

But Win was Win. His ideas were set in stone and had been from childhood.

His ideas were his father's.

Not mine. Never mine.

Finally, I had gotten Win to agree not to share his opinions on homosexuality with me. But I knew he held those opinions.

Was I in collusion by living with Win, by marrying him? Was I by proxy a narrow-minded, spiritless person?

How could I ever explain myself and my choices? Especially when more and more they seemed no longer my choices.

"Yes," I said, finally. "I know how he thinks. And talks. I hate it. But it's not me."

"We never thought it was," Danielle said, reaching for and squeezing my hand.

Mercifully, Gincy let the awkward subject drop.

And then another subject bounced into sight. I watched them strutting in our direction, three young women in teeny bikinis, swinging bright beach bags and giggling.

"I think I might just be a rocket scientist," Danielle murmured.

"Compared to the Bouncie sisters," Gincy grumbled, "you are. And I'm a physics professor. With a second degree in genetic en-gineering."

Well, the girls weren't acting like intellectuals, but why should they be, I thought. They're at the beach, a place of fun and relaxation. Okay, there was an awful lot of hair tossing going on but . . .

"Is there a hidden camera somewhere?" Gincy said. "Are we on the set of yet another Baywatch spin-off? Baywatch Vineyard?"

"Why do they have to sit so close to us?" Danielle complained when the three girls had tossed their towels not ten yards from us. "We're invisible next to them! What if Chris comes by?"

"That's the point," Gincy said. "They know what they're doing. Girls who look like that are never as dumb as they appear."

"As dumb as a bucket of hair," Danielle said.

"A big sack of stupid."

"Nice cupboards, no dishes."

"A few sandwiches short of a picnic."

"Oh, come on, you two," I scolded. "They're just having fun. Goofing around. We don't exactly sound brilliant all the time. Maybe never."

"You're a softie, Clare," Danielle snapped. "These girls are a serious threat to women like us. And it's only going to get worse the older we get. Because every year a new crop of Bouncies comes up, ready to replace wives and give middle-aged men heart attacks."

Gincy snorted. "If my husband left me for a Bouncie, he'd better freakin' have a heart attack. A big one. One that kills him. Dead. Like the roach that he is."

"Oh, crap, one's coming over here!" Danielle lifted her magazine so that it almost entirely covered her face.

"What are you hiding from?" I asked.

"I'm not hiding," she snapped. "I'm afraid I might spit and I don't want to start a girly-fight. My nails are long but look at their abs!"

The girl was now upon us—the blond one. She leaned forward and I was suddenly embarrassed being confronted with all that cleavage.

Was all that really necessary?

"Could you, like, take our picture?" she asked.

"I could," Gincy said blandly. "The question is, will I?"

The girl's smile faltered. Her pale blue eyes went blank.

"I'll do it," I said, suddenly taking pity on the girl.

Just because she was gorgeous and dumb didn't mean she was a bad person.

"How does the camera work?"

"Oh, it's totally simple," the girl replied, big, toothy smile back in place. "Just look through there and push this button. That's it!"

I climbed to my feet and followed the blond girl back to her friends. There was more giggling and then some squealing as they arranged themselves in a pose they thought was cute.

Arms around each other, butts and breasts sticking out everywhere.

Maybe they're contortionists, I thought stupidly.

"Smile," I mumbled, but lips were already open and teeth already flashing.

The blond girl snatched back the camera and thanked me with yet another giggle.

Glumly, feeling I'd somehow been abused or mocked, I made my way back to my own friends.

The sand was hot on the soles of my feet. I had to use the bathroom. My bathing suit was riding up.

"Oh, my, God, Clare," Gincy said when I'd flopped back down on my towel. "You've just shot your first *Playboy* centerfold! How does it feel to be a genuine member of the porn industry? Maybe you should join a union or something. I hear they provide good health insurance, job security . . ."

"Oh, be quiet," Danielle snapped. "Maybe we should just move."

"No way! We were here first."

While Gincy and Danielle bickered, I thought about Win.

I wondered if he was attracted to women like the three cavorting on the sand before us.

While I was out here on the Vineyard, was he spending his evenings reading *Playboy* and watching pornographic videos? Did he go to strip bars with so-called clients?

It was hard to imagine because Win had never been overly interested in sex.

Maybe, I thought uncomfortably, as the brunette squirted tanning lotion on her already brown and very flat stomach, maybe that was my fault.

Maybe Win held back because he sensed that I wasn't all that interested in sex. With him.

Maybe Win just didn't find me all that attractive.

I was the kind of girl a man married, not the kind a man fooled around with. I'd known that since adolescence.

My encounter with Finn? An aberration.

Was that part of the problem with me and Win, the lack of intense sexual attraction?

But how important was that in a marriage, how important over the long haul?

All the experts said that animal lust faded over time and was replaced by a deeper relationship built around comfort and friendship and mutual respect.

But what if the animal lust had never been there in the first place?

Maybe, I thought, *I should ask Gincy what she thinks. Maybe I should ask her how things are between her and Rick. Sexually.*

Maybe I should ask Danielle about Chris.

Maybe . . .

One of the bikini girls shrieked and her two friends took up the cry. They were in the water now, having a splash fight.

"I hope they drown," I muttered. "I hope they get shredded by a shark."

Gincy burst out laughing. "I knew you'd come around! Nobody's that generous."

Danielle patted my arm. "Welcome to the real world, honey. It ain't pretty."

August

Gincy
Blood Is Thicker

Rick and I had just finished eating a simple dinner of pasta with garlic and oil, salad, and bread—he'd cooked, of course—and I'd just dumped the dirty dishes in the sink when my doorbell rang.

And then rang again.

And again.

"Who the hell can that be?" I said, heading for the door.

I peered through the dirty peephole and saw my worst nightmare.

Holy crap. It was my brother.

Maybe I just wouldn't open the door.

Could I do that?

I mean, he had to have heard my voice. I wasn't exactly a low-talker.

What would he tell my parents? That his own sister, his own flesh and blood, had left him standing alone in the hallway like a dog.

"Shit."

"Gincy? Who is it?" Rick had come out of the mini-kitchen, a dish towel in one hand, a frown on his face.

"It's my brother," I mouthed.

"Well, let him in."

"I—"

"Yo, Gince. Open up!"

I cringed.

"Are you embarrassed of me?" Rick teased.

"Jesus, no. But just remember. You asked for it."

And I opened the door, halfway.

Tommy. In all his dirtbag glory. Wife beater T-shirt. Jeans riding below a beer paunch that had no business being on his skinny frame. Thin hair cut in a mullett.

"What are you doing here?" I snapped. "In Boston, I mean. You can't stay here tonight, you know."

"Whoa, Gince," he said, putting his hands up in the universal sign for surrender. "Slow down. Dude. Me and Jay came in for some fun, that's all."

"Jay?" I tore open the door and looked up and down the hallway. "That delinquent piece of crap is not coming anywhere near me, I hope you know that, Tommy."

"Uh, yeah? That's why he's downstairs. Dude, he's like scared of you."

I glared at my idiot brother. "He should be."

Behind me, Rick cleared his throat enquiringly. Oh, he'd hear the whole story later, all right.

"So, why are you here?" I repeated. "In my apartment." Though technically he was still in the doorway.

"Can't a guy say hey to his sister?"

"Hello. Now time to go. Don't let the door hit you on the back of the head on the way out."

Tommy shook his head. "Man, what is your damage? Me and Jay, we were like thinking you could tell us where to go have some fuuuunn. Like, get some beers and par-tay."

"No. I can't. You'll just have to find some fuuuunn on your own. Now—" I pointed into the dark hall behind him.

Suddenly, Tommy peered over my shoulder and scowled. Damn. He'd finally noticed Rick. "Who's this, your landlord?" he said in that mocking way all dumbasses have.

"No." I swallowed hard. Here we go. "He's my boyfriend."

It took almost a full minute for that bit of juicy news to sink into my brother's beer-soaked brain. Finally, a slow grin spread across his greasy face.

"Whoa, what's Mom gonna say when she finds out you're seeing some old dude?"

Rick could barely control his laughter. I shot him a warning glance and he backed into the living room, mumbling, "Hey, I'm only thirty-five."

"Mom's gonna say nothing," I snapped. "Because she's not going to find out. You keep your mouth shut, Tommy!"

"Make me!"

"You stink," I spat.

Tommy sneered. His cheesy, three-haired mustache twitched. "Yeah, well, you stink on ice."

Ah, there we were, my brother and I, the proud progeny of the Gannon-Bauer line.

I vowed right then and there never ever to reproduce. And I wondered how I could get Tommy's lines cut so he could avoid sending more stooopidity out into the already sadly stooopid world.

After another round of pointless wrangling, I told Tommy to go to Dick's Last Resort on Huntington and take the night from there. With a final smirk, he oozed off into the dark. I thoroughly enjoyed slamming the door after him.

"What?" I demanded, whirling to Rick. "Go ahead and say it." If he broke up with me over this . . .

Rick's lips twitched. "So, ah, that was your brother. Interesting. I mean, he seems—"

"Go ahead. Say it. He seems like scum. That's because he is scum."

Rick came close and kissed me on the forehead. "What I was going to say was that he seems very different from you."

I beamed. "Really? Thanks. I mean, I know that but sometimes I'm afraid some weird genetic trait is latent in me and suddenly I'll sprout a mullet and start drinking beer for breakfast."

Finally, Rick burst out laughing. "I'm sorry, Gincy. But the idea of you with a mullet is ludicrous. It's so never going to happen."

"Yeah," I admitted, "I know."

"You want to tell me what happened with this Jay character?"

"No," I said emphatically. "Someday. You wanna fool around?"

Rick did, so we did.

Later, after Rick had gone home, I thought of Trey Carrington and how he tolerated, even loved, his younger brother. Was Trey a masochist or simply very mature?

What, exactly, do we owe to family, those people foisted upon us at birth, those people from whom we descend, those people who share our DNA, our stumbling youth, our pudgy middle age, our incontinent old age?

I wondered if I would ever know the answer to that bothersome question.

Gincy
Misfit Air

I took the Blue Line out to Logan and met Danielle at the Delta shuttle.

Because we were staying at her parents' house I'd invested in a new travel bag. Something clean and not plastic. Appearances mattered to Danielle and I assumed they mattered to her parents.

I might not have been all warm and cuddly, but I did respect other people's parents.

Danielle saw me coming. "Gincy!" she cried. "Your bag! Is it new?"

An armed airport security guy glared from Danielle to me.

"And I packed it myself!" I told him brightly as I passed.

Clearly, I still wasn't past the age of occasional idiotic behavior in the presence of law enforcement.

Danielle grabbed my arm and smiled winningly at the scowling security guy. As if to say, "Please don't arrest my moronic friend."

And then she glared at me.

"What? Oh, okay. I'm sorry. I'll behave."

"Good. Now, about the bag. It's got to be new?"

I grinned, self-satisfied. "Why, yes it is. And it was a bargain, too. I got it at Marshall's."

"Well, I am just so proud of you. And new capris? You know, you clean up pretty good."

"Look, thanks again for all this," I said.

Danielle waved her well-manicured hand, a now-familiar gesture. "Don't mention it, Gincy. A girl only turns thirty once. Thank God."

"I mean it, Danielle. I can't believe your parents are paying for me and Clare to fly home with you. I mean, number one: It's totally generous. And number two: Why us, anyway? Don't you know other people in Boston better than you know us?"

I asked the question in all innocence. Really. With no ulterior motive to embarrass or provoke.

"Truth?" she said, with a funny look on her face. "No. I'm not really close to anyone in Boston. Except you and Clare. I mean, sure, there are some girls at work I have drinks with sometimes but . . ." With one delicate fingertip Danielle blotted away a tear from the corner of her left eye.

"But what?" I said, suddenly feeling very itchy. I'd never been good with tears. Mine or anyone else's.

Danielle laughed one of those sad, aren't-I-silly laughs. "But, I don't know, I've never been very good at making friends. I guess I've never really, really tried. I don't know why."

I shrugged. "That's okay. I suck at friendships, too. Maybe that's why you and I get along even though we're so different."

"Maybe we get along because we're so different. It's like I don't know what to expect from you. Ever. And that's interesting."

"There's a theory. It's more flattering than mine. Hey, here comes Clare."

"Why isn't Win coming, anyway?" I blurted, when she'd joined us, all perky and shiny in a lime green brushed cotton sundress.

Danielle identified the brushed cotton part for me.

"Well . . ." Clare bit back a smile. "I told him it was just us girls. I didn't really want him to come along. You know."

There was an awkward silence.

Why, I wondered, do people always say, "you know," expecting to hear, "of course," when the reality is that no one knows diddly-squat about anyone else's situation?

Were we supposed to understand Clare's pleasure in lying to her fiancé?

"Look," I said, determined to avoid unpleasantness, "we're all going to have a blast, right?"

"Right," Danielle said, but she didn't sound so sure. "Even without the guys. Especially without the guys."

Maybe. Clare hadn't invited Win. I didn't really care why but I was glad. I might have been forced to punch him.

Chris hadn't been invited, either. And though Danielle hadn't admitted her reasons for leaving him out of the festivities, I knew immediately and without a doubt her motives.

Chris was a pleasant diversion and nothing more. To invite him home would be to cause a whole lot of unnecessary complication.

In the end, she thought she was doing them both a favor.

Rick, however, had been invited. And he'd accepted.

And then, he'd cancelled.

I was pissed at him for backing out. But I understood, too. And I respected his decision.

Jeez, his kid was sick. The kid who'd lost his mother to cancer. Of course Rick had to stay home. Of course he wasn't going to dump Justin on a sitter for an entire weekend when the kid couldn't stop throwing up.

It's just that I missed Rick's company.

I wanted him with me.

I missed his intelligence, his wit, his gorgeous dark hair, his crashing into walls, his crashing into me.

It's the territory, Gincy, I told myself as we boarded the small plane for LaGuardia Airport behind a family of four, their two strollers, two car seats, and one giant stuffed teddy bear in tow.

Get used to it. You date a dad, you get the kid.

Accept that up front and you'll be just fine.

Clare

Friendly Skies

All buckled in and ready for takeoff.

It was the first time in a long time I'd been on a plane to anywhere but Ann Arbor, via Detroit. Win and I hadn't been away together on a romantic vacation for at least two years. He'd been so busy at the firm, moving fast on the partner track.

Which wasn't all bad. Lately, it was simply more peaceful to be without Win than to be with him. Not that my worries and questions disappeared the moment he was out of sight. But they definitely receded.

Life seemed broader, more breathable and airy when I was alone. Even if I wasn't entirely alone. Even if I was with my friends.

My friends. Now that was new.

I still couldn't bring myself to admit to them what had happened with Finn. But there were related issues I felt comfortable discussing. "Do you ever feel lonely?" I asked.

Danielle brushed the notion away with her hand. "Never. Not much. Sometimes. Why?"

"Gincy?"

"Uh, yeah, sometimes. More as I get older. It's no big deal," she added quickly.

"Are you ever lonely, Clare?" Danielle asked.

"I'm lonely all the time," I stated boldly. "It's worse when Win and I are alone together at home. It shouldn't be that way, should it?"

No one's going to tell you what to do, Clare, I reminded myself. *No one wants the responsibility of advising you to break your engagement.*

Danielle cleared her throat nervously. "Maybe it's pre-wedding jitters. You know, classic cold feet. Or something."

"Maybe."

"I'm not a big fan of therapy," Gincy said, "but maybe you should talk to someone. About the loneliness and all. That sort of thing can wear you down. So I've heard."

I laughed and mimicked Danielle's famous dismissive wave.

"Oh, I'll be all right," I said. "Danielle's probably right. It's probably just classic cold feet."

But I knew it wasn't.

Danielle
You Can Take the Girl

My parents met us at the door to our four-thousand-square-foot, split-level contemporary house. With a two-car garage. A patio out back. And a Jacuzzi.

Mom covered my face with kisses and squeezed first Clare, then Gincy.

Mom had often been described as effusive. She was born to be a grandmother. To her credit, she was remarkably restrained when it came to pressing David and me for grandchildren.

My father politely shook my friends' hands and offered each a big, genuine smile.

"The lawn looks great, Dad," I said, noting with some dismay that his face was thinner than it had been the last time I'd seen him only months earlier. "Still doing it all on your own?"

"Of course," he boomed. "I'm not an old man yet. In spite of this birthday of yours."

Dad soon went off to the garage to check his 1972 custom maroon Cadillac for fingerprints. It was only one of the many daily checks he made of the property, though as far as I knew we'd never suffered a robbery or an act of vandalism.

Mom led us girls inside. After she had shown Gincy and Clare

to the guest bedroom, which, I noted, had been redone since my
last visit, she went off to the kitchen.

I took them to see my room, the room where I'd spent almost
every night of the first eighteen years of my life.

The room where I'd be sleeping that night.

A little haven. Or not.

"Danielle?" Gincy said, standing very still in the room's center.
"Has anything changed since you last lived here?"

I surveyed the room. Plush pink carpet.

An array of dolls on the pink bedspread.

An embroidered wall hanging of a pink and purple butterfly,
my one sad attempt at needlework.

A rocking chair I hadn't been able to fit into since about the
age of five.

"No. Not really," I said. "It's pretty much as it was when I left
for college at the age of eighteen. Oh, except for the poster of
Paris at night. I bought that the summer after sophomore year, I
think."

"Doesn't your father want to turn the room into, I don't know,
a media room?" Gincy asked.

"No. He did that already with David's room. We can watch a
DVD there later if you want. Surround sound and everything."

"This sounds so much like my family," Clare said. "My brothers' rooms are now a guest room and an office for my mother.
She does do a lot of charity work, on the organizational, fund-
raising side. All my brothers' trophies and awards are on display
in the library and Daddy's home office. And I guess their other
belongings are in the attic. But my room is exactly as I left it all
those years ago. Sometimes . . ."

"Sometimes what?" I prodded. I had my own theory about
why my room was a museum.

Clare shrugged. "Sometimes I think my parents expect me to
fail spectacularly and come crying home to live out my lonely
miserable life with them. The spinster daughter in her fading
pink bedroom."

"That's probably your own insecurity talking," Gincy said.

"And where do you think I got that insecurity?" Clare shot back.

I peered into the hall to be sure we were alone.

"Well," I whispered, "sometimes I think my parents would just love me to come home and live with them. Not forever. Just until they found me a nice husband. Until he and I bought a house across the street. I think my parents keep my room this way because they want me to feel welcome. You know. If I ever lose my mind and decide to leave Boston."

"I think it's sweet," Clare said. "I think your parents really love you."

Gincy ran her finger along a shelf laden with miniature wicker furniture. "Look at this! No dust. Your mother even keeps the room clean!"

"What about your room?" I asked.

"Yeah, Gincy. Tell us. Do your parents preserve the memory?"

Gincy snorted. But behind the gross gesture I thought I sensed a genuine sore spot.

"Yeah, right," she said. "The minute I was out the door my mother put all my stuff in boxes and stuffed them in the basement. Where everything proceeded to mold. She made my room a sewing room. Or so she calls it. Last time I was home the sewing machine was covered in about three inches of dust. The bottom line is it's her room now. For her stuff. I swear I think she sleeps in there most nights. I don't think she likes my father much. I'm not sure she ever did."

"Oh, Gincy," Clare said feelingly, "that's horrible. Where do you sleep when you go home to visit?"

"In the basement. On a cot next to my moldy possessions. Which is only one of the reasons I don't go home all that often."

What could I say to that horror story?

"Girls!"

My mother to the rescue.

"In here, Mom!" I called.

A moment later my mother appeared at the door to my bedroom.

"I've just made some delicious cookies," she said, beaming. "A nice variety. Nice and hot from the oven. Why don't you come into the kitchen for a nice snack."

And then my mother reached out and poked Gincy's arm. "You're too skinny, young lady," she scolded. "Come and eat."

And there was the reason I lived in Boston . . . .

"Mom! Don't insult her!"

Gincy shrugged. "I'm not insulted. I am too thin. I'm going to look grotesquely old by the time I'm forty if I don't fatten up a bit. Look at the lines around my eyes already. So, let's go have some of those cookies."

"Thanks, Mrs. Leers," Clare said as we trailed down the wall-papered hallways after my mother. "I love home-baked cookies. My fiancé doesn't have a sweet tooth so I don't bother to make them for myself . . ."

I smiled as I followed them all to the kitchen.

Danielle, I thought, *I don't know how it happened, but you've got two pretty fabulous friends.*

Danielle
Cry If You Want To

My thirtieth birthday party was held at Captain Al's, a combination event hall and restaurant overlooking The Sound.

My parents had booked the Sea Shell Room for four hours, at no small expense. We'd all remembered the room from my cousin Mena's wedding a few years earlier. I, especially, had been impressed by the dusky rose-colored wallpaper.

The Johnny Orchestra Band, the darlings of my parents' set, had been hired for the evening to play classics like "Satin Doll" and party favorites like the ever-popular "Celebration."

"It's like a mini-wedding!" Gincy hissed when we'd first arrived. "Jeez. I'm glad I didn't bring a gag gift."

Clare and Gincy wandered off as I greeted each guest in turn. Sarah, Michelle, and Rachel were all there, husbands in tow. Aside from those six, the three of us from Boston, and David and Roberta, every other guest—with one notable exception I was soon to meet—was over fifty.

Some might have said it was more of a party for my parents than for me. But I was pleased. I liked when various generations socialized together. It seemed real and valuable. Who was anyone without context?

Take the Rothsteins. They had been good friends of my parents' for years. For the past ten of those years they'd lived directly across the street.

Wednesday nights the two couples met for bridge or various board games.

Every other Saturday they went to dinner at the club's restaurant.

Every Sunday the men played a round of golf.

Every so often the women took the train into Manhattan and caught a show or did some serious shopping.

The Rothsteins were more like family than friends. Like my aunt and uncle. If there really was a difference at that point.

I greeted the Rothsteins at their table. Among the long-familiar faces was one new face.

Mrs. Rothstein introduced him as Barry Lieberman.

Clearly, he'd been asked to attend the party for a specific reason. Mrs. Rothstein was making a match. And really, she was doing a good job of it.

A commendable job.

Her candidate was straight and Jewish.

He was somewhere between thirty-five and forty, nicely within age range.

His haircut was good and his suit well-tailored.

He was a professional.

And as a friend of the Rothsteins, he came recommended and could be held accountable. That was nothing to sneeze at.

Barry was perfectly eligible and perfectly pleasant.

But I felt not even the tiniest spark of interest in him.

When Mrs. Rothstein moved off to greet an old friend at another table, Barry and I chatted for a bit. Then he gave me his card on which were no less than three phone numbers, one of which was for a cell phone, an e-mail address, a fax number, a post-office-box number, and a street address.

"I'll be in Boston some time in the next few weeks," he said. "I'd love to take you to dinner."

"Call me," I said pleasantly, and excused myself to greet other guests.

I would go to dinner with Barry. Maybe a spark would ignite if we went to one of my favorite restaurants. Good food and a lively atmosphere were known to do wonders for romance.

I stopped by the bandstand and watched my guests talking, laughing, eating, and drinking with relish.

How could I have asked Chris to come to this event? He would have been a fish out of water.

Right?

It would have been setting him up to fail, dropping him in a room full of professional types in Hugo Boss ties, Armani suits, and Kaspar dresses.

Right?

The truth was, I'd never seen Chris in a large, sort of formal social situation. For all I knew he was totally at ease in a suit, sipping champagne, nibbling Popsicle-sized lamb chops.

But I hadn't given Chris a chance to prove himself away from home.

Why?

Maybe—and this was a scary possibility—maybe I was more concerned with how I would handle introducing Chris to my family. Concerned with what my parents—and David?—would say about my choice of date for such a major family event.

Face it, Danielle, I told myself, as my sixty-year-old, red-haired aunt Myra shimmied by laughing up a storm. Every event is major in your family. The Leers could make opera out of your getting a new haircut.

Maybe I would be better off out of context. At least on occasion.

I slipped out onto the terrace and using my cell phone, I called Chris. He answered on the first ring.

"Hey, Danielle," he said brightly. "I knew it was you. I've got your number loaded into my cell. So, how's it going? Is it good to see your parents?"

God, how I missed him at that moment. "Oh, yeah, it's great," I said. "You know. Look, Chris, I was thinking. Um. Well, I was wondering how you would feel about coming into Boston some time when I get back. To celebrate my birthday."

"Instead of out here on the Vineyard?" he asked, sounding a bit puzzled.

Or was that my imagination?

"Um, yeah. Would that be okay?"

"Danielle, I'd love to," he replied, and all I heard was true enthusiasm. "I hardly ever get to Boston. Summer is tight for me with work but I'll arrange something. Just pick a day, okay?"

Just then the door to the terrace opened and a loud shout of laughter burst through.

"Where are you?" Chris asked, with a smile in his voice.

"Oh, just at home," I lied. "My family's kind of loud. They like to have a good time."

"Sounds good to me. Danielle, thanks for calling. It means a lot. I'm sorry but I've got to go. Johnny and I are just about to load—"

"That's okay," I interrupted. "I . . . I miss you, Chris."

"I miss you, too, Danielle. I'll see you soon?"

"Yes," I whispered, too close to tears.

We ended the call and I stood looking out over the water until I could regain my composure. When I went back into the event room, I caught sight of David standing alone by the bar.

David's presence had always made me feel better. He was predictable, reliable, solid.

"Hey," I said, joining him, "where's Roberta?"

"Frankly, I don't care where she is right now. She's becoming a royal pain in my ass."

"David!" I shot a glance over my shoulder.

Thank God no one but the bartender was in earshot, and like any good bartender, this one hadn't blinked an eye at his client's private conversation.

"That's your fiancée you're talking about," I whispered fiercely. "The future mother of your children. What's wrong with you?"

"I'm sorry, Danielle. It's just . . ." David sighed hugely. A habit we both got from my grandfather.

"It's just what? You can tell me."

First, David ordered another gin and tonic. When he was served we moved off a bit to allow others access to the bar.

"It's just that we're looking for a house, right?" he said, when we'd come to stand by the big window overlooking the water. "And this one she's fixated on looks like Scarlett O'Hara's mansion—"

"Tara."

"Whatever. Well, we just can't afford it right now. I can't afford it. I mean, maybe in five years, if I plan right and the practice grows. I'm hopeful. But not now."

Where was the problem? I wondered.

"Okay," I said. "So, tell her that."

"Ah, therein lies the difficulty, little sister. I have told her. I've told her five, ten times. But the reality doesn't seem to sink in. It's like she doesn't even hear me. Do you know she's told her mother we've put in an offer on the place? And when I confronted her about it, you know what she said? She said, 'Oh, David, you'll make it work.' Do you believe it?"

I wasn't quite sure what David wanted to hear from me. Roberta's response sounded positive. Though her lying to her mother about the offer was not good news.

"Well," I said, weakly, "at least she has faith in you."

David finished off his drink in one long swallow. "I don't see faith," he said shortly. "I see pressure. I see that she's spoiled rotten and instead of helping me she's setting me up for failure. The relationship isn't about us, a team, a family. It's just all about her."

The force behind David's words stunned me.

"Is this new?" I dared to ask. "I mean, has Roberta changed since you met her? Since you got engaged?"

David shook his head. "No. To be fair, no. I'm the one who's changed. Who's changing. Whatever. But listen to me. I'm ruining my baby sister's big birthday party by moaning about my woes. I'm sorry, Danielle."

I threw my arms around him and held him tight. "I'm worried about you, David. I want you to be happy."

"Don't worry," he said, kissing the top of my head. "I can take care of myself. Really. I promise. And I will be happy. Okay? So you just enjoy the celebration."

David walked off in the direction of our parents. I watched him go.

How could I enjoy the party after that exchange?

Was nobody happy?

Clare was marrying a horribly narrow-minded, self-centered snob.

David had finally realized what I'd caught a glimpse of earlier that summer, that his fiancée was spoiled rotten and totally self-absorbed.

And Chris . . .

Nothing was wrong with Chris other than the fact that he was who he was. And I was who I was.

And that even though I had agreed to go fishing on his boat and he had agreed to come to Boston to celebrate my birthday, the fact was that we were horribly mismatched.

Even though he made me so happy.

The band came back from break and struck up a lively tune. Couples swarmed the dance floor.

Couples in their seventies. Couples who'd been together for forty years.

Couples in their thirties and forties, many second or third spouses.

People just keep trying, I thought. *They just keep trying to be happy.*

Maybe things will work out between Gincy and Rick, I thought, turning away from the dancing couples, trying hard for hopefulness. Though Gincy was still adamant about not getting serious with a guy who came with a child.

As if summoned by my thoughts, Gincy and Clare joined me. Clare looked lovely in a pale lime green sleeveless dress with cream-colored princess heels and matching bag.

Gincy had disappeared into the bathroom that morning with one of my hair-care products and somehow had managed to produce a pixielike look that was very flattering.

I considered her efforts and good results partly my own doing. I was a good influence on the girl, no doubt.

"We want to give you our presents," Clare said brightly.

"You guys! You didn't have to get me anything!"

"Yeah. Right."

Gincy handed me a heavy box wrapped in pink glossy paper. "Anyway, if you hate it I have the gift receipt so you can return it."

"I so won't hate it," I swore, tearing open the package to find a book about Kevin Aucoin, the famously talented makeup artist who had died tragically a year or two earlier.

"Oh my God, it's . . . God, I'm going to cry, here it comes! Gincy, thank you, really . . ."

Gincy patted my shoulder awkwardly. "I asked a salesperson in Barnes & Noble what someone like you might want. You know, someone heavily into all the girl stuff. It was down to that book or the big Elizabeth Taylor one—"

"*My Love Affair with Jewelry?* I bought a copy the first day it came out."

"I figured as much," she said, laughing.

Clare held out a thick white envelope. "My turn."

It was a gift certificate for Belle Sante, a lovely spa on Newbury Street.

"Oh! Oh!" I cried. "This is enough for a massage and a facial! Oh, Clare, you shouldn't have!"

"Enjoy it in good health," she said.

Gincy poked my arm. "You know," she said, "maybe we should all have a glass of champagne. What was that stuff we had at Win's party?"

"I thought you didn't like champagne!" I teased.

"Well, you know, it's good to keep an open mind."

So the three of us raised a glass.

"To the birthday girl."

"To you guys, for coming all the way to Long Island."

"To us," Clare said.

And we clinked glasses.

Okay. Maybe I'd been wrong not to trust in Chris.

But I'd been right in trusting Gincy and Clare to come home with me.

My two friends.

Clare
When You Least Expect It

Win was reading the *Wall Street Journal* and sipping a bourbon when I walked through the living room.

He looked up, surprised. "You're going out?"

"Yes," I said simply.

I do have a life without you. Even though it's a mess right now.

"Can I ask where you're going?"

"Of course. I'm going to a reading at the library at Copley Square. One of my favorite authors is in town."

"Oh?" Win said, looking almost puzzled. "Who?"

"You wouldn't know her," I said.

"Have you mentioned her to me?"

"Yes. It's Barbara Michaels. She also writes under Elizabeth Peters."

And I own all of her books. They're right there on the shelves behind you.

Win considered. "No, you're right. I don't recognize the name."

I opened the hall closet and pulled out a mini-umbrella.

"The library smells," Win said suddenly. "It's a dump for the homeless. I don't know how you can bear it. Why don't you just go to a B&N superstore? At least they're clean. And you can get a decent cup of coffee."

I tried to smile. I did. "Because," I said, "Barbara Michaels isn't reading at B&N. She's reading at the library."

Win's eyes were glancing back to the paper. He was done with the conversation. "Well," he said, folding the paper to a new page, "don't let anyone pick you up."

I thought I would faint. My stomach clenched, my mouth watered, sweat broke out on my neck.

Oh, God, what did Win know? Maybe one of his colleagues had seen me with Finn back on the Fourth of July!

But Win's creeping smile belied any knowledge of my betrayal.

I shoved away my nagging conscience.

Win, I realized, thought he was being funny. He thought that at a silly reading and book signing there'd be no eligible men to make a pass at me, only sad homeless losers and pathetic homosexuals.

Those would be his terms.

Maybe he thought that even if there were eligible men at the event, none of them would notice me, let alone make a pass at me.

Why? Because I wasn't the type men made passes at. I wasn't sexy, outstanding, irresistible.

I was Clare.

Sweetie.

A nobody.

"I'll be fine," I mumbled. I grabbed my bag and left the room. As the door shut I heard Win calling, "What time will—," but I didn't stop to answer.

The reading and signing was attended by about fifty people, which to me seemed a great success. Afterward, clutching my autographed copy of the latest in the Amelia Peabody series, I examined the display of photographs of late-nineteenth–early-twentieth-century archaeological digs, digs that took place around the time Ms. Michaels's famous heroine was busy in Egypt.

And then I was aware of someone close on my right, also studying the display.

A man. Maybe five or seven years older than me.

I'd noticed him earlier. It hadn't been difficult given that he was the only man in the room aside from two members of the library staff.

I shot a quick glance at him. Tall. Reddish brown hair, cut close. An artfully scruffy beard. A good profile, strong nose and chin. He looked Viking-like.

I looked away, afraid he'd catch me staring.

Too late.

"Hi," he said, and I turned back to him.

"Hi."

He gestured to the book I held in my arms. "You were at the reading."

I smiled. "Yeah. I love her work."

The guy's neat, clean attire precluded his being homeless. And if he was gay, well, it wasn't going to matter to me in the end, anyway. Being engaged to Win.

And there would be no more slips. No more betrayals. Ever.

I gestured at his own book, under his arm. "You, too."

The guy nodded. "I admit, I'm a fan. My sister has Ms. Michaels's books all over her apartment and one day I picked one up, just to browse. A chapter later, I was hooked."

Well, there was no harm in talking about books, was there? I asked myself.

"Her characters are always strong and intelligent," I said. "But not perfect. You feel like you know them. You feel like you are them. At least, I do. I feel like I could be a heroine. Except . . . Except . . ."

"Go on," he urged. "Except that real life is more complicated than fiction? Because instead of just one author making decisions there are countless 'authors' contributing random, conflicting ideas and no editor to pull everything together into a meaningful whole?"

"Well, that wasn't exactly what I meant," I admitted, smiling. "But it's a very interesting observation. What I mean is that even if they're afraid or sad, the heroines in Ms. Michaels's books seek out their fate. They have adventures because they have convictions and interests and they pursue ideas and justice and rest for weary souls . . ."

I stopped, embarrassed. "I'm sorry," I said, blushing. "Am I making any sense?"

"Perfect sense. And why don't you think you're like a Michaels/Peters heroine?"

"Because I'm not."

The guy gave me an odd look. "You sound so sure of that."

"I am."

"Well, maybe you're working up to being a heroine. The heroine of your own life."

An interesting idea.

"That would be nice," I said. "Maybe I should make that my goal. Thanks."

He glanced at his watch and then looked back to me. "Hey," he said, "it's only eight o'clock. I was wondering, would you like to get some coffee, maybe continue our conversation?"

For the second time that night I felt as if I would faint. I wondered if I'd heard him correctly. But the open, anticipatory look on his face affirmed that I had.

"Oh, I'm—I'm so sorry," I said. "I'd love to have coffee with you but, you see, I'm engaged."

Stupidly, I wiggled my left hand. And only then realized that I wasn't wearing my engagement ring.

"Oh. No, I'm the one who's sorry." He laughed awkwardly. "I didn't see a ring."

I looked down at my empty hand.

At my hand the way it should be?

"It's being resized," I said. As if he cared. "Of course you wouldn't know . . ."

"Yeah . . . Well, I guess I'm going to take off. Have a good night."

"Thanks," I said, forcing a smile. "You, too."

There followed a moment of supreme mutual discomfort.

And then, with a quick smile, he left me standing alone by the photographic display.

I stood there for a moment, staring blindly at the other attendees around me.

I hadn't even asked for his name.

The stranger. An admirer.

The misunderstanding had been all my fault.

I was guilty of false advertising. I wasn't wearing my engagement ring. I'd lost so much weight the ring kept threatening to fall off my finger so Win had taken it to a jeweler to be resized.

Without the ring, I appeared to be a free agent.

I wondered. Should I have hidden in the apartment until the ring was back on my finger, good and tight?

Of course not.

But why had the stranger spoken to me?

I must have been giving off a vibe that said I was available. Right?

Danielle would know the answer. She knew everything about male dating behavior and she had a notebook to prove it.

But I would never know.

And now the stranger probably thought I was just a tease, a heartless flirt.

As if it mattered what the stranger thought. I'd never see him again. I couldn't!

What a mess, Clare, I scolded. *Everything you touch dissolves into disaster.*

Win. Finn.

My heart heavy, I left the library and hailed a cab on Bolyston Street.

Alone in the dark on the hard backseat, I tried for peace of mind.

Nothing happened, Clare, I told myself, watching the streets go by, *just forget it.*

It wasn't like the July 4th incident.

Nothing happened.

But something had.

Danielle
Meet the Parents

It wasn't the first time I'd been invited to a guy's parents' house for dinner.

Except that it was. Meaning that back in high school Seth Levenkron, my senior prom date, was living with his parents, whereas Chris had his own small place behind his parents' house.

A few days before the big night Chris had asked me if I had any food allergies or intense dislikes.

"I love food," I said. "Have you ever seen me be fussy?"

"No. It's one of the things I really like about you. You're sensual. Sensuous. You embrace life."

Yes, I do, I agreed silently.

Take that Lara Flynn Boyle! Kim Cattrall! Michelle Pfeiffer!

Saturday evening Chris and I arrived at the Childs' family property in rural Chilmark.

The Childs' property covered about twenty acres. Everything was so green and lush. The air was so fresh I felt almost lightheaded.

The three-story, nineteenth-century house was white with black shutters. Colorful petunias spilled from window boxes on the first-floor windows. There was a wild garden off to the side and behind the house, just outside the kitchen door, an herb and vegetable garden.

The first floor consisted of a parlor-like front room, now used as a bedroom, complete with fireplace; a kitchen; a dining room; a half-bath; and something Chris called a mudroom. On the second floor there were three bedrooms of varying size, each with a fireplace, one used as a home office; and a full bath.

I asked where the washing machine and dryer were located. Chris gave me a funny look and told me his mother did all the laundry down by the creek.

It took me a moment to realize he was joking. Mrs. Childs had a very nice laundry and ironing room set up in the basement.

Chris introduced me to his parents as his girlfriend. It gave me a start but no one could tell my surprise thanks to my excellent social training.

Mr. Childs, a plump, red-cheeked man, was in a wheelchair. Chris had implied that his father wasn't well but he'd never offered any details. I hadn't asked, partly out of delicacy and partly because, well, I'd never expected to meet Mr. Childs or to become involved in the Childs family.

But there I was, in their home for dinner.

Mrs. Childs was tall and fair; Chris got his height and coloring from her.

Dinner was served almost immediately. Though I was used to a relaxing cocktail hour first, what could I say?

The dining table was simply, though expertly, set with everyday white china. Sunflowers graced the table, their stems cut short so as to create a lush, low centerpiece. The napkins were deep blue to match the enameled vase that held the sunflowers.

And the food! We started with homemade New England clam chowder. The entree was a juicy roast beef. Chris had put together a salad of bright, sweet tomatoes and fresh, locally grown greens.

And for dessert, we feasted on Mrs. Childs's homemade peach-and-blueberry cobbler, served with vanilla ice cream.

After what seemed like hours—and very pleasant ones at

that!—I patted my mouth with a napkin and sat back in my chair with a sigh of contentment.

"I like to see a girl with a healthy appetite," Mr. Childs said with a twinkle in his eye.

Mrs. Childs swiped his shoulder with her napkin but I wasn't in the least offended.

"That's me." I laughed. "I don't understand skinny. It doesn't speak to me. I think it's genetic."

"Speaking of family," Mrs. Childs said cleverly, "we heard you had a birthday recently."

I thanked her for remembering and told them I'd gone home to see my parents. I omitted the fact that Gincy and Clare had gone with me, as Chris thought I'd gone to Long Island alone.

"But we'll be celebrating on our own soon," Chris said, taking my hand. "In Boston."

I didn't miss Mrs. Childs's quirked eyebrow as she looked at her son and then, briefly, to our joined hands.

Gently, I slipped out of Chris's grasp. I was pretty certain Mrs. Childs liked me. Most people did. But I was also pretty sure she didn't understand my relationship with her son.

That made two of us.

Deftly, I turned the conversation to a more general, less personal topic.

About an hour later, Chris and I took our leave and went to his own home, which he said he was eager to show me. I wondered if he was going to suggest we have sex and I had my answer all prepared.

It was a gentle no.

The house was a smaller version of his parents', built in the 1970s for a bachelor uncle. Chris had inherited it at the age of eighteen, the uncle long since having passed away.

The rooms were spare but not spartan, the style simple but not cold bachelor pad. While looking at a framed photograph of the Gay Head lighthouse during a storm, I wondered who had decorated Chris's house. His mother? A former girlfriend? Or Chris himself?

There was so much I didn't know about Chris Childs. He wasn't the sort to talk much about himself and I had neglected to ask. Neglected or chosen not to ask?

Did he have a brother or sister? Had he ever been married or engaged? How old was he, anyway?

Oh, my God, had he even gone to college?

It struck me then, absolutely for the first time, that if Chris were eligible husband material, I would have acquired the answers to those questions and many more before the end of the first date.

I shuddered, mentally. I so didn't want any bothersome thoughts to spoil an otherwise pleasant evening.

"Your mother is wonderful, Chris," I said, thinking also that she was shrewd and protective of her baby. "You're so lucky. And your father is a sweetheart! He's so cute!"

Chris grinned. "I'll tell him you said so."

I playfully swatted his arm. "Oh, don't do that! I'd be so embarrassed! But really, your parents are so nice. The perfect hosts. And my God, can your mother cook! I'd be as big as a house if I lived near her. And I'm not sure I'd mind!"

Chris got a funny look on his face. He crossed the room to a side table, opened a drawer, removed something from it, then returned to me.

"I have something for you, Danielle," he said, and I swear his voice was unsteady. "I don't know if you'll like it. It's okay if you don't. I mean—"

My heart began to race. "Chris. Stop worrying. I love presents!"

He handed me a flat, square, white box; two tiny pieces of clear tape held it closed.

Jewelry, I thought. My heart continued to speed. *It's jewelry.*

Okay, wrapping paper would have been nice, or at least a big shiny bow, but it was what was inside that mattered.

A bracelet. If the size and shape of the box was any indication, it had to be a bracelet.

Fingers quivering, I sliced the tape with my nail and lifted the lid of the box.

And there it was.

It was a bracelet, all right. And it was made of thin panels of pale shell, sort of opaline, glued to a metal circle. Not even silver, just some low-grade jewelers' metal.

"I've never had a shell bracelet before," I said truthfully. Brightly.

Though I almost felt like crying. I don't know what I'd been expecting. I don't know what I'd been dreading.

"I figured as much," Chris said earnestly. "I mean, I've never seen you in anything like it but when I saw it, I don't know, I just thought of how beautiful it would look against your skin."

He really was so sweet. I smiled and reached up to kiss him softly on the lips. Chris took me in his arms and wouldn't let me go.

"Danielle," he said, his voice husky, "there's something I want to ask you."

His closeness lulled me. For a moment.

And then I was struck by a dreadful thought.

A shell bracelet just could not be an engagement offering, could it?

It had better not be! Because then I would have to turn Chris down for more than one reason.

"Hmm?" I murmured, pretending I was still under the spell of his embrace.

"We've been seeing each other for a while now—"

"Ten weeks," I said, unaware until that moment that I'd been keeping track. "Twenty times. Ten actual dates. Not including the two times we bumped into each other."

"Oh," Chris said. "Okay. Well, I was thinking, there's no one else I want to be dating. I was wondering if you felt the same. Because if you do, well, I thought we could see each other exclusively. Just us two."

The wonderful meal I'd just eaten threatened to come back up in a torrent of panic.

Oh, God, I thought, *why is this happening?*

Stupid girl, accepting an invitation to his parents' house for dinner!

"Silly," I said, trying for a softly teasing tone, one fairly seductive and reassuring, "of course I love being with you."

"But will—"

"I mean, we have such a nice time. Don't we? Everything's just so nice."

Chris looked down at me and though I tried, I couldn't read his face.

In so, so many ways Chris was an unknown.

Had my words fooled him into thinking I'd agreed not to see anyone else? Or had he read the real meaning behind them?

Chris wasn't stupid. If he had understood me, then he was saving his dignity by pretending not to have.

I tried to salvage what I could of that evening's romance. I drew back from him just a bit and held up the arm with the bracelet.

"Look," I said, "if you turn it this way it flashes the palest pink. I love pink."

Chris smiled briefly. "I know," he whispered.

Then he drew me back to him and said nothing more.

How can I not love this man, I asked myself as we embraced.

Because you're not allowed.

Gincy
Playing House

I took the plunge.
Made the leap.
Bit the bullet.
How else would my father describe my brave action?

I screwed my courage to the sticking point and invited Rick and Justin to spend a day in Oak Bluffs with me.

It was a nerve-wracking prospect, but something happened during the week that completely took my mind off the impending weekend visit.

I received a letter from The Doctor.

Let me set this up.

After years of ignoring the reality of my health—i.e., self-diagnosing and skipping yearly physicals—I'd finally succumbed to Sally's pressure and made an appointment with a doctor. Really, it was more to shut her up than because I really cared about my vital signs.

The visit went okay. There was some minor poking and prodding, nothing annoyingly invasive.

And then The Doctor, a superfit-looking woman about thirty-five years old, wanted to draw some blood.

"What for?" I asked. Somewhat belligerently.

"I want to check your cholesterol levels," she said, scribbling in my chart. "And I want to test for a thyroid problem."

"Thyroid?"

"Your eyes look a little bulgy," The Doctor said matter-of-factly.

Doctors, it seems, can insult your looks and get away with it. That has to be a perk of the profession.

"Can I say no?"

I fully intended to say no.

"You can," The Doctor replied, looking steadily at me.

Suddenly, I felt ashamed. Had I really been acting like a pissy child?

"It's your life," she went on. "But if I'm going to treat you properly, you need to work with me, not against me."

"Okay," I murmured.

So my blood was drawn by a large Jamaican woman full of attitude. She made the procedure bearable; I imagined her sitting on a struggling patient and enjoying it. When she was done she told me I'd get the results in a few days, via snail mail.

I forgot about the test about five minutes after leaving the doctor's office and making my way back into town from Chestnut Hill on the Green Line D extension.

About a week later, as I was leaving for work, I found an envelope on the floor of my building's lobby, addressed to me. It must have been put in someone else's box, someone who kindly tossed it on the floor for me.

It was an envelope from The Doctor.

My heart started beating madly and I stuffed the envelope in my bag. As soon as I got to the office I dialed Sally's extension and told her to hightail it to my office.

"Look!" I hissed, waving the envelope in her face. "This is all your fault."

"What?" Sally said, snatching the envelope. "Oh. It's probably the results of your blood test. What's the big deal?"

I snatched back the envelope.

"The big deal is . . . The big deal . . ."

"Gincy, just open it. If there's bad news at least you'll know so you can do something about it. Fix the problem, find a solution, solve—"

"Shut. Up."

I tore open the now-mangled envelope and read the contents. Then I read the contents again.

"Well?" Sally prompted. "Don't keep me hanging."

I cleared my throat. "It says, and I quote, 'Your levels are essentially normal.' "

Essentially normal?

What did that mean, essentially?

No, what did that mean, exactly?

Another question: What the hell was a level? Levels of what?

"That's how doctors talk," Sally explained. "Don't worry about it."

"Don't worry about it?" I shrieked. "It's my blood, I'll worry about it if I want to. You know, before you made me go to the freakin' doctor, I never even thought about my blood. About my—what is this? My freakin' expialadocious? What does this mean? How do they expect you not to worry when they don't explain these stupid medical codes—this could be ancient Egyptian for all I know!—and they tell you your blood is essentially normal?"

"Calm down, Gincy," Sally said. "You can ask the doctor when you go back."

"Go back? Why would I go back?"

"For a follow-up. Didn't she tell you to make another appointment?"

"No. And I'm not going to. I'm going to try really, really hard to forget this whole thing ever happened. Essentially normal. Jesus Christ. What next? Slightly insane? A little bit pregnant?"

Sally shook her head and walked off. In retrospect, I couldn't blame her.

The whole thing was still bugging me when Rick and Justin stepped off the ferry that morning in August, but I vowed not to mention The Doctor until Rick and I were alone.

First I brought the guys to the house to meet Danielle and

Clare. We stayed only about five minutes but it was long enough for Rick and Justin to make a good impression on my roomies.

On the way back out, I turned to catch any nasty faces. Instead, Clare smiled broadly at me and Danielle shook her right hand and mouthed, "Hot!"

From the house we went straight to the Flying Horse Carousel on Circuit Avenue, Oak Bluff's main street. Rick hoisted Justin on a prancing purple horse while I got us ice cream cones. Then we plopped down on a bench from where we could keep an eye on the rotating kid.

While Justin went round and round on his purple horse, I told Rick about my visit to The Doctor and about the blood test results.

"That sounds good," he said, finishing off his ice cream cone.

"Don't you think the language is a little vague?" I pressed. "Essentially normal?"

"That's how doctors talk," he said, wiping his mouth and balling the napkin. "They learn early on to avoid definitive statements. Other than, "He's dead," of course. It's a way of protecting themselves against malpractice suits. And probably also a way of admitting that they're not gods. That they might have missed something lurking in the shadows."

Well, that was disturbing.

"So, you're saying precision isn't a big thing for physicians?"

Rick shrugged. "In their language if not in their actions, no, it's not."

"That's criminal," I said angrily. "Why do people bother going to doctors anyway if all they're going to hear are diagnoses like, well, you look like you have a thyroid problem but the tests say you don't so let's just wait and see if you curl up and die before tomorrow?"

Rick laughed. "Would it make you feel better if I told you my own favorite doctor diagnosis?"

"No. Yes."

I wondered how he could be so matter-of-fact, so Zen about medical stuff, when his wife's freakin' doctors couldn't prevent her from dying of cancer at the age of twenty-nine.

Oh, my God, I realized. *That's my age. I'm twenty-nine. And I could die . . .*

"Gincy?"

"What?" I blurted.

"Are you okay? You just went pale."

Yeah, pale like a corpse. Like the corpse I soon could be!

"I'm fine," I lied. "Just tell me the story. And it had better be funny."

Rick took a deep breath. "Okay," he began, "well, it was about six years ago, I guess, and Annie had just been diagnosed. She was feeling very depressed and tired so I decided I'd try to do more around the house. You know, take some of the pressure off so she could concentrate on getting well."

Like that worked, I thought grimly.

"Anyway, one day I pulled out the vacuum and the dust mop and the Ajax and put on the TV for some background noise and got to work. At one point, I was bending over dusting a baseboard—"

"You dust baseboards?"

This was an interesting fact.

"Not anymore," he assured me. "So, I was dusting a baseboard when something on the TV caught my interest and I straightened up to check it out and crashed my head into the edge of a heavy wood shelf."

"Ow."

Rick touched the very top of his head with one finger, as if it still hurt. "Yeah, ow. I blanked out for a minute and the pain was bad but I didn't want to cause more trouble for Annie, so when she got up from her nap for dinner I didn't mention it. But four days later I still had a headache and my eyesight was a bit blurry so I went for a CT scan."

I felt my stomach drop to my knees. My knees throbbed with the weight.

"Was it scary? They put you in a tube, right?"

Rick shrugged. "No, it's no big deal, you just lie there. I kind of fell asleep. Anyway, when it was over, I asked the technician if he saw anything. And he told me that he'd leave the official readings to my doctor but that he saw no gross abnormalities."

Rick laughed. I mean, he guffawed. "It still cracks me up. No gross abnormalities. Implying, of course, there were only millions of tiny abnormalities."

I didn't get the humor. "Rick, how can you laugh about that?" I cried. "First of all, the technician guy should never have just blurted out that information. Was he trying to be funny? He probably wasn't even qualified to give an opinion!"

I grabbed Rick's arm and shook it, as if that would make him understand my point.

My fear.

"And, God, you could be a freakin' walking time bomb! What if all those little abnormalities get together and decide to make one big-ass—i.e., gross!—abnormality, and POW! you're dead."

Rick slipped out of my grasp and gave me a one-armed, cheer-up kind of hug. "Gincy, the doctor read the scan and concluded I didn't have a concussion, so there was nothing to worry about. There is nothing to worry about."

I wasn't appeased. "Essentially normal, my ass," I muttered.

"Look," Rick said, "here comes Justin. Guess he's finally tired of the merry-go-round."

"Okay. I get it. We'll drop the subject. For now."

The rest of the afternoon was spent having fun. Which I managed to do after some serious effort at putting the gross abnormalities story out of my mind.

Rick and I had fried clams for lunch; Justin went for a hot dog. Rick bought a second ice cream cone, which he managed to drop two seconds after the purchase.

"Dad," Justin said, matter-of-factly, "you might want to try a cup next time."

After lunch, Justin and I had a contest to see who could toss small rocks farthest into the ocean. I won, fair and square. Justin was a good loser so it all worked out.

Using a one-time-use camera I'd bought in CVS we took goofy pictures of each other splashing in the surf. A passing couple in their late sixties or so offered to take a picture of "the entire family." Without missing a beat, Justin grabbed my hand and Rick's, and suddenly we were a unit.

Rick winked at me over Justin's head. It was a weird moment but also really wonderful. I felt tears prick my eyes and was glad I was wearing sunglasses.

Later, I watched as the ferry pulled away from the dock, taking Rick and Justin back to Boston. The sun was almost down. My guys appeared on deck, almost shadows now, and we waved to each other until we were all lost to sight.

I was sad to see them go.

I hoped that made me essentially normal.

Gincy

It's All in the Presentation

On a wild and crazy whim, Clare and I had stayed home that night instead of wasting money at a bar. We poured our own beer and ordered a pizza.

Clare was reading some mystery set in late-nineteenth-century Egypt and I was enjoying a biography of Benjamin Franklin when Danielle came home around eleven o'clock, dragging her date behind her.

Clare, wearing only a thin cotton nightgown, grabbed a throw pillow to her chest and remained curled up in her chair. Dressed in a T-shirt and jean shorts, I got up to shake hands with this newest in a long line.

It was like shaking a few strands of limp pasta. The guy's wrist was the circumference of a matchstick.

Danielle introduced him as Stuart and announced he'd only be staying a moment.

Stuart blushed furiously and looked to Danielle. She pointed toward the bathroom. While he was gone, Clare and I shot each other questioning looks. Danielle hummed and emptied her purse on the kitchen counter.

After a moment or two Stuart scurried back and Danielle walked him to the door. There was no kiss, not even a peck on the cheek.

His head bobbed as if he were an overly humble Japanese man begging pardon for some social misstep.

"So," I drawled when Danielle returned alone. "How was your date?"

She shrugged and didn't meet my eye. "Fine. He asked me out again and I said yes. He's a lawyer, you know."

"He's a lawyer?" I said. "Jeez, I hope he's more alive in the courtroom. The guy's got no affect. He's without affect. He's affectless."

Danielle pouted. "That's not true. Okay, maybe it's a little true."

"I could hardly hear him when he said hello," Clare said, joining us now in the kitchen. "He seems far too gentle for court."

I laughed. "He's too skinny for court."

"What!" my roomies cried in unison.

"Just what I said. He's too skinny for court. He makes no impression. One breath and I could knock him over. He's the weenie guy at the beach the macho dudes kick sand at."

"That's so mean!"

I shrugged. "I'm not saying he's not super-intelligent. Maybe. Or nice. Or rich. Family money or something. But I can't imagine he's successful, at least not if he has to argue cases in court in front of a jury. If the guy sits behind a desk all day making whiz-bang deals, okay, I can see that. Maybe. Maybe he uses his meek appearance to throw off the opposition."

"Do you really think appearance has that much to do with professional success?" Clare said, doubtfully.

"In this case," I said, "yes. Tall men are more noticed than short men. Well-built men are considered more powerful than fat or skinny men. Juries are going to be persuaded by the hero guy, the handsome guy, the guy women want to date and men want to be. Or hang out with."

"I think I'll break our next date," Danielle said suddenly. "Gincy's got a very good point. Plus, I don't know, his name does nothing for me. Stuart. Stuart-shmoouart. Blah."

I grinned. "Stuart Little. See? A mouse, not a man."

"You're breaking up with a guy because of his name!" Clare

cried. "I don't believe you. How would you feel if a guy broke up with you because he didn't like your name?"

Danielle shrugged. "His loss. Besides, how could any normal man not like 'Danielle.' Please. Although one guy called me Dani-elle on our first date and, let me tell you, that was the end of that relationship."

"Why are you dating other guys, anyway?" Clare asked then. "I mean, you've been to Chris's house and met his parents. Isn't that kind of big?"

Danielle actually flushed and turned to open the refrigerator. "Is there any diet soda left?"

"She doesn't want to discuss it," I explained. "Chris isn't in the running. She doesn't take him seriously. She's intending to break his heart."

Danielle slammed the fridge door and whirled around. "Oh, please! Chris isn't in love with me!"

"Of course he is," I answered calmly. "You're just in denial."

Clare walked over to Danielle and put a hand on her shoulder. I'd never seen her touch anyone before. The girl was just full of surprises.

"Danielle, I think Gincy's right. It is pretty obvious. He looks at you like—like he's glad to be alive just so he can gaze at you."

"He—" Ah, Danielle couldn't deny it.

"And you're in love with him, too," I said.

"I am not!"

"Okay, then. You have strong feelings for him."

"No, I don't!"

I shot a look at Clare. It said, "Watch this."

"Oh, yeah?" I pointed to Danielle's right wrist. "Then what's that thing you're wearing?"

Danielle nervously—guiltily?—touched the wide bracelet on her arm. "What thing? Oh, this? It's nothing. It's just a shell bangle. Nothing."

"And who gave it to you?"

"All right," she cried, "Chris gave it to me. At his parents' house. But it doesn't mean anything. It's not like—like a promise ring."

"Then why are you wearing it? It's not gold. It's not diamonds. It's so not—"

"Okay, okay. Just—just stop. It does mean something to me. God."

"Why is it so hard to admit that you really like Chris?" Clare asked, far more gently than I would have. "He seems awfully nice."

Danielle clutched her head. The shell bangle slid farther down toward her elbow.

I think I'd like one of those, I thought.

"Because it's just not going to work out, okay?" Danielle answered, clearly near tears. "It's just not."

Clare didn't push for an explanation. I'm sure she knew as well as I did what Danielle's answer would be.

"Then why don't you cut him loose now?" I asked, "if your mind is made up? Don't drag him along, letting him think you guys are building something special when you have no intention of seeing him after the summer."

Clare shook her head at me, ever so slightly.

"Can we please change the subject?" Danielle cried, eyes glistening. "Or I'm out of here. I mean it. I don't want to talk about Chris anymore."

"Of course," Clare said before I could further antagonize anyone. "I think there's some diet soda on the porch. I'll go get some. It's warm but we have ice."

"Thanks," Danielle whispered.

Gincy

Personal Responsibility

After the grilling I had given her the night before, I wasn't sure Danielle was ever going to talk to me again.

But Danielle was remarkably buoyant. Maybe inside she was all coiled up about Chris, but when she appeared for breakfast I couldn't detect a trace of sadness or anger.

As I'd noted before, she was generally a good sport. That, and a damn good actress.

By ten o'clock we were installed at our favorite area of the Oak Bluffs town beach. The Bouncies were nowhere in sight. The day boded well.

I was half asleep, my hat over my face, when Danielle asked, apropos of nothing, "Does Rick have a nickname for you?"

I lifted the hat and squinted at her. "What? No. Sometimes he calls me Gince. That's just when he's being lazy."

"No," she said, "I mean a pet name, something only he calls you."

I scowled and sat up on my towel. "I'm not big on pet names. I find the whole concept sickening. My own name is good enough."

Danielle grinned. "You mean you don't call him Rickie-wickie or Loverboy?"

I reached for Clare's sunblock and squirted some on my pasty legs.

"He'd spit in my eye if I did," I assured Danielle. "And I'd deserve it. Well, he wouldn't actually spit. I'm the hot-tempered idiot in the relationship. Rick is annoyingly mature."

"Back when we were first together," Clare said then, "Win used to call me Clare-bear. His little Clare-bear."

"Ugh."

"Oh, I think it's kind of cute," Danielle said. "So what does he call you now?"

Clare made a face. "It's kind of embarrassing."

"Why?" I asked, returning her sunblock. "Too icky?"

"No," she said with a sigh. "Actually, it's embarrassing because all his friends at the office and from law school call their wives the same thing."

"Which is? Don't keep us hanging here!"

"Sweetie."

"Okay," Danielle said with a roll of her eyes, "that's pretty condescending."

"Sweetie?" I repeated. "As in, 'Sweetie, will you get me another beer?' and 'Sweetie, call my mother for me, would you? You really should call her more often, you know. Good little wives call their mothers-in-law at least once a week.' "

"And, 'Sweetie, have you done my laundry yet?' " Danielle added.

"Something like that," Clare admitted. "But I don't think Win means it to be condescending. I think he just calls me sweetie because all the other guys use the term."

"Ah, that's what bothers you, isn't it?" I said, putting my hat on my head where it belonged. The sun was super-strong. "The fact that you're no longer a special individual to him. You're just one of the gals. One of the stable of fiancées and wives."

"Yes," she said fiercely. "That's it exactly."

I guess I'd hit a sore truth. Danielle shot me a warning glance and I just shrugged.

"And it also bothers me that Win is so one of the guys."

Clare sat up now, too, and wrapped her arms around her knees.

"He's so one of the crowd. Everything he does seems so, I don't know, by the book, exactly what a successful corporate lawyer is supposed to do. Buy a 7-Series BMW. Upgrade his cell phone every three months. Play golf on Saturday mornings. Buy his shirts at Brooks Brothers. Marry the college girlfriend. Move to the suburbs."

"He wants to move to the suburbs?" Danielle asked. "Where, Lincoln?"

"Or Lexington. Maybe Concord. As soon as I get pregnant with our first child."

"So don't get pregnant," I muttered.

"Oh, I wouldn't mind living in a nice suburb," Clare said, neatly ignoring the pregnancy issue. "I miss living in a real house. I just—It would be nice if I had a say in our life decisions, that's all."

"Tweetie," I said. "He might as well call you his wittle yewoh Tweetie Bird. And keep you in a cage."

"Was Win always this way?" Danielle asked. "Was he always part of the pack? Was he ever really an individual? Or was that just your perception of him?"

Clare didn't answer right away.

"Or maybe you once liked that he was solid and ordinary," I said, remembering my first impression of Win at his firm's cocktail party.

Before he'd opened his big mouth.

"Maybe Win hasn't changed so much. Maybe it's you who's changed."

Clare still had no answer.

"Put your foot down now, Clare," Danielle urged, twisting open a bottle of diet iced tea, "before it's too late."

"I hate to bring everyone down even lower than we already are," I said, "but it's already way too late. Win's not going to change. Why should he? The system works fine for him."

Danielle frowned at me. "So, what are you suggesting Clare do?"

"I'm not necessarily suggesting anything," I said carefully, speaking only to Danielle. "I'm just offering my opinion. I think the only way Clare's going to have her own life—or, at least, a say in a shared life—is by dumping Win and finding another guy. A very different sort of guy."

I turned back to Clare then. "Start all over with a new guy, Clare," I said, "fresh and clean. Set new precedents. Make new rules."

Clare frowned down at the massive diamond ring that tightly encircled the fourth finger of her left hand.

Oh, crap, I thought. *I've done it again.*

Channeled Ralph Kramden. Gone one step too far.

Me and my big mouth.

Finally, Clare looked up, first at me, than Danielle. "I appreciate your thoughts," she said, voice tight. "I do. But it's my life. And I'm the one who's going to have to live it. That way I won't have anyone to blame but myself if I screw it all up."

Well, what could we say to that?

I laid back down on my towel and took a vow of temporary silence.

Danielle

What You Asked For

I made the reservation at Grille 23.

Not that Chris couldn't have handled such a simple task. Of course he could have. It's just that I was so used to dealing with personnel at high-end restaurants it seemed silly not to make the call. And to choose the place and time.

Frankly, I would have chosen Locke-Ober for dinner but I thought the prices might be too unfairly high for Chris.

I was thinking of him all along. Even though it was my birthday celebration and, technically speaking, the birthday girl should be the center of attention and shouldn't have to do any of the work.

Chris came to my door at five that afternoon. He looked very presentable. The double-breasted suit was a few years out of style, but for Boston it was just fine.

Au courant, most Boston men were not.

His hair was a bit plastered down at first but during the course of the evening it fluffed up nicely.

And, of course, he carried a small overnight bag.

One issue was left outstanding and that was the issue of where Chris was going to spend the night. In my apartment, of course, but on the couch or in my bed? With me. Having sex.

I can't really say why we hadn't slept together before then except that I had never let it happen. I'd never set up a situation in which Chris felt comfortable suggesting we spend the night together.

I wasn't entirely sure why. I wasn't entirely sure of anything where Chris was concerned.

We took a cab to the restaurant. Chris had wanted to walk but I didn't want to arrive all sweaty, even though taking a cab meant another expense for my date.

The woman never pays for transportation.

We were seated at a corner table, per my request. I didn't want Chris to be stuck right in the middle of the hustle and bustle. I wanted him to be comfortable.

I ordered the prime rib. Chris had the filet mignon.

We hardly spoke during the meal but when we did the conversation was fine. Light and fine.

Everything was going swimmingly.

Until the waiter had cleared the meal and brought dessert menus.

"Danielle," Chris said, the moment the waiter had moved off, "there's something I have to say."

I can dash off to the ladies' room, I thought wildly. I could delay whatever was coming.

But could I stop it all together?

"Yes?" I said innocently.

Chris's bright blue eyes held mine. I couldn't look away. "Danielle, I want us to be together. I want you not to see anyone else. I want us to be exclusive."

Where, where, where to begin?

How, how, how to extricate myself from this . . . trap.

I smiled feebly. Social training only goes so far.

"But Chris," I began. I prayed for inspiration. And then . . . "We haven't even, you know."

Chris gave me nothing. He continued to gaze at me with those brilliant eyes. I was a butterfly under his pin.

I swallowed hard, leaned forward, and dropped my voice to a whisper. "We haven't even been intimate yet. How can we, you know . . ."

"Commit to each other?"

I nodded.

Chris's voice was tight. "Do you need to know how I am in bed before you'll agree not to see other guys?"

"No, no, it's not that!" I assured him.

It wasn't that, entirely.

Where to go from there!

"Of course," I went on, hoping desperately that the waiter would reappear that second, "sexual compatibility is important in a relationship. But I'm not worried about that with us, really. It's just . . ."

"Just what, Danielle?"

I felt panic rise in me.

How, how, how could I tell him that I didn't want a commitment in the first place?

Well, I did want a commitment, just not with Chris.

But you do want a commitment with him!

That bothersome little voice in my head again.

You're in love with him. How can you turn your back on love! Love doesn't come around all that often, you know.

When was the last time you were in love, Danielle?

A better question: *Have you ever been in love?*

Chris spoke again before I could answer his last question. "I'm going to be away for a while, maybe as long as a week," he said. "I don't know for sure. I hate to leave right now with one of the guys sick, but I have no choice. Johnny will cover for me as much as he can."

"Where are you going?" I asked, surprised by the sudden change in topic.

"Portland, Maine. A guy named Tristan Connor contacted us, Childs' Seafoods. He's some big restaurant guy, an entrepreneur. He was on the Vineyard recently and was impressed by our reputation. I never really thought too much about it but everybody on the island knows Childs' Seafoods. Anyway, he thinks there's money to be made by opening a Childs' Seafoods restaurant."

Chris shrugged. He seemed almost embarrassed by the prospect.

"I don't know. If things work out it could mean big business for Childs' Seafoods. That's what Connor thinks, anyway. I've hired a lawyer in Portland to help me figure it all out."

"Chris, that's wonderful!" I said, raising my wineglass as if to toast him. "You'll finally be a success!"

The second the words left my mouth it hit me how insensitive and insulting I'd sounded.

The evening was so not going according to plan.

"Oh, Chris," I cried, setting the glass down heavily and spilling red wine on the snowy table linen, "not that you aren't already a success. I didn't mean . . . I just meant that . . ."

Chris's face was inscrutable. "I know what you meant," he said evenly.

I wondered if he really did.

"Anyway," he went on, "it's a big 'if' but it's a chance I think is worth taking. And when I come back, I'm going to ask you the same question I asked tonight. I'm going to ask you to make a commitment to me."

I sat straight in my chair and tried to remain composed.

I thought back to the night Chris had given me the shell bracelet. He'd asked me then to promise to date only him.

I'd sidestepped the question, not very neatly. Chris hadn't been satisfied, but he'd let the matter go.

For the moment.

Now he was asking again, and again I was avoiding.

This time, Chris wasn't about to let the matter go.

There was something fierce about Chris Childs. Suddenly, I found his persistence attractive; he was the wild hero of old, pursuing his feisty heroine with a vengeance.

Suddenly, I found his persistence repellant.

We hardly knew each other, though maybe that was largely my fault. Still, in terms of time, in terms of days and weeks and months, we were so new.

Why was he pushing, why was he trying to lock me up as his?

I looked across the table at Chris Childs and I saw a stranger. A dangerous stranger.

"Are you giving me an ultimatum?" I said, my voice quivering with a sudden fury.

And then, in an instant, the dark pursuer was gone, replaced by a sweet man in love.

"God, no, Danielle," he said, all earnest. "I don't mean it that way. I just want us to be together. I don't want to lose you."

I took his hand across the snowy white tablecloth. "You're not going to lose me," I promised.

Liar. It's over as soon as you hand the keys to the house back to the rental agency.

Chris squeezed my hand in return. "Will you think about it while I'm away? Please?"

"Of course I will. Of course. Now, how about dessert?"

Chris stayed in my bed that night. We made love. It was our first time and it was intense and erotic and desperate.

The next morning, as I watched Chris from the living room window, on his way back home to the Vineyard, suit stuffed in his overnight bag, I wondered if it had also been our last.

Gincy

Duty

They say it's bound to happen at least once in the life of every American citizen. For almost thirty years I'd dodged the bullet. But finally I got my day in court.

I was called for jury duty.

I showed the no-nonsense notice to Danielle and Clare over drinks on the terrace of Keith's, by now our favorite bar overlooking the water.

"Jury duty?" Danielle wrinkled her nose. "Ugh. You have to get out of it."

"I don't think I can," I said, worriedly. "My boss has no problem with my doing it. Kell knows I'll still get my work done."

"Fine. Then show up and if you get called to a courtroom and asked questions by the judge or lawyers, lie. Make them believe you're unfit to be on a jury."

"I can't lie," I whispered, hoping no law-enforcement types were in earshot. "It's the government, Danielle. You can't lie to the government. Especially not in court. I think it's called perjury. Or something."

"You wouldn't exactly be in court at that point, would you?" Clare asked, also in a whisper.

I shrugged. "Court is court. The way I see it, if I'm in the build-ing, I'm in court."

Danielle gestured for our waitress and we ordered drinks and a plate of fried calamari. When the waitress had gone to place our order, Danielle sat back and sighed.

"Well, I'd lie," she proclaimed. "There's no way I'm serving on a jury. No. Way. I'd say anything to get myself sent home."

"Oh, please. You'd claim to be a racist or certifiably insane?" I asked.

"Exactly. I don't care what a bunch of strangers think of me. Look, those—people—are not my peers. I don't want any of them judging me. I don't even want to be in the same room as them."

"Those people?" Clare asked. "Who, exactly, do you mean?"

"You know, the average person. The man and woman in the street."

"On the street."

Danielle rolled her eyes. "Whatever. I mean, have you seen how the average person dresses to go to work? Sweatpants. Polyester suits. Reeboks with pantyhose. I wouldn't wear that garbage to—to take out my garbage."

"You don't take out your garbage," Clare pointed out. "You pay someone else to do it."

"Well, see?"

"Look," I said, "I'm not saying I don't agree with Danielle, sort of. I mean, most people are morons. I know that. I am fully aware of that. But . . ."

Danielle put her red-nailed hand on my arm. "But what? Go ahead, say it. You know I'm right. You don't want to spend an en-tire day in an airless room with a random bunch of morons any more than I do. The average person is not like you and me, Gincy. It's okay to admit that."

"But it's wrong," I argued, "to act on it. If I lie to avoid being on a jury panel, aren't I, I don't know, rejecting the social struc-ture of democracy or something? Like, all men are created equal. All women, too. At least, we're supposed to be."

"So, you're saying it's okay to be prejudiced against morons, and it's okay to call people morons in the first place—"

"Behind their backs," I amended.

Danielle shrugged. "Whatever. But it's not okay to say, 'Hey, I'm not going into that room because it's full of morons and I don't want to spend time with them'?"

"Yeah. I guess. It sounds stupid, I know . . ."

"You can't judge a book by its cover," Clare said suddenly. "No, I mean it. You can't. Just because someone looks, I don't know—"

"Stupid?" Danielle snapped. "Uneducated? Cheesy?"

"Any of those. Just because someone looks odd doesn't mean he is odd. Or stupid or whatever. Every person has value. Every person deserves respect."

"Not necessarily from me," Danielle retorted, looking around for our slow-moving waitress. "That's all I'm saying. Where is that girl?"

"I'm with Danielle on this one," I admitted. "I'll respect anyone who respects me back. But if someone treats me with disrespect, well, I can choose to ignore her. There's no law that says I have to like everybody."

"But," Clare argued, "there are laws that say you have to respect everybody's property and privacy and lives."

"Okay," I conceded. "If I come face-to-face with a person. But I can choose to stay far, far out of the way of morons and their property whenever possible."

"Gincy's right," Danielle said. "And there are morons being called to serve jury duty every day. I simply choose not to spend my time with them."

The waitress finally appeared and apologized for the delay. I wondered how much of our conversation she had overheard and hoped she'd heard none of it. I gave her a big smile, as if to prove that I was a nice person and not an elitist snob. She didn't seem to notice.

When the waitress had gone, Clare, who looked on the edge of having a stroke, picked up the subject.

"You would refuse to serve even if your being on a jury might save an innocent person's life? Even if you might be the only really smart person on the jury, the only chance an innocent person has to get a fair trial?"

Danielle took a sip of her fruity martini before answering. "Oh, please. The court system doesn't need little ole me."

"You're horribly elitist, Danielle," Clare said angrily. "And Gincy, you're not much better."

"Have you ever done jury duty?" I asked her, faking bravado but suddenly very self-conscious. Jeez, I'd just called myself an elitist.

"No," she admitted. "I've never been called. But you can be sure that if I am called, I'll show up and I'll tell the truth and I'll perform my civic duty."

"Well, bully for you."

Danielle swatted away an invisible bug. "That's the beauty of democracy, you know. To each her own."

I spent the rest of the evening drinking in silence.

Gincy
The Dirty Truth

Idon't know why I'd bothered to wear a suit. Most of the people gathered in the main jury-pool room were dressed for street cleaning.

Men sat slumped, legs spread, arms folded across their chests. Women clacked gum and filed their nails. Some people settled in for a nap; others sat staring into space, no book or newspaper in sight. Ten people in direct sight slurped cold coffee drinks and chomped donuts.

Was I the only one who was taking this seriously? I wondered. Suddenly, I wanted to yell out, "Hey! Wake up! Sit up straight! Spit out the gum!"

Danielle was right. The average person was a slob. The average person didn't care.

God, I prayed, *I know it's been a really long time since I talked to you. Sorry about that, really. But this is important. Please, please, please don't ever let me be arrested. Because I know I'll be innocent and I just can't face a jury of so-called peers who look like these people do! Because you just know they're not big into critical thinking. And you can just bet they have a tenuous relationship with the English language, regardless of where they were born.*

After almost two hours of being lectured by a judge on the importance of jury duty, and watching a film outlining the basics of the judicial system for those who hadn't made it past fifth grade, my number was called and, along with a small mob, I was sent to a courtroom in which were gathered a judge, a defendant, various armed guards, a court recorder, and two teams of lawyers, defense and prosecution.

My stomach knotted and I began to sweat. *Crap,* I thought, *I'm going to faint! Some trigger-happy guard will think it's a trick and he'll shoot me before I hit the floor.*

I didn't faint. And after an hour of "selection process" I was thanked and sent back to the main jury-pool room. Thanked and rejected. Maybe it was how I'd answered a particular question that eliminated me from consideration.

"Juror Number Fifty-Seven. Would you have any difficulty remaining fair and impartial toward this defendant who is being charged with molesting a three-year-old girl?"

Or something to that effect.

"Yes," I replied. "Yes, I would have difficulty. I would have difficulty not spitting in his general direction whenever he walked into the courtroom."

Yeah, in retrospect it was probably my answer that got me thrown out.

Anyway, the only good thing about jury duty in Boston was the "one day or one trial" policy. I'd done my duty to the city, even though I'd been rejected for a jury, and now I was free to go.

I left the Post Office Square courthouse in a big hurry.

The city felt ugly, dirty, hot, and sticky.

I was deeply glad I hadn't been chosen for the jury. I don't know how I would have survived such an emotional ordeal without breaking down or killing the defendant, a large, sweaty fellow with heavy black plastic glasses, whom I'd convicted at first glance.

No one who looked like that slack-jawed slob in the defendant's chair was ever innocent.

Right?

Hence my answer to the attorney.

I wondered: Why were some people so perverted? How did it

happen? Where they just born defective or did life twist them into an ugly shape? Was it a combination of both predisposition and circumstance?

And how did psychologists not go crazy dealing with the morally decrepit and criminally insane?

There was a reason I hadn't gone into the mental sciences. The presence of lunatics could not be conducive to one's own peace of mind.

All I knew was that if anybody ever touched my kid in an inappropriate manner I'd—

I came to a dead halt on the corner of Franklin Street.

My kid? As in, a kid who was mine?

My son. My daughter.

Holy crap. What was I thinking?

Was this Justin's fault?

Because I'd never said I wanted kids. Ever.

I'd never fantasized about names and tricycles and trips to Disneyworld. I'd never dreamed of how my son would grow up to be the first truly honest president and how my daughter would be the head of a global corporation devoted to preserving the environment by developing Earth-friendly products.

And now I was ready to beat the shit out of some hypothetical pervert who was eyeing my hypothetical kid in a hypothetically inappropriate manner?

Coffee. I decided to get a cup of coffee, something to calm a sudden onset of nerves. Maybe something to eat, too. I spotted a bagel store up the block and headed for it.

As I walked, I tried to rationalize. Maybe I was just reacting in a normally protective manner. Didn't everyone automatically try to protect her property, even if something wasn't technically property, like a human being or a pet?

My boyfriend. My apartment. My car. My cat. My dog.

Even if you didn't actually have something in your possession, wasn't it normal to assume that if you did have that something in your possession you'd do anything you could to protect it—and to punish anyone who tried to hurt it?

Sure. The protective instinct was perfectly normal.

But wasn't it also part of the maternal instinct?

Whoa.

For the first time in my life I'd actually imagined myself as a mother. Even if it was in a roundabout sort of way.

I flung open the door to the bagel shop.

The situation called for extra cream cheese.

Danielle
Off Its Axis

Sometimes, one phone call can change your life.

One phone call from someone you love whose personal decision has ramifications he never even dreamed of.

David called one evening as I was reading the latest issue of *InStyle*.

"Hey," I said. "It's almost ten. I thought you doctors went to bed early. You know, early to bed, early to rise . . ."

"I've got some news, Danielle," he said. His voice sounded funny. Serious and more full of energy than it had sounded in a long time.

"You and Roberta decided to go to Hawaii on your honeymoon after all?" I guessed, somehow knowing that wasn't the news David had called to tell me.

"Uh, no," he said with a small laugh. "There's not going to be a honeymoon, Danielle. Roberta and I aren't getting married."

The news took a moment to sink in.

And then I shouted, "That bitch!"

I heard David take a deep breath. "Danielle," he said, "I broke the engagement. And no more yelling. I've already got one woman furious with me."

Suddenly, I felt sick to my stomach. Literally sick.

I stumbled to the kitchen and poured a glass of cold water.

"David, how could you?" I gasped, water dribbling down my chin unheeded. "Everything was all planned. The ring, the synagogue, the dress! My God, the reception! Bacon-wrapped shrimp and Beluga caviar! Why are you doing this?"

"I'm sorry you're so upset, Danielle. I mean, I thought you didn't even like Roberta."

"I never said I didn't like her!" I cried.

"You didn't have to say anything," he replied. "I know you were trying to be nice, but I could tell what you really felt that last morning on the Vineyard."

I didn't bother to deny it.

"Danielle," David went on, "I hope you can understand. I just can't marry her. I can't marry a woman I'm not in love with. I can't marry a woman I don't respect."

I loved my brother. Of course I wanted him to be happy.

Of course.

I held the cold glass of water against my flushed cheek.

But David was ruining the plan. He was bucking the system. He was destroying the family!

"David?" I croaked, remembering the anger and disappointment he'd revealed at my birthday party. "Why did you ask Roberta to marry you in the first place?"

"I don't know," he admitted. "Well, I sort of know. It just took me some time to figure out the whole thing was a big mistake. What can I say? Better now than two years into the marriage, right?"

Right.

But maybe if they'd just go ahead and get married things would change. David would fall in love with his new wife and she would grow an inner self and . . .

"Have you told Mom and Dad yet?" I said. "They must be so upset."

"They'll get over it. They want me to be happy, Danielle. What do you think, they'd force me into a situation that would make me miserable?"

Wouldn't they? I wondered.

"No," I said. "Of course not."

But maybe if they just encouraged David to give this marriage a try everything would be all right. It happened with arranged marriages, didn't it? Sometimes? If total strangers could make a marriage work . . .

"Let's change the subject," David said. "Let's talk about something positive. Hey, what about you and that guy Chris? The one I never got to meet because he was on vacation or something. The one who couldn't make it to your party. What's going on with him?"

Chris.

I rubbed my temple with my free hand and remembered our one night of extraordinary passion. I remembered also how the next morning I'd watched from my living room window as he'd loped down the block on his way home to the Vineyard, sleeves rolled to the elbow.

"Nothing's going on," I said dully. "Nothing at all."

Gincy
Unforeseen Contingency

Sally wanted to meet at Brasserie Jo on Huntington Avenue so she could watch a review of that day's stage of the Tour de France on the big flat-screen TV set up over the bar.

"I didn't know you were into cycling," I said when I'd hopped up onto a stool.

"I'm not, really. But Sido is. She's French."

"Hey," I said to the painfully skinny, sallow woman sitting to Sally's left. Sido gave a brisk nod of the head and took a long drag of her Gauloise.

I noticed that Sally's hair was streaked with acid green. So was Sido's.

"Did you guys meet at the beauty parlor?" I asked with a raised eyebrow.

Sido either ignored my question or simply was not interested in conversation.

"I don't go to a beauty parlor," Sally said with a frown. "I do my own hair. So does Sido. We met at a club."

"You have no sense of humor, you know that?"

Sally shrugged.

I leaned in and lowered my voice. "So, are you two, you know, involved?"

Sally shot a glance at Sido's sharp profile and then turned back to me. "No! We're just friends." Now it was Sally's turn to whisper. "Sido's got a girlfriend named Barbara. She's much older and has lots of money. She keeps Sido on a very tight leash. Sido's only out alone tonight because Barbara had to go out of town unexpectedly. Some business thing. I'm paying for her drinks so Barbara doesn't notice any charges on Sido's credit card."

"That sounds like an abusive relationship to me," I said, feeling my blood rise. Sido looked tough as nails, but looks, as we all knew, were massively deceiving.

Sally shook her head and I dropped the subject. She ordered a pastis, I ordered a gin and tonic, and Sido ordered a Belgian beer. Actually, she gestured for the beer. Sido, it seemed, wasn't a woman of many words.

Had she been bullied into silence?

"How can you drink that crap?" I asked when Sally's drink arrived. "It looks like phlegm."

But drink it she did. By the third disgusting glass, Sally was becoming feisty.

"Why the hell can't women be in the Tour anyway, is what I want to knew. Know."

"You got me, kiddo," I said. "I know nothing about pro sports. I'm sure there are all sorts of rules and boards and panels and traditions—"

"It stinks is what I say!"

I looked at my friend carefully. Her eyes were droopy and bloodshot. Her mouth looked strained. "And what I say is that maybe you should lay off those nauseating drinks."

"I know when I've had enough," she snapped.

I shrugged. I'd done my job. Now she was the bartender's problem. Or Sido's.

She certainly hadn't come with me.

"I gotta go pee," Sally mumbled. She slid off her barstool and stumbled off to the ladies' room. *Great,* I thought, stuffing a few French fries in my mouth. *I'm alone with Sido the Silent.*

"She like you."

I jumped. She speaks!

"What?" I asked, turning to face Sido, who, by the way, hadn't eaten a thing all night.

"She want to be your girlfriend," she said throatily, taking another puff of her Gauloise. "Sally."

Probably for the first time in my life, I was speechless. For a moment. "What! No way."

"You see how she look at you. You cannot lie."

Well, I could lie, but maybe I wouldn't. If I were perfectly honest with myself, I had to acknowledge that maybe, just maybe I'd had some inkling of Sally's feelings.

I mean, why else would a single gay woman spend so much time with a heterosexual woman, forgoing nights out in bars where she could maybe meet the love of her life, unless maybe the love of her life was right there under her nose?

The heterosexual woman. Her best bud from work.

A little full of yourself, aren't you, I chided. *Who said Sally thinks I'm the love of her life? Maybe she just wants a little below-the-belt action.*

The idea freaked me out.

"I have to run," I said to Sido. I tossed a crumpled twenty-dollar bill on the bar and grabbed my bag, hoping to get out of there before Sally returned from the ladies' room.

Sido shrugged and lit another cigarette. I ducked out of the bar through the revolving door.

Clare
Help from Above

"**M**arriage is about compromise."
I'd heard that all my adult life.

What I hadn't fully understood was that the compromise starts far before the nuptials. And that it also involves parents and in-laws.

For Mrs. Carrington's sake I would take Win's name.

For my mother's sake, I agreed to have the bridal shower back home in Michigan so that aunts and cousins and neighbors could attend. People I hadn't seen in years. People I didn't really want to see then.

But a bridal shower is as much for the mother as it is for the bride.

Which is maybe why the closer the date came, the more panicked I began to feel about the command performance.

Briefly, I considered claiming illness as an excuse not to make the trip to Michigan. Not to appear at my own bridal shower. But I rejected the idea as far too hard to pull off.

In Boston, I'd have to fake it with Win. And if I decided to get to Ann Arbor before falling ill, I'd have to fake it with Mother.

I was already horribly mired in deception. I doubted I had the dubious skill to fool anyone with a mysterious stomachache. And lying took such enormous energy.

Lying alone probably accounted for my post-engagement weight loss.

Grimly, with the unsuspecting help of my friends, I soldiered on.

I met Gincy and Danielle one evening in Boston for drinks at a place called Out of the Blue. Somehow Gincy had gotten her hands on a discount drinks ticket, good between five and seven o'clock.

Truly, she had a knack for finding bargains. I suppose growing up in near-poverty had its advantages later in life.

When we were seated at the bar—Gincy's choice; she often preferred the bar to a table—and had ordered, Danielle pulled a newspaper from her bag and asked us to bear with her while she finished reading an article.

Danielle claimed not to read, but she almost always had a magazine or newspaper in hand. Her sometimes ditzy personality belied a curious and informed mind.

Well, informed on certain topics.

"What's up with this contemplative lifestyle?" Danielle said with a frown, finally tossing the paper on the bar. "Have you read the review of that tiny French movie about some old monastery? I don't understand the whole nun and monk thing. They just sit around all day praying? Like that will make an exciting movie! Why don't they do something useful for society?"

"They do," Gincy replied calmly. "Praying is useful. They pray for your soul because you don't have the time to. You're too busy going to the mall."

"What if I don't want them praying for my soul?"

"Too bad. They're praying. That's what they do."

"A little prayer never hurt anyone," I said, then felt like an idiot for using a cliché.

I'd noticed that in the past year my diction had gotten lazy. I'd gotten lazy.

And laziness was about not caring.

"Anyway, what do you care?" Gincy was saying. "It's a free

country. You have to let them do their thing. You don't see any nuns trying to stop you from going to the nail salon, do you?"

"Of course I have to let them do their thing." Danielle rolled her eyes. I noticed there was a line of pink shimmer just under her brow. "But I don't have to like it."

"You mean," I said suddenly, pretending nonchalance, "contemplative people pray for the souls of people who aren't even Catholic?"

"Well, yeah, I guess," Gincy said. "Sure. They're holy. They pray for everybody. They're equal-opportunity pray-ers."

I guess that's what makes them holy, I thought.

"So, say I wanted them to pray for something, for example, a cause, something special, you know . . ."

"No, I don't," Gincy said. "But go on."

"How would I go about asking a contemplative to pray for me? It. The cause."

"Yeah," Danielle said. "How would you even go about finding a contemplative nun in the first place? Aren't they secluded?"

"Sequestered. Or maybe the word is cloistered." Gincy frowned. "I don't know, exactly. I suppose you could go online . . ."

"Contemplatives have Web sites?" Danielle shrieked.

"Oh," Gincy said, as if really struck by the oddness of the idea. "Maybe not. But hey, these days? Marketing is everything. The nuns have to live, too, you know. Like, say an order feeds itself on donations from people they pray for especially well. Okay, but first they've got to advertise so people know they even exist. Right? Then they have to remind people they're still there. That's marketing."

"May I see the paper?" I asked, trying again for nonchalance.

Danielle handed it to me and while she and Gincy talked, I sought the review of that tiny French movie.

Clare
Sisterhood

Later that night, after Win was asleep and snoring fitfully, I sat down in the kitchen with my laptop and went online.

I didn't turn on any lights; the glow from the screen was enough for me to see by and I didn't want to wake Win only to have him find me typing keywords such as "prayer" and "monastery."

Unbidden, I heard his fond yet derisive laugh in my head.

Win indulges your little whims, a voice inside me whispered. *How sweet of him.*

It didn't take long before I found a rather simple Web site operated by a group of nuns called the Sisters of the White Rose of Mary. Their cloistered convent was located in a neighborhood of Chicago I knew as quite gritty; the home page indicated that the convent had been there since the early twentieth century.

Nervously, I typed my petition.

That's what they called it. A petition for prayer.

"Hello," I typed, then deleted the word. Too casual.

Maybe this is a stupid idea, I thought. But just then, I didn't have any others.

I took a deep breath, thought quietly for a moment, and then the words came.

"Dear Sisters: Thank you for considering my petition. You should know that I am not a Catholic. However, my friend Virginia, who was raised in your church, assures me that you do not turn away anyone in need of your help."

And then I explained my situation. Truthfully. Almost. Instead of admitting to having cheated on Win, I spoke of having thoughts about other men.

These women might be more worldly than nuns of the previous century, but I didn't want to shock them unnecessarily. Also, I didn't want them to consider me a lost cause.

"Please," I typed, "pray for me. I want to make the right decision. Thank you. Very sincerely yours, Clare J. Wellman."

Gincy
Mommyzilla

Three times she'd come to the office. Three times in one week!

At least to me, her reasons were patently bogus.

Mommyzilla.

The monster after my boyfriend.

Rick told me the monster—Laura DeCosta—had a daughter who went to Justin's summer day-care program. Rick had met her a week or two earlier at a parents' meeting.

Mommyzilla was a single parent. Divorced.

How convenient.

And I just knew that she knew Rick and I were involved.

Maybe Rick had told her. Maybe she'd just sensed our bond on that first visit to the office. Either way, she was out to eliminate me.

I just knew it.

Let me tell you about the first attack.

Mommyzilla invaded on a Monday morning about ten o'clock.

It seems she'd promised to give Rick a recipe for the oatmeal raisin cookies Justin had liked so much, and instead of e-mailing it or jotting it on a card and sending it the old-fashioned way, she'd chosen to make a surprise appearance at his office.

At my office.

A special visit in from Charlestown just to hand-deliver a freakin' cookie recipe?

My ass.

Rick introduced us. Laura DeCosta barely acknowledged my greeting, and turned back to Rick. They headed for his office— why?—and until I saw her pass back through the hall on her way to the elevators, I couldn't concentrate.

Mommyzilla was up to something. My father didn't raise a stupid daughter. I knew trouble when I saw it pad down the hall in flip-flops and a ponytail.

The second attack came on Wednesday at about three.

I sensed someone watching me, looked up from my computer screen, and there she was. A foot or two into my office. Just standing there in her bright yellow T-shirt and flip-flops.

Again with the flip-flops. Today they were bright yellow to match her T-shirt.

Too freakin' cute.

"So, do you have children?" she asked, without preliminary niceties.

No, I thought. *But I do have manners. If I didn't, I'd kick your sorry ass out of my office right now.*

"No," I said, as evenly as possible.

I wanted to convey absolutely nothing. No feelings.

No regret, no desire, nothing.

"Oh," she said, with an odd little smirk. "Well."

And then the bitch just walked out of my office.

I'd been totally dismissed. No one had ever done that to me before.

Well, I could have kids, given the chance! I wanted to scream after her. *I have the same equipment as you! And mine's younger!*

But I sat there at my desk, paralyzed by disbelief.

According to Rick, Mommyzilla had popped in just to say hi. And to deliver a book she'd come across while browsing in Barnes & Noble. A book she just knew Justin would loooove. And it had been a bargain, too, only $4.99.

Rick didn't seem impressed with the gift.

He didn't seem nervous and secretive, either, as if he were hiding a sordid truth from me. His girlfriend.

He seemed perfectly normal, if a bit annoyed at having been interrupted, first by Mommyzilla and then by me, who'd charged into his office immediately after the monster had gotten back on the elevator.

"You want the book?" he said, tossing it aside and beginning to type. "Justin already has it."

The title was *One Hundred Best-Loved Fairy Tales*.

"Okay," I said, though I was loathe to touch it after Mommyzilla had sweated all over it.

But beggars can't be choosers. The book was a freebie. I'd send it to my pregnant teenage cousin as a wedding/baby gift, though I wasn't quite sure she could read.

I went back to my own office and kept the earlier encounter with the monster to myself.

Thursday was blissfully monster-free. And then Friday morning, another invasion.

That time, I had some advance warning. I'd stopped at the receptionist's desk for messages on my way back from the ladies' room. Ken, phone at his ear, shook his head as I approached.

"Rick," he said as I passed. "While you were on the phone you got a call from a Laura. She didn't want your voice mail. She said she'd be here sometime before noon. What? I don't know, she didn't say."

Desperate times called for desperate measures.

Once safely back in my office, I summoned my friends.

Okay. That's what Danielle and Clare had become.

My friends. Through no fault of mine.

They stepped off the elevator within a half an hour. On our way back to my office, I introduced Danielle and Clare to Sally.

Sally greeted them with her usual gruff indifference and then claimed an urgent need to use the copy machine.

"She's interesting," Danielle commented with a raised eyebrow.

"She's all right," I defended. "She is what she is. Anyway, she's not the problem." Okay, a tiny lie. "Mommyzilla is the problem.

And here she comes!" I hissed. "Right on schedule. Now, just watch and tell me what you think."

I shoved my friends into my office where they would pretend not to be spying on me.

I hovered in the doorway. Mommyzilla approached.

"Hello!" I said brightly, noting yet another pair of flip-flops. These were decorated with ladybugs.

Mommyzilla slowed. She tilted her head and looked at me quizzically.

"Oh," she said, stopping momentarily. "I didn't recognize you."

I prayed for calm.

"Gincy," I said, ever more brightly. "We've met twice this week."

Mommyzilla smiled for about a tenth of a second. And then she walked on!

Shaking, I watched her go.

Then I dashed back into my office.

"She's stopped by the office three times this week," I hissed to my friends. "Doesn't she have anything better to do, like go grocery shopping or get her lip waxed? I'm telling you, she's after Rick."

"What's her name?" Clare asked matter-of-factly.

"Laura DeCosta. She's divorced. She's got a four-year-old kid. Kristen or Kirsten or Kris Kringle or something. I don't know."

Danielle folded her arms across her chest and frowned at me. "I cannot," she said, "believe you find that woman a threat."

"Well, I do find her a threat."

"But why?" Clare said. "She didn't seem at all special."

I balled my hands into fists. "I'll tell you why she's a threat," I said fiercely. "Because she's proven she can do it. Go the distance. You know, get married, have the kid. She's an adult."

"That's debatable," Danielle murmured. "Ladybugs?"

I raged on. "What have I done with my life so far? Nothing. Nada. Face it: It would be way less of an adjustment for Rick if he got together with her. Laura knows how to be married. She knows how to be a mother. I bet she can make a sandwich and clean a toilet at the same time. While doing the laundry. And cleaning up after the dog."

"Gincy." Danielle grabbed my arm, careful, I noticed, not to lacerate me. "Gincy, listen to me. Clare and I saw what just happened out there. The woman treated you with disdain. Rick can't possibly like that kind of person. Not the Rick you've described."

Yeah. But had I been describing the real Rick?

"I've never been treated with disdain before," I said, carefully removing Danielle's hand. "Was that disdain? I thought it was disrespect."

Clare shook her head. "No, it was disdain. Also known as contempt or scorn. Trust me. I know. And don't ask why. I just know."

Danielle glanced into the hallway to be sure we were still alone. "I still don't understand what, exactly, you find intimidating about this Laura person. I mean, she wasn't even wearing any makeup. No offense, honey. But, seriously, it can't be her looks."

"There's more to life than looks, you know," I shot back.

Like pregnancy and childbirth and motherhood.

And mortgages and hospital bills and divorce lawyers.

Danielle sighed. "Oh, you poor, innocent thing. Honey, it's always all about looks. At least at first. And trust me, this woman doesn't have them."

And I did? *There's a flaw in your argument, Danielle,* I thought.

"But she does have a kid," I countered. "And she's got Rick's attention."

Clare smiled kindly. "Gincy, I think you're in love."

I flopped into my desk chair and Clare closed the door to my office.

"God. I know. It sucks, doesn't it? Especially since I'm going to lose Rick to a woman with a good forty pounds on me."

"You're not going to lose him," Clare said firmly.

"At least not to that cow!" Danielle exclaimed. "No wonder her husband dumped her. You can be sure she didn't dump him, because when you look that bad you'd be crazy to dump your man unless he was a brutal wife-beater."

I had to laugh. "Thanks, Danielle. You're so reassuring. And so awfully kind. I like that about you."

"I'm just telling you the truth," she said, unperturbed. "You're cute and smart, and even though you're full of piss and vinegar, as my grandma used to say, you're a good person. Now, come on, we're taking you to lunch."

"I usually work through lunch hour," I protested.

"Skipping meals isn't healthy," Clare pointed out.

"And men don't like skinny women."

"Or cows?" I said, feeling the laughter rise again.

Gincy

The Bull by the Horns

That night, after Justin had gone to bed, exhausted after a day spent on a field trip to the Franklin Park Zoo, I confronted Rick.

"I need to know something," I said. God, I was nervous. "I need you to tell me the truth."

Rick sat on the couch, sorely in need of replacing, and motioned for me to join him. "Okay. Shoot."

I looked him straight in the eye.

His eyelashes were longer than mine.

"Are you interested in Laura DeCosta?" I asked. "Don't lie, Rick."

He actually flinched. "Kirsten's mother? Or is it Kristen? Whatever happened to names like Kathleen? Anyway, you mean interested as in, am I attracted to her?"

Don't laugh, Rick, I prayed. *Whatever your answer, don't laugh at me.*

He didn't laugh. In fact, he suddenly looked kind of grossed out. "Jesus, Gincy, no, I'm not attracted to her at all. Did I do something to make you think I was? I'm so sorry. Tell me what it was and I'll make sure I never do it again."

Whoa. Seriously right answer.

I felt relief flood every inch of me. It was very very sweet.

"No," I said, "you didn't do anything. I guess . . . It's all me. I just . . ."

"You never have to be jealous," Rick said, saving me having to speak the word. "It's you and me. Right?"

"Yeah. I guess."

Rick took my hands and said, "Don't guess. It's a fact."

"So, you're sure I'm your type and Laura's not?"

Rick grinned. "Well, don't think I'm a creep for saying this, but, aside from all the other reasons I'm not attracted to the DeCosta person, like the fact that she's the most boring person I've ever met, and why is she showing up in the office every other day on some bogus errand?, she's not exactly good-looking."

"Danielle called her a cow," I told him.

"Well, I wouldn't call her a cow, exactly. Maybe a heifer . . ."

I slapped Rick's arm playfully.

Rick grasped my hands in his. "Here's the deal, Gincy," he said. "I love you."

Oh, boy. There it was.

The moment I'd been dreading.

The moment I'd been craving.

Could I say it back?

Rick sat quietly, patiently, my hands resting in his.

"I love you, too," I said. My voice was a bit wiggly but God, I'd said it!

We hugged for a long time.

Take that, Mommyzilla.

Clare
Pleasantville

The wedding shower.

My wedding shower.

Though Danielle had hinted that she would be happy to come with me to Michigan in case I needed any assistance—whatever that meant; probably, I thought, something to do with crystal—I didn't ask either Danielle or Gincy to join me.

Honestly, I don't think Danielle was particularly offended. Gincy, I know for a fact, was downright relieved.

"That freakin' baby shower was enough lady-party for me for years," she told me. "But have a good time and all."

Win and I took a cab to Logan. We made our way through security with the usual minor annoyances. I was asked to remove my shoes. Win's laptop rasied suspicions.

Just before takeoff, Win took my hand in his. "I'm so happy, Clare," he said. "I really believe this is the best thing for the both of us. Don't you?"

His eyes were sincere behind his gold-rimmed round glasses. He always wore his glasses and not his contacts when flying. He suffered from dry eyes.

I didn't hate Win.

Sometimes I didn't much like him, either.

And as for love? I knew I was no longer in love with him. I hadn't been for years.

But I did love Win in the way you love someone you know so well it's almost like loving yourself.

Or, at least, being used to yourself. Win was just there like I was just there.

My love for Win was a habit.

Now the question was: A good habit or a bad one?

"Clare?" Win said, squeezing my hand. "I asked you a question."

I shook my head and smiled. "Sorry, Win. There's just so much on my mind . . . Of course I think it's the right thing. Of course."

Mother and Daddy were waiting for us when we emerged from the Detroit airport with our luggage.

"My girl," Daddy said, kissing my forehead. "I'm so proud of you."

"Why, Daddy?" I asked, feigning innocence.

I'd been at the same job for several years. Had I accomplished something extraordinary without being aware of my feat?

"You're finally getting married," he replied.

Ah. The apex of my career as a woman. Until I had children, of course.

"I was beginning to think I'd never be a grandfather."

And there it was.

"You have James, Junior," I pointed out.

Daddy shook his head. "It's not the same," he declared, and I declined to pursue the topic.

"Everyone is just so excited to see you," Mother gushed, linking her arm with mine as we walked toward the car.

Behind us I heard Win and Daddy chuckling, no doubt sharing golf stories and fishing tales, bonding as men like Winchester Carrington III, Esquire and Doctor Walter Wellman would.

"Aunt Isabelle's coming, and all your cousins," Mother was saying. "And guess who's also coming to the shower? Marianne Brightman, all the way from Chicago! I know you haven't seen her since high school so I thought it would be a nice surprise to invite her. Do you know she has four children!"

"Wow," I said. "Four. That's . . . that's a lot."

I thought about the bustling airport terminal behind us. I thought of all the families heading for and returning from vacations, of all the old and infirm in wheelchairs, of all the young and obese in motorized carts driven by bored airport personnel, of all the happiness and sorrow each person carried with him or her.

I thought: *I could tell Mother I need to use the ladies' room. And once inside, I could just slip away into the crowds.*

I thought: *I could just never come back.*

I kept on walking.

"And Clare, you really must decide on your maid of honor!" Mother was urging now. "People need to make travel plans and all. And you really must choose a dress and a color scheme right away or the maid of honor will be stuck with some dreadful gown off the rack. And the bridesmaids—"

"No bridesmaids," I said. "Just a maid of honor."

"Oh, but—"

"The wedding is going to be small."

Mother looked wounded.

"I mean intimate," I amended. "It's a trend. Intimate."

"Well, all right, I'm sure you know best . . ."

Like hell I do.

"I'll ask Jessica to be my maid of honor," I said, deciding on the spot.

What did it matter that I hadn't seen or talked to my cousin in years? We'd been close as children. And I had to pick someone.

Mother brightened immediately. "Oh, Jessica will be so pleased!" she cried.

I wasn't at all sure she would be, but I smiled and nodded.

"The people at the Gandy Dancer have been just marvelous about arrangements," Mother went on.

I thought about taking a nap in my old room. And then I remembered that Win would want to come with me.

Clare
The Show That Never Ends

My cousin Jessica was indeed thrilled to be chosen maid of honor. Even after the registry had been handled and the shower planned and much of the footwork already completed in Boston.

Maybe that was why she was thrilled. There wasn't much left for her to do but show up a few days before The Big Day with her dress. And I'd made that easy for her, too, by suggesting she choose something she really could wear again as long as it wasn't black.

"Ohhh, I'm so jealous!" she squeaked as we arrived at the Gandy Dancer, once a train station and still retaining much of that historical charm. "Marrying a handsome, successful guy like Win Carrington. I hope I'm lucky enough to find someone like Win before I turn thirty. Does he have a brother? Maybe you can introduce me to some of his friends when I get to Boston!"

Mrs. Carrington was there, of course.

"Well, dear," she said, pulling me aside just before I was to open the gifts. "Have you thought about my dress?"

Her pale blue eyes sparkled with hope.

Around me women laughed and chatted. Everyone was all dressed up. Everyone was so excited to be part of a wedding.

They were excited all because of me.

"Yes," I said to my future mother-in-law. "I would love to wear your dress."

Mother will understand, I thought as Mrs. Carrington wiped tears from her eyes. *I'll make sure I make her happy, too.*

I got lots of crystal, all from Tiffany. I forget the name of the style. Danielle had chosen it for me. She would be very happy, I thought. Maybe I'd give her one of the pieces.

Jessica urged me to make a toast. I did and I thanked everyone. Finally, I said, "This is for the most important person in my life. My mother. Without her I would be nothing."

Mother cried and hugged me. Mrs. Carrington bawled. Everyone clapped.

Then it was time for the cake to be served—a mini-wedding-style cake, complete with plastic bride and groom. I tried to refuse a slice, but a worried look from my mother made me accept the plate from Aunt Isabelle.

By that time the event had taken on the feel of a dream. Or of a circus. Noise. Color. Frenzy.

"Every woman's dream . . ."

"You just don't know true happiness until . . ."

"The day every woman's dreamed of since she was a little girl . . ."

"You're going to be one of us now!"

I smiled, as I was expected to do.

Clearly, marriage was only partly about your husband. It was mostly about other wives. It was about being one of the group, a member of an exclusive club, with spin-offs for those wives who were divorced and had been replaced by younger women, for those second wives with their stepchildren and new babies, and for those wives left widowed.

Marriage was about belonging.

Well, I thought, *it would be nice to belong.*

Wouldn't it?

I didn't have time to answer my own question because just then a high-pitched, multi-voiced shout of glee went up as Win and my father and Mr. Carrington and Win's cousin Alan, his best man, appeared in the doorway of our private party room.

It was as if a band of conquering heroes had returned from years at war. The women were suddenly ultra-animated and giggly. The children, many of them my cousins, shouted with joy and rushed to greet Win and his cohorts.

I sat still on my throne, the queen with the crown of ribbons and lace, and watched.

Win beamed with pride and pleasure and magnanimity, as if he alone had created the scene before him. The king.

In fact, all four men glowed with responsibility. Even Alan, who looked as if his glow was largely due to the many gin and tonics I guessed the men had been downing at Mr. Carrington's club.

Alan's gaze swept the room and alighted on Jessica. He favored her with a wink.

"Oh, he's cute," Jessica whispered, pulling on my arm. "Who is he? Is he single? He must be, he winked at me!"

The men made their way into the room. Win came straight to me and everybody applauded as he bent to kiss my cheek.

"You look like a queen," he said, and I saw tears in his eyes. "I'm so happy you're going to be my wife."

And then he knelt at my feet, my vassal, my knight.

I leaned forward and we clasped hands. "I'm happy, too," I said. "Really."

And at that moment, I thought that maybe I was.

Gincy

In Vino Veritas

"Gincy! It's me, Sally. Let me in!"

Freakin' midnight. And I'd been in such a sound sleep.

Bang, bang, bang!

What, was she using her fists or a battering ram?

"I'm coming!" I grabbed a robe and shoved my way into it.

Bang, bang, bang!

"Jesus Christ," I muttered, making my way to the door, "hold on already."

No one had to go to the bathroom that bad . . .

I unlocked and opened the door. Sally practically fell into the room. She looked a mess, all bleary-eyed and rumpled.

And she stank of booze.

"You're drunk," I said unnecessarily.

"I know."

"You should go home."

Man, I so didn't want her to stay in my apartment.

"I don't think I can."

I sighed. "Look, if you're too loaded you can sleep—" Where? I didn't have a couch, per se. Just an old beanbag thing. "On the floor. I've got an extra blanket."

"Why not in the bed, with you?"

"Because you're drunk, that's why. I don't want you snoring in my ear and puking on my sheets. Correction: On my one and only sheet."

"Is that the only reason? Maybe you don't want me in your bed 'cause you're afraid of what might happen, huh?"

Weren't snoring and puking enough to be scared of?

"What are you talking about?" I asked, though I had a sneaking suspicion I knew exactly what she was talking about.

Sally stumbled forward. I noted her mascara had started to slide down her cheeks. "I love you, Gincy. I'm in love with you. You have to know that, right? I mean, God!" Here Sally broke into wild laugher. "I've been so obvious!"

And I'd been so stupid.

Sido, Sally's skinny French friend, was right. How could I not have seen this episode coming?

I took a step back to avoid her drunken embrace. "Sally, come on, you know I'm seeing Rick."

"What can he give you that I can't?" she demanded.

If you weren't shit-faced, I thought, *you would never have asked such a moronic question.*

Be kind, Gincy. Firm but kind.

I took a deep breath and looked her right in the eye. "I'm in love with Rick, Sally. It's not about you. Look, I'm not gay. I don't know what else I can tell you. I'm sorry."

She stood there, eyes averted, mouth opening then closing as if she were trying to say something.

"Sally?" I said. "Do you understand?"

Still, Sally had no words.

She tried to leave, but friends don't let friends stumble through the streets drunk. Finally, she gave up trying to grab the doorknob and collapsed on the floor. I covered her with my spare blanket and unfolded a plastic garbage bag in case she got sick in the night.

Or decided to suffocate herself.

Sally was snoring within seconds. No such luck for me. I lay awake most of the night feeling like a fool.

Around six o'clock I finally fell asleep.

When the alarm clock woke me, swollen-eyed, at seven-thirty, Sally was gone.

September

Danielle
Act of God

I enjoyed the ritual of preparing for bed.

Lotions and potions, creams and emollients. The simple, soothing rituals demanded almost no concentration and allowed my mind to wander.

That evening in early September as I prepared for bed, my mind wandered to Clare.

Since the wedding shower, Clare seemed rededicated to Win.

Or dedicated for the first time, at least for the first time since I'd known her.

I wondered what had happened out there in the wilds of Michigan.

Maybe, I thought, *she'd just decided to shut up and play the hand she was dealt.* I could understand that. Clare had chosen to fulfill her obligations. She had chosen to perform her duty to family and tradition and . . .

Herself?

I squeezed toothpaste onto my electric toothbrush and began to brush.

Or maybe, I thought, *just maybe, Clare had fallen in love with Win again. Maybe she'd remembered why she'd fallen in love with him in the first place.*

I didn't know and Clare wasn't telling.

And she wasn't the only one with a big secret.

I frowned at my reflection in the mirror over the sink. Was that another line? I reached for the little jar of eye cream.

Secrets could take their toll on your appearance.

See, I hadn't told Gincy or Clare about my one night of passion with Chris. They didn't even know he'd come to Boston to have dinner with me. Every time in the past days they'd asked about us, I'd neatly avoided answering.

Once, Gincy had pressed for a real answer, eyes narrowed for the kill, but I shut her down with a look I usually reserve only for potential perverts on the T.

Chris.

He was still in Portland but we'd spoken twice. The meetings and negotiations with Tristan Connor, the investor and idea man, were going well, and we talked mostly about the potentials for his business. He never once mentioned the Unanswered Question, and I was grateful, though the Unanswered Question was there, looming.

The third time Chris called I didn't answer the phone.

I couldn't.

I'd made absolutely no progress in terms of understanding our relationship and I wasn't sure I could handle another conversation in which we studiously avoided the topic we both cared most about.

Yes, I thought, looking carefully at my reflection. *Another line.* And my pores were stretching by the second.

The entire situation was wreaking havoc on my skin. I knew that if I didn't come to a conclusion soon about Chris and what it was we had together, I was going to need an appointment with a very, very good dermatologist.

I flipped off the bathroom light and went into the bedroom.

What was driving me most crazy was that I'd always been so decisive about practically everything.

I knew immediately whether I liked or disliked a dress or pair of shoes. I knew immediately whether a certain fabric would work on a certain piece of furniture. I knew immediately when a man was history.

Until Chris.

Did I love Chris? I wondered, undressing. I still wasn't sure.

People married the person they loved. That was huge. How could I love Chris if I wasn't even able to commit to dating him exclusively?

I wondered: Was there a difference between loving someone and being in love with that someone?

Yes. Wasn't there?

So maybe I was in love with Chris.

Yes, I thought, *I probably am in love with him.*

Probably.

Though how much of those feelings could really be called lust?

And did it even matter?

What I had going was a classic summer romance. Every single woman hoped to find a special summer romance, something wonderful to remember for the rest of her life.

Love, lust, who cared?

I did. I cared. And so did Chris.

Chris wanted more.

And I kind of wanted more, too.

Kind of.

I thought again of my parents and wondered why, why, why I was even considering making a commitment to Chris. He was so totally not acceptable as a husband. Why didn't I just let him go?

A better question: Why couldn't I just let him go?

With a noisy sigh I crawled into bed and stretched out flat. The air-conditioning was on high and before long I was chilly, but I left the covers at the end of the bed and stared up at the ceiling.

Suddenly, I remembered the conversation my friends and I had had about those Catholic nuns and monks who spent their lives praying for people.

I'd never been much for the whole religion thing. At least, the prayer part and all, the kind of stuff you did alone, like yoga and meditation.

But I needed help, bad. Chris would be back on the Vineyard in a few days. I had no time to hunt down some professional pray-er and explain the whole situation.

I was on my own.

"God," I said to the ceiling, "this is Danielle Leers. And I'm in trouble. I've got this big decision to make and I don't know what to do. I won't bother you with the details because you're supposed to know everything, right? So could you maybe send me a sign or something, so I can know what to do about Chris? Maybe you could perform one of those things, what do you call them, an Act of God? So I won't have to do this all on my own. Thanks."

Well, that was weird, I thought as I pulled up the covers and turned out the bedside lamp. *Weird but okay.*

Gincy
Every Woman Is an Island

Sally wouldn't talk to me at work the day after her drunken declaration.

Instead, she made a point of avoiding me entirely. The one time we accidentally met by the elevator she shot me a look full of death rays and took the stairs.

I was sorry for hurting her but I was glad that things were out in the open.

You'll miss her company, Gincy, I told myself. But it had been like the company of a mascot. And that just wasn't right, for either of us.

I sat at my desk and tried to focus on work, but my conscience was not through giving me a hard time.

I thought back to the invasion of Mommyzilla and how that third time she'd come to the office she'd treated me with disdain. Contempt. Scorn.

Even my friends had said so.

Wasn't there something of disdain in the way I'd treated Sally all along?

I put my head in my hands, hiding from myself in shame.

I'd made a joke of her to some extent, hadn't I? It was a disgusting admission but it was true. I could be a disgusting person.

I'd underestimated Sally's person. I'd underestimated her capacity for joy and pain.

I was beginning to think I didn't understand anything about love and kindness and friendship. That maybe I never really had.

I was beginning to think I didn't understand anyone, least of all myself.

And then Kell, his face grim, called a meeting of our department.

It was horrible news.

A woman named Gail Black from the graphics department had committed suicide the evening before.

She'd left no note; at least, none had yet been found.

Friends—of which she had few—reported no odd behavior in the months, weeks, days just before Gail's suicide.

Family claimed Gail had always been a good daughter, responsible, caring.

Coworkers, like me, realized we knew virtually nothing about the quiet, pleasant woman three cubicles down the hall.

Everybody was puzzled. Everybody was shocked.

We all straggled out of Kell's office, subdued, stunned.

And all day long I couldn't help but think about—dwell on—those last few minutes of Gail's life.

What had she been feeling?

Had she felt sad or lonely? Or had she been beyond feeling bad, beyond any concern with life?

Had she forgotten for a split-second that she was about to die—the habit of life being so strong—and wondered what she'd have for dinner that night?

And as she walked up that last dark staircase to the roof, had she been trembling? Had she been excited, eager to cast off this troublesome life and enter a new and better place?

Had she believed in an afterlife? Or had she simply craved oblivion?

And at the crucial moment, had she taken a bold step into the still air, or had she simply allowed herself to fall, angling her upper body far enough so that gravity grabbed hold and she tumbled, headfirst . . .

And had she then panicked and tried to stop herself, arms windmilling, mind screaming . . .

Had she been dead before she hit the filthy pavement?

What a horrible, public way to die, I thought.

What could possibly make someone choose such an openly humiliating death?

In my mind I saw Gail's paisley-print skirt bunched up over her panties, her legs splayed shamelessly, her face a mess of gore. How could she have wanted anyone to see her like that?

Maybe she'd been beyond caring about appearances. Maybe she'd so hated herself that she craved the postmortem violation. Maybe she'd been so far gone into gloom she never even thought of—after.

But how could she not have, an angry voice in my head countered. Suicide—especially one so public—was in some ways an act of aggression, wasn't it?

At least, it seemed so to me.

An unmistakable "fuck you" to the world.

"Okay, here I am, splattered across your public sidewalk. Now, clean up the mess! You didn't notice me while I was alive, you didn't hear my cries for help, well you're damn sure gonna have to deal with me now that I'm dead."

I could toss around idea after idea, I realized, but I'd never know what made forty-one-year-old Gail Black climb those gray concrete stairs to the roof of her apartment building, knowing she wouldn't be coming down in quite the same way.

Suicide was also the ultimate act of secrecy.

I shut the door to my office and slid down to the floor, my back against the door.

And I cried.

Clare
Chance Encounter

I was browsing through the fiction stacks when I saw him again. The stranger. The admirer. The Viking-like guy from the reading.

My first instinct was to scurry around the rack and into the next aisle.

I was getting married. I was dedicated to Win. The trip to Ann Arbor had changed things.

It had. I hadn't complained once to my friends since coming back East.

"Hi," I said.

He startled and looked up.

The stranger. The admirer.

Had I noticed just how beautiful he was?

Butterflies fluttered madly through my body.

And then he smiled. "Hi. Wow. This is a coincidence. Well, maybe not really. I mean, we met at the library and now here we are, at the library again . . ."

I smiled back. "It's nice to see you. You look well."

"Thanks. Oh, by the way, my name is Eason."

"Clare," I told him.

Around us, homeless men sat at blond wood tables reading

the daily papers, teens typed madly at computerized card catalogues, and book-group ladies searched for new ideas.

All oblivious to the man and woman making awkward conversation among the stacks.

Star-crossed lovers?

Eason bounced on the balls of his feet, clearly uncomfortable. "So," he said, "how are the wedding plans going?"

I'm not getting married. Would you like to go out with me?

"Fine. Okay." Oh, at that moment I felt so very conscious of my engagement ring.

It felt like an anchor on my hand, weighing me to the ground, when all I wanted to do was float free. At least for a while . . .

Remember Ann Arbor, Clare. Remember how everyone was so happy. Remember how you felt everything would be okay in the end.

"By the way," I said quickly, hoping to keep Eason there for just a bit longer. Hoping to memorize his face. "I never asked what you do. That night, at the reading."

"I teach high school," he said. "Public school system. I know. It sounds insane—so much work and so little pay—but I really like teaching."

"It doesn't sound insane at all!" I blurted. "I'm a teacher, too. I teach fifth grade at York, Braddock and Roget."

"Oh. Great. It's a wonderful school."

"Yes," I said. "It is."

Silence followed, then Eason pointed to the plastic-covered hardback he held in his left hand. "Well, I should get going. I found what I was looking for . . . I mean, the book."

I smiled, nodded, shrugged.

"Okay," he said, backing away a step or two, "well, it was good to see you again. And really, I'm sorry I asked you out that time. I didn't mean to—"

"No," I blurted. "I mean, that's okay."

I'm the one who's sorry. So sorry.

Eason hesitated a moment. Our eyes locked.

And then, he was gone.

Danielle
All the Right Moves

Barry Lieberman called to say he was coming to Boston on business.

I agreed to have dinner with him, partly as a courtesy to Mrs. Rothstein and partly in an attempt to get my mind off Chris.

And to be honest, partly because Barry fit perfectly the profile of a potential husband and, well, I certainly wasn't getting any younger.

For better or worse, even during the worst moments of the whole Chris affair, I never quite lost my practical perspective.

Barry picked me up at my apartment right on time. He was very sweet and just amusing enough to be entertaining but not obnoxious.

He also was nice-looking, in a slightly hairy way. Like that actor, Peter Gallagher.

I mean, Barry's haircut and eyebrows were a lot neater, thank God. There was some hair on the backs of his hands, which made me suspect there might be some hair on his back, too.

But he was so clean and neat overall the thought didn't really bother me.

Besides, I thought, *there's a very good chance I'll never see him naked, so what does it matter if his chest is as hairy as Austin Powers's?*

We had dinner at the Oak Room in the Copley Fairmont. Then we went for drinks to the Top of the Hub. Barry admitted he was a sucker for tourist traps.

That was another positive. He was unaffected, and not in a studied way. I mean, he was real.

Still, I felt no great spark.

But Barry felt otherwise.

While gazing out over the city of Boston he told me he had tickets to an opening-night performance at the Metropolitan Opera and asked if I'd be interested in coming to New York for that late-September weekend.

A night at the opera! Not that I was such a huge fan, but that meant an opportunity to dress up, to see and be seen.

And an autumn weekend in New York! I could shop. And I could check out some new restaurants. I could . . .

Remember, Danielle, I told myself, *Barry will be there with you. You'd be going to New York primarily to be with Barry.*

I told Barry I'd check my schedule and call him within the week.

Barry brought me home, and at the door to my apartment he kissed me good-night. It was very appropriately done, just enough to remember him by. And his face was smooth. He was a good shaver.

When Barry had gone I changed into a nightgown and flipped on the TV. For a while I watched a mystery show on Lifetime, but I wasn't really paying attention.

My mind was awhirl with thoughts of the men in my life.

Dad.

David.

And . . .

Sitting there on my couch, watching some red-haired actress solving a crime of domestic abuse, I decided that if I weren't so preoccupied with Chris, I could really like Barry.

In spite of his being perfect husband material.

Gincy
Hope and Glory

When Justin had gone to bed and I'd finished loading the dishwasher, I joined Rick in the living room.

"The Gail situation is really bothering me," I admitted, flopping down next to him on the couch. It groaned loudly and I wondered just how much longer the old thing was going to last.

Rick aimed the remote at the TV and shut off the nature show he was watching on Discovery.

"Gail's suicide is going to stay with everyone for a while," he said softly.

"I suppose. But I didn't even know her! I mean, I knew who she was, but honestly, I don't think we ever spoke. And yet every time I think about what happened I feel sick. Almost physically sick."

"You could see a grief counselor."

"No, no, no," I protested, "I'm sure I'll be fine. Maybe I'll get a book or something. Yeah, that's an idea. I'll go to Barnes & Noble at lunch tomorrow. I just need to understand a bit more."

A strange look crossed Rick's face. He opened his mouth as if to speak but shut it again.

"What? No, tell me," I begged. "You were going to say something."

Rick sighed. "It's not that I'm trying to keep secrets from you, Gincy," he said. "I just don't want to burden you."

"Well," I said, fighting a horrible feeling of doom, "you've already freaked me out with this setup so you'd better just spill it."

And he did. "At one point," Rick told me, "Annie thought about suicide. She was miserable and her latest prognosis wasn't good. She was just so tired of everything."

Now there was a bombshell. And I'd begged for it.

"I'm so sorry," I said, and I was. Would he go on?

Yeah.

"You know, the last months of her pregnancy were colored by cancer," Rick said. "I can't imagine what she went through, even though I was with her the entire time. And then Justin was born and she couldn't even be there for him, not really. Anyway, that's how she felt. Like she'd failed our child, even though he was perfectly healthy. And he was happy, too, which surprised both of us. We were so worried he was going to drink in all the sadness and be a miserable little guy."

"Justin is pretty amazing," I said. "He's the only kid who's ever liked me. I think he's got some natural anti-negativity shield or something."

Rick sort of smiled, but it was Annie he was thinking about again, not me and Justin.

"I didn't even know what to say to her," Rick admitted angrily. "How could I ask her to hang on when every doctor was telling us there was no hope? Hang on for what? So I could see her emaciated face for a little while longer? How selfish could I be? Or so Justin might, just might, bond with a mother he'd never consciously remember?"

I wanted to know if Annie had asked Rick to help her die. And I didn't want to know.

"It must have been horrible," I said inanely.

"It was a bad time, Gincy. The worst."

Could I ask? Was I supposed to ask?

"What happened, Rick?" I said.

Rick sighed deeply. "I don't really know what happened, but Annie decided to live on. Something clicked over and she seemed more peaceful from that point on. Until the end, which wasn't far off. Too soon and too far."

Rick grabbed my hands and leaned close. "Gincy, I didn't want her to die," he said passionately, "but I didn't want her to live, either. Not the way she was living. Do you understand that?"

"Yes," I said softly. "I think I do."

Gincy
An Offer She . . .

I stayed over that night and we slept wrapped in each other's arms, something that wasn't our usual habit.

The next morning I woke before Rick and started the coffee. Then I roused Justin and got him ready for day camp. When the bus came by at seven-thirty, I helped him up the steps and went back up to the apartment.

Rick was just out of the shower and drinking coffee. He looked refreshed, better than I felt. I'd dreamed all night of bad things, murder and mayhem, losing my job, my parents dying, Rick's leaving me.

After my own shower, I joined him in the living room with my third cup of coffee.

"I was thinking," he said suddenly.

Oh, God, I thought. Thinking is rarely a good sign. Telling someone you've been thinking is just about the worst sign there is.

I knew because in the previous ten years I'd told lots of men that I'd been thinking.

"Oh?" I said squeakily.

"Yes. About us. About our moving in together, seeing how it goes."

You know that old expression, you could have knocked me over with a feather? Another one of my father's all-time favorites.

Well, let me tell you. If Rick had had a feather, I'd have been on the floor.

"You mean," I said carefully, "I'd move into your place?"

"Yeah. There's plenty of room and you hardly have any stuff, so moving will be easy. We can rent a van and do the entire move in a few hours."

I got to my feet and narrowly avoided spilling the dregs of my coffee. I put the messy cup on a shelf half-stacked with books and turned back to Rick. "Jesus, Rick, it's not that. Your apartment is a palace compared to mine! It's just—whoa. Wow. I don't know what to say. Wait, here's something: Where did this come from?"

Rick grinned up at me. "It came from the fact that I love you. Maybe I should have started this conversation by restating that bit of information."

I threw my arms in the air and let them smack back against my sides. "Well, I love you, too. We know we love each other."

He looked at me keenly. "You sound angry about it."

"No!" I cried, flopping back down next to him. "Well, it's just that I didn't expect to fall in love. Now, this year, this summer. But I did and it's great," I said, grabbing his hand and squeezing. "Unless you cheat on me and then you're in seriously big trouble. I will so kick your ass."

"If I were thinking about cheating on you, would I be suggesting we move in together?"

"No," I admitted. "I guess not. But Rick, this is huge. We've only known each other for a few months. Not even."

"Yeah, but why wait? Life is short, Gincy. When something good happens, you embrace it."

This man would love my father, I thought. *At least, the clichéd wisdom part.*

"I've never been in a long-term relationship, you know."

Rick nodded thoughtfully. "I'm aware. You've told me at least a dozen times. But you're doing okay so far, aren't you?"

"What do you think of my relationship performance?" I asked, half-teasingly.

"It doesn't matter what I think. You're the only one who knows if you're doing okay. If you feel right."

"I feel fine," I admitted. "I guess. I don't think I've screwed up. Too badly. Yet."

"Maybe you're a natural."

"Hmmm." I felt my mind drift and suddenly found my knees very fascinating.

"Is there someone else?" Rick asked abruptly, and I realized that of course he would wonder.

I looked back to Rick.

His expression was heartbreaking. And suddenly I thought of the photo on Justin's nightstand, the photo of Rick taken when he was about three years old. Little overalls. A little baseball cap. Little sneakers.

I realized then that you knew you were in love when no matter how angry you were at a guy, a photo of him as a little boy reminded you of what you liked about him, of what he really meant to you. You felt flooded by tenderness, and even if the guy had farted at the dinner table or smeared bike grease on your best towels, you forgave him.

And Rick had done nothing wrong but throw an enormous monkey wrench into our works.

"No," I answered truthfully. "There's no one else." And then I took a deep breath. "Honestly? For a while, at the beginning, I kind of hoped there would be. But with you in my life, there just wasn't room for anyone else. There isn't room. That's a good thing, but at first it scared me. You know."

Rick sighed and his relief was obvious. "I do know. I feel the same way. Love is always scary, even for people like me who've been married. Maybe especially for people like me, who've lost love so brutally. I don't know. I shouldn't assume my situation is any harder than anyone else's."

There was something I needed to know. "Annie was really devoted to you though, right?" I asked carefully. "It was horrible that she died so young and that Justin never got to know her. But she never cheated on you, did she? She never betrayed you?"

"No," Rick said emphatically. "We were good. Maybe that's part of why I can love again. I had a good experience. It gave me hope."

No "once burned twice shy" here.

But was I as resilient and brave as Rick?

"What if . . ." Jeez, how to say it? "Rick, I can't help but think you're going to compare me to Annie. Compare what we have to what you guys had together. And I can't be—"

"Try not to think that way, Gincy. I don't want the past. I want the present. And the future. With you. Please believe me."

I wanted to believe him.

And then I leapt from the couch again. "Oh, my, God, what about Justin! How's he going to react to all this?"

Rick sighed and messed up the hair on his head. By now, it was a familiar gesture. "Justin likes you, Gincy," he said. "A lot. I know we'd all have to adjust and grow into a family, but I really believe we can do it."

Holy crap. A family. Did that mean . . .

"Wait a minute," I said. "I think I've been a little slow on the uptake here. Are you thinking that if I move in it'll be like a trial run? Or something."

If Danielle tried to make me wear white . . .

Rick nodded. "Yeah. For the long haul. For marriage. I wouldn't ask you otherwise. It wouldn't be fair to you or to Justin. Or to me."

No, I thought, *it wouldn't be fair.*

"Rick," I said, "I've got to think about this. Okay? This is huge." I checked the clock on the VCR. "Look, we both have to leave for work now. Maybe I should just go home tonight, by myself. Try to—try to figure things out."

Rick opened his mouth but closed it without saying anything. Like, "Don't run off, okay? Let's figure this out together."

And then he got up off the couch. It wailed in relief. "Of course," he said. "And whatever I can do to help, let me know. Promise?"

I took his hand. "Yeah," I said. "Promise."

Gincy

Sharper Than a Serpent's Tooth

The phone rang at nine o'clock that night.

It was my father.

"Who's dead?" I blurted.

"What?"

"Someone must be dead. You never call me. Who is it? Oh, my God, is Mom okay?"

Okay, I didn't really like my mother but I didn't want her dead. Yet.

My father sighed. "Virginia, you get that morbid habit of thinking from your mother's Aunt Bessie. All that woman could talk about was death and dying and—"

Poverty and disease and sin . . .

"Dad! Why are you calling me?"

Dad cleared his throat. "Well," he said, "this is a bit awkward, Virginia. You know I've never interfered with your, uh, with your personal life . . ."

Ah. "Tommy told you about Rick?" I asked, sparing the poor man.

"Now, Virginia, I know your brother doesn't always show it, but he does care for you—"

"Dad," I interrupted, "what did Tommy tell you?"

In short, that I was seeing some "creepy old guy."

"You've always had good sense, Virginia," Dad went on, cutting off my shriek of horror. "And you've been on your own for some time now. Maybe you don't think you need your father's advice, but here it is. I want you to be careful. Men, well, most men aren't what they seem. This person might seem on the up-and-up but you have to be very careful. He's not taking money from you, is he?"

Poor Dad.

Poor me.

Such deep miscommunication.

As gently and as firmly as I could I told Dad the truth about Rick.

That he was only thirty-five. That he was a well-respected professional and a good father. Dad wasn't glad to learn that Rick was a widower, but he was glad to learn he wasn't divorced.

And that he wasn't taking money from me.

As if I had any to give.

I did not tell my father that Rick had just asked me to move in with him. One step at a time.

I think I reassured Dad that I hadn't allowed myself to fall into the clutches of a dastardly villain. By the time we said good-bye, his voice wasn't quite so grim. And he actually asked me to call him if I needed anything. Like advice.

It was probably the best conversation I'd ever had with my father. And it had taken almost thirty years to happen.

Later that night, while lying sleepless in bed, I was overwhelmed by a sense of my own frailty. Every hurtful, selfish thing I'd ever done was suddenly right before me in a glaringly bright light.

I'd been a rotten friend. I should have taken Sally more seriously as a person. Maybe I'd led her on without even realizing it. Even if I hadn't, I should have been sensitive enough to pick up on her feelings and maybe spend less time with her.

But sensitivity had never been my strong suit.

And maybe I hadn't been a very good daughter, either. I hadn't given my father much credit for anything, least of all for caring so much.

There was a slight breeze coming through the window. I pulled the sheet up around my neck and suddenly felt like a little kid, sent to bed without supper for some stupid infraction.

Gincy, I told myself sadly, *you have an awful lot to learn.*

How could I possibly move in with Rick and Justin and take on all that responsibility when I was such a screw-up?

Clare
Charity Begins

It was a letter from the convent of the Sisters of the White Rose of Mary.

I was glad that Win hadn't seen it before I could retrieve the bulky envelope from the mailbox.

Once inside the apartment I tore open the Sisters' response to my plea. I'd made my decision to go through with the wedding, but still, I was curious to hear the Sisters' words of wisdom.

I put aside the card on which was printed a poorly painted bleeding heart, and with it the card on which an insipid Jesus looked up at me with watery blue eyes.

Horrible. I'd never understand the appeal of such things.

There was a handwritten letter from someone named Sr. Richard Marie, blue ink on white paper. The penmanship was perfectly regular, a lost art. Certainly none of my students wrote half as legibly. Neither did I, come to think of it.

I read. "You must turn your mind to your duty," Sr. Richard Marie advised, "and to the promise you made to your fiancé as well as to God."

But I don't know God, I thought. *I was never really introduced. Not properly.*

I read on, spirits falling. "Think always of Our Blessed Virgin

Mary, both wife and mother, and of the sacrifices she made in the name of love. Follow her example always and you will walk in the Grace of God."

Her example. I didn't know much about the Virgin Mary—aside from the obvious—but I knew enough to guess that she didn't snap at Joseph the way I'd been snapping at Win in the past months.

Poor Win. He tried, he really did.

He wasn't a bad man. He had his flaws and his faults, but so did I. So did everyone.

No one is perfect, Clare, I reminded myself.

And then I heard my mother's voice in my head. She was angry, and something else. Manic.

Are you thinking there's someone out there so much better than Win? Are you? she demanded shrilly. *So utterly made for you that it's worth throwing away what you have in hand, what you've worked at for over ten years?*

Mother fell silent and I thought about her questions.

I'd been with Win for over ten years.

What was there to show for it? What had I earned? What had I received?

What had I given?

And then I wondered: Was longevity alone an accomplishment? Were forty bland, possibly soulless, years of marriage better than forty years of shorter-term alliances?

Especially if those alliances brought intense emotion and unexpected flashes of supreme passion and knowledge of the sort you just couldn't find in a long-term, exclusive partnership.

Of course longevity is an accomplishment, Mother shrieked. *If it isn't, then what have I . . .*

I looked back at the handwritten letter.

"Remember," Sister Richard Marie wrote, "Jesus Christ gave up His life. He suffered and died for our sins."

The poor man, I thought, folding the letter. *Why had he bothered?*

Gincy
Domestic Trappings

We dropped Justin off at a neighbor's house for a play date and walked to the Congress Street loft district.

I'd never been to the furniture store called Machine Age. Rick promised I'd enjoy it.

I didn't.

"What do you think of this couch?" Rick nodded at some long thing covered in a nubbly pea green material.

"It's not exactly the style I'd considered but . . ."

Rick sat down on the monstrosity. Was he color blind?

"I don't know," I said. "It's okay."

The place made me nervous. Everything was so expensive and severe. And ugly.

"Pretty comfortable," Rick went on, running his hands over the seat. "Tough fabric. That's important, considering Justin's been begging for a dog. Maybe I should just get a secondhand couch. Or go to one of those outlets on Route 1. Jordan's or something. With a kid and a dog, and let's face it, the way I spill stuff, the thing's going to be destroyed before long . . ."

"Rick!" My own voice startled me. A salesperson glared. A customer hurried off to another section of the store.

Rick frowned. "What's wrong?" he said, rising from the couch. "Do you feel sick?"

I took a step back from him. "No. I mean yes, in a way. Rick, I just don't understand how you can be making this life choice."

"Buying a couch is a life choice?"

He wasn't joking.

"No, no," I said, clutching my head. "Marriage. I'm talking about your getting married again. To me! After all the pain of losing Annie and . . . Rick, what if I die? What if I screw us up? What about Justin?"

Rick didn't try to reach for me. He'd been good from the start at reading my antipathy to being touched at certain peaks of emotion. "Life can't be about expectation, Gincy," he said quietly, "or it's all a waste. Nothing's ever as you expect it to be. Life has to be about risk. If you want to be happy there's no other way."

Fine words but . . .

"But what if you take the risk and you aren't happy?" I pressed.

Rick shoved his hands into the front pocket of his faded black jeans. "Look," he said, "when I married Annie we'd already known each other for five years. Getting married, then Annie's getting pregnant, it was like my life was all set, everything in place, the road all paved to the distant end. I was sure of Annie. But what I didn't realize was that I couldn't be sure of life. When she got sick, I was totally shocked. I'd never even considered one of us could die before being grumpy old grandparents."

"What's your point?" I said, though I knew what he was trying to say.

"My point is that if I had to do it over again, knowing I'd lose Annie, I would. I'd take what I could get and be grateful for it."

I didn't answer.

"Sometimes," he went on, "life kicks you in the teeth. And there's nothing you can do about it but go on. Maybe your grin's a little lopsided for a while, but what's the alternative? Give up?"

I shrugged and thought of Gail. Had she given up? Was that what suicide was all about?

Maybe. Maybe not.

"Well, I couldn't give up," Rick went on, his tone urgent. "I had Justin. He was only a few months old. Annie would have been seriously disappointed in me if I'd fallen apart. In a way, Justin saved my life."

And then, I snapped. I swear I went insane.

Annie, Annie, always Annie. Justin was Annie's child, not mine. He'd never be mine.

"Annie was prettier than me," I blurted, choking back tears. "How can you ever love me like you loved her?"

Rick looked absolutely stunned. He reached for me then, but I turned and ran out of the store, startling the owner who probably thought I was an escaping thief.

Once on the sidewalk I turned right and kept going. Behind me, I heard Rick's running feet.

"Gincy!" he called, and he sounded panicked. "Come back!"

Tears streamed down my face. I kept running. Behind me, Rick's voice grew tinier and tinier until finally I could no longer hear him.

Maybe he'd stopped calling for me. Maybe I was just too far out of range for anything to reach me.

Eventually, I slowed to a stumbling walk. My chest heaved from the physical exertion as well as from the overflowing of my heart.

I thought of Gail again, dead so suddenly, though maybe her death had been long in coming.

Had anyone loved her?

Was love ever enough to save a person from despair?

I thought of Sally, bestowing her love on someone who just couldn't give love back. Our friendship was ruined, and I blamed myself.

And I blamed love. Love got people into trouble.

On Summer Street I stopped and leaned against a building. A middle-aged man passing by, briefcase in tow, scowled at me as if I was a druggie and maybe just then I looked like one, all hollow-eyed and sad.

Why couldn't anything be guaranteed? Why couldn't you

know with confidence that a marriage would last, that a child would grow up to be healthy and wise, that you would die peacefully at a ripe old age, surrounded by loved ones?

I pushed off the building and stepped blindly off the curb.

A horn blasted and I stopped dead. An SUV rounded the corner and missed me by inches.

"You are one stupid bitch!" the woman in the passenger seat screamed at me.

I didn't even want to yell back.

Maybe she was right. Maybe I was one stupid bitch. A stupid bitch full of piss and vinegar.

I walked on in search of a T station.

This is what you wanted when you moved to the big city, Gincy, I told myself.

Experience. Challenge.

Life.

Can you deal with it, after all?

Danielle
Nothing Good Ever Came Easily

"So, what are you going to tell him?" I asked.

Gincy and Clare sat on my couch and I presided from a leather armchair I'd gotten on sale at Adesso.

I'd never imagined Gincy to be such a drama queen. Actually running from a store, tearing down the street, ignoring the pleading cries of her lover?

"I think I already told him my answer," she snapped. "You don't run away from someone who's shouting for you to stop without sending a pretty clear message."

"I'm sure he hasn't cut you off," Clare said gently. "I'm sure he understands."

"Understands what?" Gincy cried. "That I'm stringing him along until I work up the nerve to say no? Which ends our relationship. It has to. And it makes me sick to think about losing him."

"So you're definitely going to say no?"

"Yeah," Gincy said, rubbing her temples. "I have to. I'm just not ready."

"No one's ever ready," Clare murmured.

"It . . . It feels like there's so much death," Gincy went on, more to herself than to us. "Annie is dead but she's not, you know? But the fact that she died and they didn't just divorce . . . Sometimes it creeps me out. I can't explain it."

This girl had to get it together.

"So," I said, "you'd rather Rick have a bitchy, money-grubbing ex-wife prowling outside his apartment door? You'd rather him be a divorced dad instead of a widower? Believe me, you're better off with Annie dead than with her living on his paycheck and slamming your character to Rick's former so-called friends."

Clare's eyes widened to ridiculous proportions.

"You're despicable," Gincy said, her voice shaking with fury. "Do you even have a heart? That is one of the coldest things I've ever heard."

"I'm just trying to be realistic," I replied, perfectly in control. Not cold. Never cold.

"Look," she went on, "I'm not you. We're not even close to being members of the same species. So don't start spouting your screwed-up philosophy of men and women to me, okay? Like you know what you're doing? Like you know anything about commitment?"

I gripped the arms of the chair and felt something inside just break in two.

All right, I thought. If Gincy could reveal herself to be a drama queen, I could reveal myself to be one, too.

That or a doomed heroine. Because I was the victim in the whole affair, wasn't I?

"I'll have you know," I said calmly, "that Chris asked me to make a formal commitment to him. And that he's waiting for my answer."

Clare gasped. "The bracelet . . ."

"After that," I said. "When he came to Boston to take me to dinner for my birthday."

Gincy shook her head. "You never told us . . ."

"I don't tell you everything," I snapped. "I can handle my own life."

"I don't understand," Clare said gently. "Did he ask you to marry him?"

"No," I admitted. "But the idea is the same. He wants us to be exclusive."

"Which means he wants to get married at some point," Gincy said, undeterred by my anger at her. "Step one, go steady. Become his main squeeze. His one and only."

Married at some point . . .

The moment of truth had arrived. Suddenly, I knew I'd made my decision.

"Yes," I said, "except that I won't be marrying Chris Childs. Or making a commitment to him. Ever."

The words, now out of my mouth, horrified me. But I would not take them back.

"Are you in love with him, Danielle?" Clare dared to ask.

I sat staring at my knees for a long moment.

"Dan—"

"Yes, no, I don't know!" I cried. "It doesn't matter because I'm not allowed to marry Chris!"

"Who says so?" Gincy shot back. "Have you ever actually talked to your parents about marrying someone not Jewish? Have you? Because it's about Chris's being Christian, isn't it?"

No, I hadn't ever talked to my parents about marrying a non-Jew. But I knew what was expected of me.

"You don't understand," I cried. "To the Leers, a fishing business is not a glamorous thing. It's the old country, it's drudgery and poverty and dying before you're fifty without a tooth in your head."

Clare cleared her throat. "Danielle," she said, "I met your parents. They don't strike me—"

"Once! You met my parents once! I know them, you don't." I got up from the chair and began to pace the living room. "Believe me, my mother won't care that the Childses have hundreds of acres or whatever, or that they live in a beautifully restored nineteenth-century house overlooking a pretty pond. Esther Leers will care that Chris's father didn't finish high school. She'll care that Chris didn't finish college. My God, she'll be horrified to learn that his mother wears an apron to walk to the mailbox at the end of the drive."

"Do you really care that much about what your mother thinks?" Gincy asked, and I thought I saw a look of sympathy cross her face.

I didn't want her sympathy.

"I care enough," I said, "to want my parents and aunts and uncles and cousins to come to my house for the holidays. I don't want to isolate them. I don't want to make them feel I'm betraying all they've worked so hard to give me. I'll do what I have to do to keep my family."

"Even if it means giving up Chris?" Clare's voice was hushed.

For a moment I couldn't reply. "Yes," I said finally, my voice choked. "Even if it means that. I want tradition more. I can't—I won't!—be an outsider to my own family. They have expectations. I have to live up to them."

"What are those expectations?" Gincy asked. "Exactly. I mean, have your parents ever sat down with you and handed you a checklist? Or are you just assuming—"

I cut her off. "Giving up Chris is a sacrifice? So big deal. Like other people in my family didn't make sacrifices? Please. Giving up Chris is a minor sacrifice compared to what my Great-aunt Ruth gave up in the war. To what my grandparents lost. The prejudices they faced. My sacrifice is nothing compared to theirs. And it's one I'm totally willing to make."

There was a horrible, heavy silence. Finally, Gincy stood and walked to the door of the apartment.

"I don't think this is about sacrifice," she said quietly, her hand on the knob. "I don't think it's about your family at all. I think it's all about you and your own cowardice. I think you're chickening out of your own life. And I'm sorry for you."

Clare covered her face with her hands.

I was sorry for me, too.

Gincy
Braveheart

I'd called Danielle a coward. I was not unaware of the irony. I decided to break up with Rick face-to-face, though the coward's way out was so tempting. A phone call, an e-mail, an old-fashioned Dear John letter.

I called and asked if it would be okay to come over. Rick told me that Justin was at a friend's house and that it would be fine. His voice was flat.

I let myself in; Rick often forgot to lock the door. He wasn't in sight; I imagined he was in the bedroom.

I took a moment to look around, to remember. And something odd happened.

For the first time, the framed photos of Annie, alone and with Rick and Justin, didn't seem threatening. In fact, I realized, the photos seemed perfect right where they were.

Annie was Annie. Gincy was Gincy.

Rick and I were who we were.

We were the couple in the photo taken on the beach, the photo taken by Justin with my one-time-use camera. The couple with their arms slung over each other's shoulders, smiling into the sun.

Past, present, future. We were going to hold it all in our hands.

I went into the bedroom. Rick was standing at the window, looking out at the darkening sky. I knew he'd heard me come in, but it was a moment before he turned.

His eyes were tentatively hopeful. Not assuming. Not defeated.

And in that moment I realized that I loved him for allowing me this freedom.

This is the face I will cherish forever, I thought.

Wow.

Rick took a tentative step toward me. "Gincy?"

"You know," I said, feeling a big old smile dawn on my face, "I think we should go to Jordans for the couch. I'm not any less destructive than a five-year-old or a dog. Or you. I mean, all of us together? Maybe we should just buy disposable cardboard furniture or something."

And then we were in each other's arms, crying, laughing, kissing.

The necessary leap of faith. Someone had to take it.

So Rick did. And I followed.

Danielle
The Cruelest Month

I'd been avoiding Chris since he'd come home from Portland. He had to know the reason for my missing his calls. For my staying in Boston one weekend due to a sudden and severe summer cold.

He had to know the reason, but I had to speak it to his face. I owed him that much. Finally, I called Chris and we made plans to meet on the Vineyard.

Once there, the conversation was brief and awkward.

"I don't understand why we just can't go on the way we are," I said. "Why do we have to change things? Everything's so nice the way it is."

"For who?" he asked.

I had no answer. Things weren't really nice for either of us.

"Look," Chris said, pointing to his heart. "I've got to take care of this. I don't think I can do that with you. Not without further commitment, Danielle. I'm sorry."

"How do you even know I'm not already committed to you?" I cried stupidly.

Chris had the decency to look embarrassed. For me? "I saw you with another guy one night. I know you've been seeing other people on the island."

"Have you been following me?" I demanded, though I knew the notion was absurd.

"No, no. But the Vineyard's a small place. My friends talk. It's okay. I mean, we never had an agreement."

No. We hadn't had an agreement.

Chris went on. "And I don't know about back in Boston. If you're seeing someone else there, too. I guess I just don't know much at all about your life, Danielle."

"That can change," I said, though I knew I was lying. Words just kept coming, making no sense. I was clinging to Chris at the same time I was pushing him away.

And he had had just about enough. "Danielle," he said, angrily, "you're making this too hard. For both of us. Face it. You don't want what I want."

"I do! I do. Just—"

"What?" he shot back. "Just not with me? That's nice. And I thought we had something special."

"We did," I said lamely.

Chris grunted. He was furious. "Not special enough for you to say yes without having to qualify your answer. I'll be with you— but. I'll be with you—except. I'll be with you—until. Until what? Until a more eligible guy comes along? Come on, Danielle, I'd have to be stupid to accept a relationship on your terms."

I shook my head. "So I should accept a relationship on your terms?"

"No. We should build one on our terms. But there is no 'we.' "

I couldn't argue any longer.

"Look," he said, after a moment, his voice gentler. "I've got to go. I've got to get out of here. I hope things work out for you, Danielle. I hope you get what you want."

I watched as he drove away.

I, too, hoped I got what I wanted.

Whatever the hell that was.

Gincy

Leaving the Nest

Moving was hell.

Packing sucked. And I just bet unpacking would suck, too.

I wondered if I'd miss my little Allston apartment. I mean, it was pretty much of a dump but it was my dump.

And the contents of the apartment. The lopsided wooden table I'd bought in college and had been lugging around with me ever since. The warped plastic colander I'd found at a flea market. The green folding chair that doubled as a laundry drop.

None of those things would come with me.

Miss the place?

Not so much, I realized. Because it was time to go, time to move on. It felt okay, the decision I'd made so surprisingly, on the spur of the moment.

And Justin was okay with it, too. Sure, we'd all stumble through a period of adjustment, but the fact that Justin had already asked me to share his room boded well for our future.

There was only one major chore left to tackle.

I still had to tell my parents that I was moving in with Rick.

The guy with the kid and the dead wife.

Or did I have to tell them?

Maybe, I thought, *maybe I just won't say anything.*

I'll cancel my phone service and just use my cell phone and . . .

But what about the mail?

And what if Tommy shows up again, unannounced? He'll frighten the new tenant to death . . . The Mullett Monster.

I stared at the stupid phone.

It bothered me to realize that I was actually afraid of my parents' reactions. Well, not so much of their anger as of their disappointment.

What did they want me to do with my life?

Would my being with Rick fit into their hopes?

Did they have any hopes for me? Had they ever?

I wondered: Are we ever not children, hoping to please, needing to rebel, craving attention in some form or another?

What a chore to be a parent!

If things went okay with me and Rick, if I became Justin's official stepmother, would I fall apart under the pressure?

And what would happen if we had a kid together? Would I scar him for life before his first birthday, assuring years of therapy and drugs for all sorts of problems from uncontrollable quivering to pyromaniacal tendencies to severe panic attacks in the presence of vegetables?

That way lies madness, Gincy, I warned myself. *In more ways than one.*

One foot in front of the other. Like Dad always said.

Dad.

I picked up the phone, hoping my father would answer.

Luck was with me.

"Hi, Dad?" I said, voice quivering. "It's me. I have some good news."

Danielle
Singleton

I decided to go alone to Clare's wedding.

David would have been my escort. But he'd taken a few days off and was visiting his best friend from medical school in Colorado. Regrouping, he said.

I wished him well, as did our parents. To my total surprise, they were thrilled with David's decision to break his engagement to Roberta.

It seems they'd seen her for what little she was right from the start. But they hadn't issued a word of warning. They hadn't interfered in David's life.

They'd let their thirty-six-year-old son make his own discoveries and decisions.

My parents' actions had made me start to reconsider some of the notions I held about them.

About the four of us as a family.

About their expectations and my own.

About bravery and independence.

About the fact that I wasn't David and never had been.

In short, I was a wreck. Nothing was stable, nothing was right. Everything I'd been so sure of now seemed dubious and questionable. Everything was a shade of gray.

Deception. Indecision. Uncertainty.

I'd ruined things with Chris by not being honest. I mean, maybe we hadn't been meant for each other but if only I'd been honest with him up front, I could have saved us both a lot of heartache.

I wasn't going to go through the same nonsense with Barry. So I called him and gently explained that I'd been involved with someone for several weeks and that our relationship had come to a sudden and unexpected end. I told him I felt all discombobulated and that it wouldn't be fair to Barry to spend more time with him when I was in no position to start another relationship.

Barry was very polite and understanding. At least, he acted like he was, and for that I was grateful. He didn't let me off the hook entirely, though.

"Danielle," he said, "if you were involved with someone, and I'm guessing it was a pretty important relationship if you're so upset that it's over, can I ask why you agreed to see me in Boston?"

"I'm not quite sure," I admitted. "But I'm glad I did see you. I know that sounds selfish and it is, but I like you. I had a really good time with you."

Barry chuckled ruefully. "Well," he said, "I'm sorry. For both of us. I hope you feel better soon about—about the breakup. As for me, well, I'm not going to lie and say I'm not disappointed. I like you, too, Danielle."

"I'm sorry, Barry," I said, tears threatening. "Really."

"Look, maybe in a few months, if neither of us is—"

"Maybe," I agreed. "In a few months."

Listlessly I went about choosing an outfit and hairstyle for Clare's big day.

I still had deep reservations about Win, but Clare was my friend and I was determined to support her choice.

Besides, I thought, *what do you know about true love, Danielle? What did you ever know?*

Clare
Fortitudo

The night before my wedding.
My last night as a single woman.

Though maybe the night before I'd met Win all those years ago had marked that occasion.

Either way, come the next evening I would be Mrs. Winston Carrington III. Clare Jean Wellman Carrington.

A lot of names to carry around.

A lot of roles to play.

We had the bridal suite at the old Ritz. It was ten o'clock and in everybody's opinion I was supposed to be in bed. But I just couldn't sleep.

I knew Win and some people in town for the wedding were still at the bar downstairs. I slipped into the dress I'd worn for dinner and took the elevator to the ground floor.

I halted just outside the door to the almost-empty bar.

Win's voice rose and fell like a tide. And I heard the rest of my life laid out. No surprises. Nothing new. All according to plan. Win's plan.

It wasn't a bad life. But was it really mine?

And if not, whose fault was that?

"Clare will probably want to get pregnant right away," Win was saying. "I want her to quit working as soon as she does, of course. It's not like we can't live comfortably on my salary. More than comfortably."

I heard the low rumble of male chuckling.

Oh, yes, Win. We all know you make lots and lots of money.

"I figure for the next few years we'll vacation back home, at the lake. That way the grandparents will each get their fair share of the kids. I know Clare wants to go to Paris, but that can wait. Maybe I'll take her for our tenth anniversary."

Ten more years . . .

It won't be a bad life, Clare, I told myself as I rode the elevator back to the bridal suite.

There will be consolations.

Clare

Impromptu

I stood at the altar.
Win stood next to me.

Behind us, our friends and family were gathered.

The reverend was reading from a sheet of paper.

And I was thinking.

Sometimes, I thought, *we women forget that men have feelings and emotions.*

Sometimes we forget that men were once little boys in need of cuddles and kisses. That in some ways men are always little boys, much as we women are always little girls.

Sometimes, I thought, *we women forget that men are as much in need of love as we are.*

And we really, really should never forget that.

I couldn't marry Win, as much for his sake as for mine.

The initial blessing had just been read.

The reverend looked smilingly at us.

Enough.

"I can't marry you," I blurted. "I can't do this."

The reverend frowned and stepped closer to Win and me. "My dear," he whispered. "Do you feel all right?"

Win was frowning, truly puzzled.

"I feel fine," I said firmly.

I didn't know if our friends and family could hear me. I didn't care.

"I feel fine," I repeated, "because I've told my last lie. I'm through with lies. My soul can't take the strain of one more false-hood."

Win's face darkened. The truth was dawning. "What are you saying?" he hissed.

He took a step toward me and reached for my elbow. His fingers dug into my flesh and I yanked my arm away. The reverend gasped and a murmur arose from those in the pews.

And then I began to run.

Gincy

She's Come Undone

I'd heard about a bride or groom abandoning the other at the altar but I'd never, ever thought I'd witness such a truly dramatic event.

It seemed unreal, like a movie, Clare fleeing back down the aisle, the reverend hurriedly ushering Win and his best man behind the altar, some old lady screaming, kids running after Clare, probably thinking it was all a big game.

A full minute later and Danielle's mouth was still hanging open. Gently, I pushed on her chin and shut it.

"Wow," Rick said. "Wow."

"I can't believe she did it," Danielle said. "I just—I'm stunned."

"I'm proud," I declared. "Win was a jerk. Clare can do much better."

Danielle began to fan herself with one of the programs we'd been given on the way in. "Yeah, but on the altar! She couldn't have dumped him backstage or whatever?"

"I'm with Danielle on this one," Rick said, and I glared. "Okay, maybe she just couldn't work up the nerve until the big moment. But you have to admit that even if the guy's a jerk, this has to be harsh on his family."

"I guess I'll have to return this gift," I said, poking at the perfectly wrapped box on the pew next to me. "I even used her registry."

"And she looked so lovely in that dress," Danielle murmured. "What a waste."

The exodus was continuing.

Mr. and Mrs. Carrington passed us first. Mrs. Carrington looked as pale as rice. Mr. Carrington's face was a dangerous purplish red.

Trey, looking dapper in his tuxedo, followed and winked at us.

And then came the Wellmans, carbon copies of their not-to-be in-laws. White and red. Shock and fury.

The church emptied rapidly after that, but we three still sat, stunned.

Finally, Rick stood. "Well," he said, pretending to haul us both up off the pew. "I know it's been a shock and all but I, for one, could use a drink."

Danielle smiled feebly. "Look at us. We're all dressed up. We just have to go someplace. Plus," she added, "I'm really kind of down right now. I could use some company."

I don't know what possessed me. I don't. But when we all had shuffled out into the center aisle, I gave Danielle a great big hug.

"Thanks," she said, her eyes tearing.

"Don't mention it," I answered, my own eyes welling up. "I mean it. Don't ever mention it again."

Clare

Postmortem

My father, furious, went back to Michigan on the very next plane to Detroit. My brothers and their wives dutifully joined him.

My mother, oddly calm, offered to stay with me for a few days. I hesitated before thanking her and accepting her offer.

That first night I holed up alone in one of the rooms of the hotel suite my father had abandoned.

The second night I slept in the king-sized bed with my mother. I cried for hours. My mother cried at intervals. Neither of us got much sleep.

At one point, very late, I thought I heard my mother whisper these words: "I'm sorry, Clare. I'm so sorry."

The next morning the words seemed like a dream and I didn't ask my mother to verify their reality. It was good enough that I had heard them, no matter the source.

I moved out of the loft immediately and rented a small apartment in the Fenway area. Mother flew home.

Finally, I called Gincy and Danielle. Each had left messages on my cell phone but I just hadn't been ready to talk. We met a week to the date after the wedding that wasn't. Gincy had another drink coupon for the Good News Bar and Cafe.

"I don't feel at all bad for Mr. Jerry McJilted," Gincy declared. "He was an idiot and he still got a vacation out of it. Win and his best man on the shores of Tahiti. I wonder if . . . Ugh. I forgot Win and Alan are cousins. Anyway, Clare, I think you should have kept the ring and then sold it and used the money for a fabulous vacation for yourself and your girlfriends."

"I had to give the ring back," I said. "It cost Win a fortune. It wouldn't have been right to keep it. Besides, I didn't even like it."

Danielle's eyes bugged. I noted she looked a bit haggard but I said nothing.

"What!" she cried. "It was a three-carat cushion-cut central diamond with two carats' worth of diamonds in the band! A platinum band!"

Gincy grinned. "I thought you only liked yellow gold?"

"I'd have made an exception. My God, the thing was gorgeous!"

"It was too much for me," I admitted. "Too big and flashy."

Danielle leaned against the back of her stool. "Water. I need water! I mean it, someone call the bartender!"

I smiled, glad to be with my friends again.

"Anyway," I said, "I'm sorry I broke the engagement the way I did. I think I'll always be sorry. But I just couldn't do it until that critical moment. It was now or never, do or die. And I just couldn't die."

Gincy raised her beer bottle. "You're a brave woman, Clare," she said. "I really admire you."

I smiled ruefully. "I hope I feel brave when I'm all alone at night in my new little apartment. I'm completely without all the amenities Win had installed in the condo. I mean, I hardly ever used the dishwasher but at least I had a choice. Now, I'm lucky to have a microwave."

"Can't your parents help you out?" Danielle asked, in all innocence.

So I finally told them about the monthly allowance my parents had been sending me. And about how as punishment for running out on my wedding, my father had sworn he'd never give me another cent.

"My mother's furious with him," I said. "She can't believe he wants to cut me off entirely. I don't know why she's surprised. I half suspected it would happen. But I am grateful for her support. Staying with me after the—well, after the almost-wedding. Helping me to find an apartment and move out of the loft."

I shrugged. "Who knows? Maybe this will be a turning point for her, too. Daddy's been pretty condescending to Mother for the past forty years. Maybe now it's finally time for her to fight back. Stand up for herself. You know, before my mother married she was accepted to several very good graduate programs in art history. Maybe now she'll go back to school . . ."

I trailed off, not wanting to put too much energy into vague possibilities.

"One person is brave enough to change and others follow," Gincy said, and I knew she was thinking of Rick and herself. "You are brave, Clare. And maybe you've helped your mom to be brave, too."

Maybe. But my only intention had been to save my own life.

"I wish I could have been brave years ago," I admitted, "before things got so—so settled with Win. Before I hurt so many people."

"We all wish we could have done things differently," Danielle said softly.

"I'm sorry about you and Chris," I said.

She shrugged. "It's okay. You never know what will happen."

Gincy eyed her shrewdly. "What's going on in that fluffy brain of yours?"

"Nothing. So, how's everything with you and Rick?"

"Ah, conveniently changing the subject. Things are fine. We've already had one fight over our stuff. You know, he thinks his stuff is more important than mine, which it's not, and I think my stuff is more important than his, which it is."

I laughed. "Sounds like you're doing just fine," I said.

I hoped she was. I hoped Danielle would be okay.

And I so hoped that I would be, too.

Danielle
Who's Sorry Now

My friends had inspired me.

Both had taken such enormous risks. Both had been so brave.

Gincy's bravery seemed to have snuck up on her. She'd gone to Rick's apartment to end their relationship. Both Clare and I had been ready for a phone call of distress. We'd been ready to rush to her apartment and sit up with her all night as she stamped out her grief.

Instead, we'd each gotten a brief call made from Rick's apartment telling us to go to bed. Telling us that she was fine. Promising that she'd tell us more in the morning.

"Be happy for me," she'd said. "I'm so freakin' happy I could plotz!"

Clare's declaration of independence had been a touch more deliberate. She'd been unhappy and discontent for months. In passive-aggressive ways she'd tried to show Win her anger and her disappointment. And, as usual with such methods, she'd failed.

Finally, at the very moment of truth, she'd found the courage to speak honestly.

My friends were strong women. Not perfect—who was?—but they were really trying.

I wanted to be worthy of them. So I thought I'd give it one more try.

I missed him in Menemsha, where the Childs' Seafoods major boats were docked. Johnny told me he'd gone in to Oak Bluffs.

I found Chris just coming out of the Rattlesnake, one of his favorite hangouts.

I wasn't at all sure he was glad to see me. His face was a rapid play of emotions. Surprise. Pleasure. And annoyance.

And certainly his greeting was less than encouraging. "Danielle," he said flatly. "What are you doing here?"

"I had to see you," I said. "I want us to . . ."

The air was wet and chilly, more than hinting at fall. I shivered, and Chris unenthusiastically suggested we go inside.

He indicated the barstool on which I should perch. He remained standing.

"Let me go first," he said. "One of the reasons I was first attracted to you was because you were so different from any woman I'd ever known. You were so exciting. Every moment with you was a surprise. A good surprise."

"Thank you," I whispered. "I felt the same. I feel the same. I—"

"Let me finish, Danielle." Chris pushed his hair off his forehead with both hands and sighed.

Was I such a burden?

"I think I was wrong to get together with you," he said, looking me square in the eye. "I don't think two people from such different lives can make it work. Not for the long run. Not for a lifetime. I should never have asked you to make a commitment to me, Danielle. It was unfair. I'm sorry."

"No," I pleaded, reaching for his arm. "It wasn't unfair, what you asked. I—"

Chris recoiled as if I were somehow contaminated. "I'm sorry, Danielle. I just can't do this. And . . . I think you've got to move on. You're bad news for me. You're going to be bad news for any guy until you figure out what it is you want."

To say his words stung me, to say they were a slap in the face, to say they wounded my pride—all would be a terrible under-statement.

No one—no one!—had ever said such a horrible thing to me.

And the worse part about it all was that Chris was right.

I was bad news even to myself.

"I hate that you're so smart," I said finally, my voice thick with emotion. "I can't even tell you to shut up because I know you're right."

Chris gave me a sad sort of smile. "I'm not any smarter than you are, Danielle. I just got here ahead of you, that's all. And I'm still alone, so what does it really matter?"

"I don't want to end up alone," I said, inanely.

"That's up to you, Danielle," he said, not unkindly. "Your life is totally up to you."

Gincy
Best-Laid Plans

Danielle lay facedown across her bed.

I wanted to shake her silly for having gone back out to the Vineyard in search of Chris. Sure, maybe it was partly my fault that she'd gone, all that stuff I'd said about her chickening out and all.

What had I been thinking? I'd never even been totally convinced Chris was the right guy for her!

Me and my big mouth.

"The only reason I took the house this summer was to meet Mr. Right," she sobbed. "I didn't do it to have fun or to get girl-friends."

"But you did have fun," I reminded her. "And you did get girl-friends. You got me."

"And me," Clare added, handing Danielle another tissue.

"It's what we all got. Friends. I'd say it was a pretty good deal all around."

"You got Rick," Danielle mumbled, wiping at her wet cheeks.

Okay. Good point.

"For now," I admitted. "Maybe it will last. I hope it does. But let's face it. Romance is a huge crap shoot. Finding someone who'll last over the long haul . . ."

"And sometimes the long haul itself brings out the inherent problems," Clare added. Not helpfully.

Danielle wailed magnificently. "I just . . . I just regret so much! I regret ever going out with Chris in the first place. What was I thinking!"

"You were thinking, 'what a cute guy! and he's so nice, too,' " Clare said. "Why shouldn't you have gone out with him?"

But our words of comfort were falling on deaf ears.

"I regret not inviting Chris to my birthday party. I regret not making a commitment to him. As if I had it in me to make a commitment to anyone!"

"Maybe," Clare said tentatively, shooting me a look of helplessness, "maybe deep down you really didn't want to get all tied up with Chris. That's okay, too."

Danielle sobbed. "If deep down I didn't want to be tied to Chris, then I regret that, too!"

Poor kid, I thought. This was going to take some time.

I patted her shoulder. "You know what Katharine Hepburn said about regrets?" I asked.

Danielle shook her head and snorted into a tissue.

"She said that if you don't have any, you must be stupid."

Danielle sobbed even more loudly. "Easy for her to say! She was rich and gorgeous! And she had Spencer Tracy forever. Almost."

"I suspect their relationship wasn't all it was made out to be by the romantics," Clare assured her quietly. "Try not to focus on what other people have or don't have. Just think about how Danielle can be happy again."

Danielle flipped over to her back and sat up on the rumpled bed. She looked like hell. It was the first time I'd ever seen her looking less than perfect and I was pretty sure it would be the last.

"Maybe," she said, "we could make a promise to each other. Maybe we could promise we'll try to stay friends for as long as we live. No matter where we each wind up in life. Maybe we should promise that we'll meet once a year, even when we're old and creaky and incontinent and in wheelchairs and no one loves us and—"

"Jesus, Danielle," I cried, "can you be more depressing? Look, you're the only one who's thirty. Give us the chance to grow old after you and then we'll talk about the future. Sheesh."

Clare smiled. "I think Danielle has a very good idea. I can see us all forty years from now, crazy old ladies sharing our life stories . . ."

Danielle frowned anew. "I am saying this now. I am so not ever wearing a purple dress with a red hat or a caftan or a housedress or corrective shoes. I don't care how senile I get. Shoot me if I even think about it."

I rolled my eyes.

"Okay, we promise," Clare said.

And finally, finally, Danielle smiled. It was a good thing to see.

Epilogue

Gincy

All's Well That . . .

We didn't see much of each other after our lease on the Oak Bluffs house ended. We did keep up via e-mail, but without the excuse of a common destination—Martha's Vineyard—we each retreated to our separate lives.

I suppose it was normal. I suppose it was to be expected.

I mean, there was daily life to get through, jobs and responsibilities, and everyone's annual cold or flu.

Life.

Like turning thirty. Like celebrating the holidays for the first time with Rick and Justin. Like getting a promotion.

But by the time February grumped in I was ready to think again about my friends. And about the summer. I told Rick I had something kind of crazy in mind and he just shrugged.

"What else is new?" he said.

We met at George, just us three.

"So, what do you say? We rent a house?"

Danielle groaned. "Just not the same dump, please!"

."Oh, I think it would be nice to rent the same place," Clare said. "It's got memories now."

I laughed. "Oddly, I'm with Danielle on this one. Maybe it's living with Rick or maybe it's age but my taste is improving. I say we start the search now and get something decent."

Clare shrugged. "What about girls-only weekends?" she suggested.

We each thought that a good idea.

"Does Justin qualify as a guy?" Clare asked then. "I mean, he's only a child. Are you really a guy at the age of five?"

"Does he pee standing up?" Danielle asked.

"Uh, yeah," I said. "Of course."

"Then he's a guy. But okay, he can be the exception on girls-only weekend."

"He'd better be! I mean, he could be my own kid someday."

"Gincy!" Clare cried. "Are you and Rick talking about getting married?"

"Holy crap, not yet! But, you know, we are living together. You don't live with a guy with a kid without the topic of marriage coming up every once in a while."

"What's once in a while?" Danielle demanded.

I squirmed. "I don't know. Like, every week. Or so. Once every week or so. Twice a week, tops."

"I can help you plan the wedding!" Danielle said brightly.

Clare shot me a look that said, "Don't go there. Ever."

"You want to hear something funny?" I said. "Well, not funny, exactly. Get this. My father, a man who'd only been to Boston once when he was about nineteen, has visited me twice since I moved in with Rick. I know the first time was to make sure I wasn't living with some drug addict in a hovel."

Danielle nodded approvingly. "He only did what any good father would do."

"How does he get along with Rick?" Clare asked.

"Fine," I told them. "You know, Dad's not exactly a great conversationalist, but so far no punches have been thrown. And Dad and Justin have totally hit it off. I mean, we have to tear Justin away from Dad when it's time for bed. He calls him Pop. Isn't that cute? It's like they're buddies. Like, Rick's a menace with any kind of tool and Dad's a whiz, so suddenly, Dad's become this Construction Man hero-type. He even gave Justin his own set of tools. And believe me, they've put them to use on all the stuff Rick never got around to fixing. Like the bedroom door, which was hanging by one hinge. Thank God for screwdrivers and the macho guys who know how to use them."

"I never thought I'd hear you so psyched about family," Clare noted.

"Me, neither," I admitted. "But if there's one thing I've learned since we all met last May it's 'expect the unexpected.' I mean, my father had been telling me that since I was a kid but I never listened. You know, there's something to clichés. People use them for a reason."

"So what about your brother?" Danielle asked. "Tommy, right? Have you guys gotten any closer?"

Sure, I thought. *Let's talk about the one area in which I've made no progress.*

"You know," I said, "I only have so much energy. It's huge I'm with Rick and Justin. It's huge I'm actually getting to know my father and he's getting to know me. I just can't handle Tommy right now. Maybe some day. Or not."

"Okay, so what about your mom?"

I glared at Danielle. "You never let up, do you? Jeez. I don't know. Sometimes I think I'll never have a decent relationship with my mother. Who knows? She's never made an effort, but then again, neither have I. Right now, I'll take what I can get. End of this conversation."

"What ever happened to your friend Sally, from work?" Clare asked in all innocence. "How's she doing?"

I hesitated. I'd told Rick about what had happened that night in my apartment. But I hadn't told Danielle or Clare, less to protect Sally's privacy than to hide my own culpability.

But now, I revealed all.

"Ouch," Danielle remarked.

"Yeah, ouch. But I hope she's happy. She left Boston for a job out in California," I told them. "I don't expect I'll ever hear from her again."

"That's okay, honey," Danielle said, patting my hand as if she were my grandmother. "You have me and Clare. And we're all the girlfriends you need."

Oh, yeah.

Clare

The Start of Something

I was glad when Gincy called and suggested we get together. Life had been super-full since the aborted wedding, but still, I missed my girlfriends.

"My father still isn't speaking to me," I admitted. "It broke my heart at first. He just couldn't understand. Or he wouldn't. He says I embarrassed the family and that's an unforgivable act."

Gincy scowled and held her tongue. I knew it cost her.

"Either way," I went on, "I'm still not happy about the situation. But I am rethinking just about everything in my life. And I'm realizing Daddy wasn't such a great father to me. In a way I don't care if he won't speak to me because I have nothing to say to him. Yet."

Danielle sat back as if stunned. I knew family meant all to her.

"Do you ever hear from Win?" Gincy asked, tossing back the last of her beer.

I laughed uncomfortably. "Oh, no. I think that as far as Win's concerned I'm just too big of an embarrassing memory."

"I bet he's getting dates with his sob story of being left at the altar by his bitch of a fiancée," Gincy said.

"Maybe. His mother called me once, back around Christmas. It was horribly awkward. I'd sent a note of apology in October when I returned her dress, but . . . Well, let's just say all is not for-given."

"You poor thing," Danielle murmured.

Yeah, poor me. The victim. Or the victimizer?
I wondered.

What was the point in telling my friends now, all these months later?

What was the point in not telling them?

"I cheated on Win once," I blurted. "Last summer."

"What!" Danielle cried, leaping from her stool and grabbing my shoulders. "And you didn't tell us?"

"Ow," I said, removing her hands. "I'm telling you now."
And I did.

And then I filled them in on Eason. My new guy. The library guy.

"Sooo," Danielle drawled, "are we hearing wedding bells in the foreseeable future?"

"God, no!" I cried. "I had way too close a call back in September. There's no way I'm talking about marriage again for a long, long time. If ever."

"This guy Eason doesn't push?" Gincy asked.

"No, not at all. He respects my need to go slow. With the com-mitment part."

Danielle's eyes gleamed. "So you are having sex?"

"Of course!"

"And . . ."

"What? I'm not talking about that. It's personal."

"Personal?" Gincy repeated. "You just told us you cheated on your fiancé! Look, just tell us this. Compared to Win, how would you rate Eason?"

I hesitated. "Well, if Win was, say, I don't know—this is embar-rassing!"

"Oh, come on," Danielle coaxed. "After all we've gone through with you? Dealing with your furious father and your swooning mother after you'd run screaming from the church?"

"I wasn't screaming. And I didn't run. Exactly. But, okay. You're right. I owe you something. Okay. If Win was a—five—"

"Poor thing!" Danielle cried. "No wonder you left him at the altar."

"—then Eason is a . . ."

"A what?" Gincy was grinning. "A nine? A ten?"

"No." Could I say it? "A twenty."

"Whoo-hoo! Girlfriend hit the jackpot!"

"How did you two hook up finally, anyway?" Danielle asked.

"I know it sounds impossible, but we met again in the library in early November. It was the third time."

Gincy nodded wisely. "Ah, the charm."

"You do go other places, right?" Danielle asked. "I mean, like restaurants and movies?"

"Oh, sure. And when spring comes we're going to do some camping. Win wasn't a big fan so we never went. I've really missed the outdoors, and Eason's got all his own equipment. It should be fun. We'll do some hiking, too."

"Do you think you'd consider leaving Boston someday?" Gincy asked suddenly. "For some small town with like, a general store and a local swimming hole? God, I couldn't wait to get out of that kind of environment!"

"Well, you know how I feel about the L.L. Bean lifestyle," I joked. "Anyway, I'm not making any plans for the future yet, with or without Eason. He knows how I feel. He seems okay with it. We'll just have to see how it goes."

"You sound awfully Zen-like."

I laughed. "Either that or I'm still just so horribly tired from having faked my life for so long. I guess on some level I just don't care what happens with Eason in the end. I just want to be honest this time, with myself and with him."

Gincy eyed me carefully. "It's almost as if you're a completely different person from the girl I met last May. You were so hesitant. But there was also a sense that you were about to explode."

"And I did, didn't I?"

Danielle rolled her eyes. "Honey, it was spectacular."

Danielle
Back to the Beginning

I knew the subject was going to come up.

"Did you ever tell your family about Chris?" Clare asked me. "About what happened in the end?"

"No."

Gincy looked doubtful. "Not even David? He'd understand. And you two are so close."

I sighed. "No," I repeated. "Why should I bother talking about it? It's all over now, anyway."

My friends looked at each other and then back to me.

"But you were in love," Clare said gently. "Weren't you?"

How could I help my friends understand? "I don't think I was," I said. "Not really. I mean, Chris meant something to me. But in the end . . ."

I took a deep breath. Those two were always causing me grief. Testing me. Someday they'd give me a heart attack. "Okay, look," I said, "I kept that silly bracelet Chris gave me. The shell one. It's in a box and I'll never wear it again but I just couldn't bear to throw it out. I'm still not sure if Chris is a good memory or a bad one. Maybe I'll never figure it out."

"But the bracelet will remind you of an important lesson, right?" Gincy looked at me in expectation.

I looked back at her challengingly.

"Danielle," Clare said quickly.

Good girl. Once again defusing a potential fight.

"Last summer I was so preoccupied with my own situation with Win I didn't spend much time thinking about yours. But later, when I took the time to consider, well, I thought it seemed kind of odd that Chris was pressing for a commitment so early in your relationship."

Gincy nodded. "Yeah. I thought so, too. Okay, Rick wanted a commitment from me early on, too, but he didn't demand. He asked. Danielle, I'm thinking maybe it's way better you backed off."

"I think I might have idealized Chris, just a bit," I admitted finally. "I think I might have focused so much energy on him because the idea of finding Mr. Right and getting married really terrified me. Even though I thought that what I wanted was to hurry up and get married."

Gincy grinned. "Serious insight! Have you been seeing a therapist?"

"No, of course not. I'm not as empty-headed as you think I am."

"I never said you were empty-headed!" Gincy protested.

I just rolled my eyes at her.

"So," Clare asked, "are you seeing anyone special?"

"Yes," I told them. "I most certainly am. It started slowly, but we're picking up speed as we go."

"Well, who is he?" Gincy demanded.

I'd forgotten how fun it was to annoy her. She was so easily aggravated. Really, she was the one who should have been in therapy, learning patience.

"It's Barry, the guy I met at my birthday party last August. The Rothsteins' friend. And before you make any judgments, let me say that I really like him. Really. We're very suited for each other."

"But didn't you dump him?" Gincy demanded.

She really was impossible.

"I didn't dump him. I—Oh, never mind! Anyway, I called him again just before I was flying home for Christmas. And yes, my

parents have a tree, why not. Anyway, luckily Barry was available.
Since then we've been seeing each other about twice a month.
He comes here and I go there. And we try not to spend the en-
tire time with my parents."

"And in between?" Clare asked.

I knew someone would ask.

"Are you seeing other guys?"

"No. And that's fine. I'm working on falling in love."

"What about your system?" Gincy asked. "Still keeping that
notebook? How does Barry rate on, oh, I don't know, hairstyle?"

"I abandoned the system. No more checklists. And his hair is
great, by the way."

Both Gincy and Clare spontaneously clapped.

"Good for you!" Clare said.

We ordered another round of drinks and some appetizers.

"So," Gincy asked when the waiter had gone, "you never heard
from Chris after that last time? Just after Clare's, uh, non-
wedding?"

I cringed. But I'd admitted everything else . . .

"I sent him an e-mail in early November. And before you yell,
yes, I know it was stupid."

"What did you say to him?" Gincy asked.

I sighed. "God this is embarrassing. I told him I could come
out and see him if he liked. And other stuff. You really don't
want to know."

"Oh, Danielle."

Clare patted my hand.

I tried to smile but I'm afraid it came out a grimace. "Anyway,
he e-mailed back. His spelling was abysmal. He told me he'd
moved on. He'd met some girl who'd moved back to the Vineyard
after like fifteen years away. Some girl he'd known when he was a
kid. God, I wouldn't be surprised if he was married by now! And
he asked me not to contact him again. Can you imagine? I felt
like a stalker."

Gincy's face turned red and I knew her well enough by then
to know she was just aching to punch Chris in the face.

I loved her the more for it.

"That's horrible, Danielle," Clare said, consolingly. "But it's also probably for the best. At least he didn't play around with your heart. At least he was honest about his situation—"

"Right," I cut in. "Just like I was with him. Don't remind me."

Our drinks arrived and I took an appreciative sip of my martini.

"Jumping way ahead," Gincy said, "what happens if you and Barry decide to get married? Is he going to leave New York for you? Move to Boston?"

About some things the girl would never learn.

"Gincy, don't be silly. Men never change cities for women. Of course I'll move back to New York. Anyway, it's not like it will be a sacrifice. I love New York. It's my home."

"Yeah, but what about your job?" she pressed. "Your career?"

I smiled at her fondly. "That is a joke, right? You can't think I really care about my job. Gincy, I've been waiting all my adult life to quit work. I've always considered work just something to do until I decide to get married."

"And if you don't decide to get married?" Clare asked.

Good question.

"Well," I said, "if I don't get married . . . Ugh, then I'll just have to keep working. Can we please change the subject?"

"You, Danielle Sarah Leers, are priceless."

"I know!" I said.

And I finally believed it.

S0-CFC-196

℮lmer Towns may have already become to you what he has to me—a very helpful friend! Think then of the blessings of a helpful friend assisting us to study the personal characteristics of the "Most Helpful Friend"—the Holy Spirit—whom Jesus sent as the ultimate Helper.

As always, Dr. Towns is practical, thorough and inspiring—and with the Holy Spirit as *both* the subject *and* his Helper in this project, we have reason to expect a book packed with refreshing insights and useful study resources.

JACK W. HAYFORD, D. LITT.
Senior Pastor
The Church On The Way

THE NAMES OF THE HOLY SPIRIT

OF THE

*Understanding the Names
of the Holy Spirit and
How They Can Help You
Know God More Intimately*

ELMER L. TOWNS

Regal

A Division of Gospel Light
Ventura, California, U.S.A.

Published by Regal Books
A Division of Gospel Light
Ventura, California, U.S.A.
Printed in U.S.A.

Regal Books is a ministry of Gospel Light, an evangelical Christian publisher dedicated to serving the local church. We believe God's vision for Gospel Light is to provide church leaders with biblical, user-friendly materials that will help them evangelize, disciple and minister to children, youth and families.

It is our prayer that this Regal Book will help you discover biblical truth for your own life and help you meet the needs of others. May God richly bless you.

For a free catalog of resources from Regal Books/Gospel Light please contact your Christian supplier or call 1-800-4-GOSPEL.

Scripture quotations in this publication are from the *New King James Version.* Copyright © 1979, 1980, 1982 Thomas Nelson, Inc. Used by permission.

The following versions are also used:
KJV—King James Version. Public domain.
Scripture quotations marked *(NIV)* are taken from the *Holy Bible, New International Version®. NIV®.* Copyright © 1973, 1978, 1984 by International Bible Society. Used by permission of Zondervan Publishing House. All right reserved.

NOTE: The above Bible versions are used intermittently for the Scripture references in the appendices.

© Copyright 1994 by Elmer L. Towns
All rights reserved.

Library of Congress Cataloging-in-Publication Data
Towns, Elmer L.
    The names of the Holy Spirit / Elmer L. Towns.
        p. cm.
    ISBN 0-8307-1676-9
    1. Holy Spirit—Name. I. Title.
BT121.2.T68 1994   93-45026
231'.3—dc20   CIP

5 6 7 8 9 10 11 12 13 14 / 02 01 00 99 98 97

Rights for publishing this book in other languages are contracted by Gospel Literature International (GLINT). GLINT also provides technical help for the adaptation, translation and publishing of Bible study resources and books in scores of languages worldwide. For further information, contact GLINT, P.O. Box 4060, Ontario, CA 91761-1003, U.S.A., or the publisher.

Contents

SECTION III
The Nature of the Holy Spirit

Introduction

I have been fascinated with names all my life, perhaps because my name—Elmer—is not a common one. I have both liked and disliked my name since I was a small boy. I remember some friends making fun of my name in the first grade. It seems there was a comedy character on radio named Elmer at whom people laughed—he was considered dumb. When I asked my mother why I had that name, she told me it was because "I loved your father." I was named after him. So I liked the name after that, no matter what others said.

My fascination with names led me to write *The Names of Jesus* (Accent Books, 1988). In the appendix, I listed more than 800 names, titles and references to Jesus.

Then I wrote *My Father's Names* (Regal Books, 1991), primarily analyzing the names of God in the Old Testament. I listed in the appendix more than 100 of His names and titles.

Because the Holy Spirit is the Third Person of the Trinity, I naturally wanted to write a book on His name. This book finishes the trilogy. I have listed more than 100 names, descriptive phrases and titles for the Holy Spirit in appendix 1.

In this study, however, you will learn more than the Spirit's names. You will also learn about His personality, and what He does for you today. This book is, therefore, more than a doctrinal study of the names of the Holy Spirit. I want you to learn about Him, to know Him and to experience Him in your life.

People usually do not think of the term "Holy Spirit" as a name. Instead, they think of the phrase as a description. Maybe this is because they do not think of the Spirit as a person. People think of Him as an influence and give Him a title just as they give a title to boats, cars or hurricanes. They think of Him as an influence, as "the spirit of democracy," or "the spirit of the Yankees."

Because people pray to "Our Father in heaven," or they pray, "Dear Jesus," they know of the Father and the Son as persons. But most people never pray to the Holy Spirit, perhaps because they do not think of Him as a person. Some do think the command, "Pray the Lord of the harvest" (Matt. 9:38) is directed to the Holy Spirit; also, "the Lord is the Spirit" (2 Cor. 3:17). And Scripture shows examples of prayer to the Lord as the Spirit present among His people— instances in which the Spirit responds to the prayers being offered (see Luke 2:25-29; Acts 10:9,13-15,19; 11:5,7,8,12; 13:2; 15:28).

I can't write about the names of the Holy Spirit and not write about the Trinity. When describing the Trinity, I like to use the statement written by the Early Church fathers in the Athanasian Creed: "We worship one God in Trinity and Trinity in unity, neither confounding the persons, nor dividing the substance."

To explain how the doctrine of the Trinity works, I have used the following statement: "The members of the Trinity are equal in nature, separate in person but submissive in duty." In this book, therefore, I have emphasized three things.

First, this book equally emphasizes the deity of the Holy Spirit with God the Father and God the Son—they all have the same nature, attributes and character.

Second, this book separates the personality of the Holy Spirit from the personality of the Father and the personality of the Son—the Godhead consists of three separate persons.

Third, this book emphasizes the duties of the Holy Spirit,

who was sent by the Father and the Son to carry out the work of God in the world.

When I asked some authorities to read this book, most of them were surprised. They indicated that they had never seen all these names for the Holy Spirit gathered in one place. I taught this series in the Pastor's Bible Class at Thomas Road Baptist Church in Lynchburg, Virginia, where approximately a thousand people gather weekly to study the Scripture. Just as in my two previous books, *The Names of Jesus* and *My Father's Names*, the congregation was fascinated with the content, wanting to know more. I feel my best books have been hammered out in the arena of a class's receptivity before being offered to the publisher.

This book is aimed beyond the study of Bible facts. I want you to feel the Holy Spirit living through you. I wrote this book to do more than fill academic curiosity. It should help you live successfully for God. Each chapter, therefore, concludes by offering principles to be applied to life.

One name or title is missing in this study: the term "ghost," as in Holy Ghost. The original *King James Version* (1611) translated the word *pneuma* "Ghost" as in, "Ye shall be baptized with the Holy Ghost" (Acts 1:5), and, "after that the Holy Ghost is come upon you" (Acts 1:8). This has resulted in confusion in some minds.

Some think the word "ghost" refers to a phantom, as in "the ghosts of Halloween." But the word *pneuma* should be translated "Spirit." The word "ghost" had a different meaning in 1611 than it does today and this difference blurs the personality of the Third Person of the Trinity for some. The solution to this confusion is simple. Every time the term "Holy Ghost" is found in the original *King James Version,* it should be translated "Holy Spirit." If you prefer to use the name Holy Ghost, do so, as long as you understand the meaning of the name you are using. For the Holy Spirit is the furthest thing from a phantom. He is very real.

His primary name, Holy Spirit, has a twofold implication. First, when we take the Holy Spirit into our lives, He should make us holy, as His name implies. "Or do you not know that your body is the temple of the Holy Spirit who is in you, whom you have from God, and you are not your own?" (1 Cor. 6:19). Second, when we live by the principles of the Holy Spirit, He will make us spiritual, because we become like Him. You should become holy and spiritual as you study the Holy Spirit.

I want to thank the many people who have helped me understand the Holy Spirit. My theology of the Holy Spirit was transformed by reading *He That Is Spiritual* by Lewis S. Chafer (Zondervan, 1964), founder of Dallas Theological Seminary. Before this, I was afraid of the Holy Spirit because of some extremes I saw in some churches. I had an unfortunate experience as a young believer and was turned off to any emphasis on the Holy Spirit throughout my life.

I also want to recognize John R. Rice for convincing me that power in service comes from the Holy Spirit. He urged me to seek His power. I appreciate how Larry Gilbert clarified my thinking about the gifts of the Holy Spirit. Dr. Douglas Porter, a former student and a graduate of Liberty Baptist Theological Seminary, challenged me to think about the many names of God. We discussed these matters for hours, and he helped in the research for this book.

Many have contributed to my thinking about the Holy Spirit, but in the last analysis, we are all a product of our teachers and friends. Just as every tub must sit on its own bottom, so I must take responsibility for all the weaknesses and omissions of this volume.

May God make you more holy and more spiritual as you study these terms for His Holy Spirit.

Elmer L. Towns
Lynchburg, Virginia
Summer, 1994

SECTION I

Jesus and the Holy Spirit

CHAPTER 1

The Helper: Jesus' Favorite Name for the Holy Spirit

THE MINISTRY OF THE HELPER

Preconversion Ministry

1. Helper/Prosecuting Attorney   His role in convicting us of sin.
2. Helper/Crossing Guard   His role in restraining us from sin.

Ministry at Conversion

1. Helper/Interior Decorator   His role of renewing spiritual life.
2. Helper/Apartment Manager   His role of indwelling the believer.
3. Helper/Notary Public   His role of guaranteeing our salvation.

Postconversion Ministry

1. Helper/Administrative Assistant   His role in filling us for service.
2. Helper/Search Committee   His role in setting us apart to God.
3. Helper/Teacher   His role in explaining spiritual truth to the believer.
4. Helper/Lawyer   His role in presenting our prayers to the Father.

What is Jesus' favorite name for the Holy Spirit?" I asked a minister as I was writing this chapter.

"I never thought about it before," my pastor friend responded. I then explained this book and what I wanted to accomplish with it. Then my friend said to me, "I think Jesus' favorite name is 'Holy Spirit.'"

Obviously he thought of the Third Person of the Trinity as the Holy Spirit because of His title. But is a title the same thing as a name? The title "Father" for the First Person of the Trinity is designated a name (see John 17:1). This was

Jesus' favorite name for God. The Second Person of the Trinity is Jesus: "You shall call His name JESUS" (Matt. 1:21). Yet, Jesus' favorite name for Himself was "Son of Man," a title He used more than any other.

The name or title "Spirit" is used approximately 500 times in Scripture in reference to the Third Person, and the combined term "Holy Spirit" is used approximately 100 times. The expression "Holy Ghost," used 91 times in the *King James Version,* should be translated Holy Spirit.

My name is Elmer, but when I first had children their favorite name for me was Dad. My wife calls me "Sweetheart." That could be her favorite title for me.

My minister friend told me Jesus' favorite name for the Third Person of the Trinity is "Holy Spirit." He thought so because it is used so many times in Scripture. But I disagree.

Jesus' favorite name for the Holy Spirit was probably "Helper." Of all the things the Holy Spirit does, He helps us obtain the personal salvation that was accomplished for us on the Cross. In the *King James Version,* the name "Helper" is translated "Comforter." Jesus promised, "And I will pray the Father, and He will give you another Helper, that He may abide with you forever" (John 14:16). The Greek word "helper" is *parakletos,* and may be translated "helper, comforter, advocate or one called alongside." This term is related to the compound verb with the prefix *para* meaning "alongside" and the verbal base *kaleo* meaning "to call."

Although the name "Helper" for the Holy Spirit occurs only four times, I think it is Jesus' favorite name because it best identifies what the Holy Spirit does. Each time this name is used in Scripture, it is used by Jesus Christ (see cf. John 14:16,26; 15:26; 16:7). Jesus repeated the name "Helper" during the Upper Room Discourse, perhaps the most intimate of all the recorded sermons of Christ. I think it is Jesus' favorite name for the Holy Spirit because it relates to salvation.

After I asked my friend the question, "What is Jesus' favorite name for the Holy Spirit?" he finally came back and said to me, "I didn't think of the Holy Spirit as having a name."

WHY WE DON'T RECOGNIZE HIS NAMES

My friend is similar to a lot of people who think of the Holy Spirit as an influence, an attitude or a corporate opinion. Some of the titles in the *King James Version* have contributed to misinformation about the Holy Spirit's name. The name "Holy Ghost" makes people think of Him as a Halloween spook, and the name "Comforter" makes people think of Him as a quilt on a bed, or someone who comes and comforts people at a funeral.

Perhaps people do not recognize the names of the Holy Spirit because of certain implications in Scripture. First, Jesus promised that the Holy Spirit would come but He also emphasized a major thrust of His ministry would be glorifying Christ (see John 16:14). Because the Holy Spirit talks more of Jesus than Himself, many Christians have concluded they should not glorify the Holy Spirit. They do not speak to Him and do not know Him. But as the Third Person of the Godhead, the Holy Spirit should receive glory just as much as the Father and the Son.

Another reason people do not recognize the Holy Spirit's name is because of His task. The Father initiates the process of salvation, and the Son carries it out on Calvary. But the Holy Spirit works in the heart of the believer to effect that which the Son has done.

This work of the Spirit can be compared to the construction of a large building. The owners of the building who initiate its construction are remembered as well as the engineer and the architects. But most people do not remember the workers who do the actual work. In a similar way, most people do not give attention to the Holy Spirit, who actually applies salvation in our hearts.

Another reason the Holy Spirit is not recognized is because He did not come in the flesh. No one doubts that Jesus was a person or that He had a corporeal body on earth. The most obvious physical manifestation we see of the Holy Spirit is when He descended as a dove upon Jesus at His baptism (see Mark 1:10), and as tongues of fire on the Day of Pentecost (see Acts 2:3).

In the Old Testament, however, the Holy Spirit is identified with the pillar of cloud and fire through which the Lord guided the Israelites at the Exodus and in the wilderness wanderings (see Exod. 13:21; 19:16-19; Isa. 63:11-14; Heb. 12:29).

Also, Paul identifies the Spirit of the Lord as the source of the glory and radiance seen on Moses' face after he had entered the Lord's presence in the cloud covering Sinai (see Exod. 19:9; Deut. 31:15; Ps. 99:6,7; 2 Cor. 3:17,18). Ezekiel shows the Spirit of God manifesting Himself in glory, radiance and fire (see Ezek. 1:27—2:2).

As you read this book, ask for "Holy Spirit eyes" so you can see Him in Scripture. You will find more than 100 references to the names, titles and descriptions of the Holy Spirit in appendix 1. One person said to me, "Wow! I didn't know He had that many names." Perhaps that is because we are not accustomed to looking for them. Many Christians have "Holy Spirit blindness." They are blinded to the Holy Spirit because of the nature of His task, or because of some bias that grows out of their experience.

STOP before continuing to read, and breathe this prayer.

Lord, give me eyes to see the Holy Spirit in my life and in the Scriptures. In Jesus' name, Amen.

WHY A FAVORITE NAME?

Most of us like the name that best describes us. Certain women like to be called "Mom" because they see their main task as raising children. When I first began preaching, I pastored the Westminster Presbyterian Church in Savannah, Georgia, during my sophomore and junior years in Bible college. Obviously, I was too young for the scriptural titles that describe a pastor, such as elder, bishop or minister. I was not ordained, so I could not be called "Reverend." Everybody in the church called me "Preacher." Because I like to preach, and thought I did a pretty good job, I liked to be called "Preacher."

After graduating from seminary, I became a professor of Christian education at Midwest Bible College in St. Louis, Missouri. Again, I love to teach. All my students called me "Prof." I enjoyed that title because it described what I enjoyed doing. When people call us by names that reflect what we do best, we usually enjoy that designation.

A certain salesman was transferred from Chicago to Atlanta, and because he considered himself a good salesman, he decided to sell his house without the aid of a real estate company. He advertised and got a few people to come and walk through his house. The salesman gave a strong sales pitch to each prospect. But his hard-sell tactics produced no sales. After six frustrating months and the loss of time and money, he finally listed his house with a real estate agent.

What the salesman did not realize was that an agent counsels customers before showing them a home. The agent qualified customers so that he showed the salesman's home only to those who had the financial ability to purchase it. Also, the agent found customers who had a desire for a home similar to the salesman's home. Once he had shown the home, the agent could continue to point

THE HOLY SPIRIT HELPS YOU IN SALVATION

Preconversion	*Conversion*	*Postconversion*
1. Reprove/Convict (see John 16:7-10)	1. Regeneration (see Titus 3:5)	1. Fullness (see Eph. 5:18)
2. Restraint (see 2 Thess. 2:7)	2. Indwelling (see 1 Cor. 6:19)	2. Sanctification (see 2 Cor. 3:18)
	3. Sealing (see Eph. 4:30)	3. Illumination (see 1 Cor. 2:12)
		4. Prayer (see Rom. 8:26,27)

out the advantages and answer questions.

The work of the Holy Spirit in salvation is similar to that of the real estate agent. The Holy Spirit works conviction in the hearts of the unconverted long before they come to a gospel service. He witnesses to the person the positive reasons for salvation and warns against procrastination. The Holy Spirit is the Helper (paraclete) who gets a decision and seals the contract. Although this analogy cannot be pushed to every aspect of the Holy Spirit's work in salvation, it is illustrative of the process.

THE HELPER IN OUR CONVERSION

Before returning to the Father, Jesus promised that He would send "another Comforter," using the Greek word *allos* for "other," which means "another of the same kind." Jesus could have used the word *heteros* for "other," meaning another of a different kind. But Jesus used the word *allos*, which means the Holy Spirit is another Helper just as Jesus is our Helper.

Preconversion Ministries

The chart on the previous page shows nine helping ministries of the Holy Spirit. First, He reproves sin (see John 16:7-10), which means He is like a prosecuting attorney who helps the state prove a case of wrongdoing. Second, the Holy Spirit is the restrainer (see 2 Thess. 2:7), which means He is like the crossing guard that protects children on their way to elementary school. He helps by holding back harm and danger.

Conversion Ministries

In His conversion ministry, the Holy spirit regenerates (see Titus 3:5), which means He is like an interior decorator who renews an old room, making it new. Then the Holy Spirit indwells us (see 1 Cor. 6:19), which means He is like an apartment manager, one who comes to live in the complex to protect it, making sure all of the equipment is functioning. Finally, the Holy Spirit is our seal (see Eph. 4:30), which means He is like the notary public. He helps to guarantee the accuracy of the signature, and if necessary will testify in court.

Postconversion Names

In His postconversion ministry, the Holy Spirit fills the person (see Eph. 5:18). He is like an administrative assistant who comes in to help get the job done. Next, He is the sanctifier (see 2 Cor. 3:18), serving as a search committee chairman who helps the group select a leader, set the leader apart and put that person in a place of prominence. The Holy Spirit is the illuminator (see 1 Cor. 2:12), like the teacher who helps believers to understand and apply the Word of God to their lives. Then the Holy Spirit helps believers to pray (see Rom. 8:26,27), which is like a lawyer who helps people by presenting their cases before a magistrate.

HOW THE HOLY SPIRIT HELPS

The Helper/Prosecuting Attorney

The Holy Spirit is sent to help people become Christians. Before they can become saved, however, they must realize they are lost. The Holy Spirit helps unsaved people by revealing their sin to them. In this role, the Holy Spirit could be called the convictor, or reprover. Like a prosecuting attorney, He convicts people of their sin, enabling them to seek salvation.

As the helper/prosecuting attorney, the Holy Spirit helps to convict us of sin in three ways. First, He helps people see their sin. Jesus said the Holy Spirit will help convict people "of sin, because they do not believe in Me" (John 16:9). Before salvation, people have difficulty believing in God. Jesus said, "He who believes in Him [the Son] is not condemned; but he who does not believe is condemned already, because he has not believed in the name of the only begotten Son of God" (John 3:18). Therefore, the Holy Spirit helps people accept salvation by pointing out unbelief and bringing them to Christ.

Second, the Holy Spirit helps prosecute people concerning righteousness. Jesus said the Holy Spirit would convict "of righteousness, because I go to My Father and you see Me no more" (John 16:10). Hence, the Holy Spirit helps people see themselves in relationship to Jesus Christ. People do not measure up to Jesus Christ, who is God's righteous standard, so the Holy Spirit helps them see their shortcomings.

Third, the Holy Spirit helps people come to Christ by convicting them "of judgment, because the ruler of this world is judged" (John 16:11). This judgment does not refer to the coming judgment of all believers at the Great White Throne, but to the judgment of Satan and sin at the cross of Christ (see John 12:31).

The Helper/Crossing Guard

As bad as things are in the world, they are not as terrible as they might be if the Holy Spirit were not present in the world to restrict the persuasive influence of sin. In the role of restrainer of sin, the Holy Spirit is like a crossing guard who restrains children from running into the path of traffic. He helps the children by protecting them from harm. As the Restrainer or Crossing Guard, "He who now restrains will do so until He is taken out of the way [at the return of Christ]" (2 Thess. 2:7).

The Helper/Interior Decorator

The Holy Spirit helps us with our new life when we are saved. The Greek word translated "regeneration" is used only once in the Bible in the context of salvation, and it relates to the ministry of the Holy Spirit. "Not by works of righteousness which we have done, but according to His mercy He saved us, through the washing of regeneration and renewing of the Holy Spirit" (Titus 3:5). Regeneration is the theological word for being "born again." Jesus told Nicodemus, "Unless one is born of water and the Spirit, he cannot enter the kingdom of God" (John 3:5). This regeneration of the Holy Spirit gives us new life, makes us part of God's family, and gives us eternal life. This is not just life unending; it is a new quality of life (i.e., God's life). The Holy Spirit is like an interior decorator who takes a shabby old house and renovates it, making it like new.

The Helper/Apartment Manager

The indwelling of the Holy Spirit is like the manager of an apartment building. He lives in the building to tend to problems, to make sure the building is not damaged and to help people enjoy the apartment complex.

One of God's purposes from the very beginning was to live with His creatures. He walked with Adam in the garden, lived in the Tabernacle among the children of Israel in the wilderness and came to dwell in Solomon's temple. Likewise, the Holy Spirit comes to dwell in Christians to help them live the Christian life. "Or do you not know that your body is the temple of the Holy Spirit who is in you, whom you have from God, and you are not your own?" (1 Cor. 6:19). The Holy Spirit uses our body as a temple. This indwelling is the basis on which He helps us in every other area of our lives.

When we realize that the Holy Spirit indwells us as our Helper, we should first yield our bodies to God (see Rom. 12:1). Second, we must assist Him by properly caring for our physical bodies, keeping them pure and clean. Third, we should glorify God in our bodies by doing those things that please Him.

The Helper/Notary Public

The Holy Spirit seals us with Himself to guarantee our salvation. The Bible teaches that the Holy Spirit is more than One who seals us; He *is* our seal. "You were sealed with the Holy Spirit of promise, who is the guarantee of our inheritance until the redemption of the purchased possession" (Eph. 1:13,14).

Our lives consist of many seals. When a man and woman agree to marry, the man usually gives the woman an engagement ring, which is the seal of his commitment to her. Paul used a first-century custom to tell how the Holy Spirit is our seal. In the ancient world, a person would seal a letter with candle wax, then place his signet ring into the melted wax as the seal. When the recipient got the letter, the unbroken seal in the hardened wax guaranteed that the content was genuine.

In like manner, the Holy Spirit is our Notary Public in

that He guarantees God's "signature." He seals the salvation God has given to us against the day when we fully experience it in heaven. It is important that we "do not grieve the Holy Spirit of God, by whom you were sealed for the day of redemption" (Eph. 4:30).

The Helper/Administrative Assistant

The Holy Spirit comes every time we ask Him to fill us for service, just as an administrative assistant is available to perform a job until it is completed. The Holy Spirit dwells in us and, when we will allow Him, He will help us in our Christian lives and service. The Bible calls this the filling of the Holy Spirit (at other places in this book it is called the anointing). Paul encourages, "And do not be drunk with wine, in which is dissipation; but be filled with the Spirit" (Eph. 5:18). This imperative is in the present tense, which means God commands us to be continually filled with the Holy Spirit for effective service.

Many people think that the filling of the Spirit is like taking an empty glass to the sink and filling it up. In one sense, we already have the Holy Spirit in our lives because of His indwelling in the experience of conversion. When the Holy Spirit fills us, He fills us with His grace and power. This means He fills us with His ability to accomplish much for God. Jesus promised His disciples the power to witness (see Acts 1:8), and on the day of Pentecost they were filled with the Spirit (see Acts 2:4). On another occasion, Peter needed filling (see Acts 4:8). And later, in a prayer meeting, the building shook when the people were filled with the Holy Spirit (see Acts 4:31). These verses indicate you can be filled many times.

The Helper/Search Committee

The Holy Spirit is our sanctifier, which means He helps us

become holy. Actually, the word "sanctify" means to set apart. A twofold action occurs when the Holy Spirit sanctifies. First, He sets us apart from sin. In this action, He works in our hearts to motivate us to repent of and turn from sin. In the second action, the Holy Spirit sets us apart to God. We are motivated to seek God and His righteousness.

The Helper/Search Committee actually does the work of searching us out, just as a pulpit search committee seeks the proper person for the position. Then the Helper/Search Committee recommends the person and prepares the way for the candidate to get the position. The Holy Spirit or the Helper/Search Committee works *internally* in our lives to make us holy, and *externally* in heaven to secure our position/standing before God. In heaven we are declared righteous (justified), standing perfect before God.

The Helper/Teacher

The Holy Spirit illuminates the believer to see spiritual truth. In this role, He is the teacher of spiritual truth. "The god of this age has blinded, [those] who do not believe" (2 Cor. 4:4). This means the unsaved person cannot understand spiritual truth. But when a person is converted, the Holy Spirit becomes the Helper to teach or illuminate so the person can understand spiritual truth.

The job of teaching or illuminating the believer has several names in the New Testament. At one place it is called "the anointing." "But the anointing which you have received from Him abides in you, and you do not need that anyone teach you" (1 John 2:27). This does not mean the believer should not have human teachers, but that the Holy Spirit is the Teacher who causes the believer to understand, whether or not a human teacher is involved in the learning process. The apostle Paul noted, "The natural man does not receive the things of the Spirit of God...because they are spiritually discerned" (1 Cor. 2:14). In contrast, "We have received, not the spirit of the world, but the Spirit who is from God, that we might know the things that have been freely given to us by God" (1 Cor. 2:12).

Returning to the illustration of the Helper/Teacher, John the apostle puts these two together: "But the Helper, the Holy spirit, whom the Father will send in My name, He will teach you all things, and bring to your remembrance all things that I said to you" (John 14:26).

The Helper/Lawyer

The Holy Spirit is our Attorney who presents our case before the judge. A lawyer is usually hired by a defendant because, (1) the lawyer knows the law; (2) the lawyer knows the legal system; and (3) the lawyer has the ability to argue (logically present) the matter before the judge.

The Holy Spirit also is the Intercessor who prays for the believer and with the believer, and in the place of the believer. Why? "For we do not know what we should pray for as we ought, but the Spirit Himself makes intercession for us with groanings which cannot be uttered" (Rom. 8:26).

We are not always aware of the perfect way to approach God in prayer. Perhaps we come begging when we should be worshiping Him. We are human and God is infinite. So the Holy Spirit makes sure the believer always prays properly. That means no matter how the believer prays or what the believer prays, the Holy Spirit makes the words come out right when presented to the Father in heaven. "The Spirit also helps in our weaknesses...[making] intercession for us with groanings which cannot be uttered" (Rom. 8:26). What is the result of the Holy Spirit's work as our Helper/Lawyer? "He makes intercession for the saints according to the will of God" (Rom. 8:27).

LIVING WITH THE COMPLETE GODHEAD

Often, after knowing someone for some time, we see that person in a new setting and learn something new about our friend. Perhaps we discover a new common interest or shared experience or similarity in certain skills in the process. Our new knowledge helps us better understand our friend and may contribute to a better relationship.

Many have known God and walked with God, but they are ignorant of the Holy Spirit and how He can make their lives complete. Knowing about the Holy Spirit is the first step to knowing Him and allowing Him to work in your life.

Many Christians limit their understanding of the Holy Spirit to a single experience they have had with the Holy Spirit or to a particular work of the Holy Spirit. This person may emphasize the gifts of the Holy Spirit, the filling of the Holy Spirit or the illumination of the Holy Spirit. Obviously, this is a narrow understanding of the Holy Spirit.

The Principle of God's Dwelling Place

As the Spirit of the LORD, the Holy Spirit is the key to our having a vital relationship with God. From the beginning of time, it has been God's desire to dwell with people and have fellowship with them. Originally, He prepared a garden where He apparently met with Adam and Eve on a regular basis. Later, He gave Moses the plans for the Tabernacle, and His glory rested in the Holy Place in the center of His people. When the Tabernacle wore out with age, Solomon built a temple, which again was filled with the glory of God. Then, in the fulness of time, "The Word became flesh and dwelt among us" (John 1:14). As Jesus prepared to leave, He promised He would send another Helper. In this age, the Holy Spirit is the means by which God dwells in and among people.

The name "Spirit of the LORD" occurs 25 times in the Old Testament. In every case, a relationship between the Holy Spirit and a specific person is either clearly stated or strongly implied. The use of this name for the Holy Spirit illustrates the desire of God to have a meaningful place among His people.

The Principle of Insight for Living

A second principle implied by the names of the Holy Spirit is that He imparts insight for living. The name Helper/Teacher suggests the Holy Spirit is willing to give us insight and help us make decisions. Also, this name implies the guidance and leading of the Holy Spirit in our lives.

At times, Christians find it difficult to discern God's will concerning a particular decision. God directs Christians in two primary ways in making decisions. "A man's heart plans his way, but the LORD directs his steps" (Prov. 16:9). First, God leads in our decision making by giving us the ability to think through the issues and come to a conclusion.

Second, God reserves the right to intervene in our circumstances, through counsel with others, or in some other way to redirect our steps toward a better decision. In both cases, the Holy Spirit living within the Christian helps the Christian discern God's will.

The Principle of Power for Service

The principle of power for service is implied in the name Spirit of Might. Someone has said, "You can't do the work of God with the power of man. You do the work of God with the power of God." Unfortunately, many Christians know by experience that they can in fact witness, teach Sunday School and engage in other forms of ministry without possessing a sense of God's power upon their lives. But ministry done for

God in the flesh does not produce the kind of results that could otherwise be anticipated, nor is it as personally fulfilling as ministry done in the power of the Holy Spirit. The Helper/Administrative Assistant reminds us of the power for ministry that is available in the daily filling of the Holy Spirit.

This principle of power for service is also implied in the name Helper/Search Committee. The 25 occurrences of the title the Spirit of the LORD in the Old Testament describe the work people do for God when they have the Holy Spirit. Usually, the Bible describes the Spirit of the LORD coming upon people and enabling them to do a work for God. Spiritual power results from the sanctification and filling of the Holy Spirit.

The Principle of Reverence for God
The phrase Helper/Apartment Manager describes the indwelling of the Holy Spirit in us. Then, the Helper/Lawyer is His work for us. Although the Scripture says much about developing personal intimacy with God (i.e., knowing God), in a certain sense we must stand in awe of Him. This principle of reverence will influence our faith in God, our prayer life and our worship; as a matter of fact, it will influence everything we do. Having proper reverence for God will help us see Him in His majesty. We will see His greatness as One who is both trustworthy and worthy of our worship.

The principle of reverence for God will also help us understand ourselves better. Throughout the Scriptures, whenever a person or group of people gained a clearer understanding of the nature of God, they gained a more realistic understanding of themselves. Because man is made in the image of God, when a person can better see the primary object (God) he will better understand the reflection in the mirror. Usually, this understanding can be accompanied by personal repentance or a revitalization of the spiritual life.

Reverence for God results in understanding who we are.

This principle of reverence for God will also change the way we live. The New Testament makes it clear that the Holy Spirit lives within the believer. When we have reverence toward the Holy Spirit of God, we will be careful about what we do with and where we take our body, His temple. Many Christians would change their language, actions and the places they go to if they had an inner consciousness of reverence for the indwelling Holy Spirit.

SECTION II

The Ministry of the Holy Spirit in the Believer

CHAPTER 2

The Atonement Terms for the Holy Spirit

THE ATONEMENT TERMS FOR THE HOLY SPIRIT

Providing Salvation

1. The Eternal Spirit	His priestly role in intercession for the unsaved.
2. The Gift of God	His gift of eternal life to the unsaved.
3. The Spirit of Him Who Raised Up Jesus from the Dead	His role in resurrection.

Effecting Salvation

1. The Spirit of Grace	He accepts the sinner for salvation.
2. The Same Spirit of Faith	He enables the sinner to believe.
3. A New Spirit	He gives the repentant sinner a new nature.
4. The Spirit of Life	He makes the convert alive to God.
5. The Spirit of Adoption	He makes us heirs to God.

The Scriptures were given that people may come to faith in Christ and experience salvation. John explained, "But these are written that you may believe that Jesus is the Christ, the Son of God, and that believing you may have life in His name" (John 20:31). The previous chapter emphasized the role of the Holy Spirit as Helper in our conversion. Conversion is what enables a person to receive eternal life. But the door of salvation has two sides: man's side and God's side. This chapter describes the role of the Holy Spirit in providing salvation. This is God's side of the door. This chapter describes several names and titles of the Holy Spirit as He does His work in the atonement wrought by Christ.

THE HOLY SPIRIT IN THE WORK OF ATONEMENT

The Holy Spirit is involved in two aspects of the atonement. First, the Spirit was involved in the atoning death of Christ, which made salvation possible (see Heb. 9:14). Second, He is involved in drawing people to faith in Christ (see John 16:8-11) and applying the results of salvation.

In light of the multifaceted role of the Holy Spirit in salvation, many names describe aspects of His saving ministries. These names include the Eternal Spirit, the Gift of God, a New Spirit, the Same Spirit of Faith, the Seal names, the Spirit of Adoption, the Spirit of Grace, the Spirit of Him Who Raised Up Jesus, the Spirit of Life and My Witness.

The first involvement of the Holy Spirit in salvation is His role in making salvation possible. Although the focus of the Scriptures is on what Christ did in His atoning death, a closer examination of the biblical teaching makes it clear that providing salvation was a Trinitarian ministry (i.e., involving all three members of the Trinity). Three names are used to relate the Holy Spirit to the sacrificial nature of Christ's death, His descent into hell and His victorious resurrection to life.

NAMES OF THE HOLY SPIRIT
RELATED TO THE ATONEMENT

1. The Eternal Spirit
2. The Gift of God
3. The Spirit of Him Who Raised Up Jesus

The Eternal Spirit

In the Old Testament, the priest would take the blood of a sacrificial animal and offer it to God for atonement. In the sacrificial death of Christ, the Eternal Spirit apparently acted in this priestly role. The writer of the Epistle to the Hebrews asks:

> For if the blood of bulls and goats and the ashes of a heifer, sprinkling the unclean, sanctifies for the purifying of the flesh, how much more shall the blood of Christ, who through the eternal Spirit offered Himself without spot to God, purge your conscience from dead works to serve the living God? (Heb. 9:13,14).

The Holy Spirit was the (active) agent who offered the (passive) Lamb to God.

The Gift of God

Between the death and resurrection of Jesus, the Bible describes Jesus descending into Hades. This was done to release the Old Testament saints from the captivity of Hades, that they might enjoy the presence of God (see Ps. 68:18; Eph. 4:8). In the context of describing this work, it is also noted that Christ gave gifts to men. Although this statement has some reference to the gifts of the Holy Spirit (see Eph. 4:11), it probably also refers to the gift of eternal life (see Rom. 6:23). All these gifts are linked to the ultimate Gift of God, the Holy Spirit (see John 4:10; Acts 8:20). All these gifts are in Him—the Holy Spirit—and to get Him is to get them. Without this Gift of God, it would be impossible for Christians to enjoy spiritual gifts, eternal life or any of the other gifts and blessings of God in the Christian life.

The Spirit of Him Who Raised Up Jesus

In describing the Holy Spirit as the Spirit of Him Who

Raised Up Jesus (see Rom. 8:11), Paul linked the Holy Spirit with the resurrection of Jesus to life. Earlier in Romans, this linkage was also made through the use of another name, the Spirit of Holiness. In his opening remarks, Paul described Jesus as "declared to be the Son of God with power, according to the Spirit of holiness, by the resurrection from the dead" (Rom. 1:4). These two names imply some measure of the Holy Spirit's involvement in the resurrection of Jesus.

THE HOLY SPIRIT APPLYING THE WORK OF ATONEMENT

The Holy Spirit was not only involved in securing the means by which salvation is possible; He is also actively involved in effecting that salvation in the lives of those who respond to the gospel. The atonement names of the Holy Spirit tend to emphasize this aspect of His ministry.

NAMES OF THE HOLY SPIRIT EFFECTING SALVATION

1. The Spirit of Grace
2. The Same Spirit of Faith
3. A New Spirit
4. The Spirit of Life
5. The Spirit of Adoption

The Spirit of Grace
Because salvation is all of grace (see Eph. 2:5,8), it should not be surprising that one of the saving names of the Holy

Spirit is the Spirit of Grace (see Zech. 12:10). Grace is the unmerited favor of God toward the repentant sinner. Grace has been described through the use of an acrostic—God's Riches At Christ's Expense. The Spirit of Grace is the channel through which God's unmerited favor is applied to the believer at conversion.

GRACE

God's Riches At Christ's Expense

The Same Spirit of Faith
Paul also described the Holy Spirit as, "the Same Spirit of Faith" (2 Cor. 4:13). The Bible teaches that people could not be saved without faith (see Eph. 2:8,9). Some teachers maintain this gift of grace is sovereignly given. Others hold that God has already given to everyone the ability to exercise saving faith in Christ in response to the gospel (see John 1:12). Regardless of one's belief about the extent of this aspect of the Holy Spirit's ministry, the title Spirit of Faith suggests the involvement of the Holy Spirit in a person's response to salvation. Also implied in this name is one means by which we may grow in our faith in God. As we develop our relationship with the Spirit of Faith, we will increase in our faith as we live by the faith of God (see Rom. 1:17; Gal. 2:20).

A New Spirit
The prophet Ezekiel spoke of a time when God would save Israel by giving them a New Spirit (see Ezek. 11:19). When a person is saved today, he or she also receives this New Spirit. In the act of salvation, God makes us a new creation and helps us live the Christian life.

> Then I will give them one heart, and I will put a
> new spirit within them, and take the stony heart
> out of their flesh, and give them a heart of flesh,
> that they may walk in My statutes and keep My
> judgments and do them; and they shall be My
> people, and I will be their God (Ezek. 11:19, 20).

The New Spirit makes a person a "new creation"
(2 Cor. 5:17).

The Spirit of Life

Another saving name of the Holy Spirit describing His role
in effecting salvation is "the Spirit of Life." Paul explained,
"For the law of the Spirit of life in Christ Jesus has made me
free from the law of sin and death" (Rom. 8:2). Before salvation, people are described as "dead in trespasses and sins"
(Eph. 2:1), but when they are converted, they are "alive to
God in Christ Jesus our Lord" (Rom. 6:11). The difference is
effected by the ministry of the Spirit of Life in salvation.

The Spirit of Adoption

The Spirit of Adoption refers to the ministry of the Holy
Spirit in appointing us as heirs within the family of God.
"For you did not receive the spirit of bondage again to fear,
but you received the Spirit of adoption by whom we cry
out, 'Abba, Father'" (Rom. 8:15).

In the first century, adoption was a common means of
legally placing a child in the family as an heir. Although the
work of the Holy Spirit in regeneration makes us a part of
the family of God, the work of the Holy Spirit in adoption
guarantees our position in the family as heirs. By regeneration, the Holy Spirit gives the believer a new nature and a
new spiritual desire toward God. By adoption, the Spirit

guarantees us all the rights and privileges of belonging to the family of God. This also implies that we have a responsibility to live up to that honor.

REGENERATION	ADOPTION
Born Again	Placed as Sons
Becoming a Child	Becoming a Son
Experiential	Legal
Receive God's Nature	Receive Rights as Heir

ENJOYING THE ATONEMENT NAMES OF THE HOLY SPIRIT

The atonement names of the Holy Spirit serve as a reminder of the greatness of God's provision of salvation. Salvation is a gift of God, something He intends for us to enjoy rather than work for. So the saving names of the Holy Spirit should be a source of enjoyment in our lives. This is more likely to be the case when we understand and apply four principles arising out of these saving names.

The Principle of Complete Provision
When a child goes to camp, he will find the experience more enjoyable when he realizes his mother has packed everything he needs to have a great trip there and a great experience at camp. The saving names of the Holy Spirit remind us that God's provision in salvation is complete. The Father has packed complete provisions for every emergency on life's journey.

The Bible uses at least 131 different expressions to describe the salvation experience. Why are so many expressions used? One reason relates to what is involved in God's complete provision, which we call salvation. Just as the supply checklist on a trip to camp may include many things that may be summarized as necessary supplies, so God's salvation checklist contains many individual expressions of salvation that are summarized in the word "salvation."

Consider some of the provisions of the Holy Spirit in salvation. For our guilt, He offers forgiveness (see Eph. 1:7). For our sense of rejection, He offers acceptance (see Eph. 1:6). For our alienation, He brings us close to God (see Eph. 2:13). He replaces our deadness with life (see Eph. 2:1). Our bondage is exchanged for liberty (see Gal. 5:1). Our poverty is replaced by His riches (see Eph. 1:3). And the list continues to meet every human need. Certainly much is to be enjoyed in the Holy Spirit's complete provision of salvation.

The Principle of Family Security

A second principle implied in the saving names of the Holy Spirit is the principle of family security. These names indicate the Holy Spirit's ability to complete the good work of salvation that He has begun in every believer (see Phil. 1:6), and His power over anything that would threaten the believer (see John 17:2). Our spiritual assurance is guaranteed by the person and work of God. If God were to take away eternal life from anyone, it would be a denial of His nature and work. God is true and just. He cannot deny Himself. Therefore, anyone who has eternal life has it forever. Beyond the nature of God, Christians have the promise that nothing can separate them from the love of God (see Rom. 8:33-39).

When my children were growing up, I often motivated them to good behavior, telling them, "You're a Towns." I reminded them that their grandmother often motivated me with the same admonition. Some object to the doctrine of our eternal position in the family of God, fearing that it may lead some into sinful lifestyles. Actually, just the reverse can be true. Most people do not actively live to dishonor their family. They know they have the family name and would not want to drag it through the mud. Family honor is a motivating factor, encouraging people to live up to the family name. So an understanding of our position in the family of God ought to motivate us to live up to the honor of that great family.

The Principle of Family Identity
Also implied by these names is the principle of family identity. Many people have searched out their family tree to discover they are distantly related to some important ancestor. When they learn this, they may change their lifestyle as they subconsciously begin to live as that famous ancestor lived. The saving names of the Holy Spirit refer to our being brought into the family of God and our identification with the Son of God. In at least one sense, the Christian life is simply letting Jesus live His life through us (see Gal. 2:20).

The Principle of Continuing Support
The final principle arising from the saving names of the Holy Spirit is that of continuing support. Although many of these names relate to various aspects of salvation, some, like the name Helper, indicate that what the Spirit has begun in salvation He will continue in His teaching and maturing ministries in our lives. These ministries of the Holy Spirit are considered in greater detail in the next chapters, but they are introduced in the saving names of the Holy Spirit.

CHAPTER 3

Terms for the Maturing Work of the Holy Spirit

TERMS FOR THE MATURING WORK OF THE HOLY SPIRIT

**Indwelling Names
of the Spirit**

1. A New Spirit   He gives the believer the Spirit-filled life.
2. A Spirit of Grace He helps the believer walk by grace, not law.
3. Spirit of   He motivates the believer to pray.
   Supplication
4. My Witness   He bears witness of the believer's salvation.
5. My Helper   He helps the believer grow in Christ.

**The Life of God
in Human Lives**

1. Union with God   He puts the believer in God.
2. Communion   He helps the believer's fellowship with God.
   with God

God's purpose in our lives as Christians is that we might be transformed into the image of Christ (see Rom. 8:29). This change in our character and life is accomplished through the maturing ministry of the Holy Spirit. As we have seen in other ministries of the Holy Spirit, several names tend to describe this work. Each of these names emphasizes the ministry of the indwelling Holy Spirit in the process of sanctification.

The word "sanctification" means "to be set apart." When Bible teachers use this word to describe the ministry of the Holy Spirit, they are referring to His attempts to make the Christian "set apart from the world" and "spiritual" (to reflect the character of God).

The word "sanctification" is used in three tenses. First, Christians *have been* sanctified in that they were forgiven and set apart to God in salvation. Second, Christians are constantly *being* set apart from sin through the work of the Holy Spirit in their lives. Third, Christians *will be* completely sanctified at the rapture or when they enter God's presence through death, when they will be completely free from sin. The maturing names of the Holy Spirit are those names that draw attention to the fact that the Holy Spirit indwells Christians and makes them mature. The word

THREE TENSES OF SANCTIFICATION		
Past	**Present**	**Future**
Position	Experience	Consummation
Positional sanctification	Progressive sanctification	Prospective sanctification
I have been sanctified	I am now being sanctified	I shall be sanctified
Hebrews 3:1	1 Thessalonians 5:28	1 John 3:2

"mature" means to be whole, complete or well rounded. Although many aspects of the maturing process are evident in the Christian life, the key to Christian living is the life of God living through human lives. This intimacy with God is experienced by the Christian as he or she comes to understand the Holy Spirit's indwelling of the believer.

THE INDWELLING NAMES OF THE HOLY SPIRIT

One of the results of the Holy Spirit in our conversion is that He indwells us. Several names of the Holy Spirit emphasize this aspect of His ministry, including a New Spirit (see Ezek. 11:19), the Spirit of Grace (see Heb. 10:29), the Spirit of Supplication (see Zech. 12:10), My Witness (see

Heb. 10:15) and the Helper (see John 14:26).

A New Spirit

When a person becomes a Christian, God puts within that person a New Spirit who then effects other changes in his or her life (see Ezek. 11:19). All growth toward maturity in the Christian life is the result of the New Spirit living His life through the Christian. This new life is sometimes called the victorious life, or the Spirit-filled life. The Christian should yield to the control of the New Spirit. When this is done, the believer will grow toward maturity.

Spirit of Grace

Another maturing name of the Holy Spirit is the Spirit of Grace. The Scriptures describe salvation as being all of grace (see Eph. 2:8), and the Spirit of Grace is the means by which the grace of God is communicated to people (see Heb. 10:29). But the maturing process in the Christian life is also dependent upon the ministry of the Spirit of Grace. Paul challenged the Galatians, "Are you so foolish? Having begun in the Spirit, are you now being made perfect by the flesh?" (Gal. 3:3). In this way, he reminded them that the same Spirit of Grace who brought them salvation was also the key to the maturity they were seeking.

Spirit of Supplication

The term Spirit of Supplication (see Zech. 12:10) reminds the Christian of the importance of prayer in the maturing process in the Christian life. Many Bible teachers have described personal Bible study and prayer as the two absolute essentials in the process of spiritual growth. The teaching names of the Holy Spirit help us grow as we read the Scriptures and the Spirit of Supplication helps us grow in our prayer life. Sometimes, the Spirit of Supplication prays for us when we do not know how to pray. "For we do not know what we should pray for as we ought, but the Spirit Himself makes intercession for us with groanings which cannot be uttered" (Rom. 8:26).

My Witness

A fourth maturing name of the Holy Spirit is My Witness (see Job 16:19; Heb. 10:15). Together with the Father and the Son, the Holy Spirit consistently bears witness in heaven (see 1 John 5:7). The Holy Spirit bears witness of our salvation because of what Christ has done. But the Holy Spirit also bears witness on earth, by using the testimony of our salvation to speak to unsaved people (see 1 John 5:8-10).

The Helper

The fifth maturing name of the Holy Spirit is the Helper (see John 14:26). As we have already noticed, Jesus used this term to describe the multifaceted ministry of the Holy Spirit. Part of that ministry involves helping us grow to become all God intended us to be. Whenever we face a new challenge to grow spiritually, we can be confident of the ministry of the indwelling Helper to assist us in our adjustments and guide us in our decisions.

THE LIFE OF GOD IN HUMAN LIVES

At the very heart of the Christian life is the union and communion of the Christian with God. Union with God refers to that relationship of salvation between God and the

Christian, which happens at the moment of conversion. Communion with God refers to our continuing experience of recognizing and enjoying fellowship with God. In both union and communion, the Holy Spirit is involved in helping us mature in Christ.

Union with God

The Christian's standing or his new position in heaven is described in Scripture by the phrase "in Christ." This expression is used 172 times in the New Testament in connection with virtually every aspect of Christian experience. The experience of being placed in Christ occurs at conversion as the Holy Spirit puts us into the Lord Jesus Christ and we enjoy the perfection of Christ in the heavenlies. It is usually not until much later, however, that many Christians experience the reality of this truth.

Being "in Christ" is a description of the Christian not only at conversion, but also throughout his or her Christian life. In identifying the believer's position "in Christ," Paul hints at the intimacy that exists between the Christian and Christ. As the child in its mother's womb is an individual personality while being very much a part of its mother, so the Christian retains his or her individual personality while being in Christ. This expression describes the intimacy of the Christ/Christian relationship more than any other biblical expression or illustration of that relationship.

Communion with God

Communion with God is like the tide; it comes and goes. It is another term for fellowship with God. At times, a Christian may sense a deeper communion with God than at other times. Although all Christians are united with God, relatively few experience the communion or fellowship with Christ that is characteristic of the deeper Christian life. Our union with God is an accomplished act at conversion, but our communion with God is an experience that usually involves many steps. The following six steps to fellowship or communion are suggestive of how this experience occurs.

The first step in experiencing communion with Christ is *knowledge*. The apostle Paul often used the "know ye not" formula when introducing some aspect of Christian experience (see Rom. 6:3, *KJV*). For some, merely understanding aspects of the believer's union with God is the beginning of a deeper communion with Christ. One cannot fully appreciate any truth that is not at least partially understood intellectually.

Repentance of known sin is a second step for entering into a deeper communion. Repentance involves turning from sin, and being cleansed from sin. In repenting, the Christian (1) searches his or her heart for sin that blocks fellowship with God; (2) begs forgiveness for sin (see 1 John 1:9); (3) asks God to forgive on the basis of the blood of Jesus Christ (see 1 John 1:7); and (4) promises to learn lessons from the experience so that it does not happen again.

A third step in enjoying communion with God is a *step of faith*. Often, entering into communion is a matter of acting on the Word of God. Christians appropriate the deeper life of communion by faith, just as one appropriates the eternal life of salvation by faith.

The fourth step in the process is that of *surrendering or yielding completely to God*. Yielding is a once-and-for-all response to God that governs all future responses to God. The initial yielding of your life to God is followed by a daily outworking of that yielding through obedience to the promptings of the Holy Spirit in your life. This has been characterized as telling God one big *YES!*, followed by daily telling God yes.

Step five is expressed in *obedience*. The attitude of yielding to God is expressed in active obedience to the known and revealed will of God. Christians sometimes use yielding as an excuse for their passive attitude toward working for God, but those who truly yield to God will want to work for Him.

The sixth step in experiencing communion with God is *crucifying one's self or taking up one's cross*. The Bible teaches that the old nature was crucified with Christ (see Gal. 2:20). Now the Christian must act on what has happened. Thus, when tempted to sin, we should respond as a dead person; but when prompted by the Spirit, we should show that we are alive to His leading (see Rom. 6:11).

How the Holy Spirit Works in Maturing the Christian

The maturing names of the Holy Spirit emphasize His work in making us more like Jesus. But how does the Holy Spirit accomplish this work? The Holy Spirit matures the Christian by supporting the processes that lead to growth, just as parents contribute to the physical growth of their children by feeding them, insisting they get sufficient rest, encouraging them in physical activities and so on. Although the Holy Spirit may do many specific things in an individual Christian's life to help the maturing process, a few general principles show how He helps us become more like Jesus.

The Principle of Tree Growth
The principle of tree growth recognizes that growth begins on the inside and works its way out. The psalmist noted, "The righteous shall flourish like a palm tree, he shall grow

like a cedar in Lebanon" (Ps. 92:12). The comparison between these trees and the Christian emphasizes that growth in the Christian finds its origins in the inner life rather than from some external circumstances. Palm trees can withstand many adversities and continue to experience growth; but if the inner core of the palm is corrupted, it begins to wither and die.

The principle of tree growth is also mentioned in the New Testament. Jesus warned His disciples, "By their fruits you will know them" (Matt. 7:20). By this, Jesus meant they could discern between true and false teachers by the fruit they produce in their lives. Later, Jesus used the image of a vine and branches to urge His disciples to bear fruit (see John 15:1-8). The apostle Paul also described Christian character as the fruit of the Holy Spirit (see Gal. 5:22,23).

The Holy Spirit matures Christians according to the principle of tree growth by being that life within that produces spiritual fruit in believers' outer lives. When we allow the Holy Spirit to live through us, spiritual fruit in the form of Christian character will result. When other influences become more dominant in our lives, a different kind of fruit will soon become evident.

The Principle of Grace as Needed

A second principle governing the Holy Spirit's maturing ministry is the principle of grace as needed. Many Christians may wish they could have some instantaneous experience with the Holy Spirit that would eliminate all sin and immaturity in their lives. Many would like instant maturity, but that is not how the Holy Spirit has chosen to accomplish His work. Rather, the Spirit of Grace constantly gives grace as needed for each step in the maturing process.

A parent would not bring a newborn baby home from the hospital and give it several bags of food at one time and expect the child to be fully mature within a week. Maturing of children takes many years; some parents may wonder if they will ever accomplish that task. Similarly, God does not expect Christians to become spiritual giants overnight. Rather, the Holy Spirit gives Christians grace as needed, day by day, throughout many years as He matures them.

The Principle of Glory to Glory
When Paul wrote to the Corinthians about the maturing ministry of the Holy Spirit, he noted:

> But we all, with unveiled face, beholding as in a mirror the glory of the Lord, are being transformed into the same image from glory to glory, just as by the Spirit of the Lord (2 Cor. 3:18).

The principle of glory to glory recognizes one of the processes used by the Holy Spirit in maturing believers. Apparently, maturity was not a one-time experience with the Holy Spirit that instantaneously transformed carnal Christians into spiritual, Christlike giants. Rather, it was a process by which Christians became increasingly more Christlike by focusing their attention on the glory of the Lord.

Paul also refers to this principle in his Epistle to the Philippians. There he expressed his confidence in "this very thing, that He who has begun a good work in you will complete it until the day of Jesus Christ" (Phil. 1:6). This practical spiritual growth to maturity is part of God's will for every Christian (see 1 Thess. 4:3). These changes toward greater Christlikeness could not be accomplished apart from the maturing ministry of the Holy Spirit.

The Principle of Encouragement
Through Confirmation

A fourth maturing principle used by the Holy Spirit is the principle of encouragement through confirmation. When a student struggles to master some new skill, the teacher will often draw the student's attention to the progress that has already been made. The teacher measures the progress of growth to motivate the student to continue mastering new skills. In the same way, the Holy Spirit encourages us to become more like Christ by occasionally causing us to realize how much we have already changed.

This is an important principle to remember as we struggle to break harmful habits or develop healthy spiritual disciplines in our lives. Sometimes, recognizing the enormity of a significant change that needs to be made in our lives can overwhelm and discourage us in our spiritual growth. At those times especially, we need to pause and realize what the Holy Spirit has already done in this work of making us more like Jesus. In most cases, the big challenge before us becomes more realistic when we recognize the bigger change that has already been made.

The Principle of Available Assistance

The fifth maturing principle governing this aspect of the Holy Spirit's ministry is the principle of available assistance. No Christian ever needs to feel he or she must struggle alone against the world, the flesh and the devil. The Holy Spirit lives within every Christian and is constantly working to help us become like Jesus.

Paul reminded the Corinthians:

> No temptation has overtaken you except such as is common to man; but God is faithful, who will not allow you to be tempted beyond what you

are able, but with the temptation will also make the way of escape, that you may be able to bear it (1 Cor. 10:13).

This verse illustrates two ways the principle of available assistance is at work in our lives. First, the Holy Spirit has set reasonable limits on problems He will allow to come into our lives. This is illustrated in the Old Testament experience of Job, who was protected by God (see Job 1:10). Even when God allowed Satan to introduce problems into Job's life, He set limits—knowing how much Job could handle (see Job 1:12; 2:6).

Second, the Holy Spirit will also offer solutions to any problems He allows to come into our lives. Whenever we encounter a problem that seems overwhelming, we can be confident the Holy Spirit has already prepared a way of escape to make the problem more bearable.

The maturing names of the Holy Spirit emphasize our responsibility as Christians to continue to grow in grace. In the Old Testament, the prophets often called Israel to look back to their origins and realize how much God had done for them as a nation. This is a good practice for Christians today. As you conclude this chapter, take a few minutes to make a list of the evidences of growth in your life as you review the maturing ministry of the Holy Spirit in your life since you became a Christian.

CHAPTER 4

Terms for the Teaching Ministry of the Holy Spirit

THE TEACHING NAMES OF THE HOLY SPIRIT

1. The Anointing — He removes spiritual blindness.
2. The Spirit of Revelation — He reveals spiritual truth.
3. The Spirit of Truth — He communicates the content of truth.
4. The Spirit of Knowledge — He makes believers know facts about God.
5. The Spirit of a Sound Mind — He takes away fear and enables rational thought.

When you read the Scriptures, and a verse seems to "leap off the page" and you see a truth you have never seen before, that is the ministry of the Holy Spirit causing you to see that truth. At other times you may be listening to a sermon or Bible lesson and a light flashes on. You see Christ clearly. That is the work of the Holy Spirit. The Holy Spirit is the Illuminator, the Teacher, the One removing your spiritual blindness.

When you pray, "Open my eyes, that I may see wondrous things from Your law" (Ps. 119:18), you are asking the Holy Spirit to show you new things from the Bible.

The Holy Spirit is your Helper. Just as a kindergarten teacher helps students recognize the letters of the alphabet or helps them add two and two, so the Holy Spirit helps babes in Christ recognize basic Christian truth, or helps mature believers understand the deeper Christian life.

The Holy Spirit is our Teacher. Jesus promised to send the Spirit, adding, "He will teach you all things, bring to your remembrance all things that I said to you" (John 14:26). Although this reference may relate directly to the disciples, it surely applies to us today. Then Jesus promised that the Teacher would "guide you into all truth" (John 16:13).

Paul also identified the teaching ministry of the Holy Spirit when he reminded the Corinthians, "These things we also speak, not in words which man's wisdom teaches but which the Holy Spirit teaches, comparing spiritual things with spiritual" (1 Cor. 2:13). Later, John also emphasized the teaching ministry of the Holy Spirit, reminding Christians:

> But the anointing which you have received from Him abides in you, and you do not need that anyone teach you; but as the same anointing teaches you concerning all things, and is true, and is not a lie, and just as it has taught you, you will abide in Him (1 John 2:27).

In this passage, "the anointing" occurs when the Holy Spirit comes upon a believer and anoints the believer with Himself. The believer receives the Holy Spirit, who teaches the believer spiritual things.

We usually think of Jesus as a Teacher; this was the name used to address Him, more than any other name. The title Teacher is apparently never used to describe the Holy Spirit as it is used to describe Jesus, but the Holy Spirit performs all the duties a teacher does: He guides, reveals, teaches, tells, shows, leads and, even as a human teacher will do, reproves, corrects and convicts.

THE HOLY SPIRIT AS TEACHER

This chapter will describe the Holy Spirit in His teaching ministry by using several terms:

THE TEACHING NAMES OF THE HOLY SPIRIT

1. The Anointing (see 1 John 2:27)
2. The Spirit of Counsel (see Isa. 11:2)
3. The Spirit of Revelation (see Eph. 1:17)
4. The Spirit of Truth (see John 14:17)

The Anointing

When John described the Holy Spirit as the Anointing, he emphasized His direct teaching ministry (see 1 John 2:27). Some have taken this statement to justify their refusal to learn from human teachers. Actually, John did not say it is wrong to learn from human teachers (he himself was teaching others as he wrote these words), but only that teachers were not absolutely necessary to help Christians distinguish the truth from error. Most Bible teachers agree John wrote this epistle to warn Christians about the false teachings of heretical teachers. In doing so, he reminded his readers that the Anointing teaches truth, not lies, and, therefore, could be relied upon more consistently than human teachers who may or may not teach the truth.

Often, the Holy Spirit has prevented new Christians from becoming involved in a religious cult by making them aware of some error in the teaching of the cult. Sometimes, they do not fully understand this direct ministry of the Anointing until they look back years later and realize how the Holy Spirit helped them discern between truth and error as they studied the Scriptures.

In addition to protection from negative lessons, the Holy Spirit will teach with His anointing. The Holy Spirit comes and removes spiritual blindness from those "whose minds the god of this age has blinded" (2 Cor. 4:4). Being worldly minded blinds us to God's plan and we cannot understand the principles of salvation. The Holy Spirit is the Teacher who shows us the meaning of the Cross.

As Teacher, the Holy Spirit also teaches us about Jesus Christ. Some were blinded "lest the light of the gospel of the glory of Christ, who is the image of God, should shine on them" (2 Cor. 4:4). The Holy Spirit magnifies Jesus Christ so we can see Him. Jesus explained, "He will not speak on His own authority,...He will glorify Me" (John 16:13,14). The main topic in the Holy Spirit's curriculum is the Lord Jesus Christ.

The Spirit of Revelation

When Paul prayed that the Ephesians might have the Spirit of Revelation (see Eph. 1:17), He emphasized the teaching ministry of the Holy Spirit in showing us things we could not otherwise know apart from His ministry. A good teacher communicates not only the facts of a lesson, but also insights that help the student understand and appreciate the relationships that tie those facts together. The Spirit of Revelation teaches Christians insights about life, helping them understand the forces at work in their lives. Those believers who learn under the Holy Spirit's teaching ministry will have a better idea of what God is doing in and through their lives.

The Spirit of Truth

Another teaching name of the Holy Spirit that emphasizes the character of His teaching is the title Spirit of Truth (see John 14:17). As the Spirit of Truth, all that the Holy Spirit teaches is characterized by truth. This means the lessons of the Holy Spirit are accurate, and His students can have complete confidence in what they are taught.

I have taught in Christian colleges and seminaries for 33

years. I wish I could say I have never made a mistake, but I can't. Just the other day, I pointed to a pronoun in a verse, and told the class it was a reference to Paul, when it was a reference to Christ. I backed up, corrected myself, and went on. But the Holy Spirit is accurate, and never contradicts Himself, because He is the Spirit of Truth.

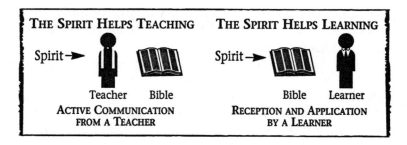

THE SPIRIT HELPS TEACHING   THE SPIRIT HELPS LEARNING

Spirit →   Teacher   Bible   Spirit →   Bible   Learner

ACTIVE COMMUNICATION   RECEPTION AND APPLICATION
FROM A TEACHER   BY A LEARNER

THE HOLY SPIRIT'S ROLE IN LEARNING

In the previous section, the Holy Spirit as Teacher was emphasized. Here we should note that some of the teaching names of the Holy Spirit apparently emphasize learning rather than teaching. The goal of all teaching is learning. I have defined teaching as, "the guidance of learning activities." No teacher has really taught until the student has learned the lesson. Here are some of the terms applied to the Holy Spirit that emphasize learning:

THE HOLY SPIRIT'S LEARNING NAMES

1. The Spirit of Knowledge (see Isa. 11:2)
2. The Spirit of a Sound Mind (see 2 Tim. 1:7)
3. The Spirit of Understanding (see Isa. 11:2)
4. The Spirit of Wisdom (see Exod. 28:3)

The Spirit of Knowledge

As the Spirit of Knowledge (see Isa. 11:2), the Holy Spirit enables His students to understand basic facts about God and His world. These spiritual lessons become the basis of the rest of His teaching ministry in our lives. The primary thrust of the teaching ministry of the Holy Spirit is to enhance our experiential knowledge of God.

For example, we know that lying is wrong, but the Holy Spirit reveals the true nature of our "fibs," as we like to call them. Then we are horrified by what we have said. We have theoretical knowledge about our actions until the Holy Spirit reveals their actual nature. The same can be said of positive truth. Someone knows about Jesus from seeing a Christmas or Easter movie. They hear a sermon or read a Christian book, but they have no experiential relationship with Jesus Christ. Then the Holy Spirit reveals Jesus Christ to this person, who is miserable because of sin. This ministry is the Holy Spirit as Teacher, who is also the Spirit of Knowledge.

From our perspective as the Holy Spirit's students, we should rely upon Him to teach us to have both a greater intellectual understanding of Jesus and deeper communion with Him.

The Holy Spirit does not whisper in our ears during an exam when we pray for an answer that we have never memorized. The Holy Spirit illuminates the Scripture as we study and learn the Word of God. He helps us learn and retain knowledge about spiritual things. The Holy Spirit works "hand in glove" with our abilities so we will have spiritual illumination.

The Spirit of a Sound Mind

Sometimes, Christians have behaved irrationally while claiming to be under the influence of the Holy Spirit. The Bible, however, promises that God has given us a "Spirit of a sound mind" (2 Tim. 1:7). This soundness is communicated to our spirits by the Holy Spirit. He keeps us from fear or other emotional pressures that would make us do dumb things or make foolish decisions. He works with our own spirits to give us confidence.

When people are converted to Christ, the Holy Spirit's ministry in their lives often results in an enhanced ability to think rationally, without their minds being clouded by the effects of drugs, alcohol, pornography and so on. Perhaps you have experienced the ministry of the Holy Spirit in your own life in a way that involved a new direction that surprised you. At other times, the Spirit of a Sound Mind enables us to learn through the rational application of truth we already know. He expects us to think through the issues involved and to come to a conclusion, much as a college student does in an independent research course. This is both a learning experience for the Christian and the teaching ministry of the Holy Spirit.

The Spirit of Understanding

A third step in the learning process involves gaining insights from "the Spirit of understanding" (Isa. 11:2). Understanding is the ability to discern the subtle differences involved between two or more options. We can't always simply look at a problem and seek to come to a rational conclusion on the basis of what is known. We can rely upon the Spirit of Understanding to give us insights we might not otherwise have. The Holy Spirit might have taught us former lessons, so at the act of making a decision, He helps us to make the correct choice.

The Spirit of Wisdom

As "the spirit of wisdom" (Exod. 28:3), the Holy Spirit

teaches us to view life from God's perspective. Wisdom is the ability to correctly apply all the facts or knowledge we have learned. A young Ph.D. may have a lot of knowledge, but he may not have the wisdom of his father who never attended college. The wise father knows how to apply the facts he knows.

As the Spirit of Knowledge, the Holy Spirit takes the facts He teaches and, as the Spirit of Understanding, He helps the believer apply them to life. The thesis of the book of Proverbs may be paraphrased as, "My Son give yourself to knowledge that you may gain wisdom." When Christians find themselves in a situation where they do not know what to do, they should pray for increased wisdom (see Jas. 1:5). One of the ways God will answer such a prayer is through the ministry of the Spirit of Wisdom.

How the Holy Spirit Teaches

All good teachers realize certain laws of teaching and learning will enhance their teaching ministry if consistently applied. Likewise, the Holy Spirit teaches us the truths of God according to certain principles. Although many teaching principles may be drawn from the teaching names of the Holy Spirit, the following illustrate how the Holy Spirit teaches us and how we can more effectively teach others.

The Principle of Readiness

Readiness as a principle in the teaching ministry of the Holy Spirit is illustrated in the way He revealed God's will to the human writers of Scripture. The Holy Spirit used 40 writers over a period of some 1,600 years to complete the 66 books of the Bible. The finished product can be read by the average reader in about 80 hours. Certainly a book the size of the Bible could have been written in less than the 1,600-plus years it took for the Holy Spirit to write it. After all, the Bible itself claims that God's Word is forever "settled in heaven" (Ps. 119:89). Presumably, the Holy Spirit could have dictated the settled Word of God to an efficient typist who could transcribe it in a matter of weeks or months rather than centuries.

One reason the Holy Spirit took His time in teaching generations of people the Scriptures relates to the principle of readiness. Before He could teach the heart of the Scriptures, which is the salvation provided by Christ on the cross, the Holy Spirit first needed to teach people the Old Testament law that showed them the need for salvation. The lessons He taught through the prophets served to reinforce our inability to keep the law. This helped make other generations ready for the message of the gospel. After teaching the means whereby we could be saved, the Holy Spirit then taught through the apostles how to live the Christian life. In every instance, a lesson was not taught until readiness had been established.

If you have been a Christian for some time, you realize that the Holy Spirit teaches you best when you are ready to learn new truth. Have you ever read a familiar passage of Scripture and learned something new you could apply to your life? Why didn't the Holy Spirit teach you that principle when you first read that passage? One reason may have been that you were not ready to learn the principle. In our response to the teaching ministry of the Holy Spirit, we need to maintain an openness to His instruction and the readiness to learn all that He wants to teach us.

The Principle of Variety
The Holy Spirit revealed truth to the writers of the

Scriptures in a variety of ways, including dreams, verbal conversations, historical events and rational thinking processes. On some occasions, the Spirit wrote or dictated the message directly. He did not simply rely upon one proven method of teaching and use it until it became ineffective.

In His teaching ministry in your own life, have you noticed the various ways the Holy Spirit seeks to teach you truth? Often, He teaches as we read the Scriptures or hear a lesson taught or sermon preached. On other occasions, He may allow certain circumstances in life to teach us important lessons. Sometimes, He speaks through the formal or informal counsel of others as they share what they have been taught by the Holy Spirit. On yet another occasion, the Holy Spirit may use Christian literature, radio or television to teach us what He wants us to know. We should not be surprised by the many creative ways the Holy Spirit seeks to teach us important lessons.

An important lesson can be learned here for those of us who seek to teach our children or others what the Holy Spirit has taught us. We should not rely upon a single means of teaching to communicate to others, but rather realize that varying our teaching methods will make our teaching more interesting and usually result in better or increased learning in those we teach.

The Principle of Life Response

A third principle implied in the teaching names of the Holy Spirit is the principle of life response. The Holy Spirit does not teach us simply to expand our knowledge, but rather He communicates truth for us to apply to our lives. When He teaches, He expects to see a life response in His students.

From time to time, it is good for Christians to evaluate how well they are applying the lessons the Holy Spirit has taught them. In the past six months, what new lessons has the Holy Spirit taught you? What difference have those lessons made in your life? What difference could those lessons make in your life if you were more responsive to the Holy Spirit's teaching?

This is also a principle that should characterize our teaching ministry. When we teach others, our primary concern should be to change their lives through truth, rather than simply communicating content as an end in itself. This is especially true when we teach the Bible, which was written "that the man of God may be complete, thoroughly equipped for every good work" (2 Tim. 3:17).

The Principle of Review

Many verses in the Holy Spirit's textbook, the Bible, teach the importance of review as a teaching principle. The Holy Spirit's repetitious style of teaching may be illustrated when phrases are repeated to emphasize a point, "Precept upon precept, precept upon precept, line upon line, line upon line, here a little, there a little" (Isa. 28:13). Repetition and review are the key to learning.

The Holy Spirit's use of review in His teaching ministry is readily apparent in the Christian life. Certain things taught to us by the Holy Spirit early in our Christian lives are often repeated periodically throughout the Christian life. Most Christians learn early that they need to pray regularly. But it is a lesson we often forget. So we need to be constantly reminded of this lesson if we are to have an effective prayer life. The same is true of personal Bible study, sharing our faith with others and a host of other lessons the Holy Spirit has to repeat for our edification.

A good teacher will periodically take time to review previous lessons. These former lessons serve as the foundation upon which new truth is taught, as well. If the foundation of a structure is weakened, the whole structure will fall. Therefore, teachers should review basic lessons with their students to ensure these foundational truths are well learned.

The Principle of New Frontiers

Finally, the principle of new frontiers reminds us that the teaching ministry of the Holy Spirit is unending throughout our lives. The Holy Spirit always can and will teach us something new if we are open to Him. Learning ought to constantly push out our frontiers.

Good teachers realize their students need to be constantly challenged with new truth. Although review is important, to constantly repeat the basics without moving on to something else will eventually frustrate students in their learning and often lead to discipline problems in the educational environment (i.e., the home, school, church, etc.). But when students are challenged with new frontiers, they respond enthusiastically toward learning.

The teaching names of the Holy Spirit remind us of a significant ministry of the Holy Spirit in our lives today. Our response to these names ought to be twofold.

First, if the Holy Spirit is teaching, we ought to be eager to learn. Learning the lessons He has to teach results in a changed life.

Second, understanding that the Holy Spirit often teaches indirectly through others, we ought to be willing to be a part of His teaching ministry in the lives of others. One reason the Holy Spirit teaches us these lessons is to equip us to communicate these lessons to others (see 2 Cor. 1:4; 2 Tim. 2:2). The teaching names of the Holy Spirit are both an invitation for us to learn for ourselves, and a motivation for us to teach others.

SECTION III

The Nature of the Holy Spirit

CHAPTER 5

Terms Describing the Identity of the Holy Spirit

The Identity of the Holy Spirit

The Holy Spirit Is a Person

1. The Pronoun "He"	He is a Person.
2. The Love of the Spirit	He has emotions.
3. The Same Spirit	He makes independent choices.

The Holy Spirit Is God

1. The Spirit as *Elohim*	He is God of the Old Testament.
2. The Spirit as *Jehovah*	He is LORD in the Old Testament.
3. The Spirit as *Shekinah*	He is the glory of God.
4. The Spirit as *Shaddai*	He is strong to nourish the believer.
5. The Spirit as *El Elyon*	He is the possessor of heaven and earth.

hroughout the Scriptures, one of the ways God reveals Himself to mankind is by assigning meaningful names to Himself. In two of my previous books, *My Father's Names* and *The Names of Jesus*, selected names of God and Jesus were considered to learn what they taught about the identity of the First and Second Persons of the Trinity. We can also learn more about the nature and identity of the Holy Spirit by examining the names Scripture ascribes to Him, the Third Person of the Trinity.

Two mistakes are commonly made in considering the identity of the Holy Spirit. First, some tend to think of the Holy Spirit as some sort of influence or concept rather than a distinct person. Second, some tend to think of the Holy Spirit as significant, but something or someone less than God the Father and Jesus. Although many arguments may be used to dispute these false views of the Holy Spirit, understanding the identity names of the Holy Spirit will help Christians understand the Holy Spirit. In a sense, every name ascribed to the Holy Spirit in Scripture is an identity name, but the names considered here particularly identify the personality and deity of the Holy Spirit.

THE HOLY SPIRIT IS A PERSON

A confused understanding of the unique personality of the Holy Spirit is accepted by at least two distinct groups of teachers today. First, some liberal theologians will acknowledge that the Holy Spirit may be a reality, but their failure to accept the Scriptures as the inspired and inerrant Word of God leads them to think of the Holy Spirit as a mythological being.

Second, some radical cults, such as the Jehovah's Witnesses, deny the personality of the Holy Spirit and refer to Him as a mere influence. Unfortunately, some otherwise conservative Christians who do not know what the Bible teaches about the Holy Spirit tend to believe similar views about the personality of the Holy Spirit.

The primary identity term of the Holy Spirit that emphasizes His personality is the pronoun "He" (see John 14:17; 16:13). Normally, special recognition would not be given to a personal pronoun as a significant name. But the use of the masculine pronoun is significant in reference to the Holy Spirit. The New Testament was originally written in the Greek language, which has three genders: masculine, feminine and neuter. The word "spirit" is a neuter noun, so when it is used apart from the Holy Spirit, the neuter pronoun "it" should be used.

Twice, the Greek neuter pronoun *auto* is used to identify the Holy Spirit (see Rom. 8:16,26). This form of the pronoun is used to agree with the article it shares with the word *pneuma* (spirit). When the translators of the *King James Version* translated this word, they suggested the translation "the Spirit itself." This is the correct meaning of the neuter pronoun of the Greek, but it suggests something different in English than was probably intended by Paul when he wrote the epistle in Greek. Paul used this form of the pronoun to make it clear he was talking about the Holy Spirit, not to suggest He was an "it," or less than a person. More recent translations have overcome this problem by translating the phrase "the Spirit Himself," which captures the apostle's meaning without suggesting something that was never intended.

The Bible says "when He has come" in identifying the Holy Spirit in John 16:8. John's decision to use the masculine pronoun *ekeinos* when referring to the Holy Spirit, and the use of the translation "He" rather than the neuter pronoun "it," demonstrates an effort to reflect the apostolic emphasis on the personality of the Holy Spirit. If the Holy Spirit were just an influence, the neuter pronoun could be used. But because the Holy Spirit is a Person, the masculine pronoun is used of Him just as it is used of God the Father and of Jesus. When John used this pronoun to describe the Holy Spirit, it was not just a slip of the pen. The Holy Spirit is a Person, as demonstrated throughout the Scriptures. The various attributes and actions of personality are attributed to the Holy Spirit.

Personality implies the existence of certain attributes: intellect, emotion or sensibility, and volition or willpower. Paul emphasized the intellectual ability of the Holy Spirit to know things, "For what man knows the things of a man except the spirit of the man which is in him? Even so no one knows the things of God except the Spirit of God" (1 Cor. 2:11). Paul further understood that the rational capacity of the Holy Spirit included wisdom and communication when he prayed, "That the God of our Lord Jesus

Christ, the Father of glory, may give to you the spirit of wisdom and revelation in the knowledge of Him" (Eph. 1:17).

The emotional aspect of the Holy Spirit is also evident in the Scriptures. Paul described the positive emotions of the Holy Spirit when he referred to "the love of the Spirit" (Rom. 15:30). He also spoke of the Spirit's ability to empathize with our inner emotional struggles:

> Likewise the Spirit also helps in our weaknesses. For we do not know what we should pray for as we ought, but the Spirit Himself makes intercession for us with groanings which cannot be uttered (Rom. 8:26).

One of the negative emotions of the Holy Spirit is His ability to be grieved: "And do not grieve the Holy Spirit of God" (Eph. 4:30). Isaiah cited an example of how Israel "rebelled and grieved His Holy Spirit" (Isa. 63:10). The Holy Spirit has the ability to respond emotionally to the ideas and experiences He encounters.

The Holy Spirit has the faculty of will and the ability to make decisions. In his discussion of spiritual gifts in the church at Corinth, Paul uses the title "the same Spirit" five times (1 Cor. 12:4-11) in describing the Spirit's independent choice to impart different gifts to different believers. When the Greek word *autos* is preceded by an article, it is translated "the same" and is distinguished from being a personal or reflexive pronoun whether or not it is followed by a noun. It is also interesting to note that Paul may be using this form to identify the other distinct persons of the Godhead in this context, although the terms "the same Lord" and "the same God" may also be names of the Holy Spirit (1 Cor. 12:5,6).

Elsewhere in the Scriptures, the Holy Spirit is also described as teaching (see John 14:26), testifying (see John

15:26), guiding (see Rom. 8:4), speaking (see 1 Cor. 2:13), enlightening (see John 16:13), striving (see Gen. 6:3), commanding (see Acts 8:29), interceding (see Rom. 8:26), sending workers (see Acts 13:4), calling (see Rev. 22:17), comforting (see John 16:7) and working (see 1 Cor. 12:11). These actions cannot be accomplished by a mere influence or force. Only a rational, emotional, active person could do all that the Scriptures teach the Holy Spirit accomplishes.

THE HOLY SPIRIT IS GOD

The identity names of the Holy Spirit also reveal His divine nature. Names ascribed to the Holy Spirit such as God, Spirit of God, the Breath of the Almighty, the Voice of God, the Spirit who Is from God, Lord, Spirit of the Lord and the Glory of the Lord, all tend to emphasize the deity of the Holy Spirit. These are only a few of the various identity names of the Holy Spirit that emphasize aspects of His deity.

THE OLD TESTAMENT NAMES OF THE HOLY SPIRIT

1. *Elohim*   4. *Shaddai*
2. *Jehovah*   5. *El Elyon*
3. *Shekinah*

The Holy Spirit as *Elohim*/God
Some of the identity names of the Holy Spirit link Him to *Elohim*, an Old Testament name for God. These names include the Breath of God (see Job 27:3), the Finger of God

(see Luke 11:20), the Fullness of God (see Eph. 3:19), the Gift of God (see Acts 8:20), God (see Acts 5:4), the Holy Spirit of God (see 1 Pet. 4:14), the Seal of God (see Rev. 9:4), the Seal of the Living God (see Rev. 7:2), the Seven Spirits of God (see Rev. 3:1), the Seven Spirits of God Sent Out into All the Earth (see Rev. 5:6), the Spirit of God (see Gen 1:2), the Spirit of Our God (see 1 Cor. 6:11), the Spirit Who Is from God (see 1 Cor. 2:12), the Spirit of the Holy God (see Dan. 4:8), the Spirit of the Living God (see 2 Cor. 3:3) and the Spirit of the Lord GOD (see Isa. 61:1).

The Old Testament name Elohim, usually translated "God," is by far the most common name for God in Scripture. This name is derived from the Hebrew word *El*, meaning "Strong One." Therefore, Elohim is the Strong One who manifests Himself by His Word. This name is used more than 2,500 times in the Old Testament, often to remind the reader of the strength or faithfulness of God. It is the name used in the first (see Gen. 1:1) and last (see Rev. 22:19) reference to God in Scripture, and is often used in connection with God's rule over His creation.

The various identity names of the Holy Spirit that link Him with Elohim tend to emphasize the divine nature of the Holy Spirit, particularly as it is manifested in the strength and faithfulness of His Word. Because the Holy Spirit is the divine Author of the Scriptures, these names of the Holy Spirit remind us of the faithfulness of the Scriptures. Also implied in these names is the ability of the Holy Spirit to accomplish His work in our lives and honor the promises of the Scriptures.

The Holy Spirit as *Jehovah*/LORD

Some of the identity terms of the Holy Spirit link Him to the name *Jehovah*, another Old Testament name for God. These terms include the Breath of the LORD (see Isa. 40:7), the Lord (see 2 Cor. 3:17), the Spirit of the LORD (see Judg. 3:10), the Spirit of the Lord GOD (see Isa. 61:1) and the Voice of the LORD (see Ps. 29:3-9). Several other references to the Holy Spirit are given in a context that suggests a relationship to Jehovah, although the name Jehovah is not a specific part of the title.

The name Jehovah, printed LORD in many Bible translations,* means "Self-existent One," according to many scholars. It is derived from the verb "to be" repeated twice. Jehovah identifies Himself as "I AM THAT I AM" (Exod. 3:14, *KJV*), implying both His self-existence and His eternity.

The name Jehovah for God is used about 4,000 times in the Bible,* usually in association with His people. It has been called "the covenant name of God," because it is often used to identify Him in His covenants with man (see Gen. 2:15-17; 3:14-19; 4:15; 12:1-3). If Elohim (God) is the primary name of God in Scripture, Jehovah (LORD) might be called the personal name of God in Scripture.

When the identity names of the Holy Spirit are associated with Jehovah, we are reminded of the role the Holy Spirit has in our relationship with God. The very name implies His desire to relate closely to His people. In the Old Testament, it was the Spirit of the LORD who repeatedly came upon the judges as God brought deliverance to His people (see Judg. 3:10; 6:34; 11:29; 13:25; 14:6,19; 15:14).

In the New Testament, the liberty of the Christian is linked to the Spirit of the Lord. "Now the Lord is the Spirit; and where the Spirit of the Lord is, there is liberty" (2 Cor. 3:17).

The Holy Spirit as *Shekinah*/Glory

Two identity names of the Holy Spirit link Him to the *Shekinah* glory that was manifest in the wilderness wanderings, in the tabernacle and in the first Temple of Israel. In this regard, the Spirit is identified as the Glory of the Lord (see 2 Cor. 3:18) and the Spirit of Glory (see 1 Pet. 4:14). Other references such as Divided Tongues, as of Fire (see Acts 2:3), the Seven Lamps of Fire Burning Before the Throne (see Rev. 4:5), the Spirit of Burning (see Isa. 4:4) and the Voice of Your Thunder (see Ps. 77:18) might also be related to manifestations of the Shekinah glory of God.

The Shekinah glory of God was a self-revelation of the presence of God in the midst of His people. Originally, the pillar of fire by night and cloud by day were the means by which God led Israel through the wilderness and protected them from the Egyptians. When the Shekinah glory filled the Temple built by Solomon, those who had come to praise and worship the Lord could do little more than stand back silently in awe of God's unique presence among them. Throughout history, revivals of the Church have been described as God manifesting His glory among His people.

When the identity names of the Holy Spirit link Him with the Shekinah glory of God, it is again a reminder of His divine nature. Also implied in these terms are the leading and protecting ministries of the Holy Spirit in the life of the believer. Personal and corporate revival comes when we recognize the Holy Spirit as God, repent of those sins that He brings to our attention, and yield to His leading by obeying the known will of God.

The Holy Spirit as *Shaddai*/Almighty
The Breath of the Almighty (Job 32:8; 33:4) and the Voice of the Almighty (Ezek. 1:24) are identity terms of the Holy Spirit that link Him to the Old Testament name of God, *Shaddai*. This name means "rest" or "nourisher." Although the Old Testament name of God *El Shaddai* is usually translated "the Almighty God" (see Gen. 17:1,2), it also means "the All-sufficient God." The characteristics of strength and the ability to supply our needs are tied to the name Shaddai.

When the name of the Holy Spirit Shaddai is used in Scripture, it is a reminder that the Holy Spirit is sufficient to meet the needs in our lives. It is interesting to note that this title of the Holy Spirit is given in the context of people who needed to be encouraged, comforted and strengthened by reminding them of the all-sufficiency of the Holy Spirit. Elihu reminded Job that the Breath of the Almighty would give him both understanding (see Job 32:8) and life (see Job 33:4). Ezekiel must have been discouraged as he was taken among the captives to Babylon. Yet young Ezekiel heard the Voice of the Almighty (see Ezek. 1:24). Likewise, when we are feeling down in our Christian life, recognizing the all-sufficient ministry of the Holy Spirit in our lives should be a source of encouragement.

The Holy Spirit as *El Elyon*/Most High

Twice in Scripture, an identity term is ascribed to the Holy Spirit linking Him with *El Elyon*, usually translated "the Most High God." The reference to His Voice by the psalmist implies he is talking about the Voice of the Most High (Ps. 18:13). In the New Testament, Gabriel referred to the Power of the Highest to describe the Holy Spirit when he explained to Mary how she would bear a son and remain a virgin (see Luke 1:35).

El Elyon is used primarily in the context of convincing Gentiles that the true God of Israel was above all the false gods of the Gentiles. The first reference of this title in Scripture occurs in the context of Abraham's meeting with Melchizedek (see Gen. 14:18). On that occasion, the meaning of this name is linked with the idea of God's rightful ownership over all He created (see Gen. 14:22). Prior to that meeting, the name was also used by Lucifer in his quest to challenge God's authority in heaven and "be like the Most High" (Isa. 14:14). Perhaps because of the significance of this name in the beginning of their continuing rebellion against God, the name El Elyon appears to be the preferred name of God used by demons in addressing Jesus (see Mark 5:7).

The identity names of the Holy Spirit that link Him with El Elyon emphasize the rightful authority of the Holy Spirit over all of His creation. Also implied in these names is the idea that the power of the Holy Spirit is supreme over whatever power may be associated with other spiritual beings. A third implication of these names of the Holy Spirit is a reminder to Christians that we are part of an ongoing spiritual conflict between God and the devil. This conflict began with the devil's refusal to recognize the rightful authority of El Elyon over all creation, and will end with the devil's realization of the supreme power of El Elyon.

DEVELOPING YOUR RELATIONSHIP WITH THE HOLY SPIRIT

When we understand the terms for the Holy Spirit that emphasize His identity, personality and deity, we should work to develop our relationship with Him. Just as Christians are "called into the fellowship of His Son, Jesus Christ our Lord" (1 Cor. 1:9), we are also called into the "fellowship of the Spirit" (Phil 2:1). Paul's final recorded prayer for the church at Corinth was, "The grace of the Lord Jesus Christ, and the love of God, and the communion of the Holy Spirit be with you all. Amen" (2 Cor. 13:14).

The Principle of Integrity
An important part of building any relationship is to be honest and up front in your dealings with the other person. Lying about yourself, your attitudes or your actions will

hinder the development of open lines of communication, which are so essential in building interpersonal relationships.

The Bible records the story of two disciples who offended the Holy Spirit when they attempted to lie to Him (see Acts 5:3). Ananias and Sapphira were not required to give the proceeds of the sale of their property to God, so anything they gave would have been appreciated under normal circumstances. But their decision to lie about what they were doing had severe consequences, and cost them their lives. Christians today who are committed to developing their relationship with the Holy Spirit should be careful to be honest before God in all they do.

The Principle of Openness

A second important part of developing a relationship with other people is that of openness to their ideas. When others sense consistent resistance to their ideas, they will soon abandon any efforts to build the relationship. In his address before the Sanhedrin, Stephen rebuked the religious leaders for resisting the Holy Spirit: "You stiffnecked and uncircumcised in heart and ears! You always resist the Holy Spirit; as your fathers did, so do you" (Acts 7:51). Christians today need to guard against resisting the Holy Spirit in their lives.

The early Christians understood this principle of openness, and were eager to obey the directives of the Holy Spirit. Peter obeyed the Holy Spirit when he was commanded to go to Cornelius's household (see Acts 10:19,20). Philip followed the leading of the Holy Spirit in his ministry (see Acts 8:39). Against his better judgment, Ananias came to Saul, obeying what the Holy Spirit had revealed to him (see Acts 9:10-17). Later, Paul and Silas were led by the Holy Spirit in their ministry (see Acts 16:7-10).

The Principle of Consideration

A third important element involved in developing a relationship with another person is being considerate of the values, interests and preferences of the other person. If a man understands that his wife prefers a particular type of flower, he contributes to their relationship when he buys that kind of flower for his wife rather than a flower he may prefer. Many relationships are eroded and eventually destroyed when couples refuse to consider their partner's values relating to finances or child rearing, or when they consistently neglect each other's interests when planning vacations or even meals.

Being inconsiderate can also hinder our relationship with the Holy Spirit. Jesus warned about the sin of blaspheming the Holy Spirit (see Matt. 12:31). Many Bible teachers believe "the unpardonable sin" of blaspheming the Holy Spirit involved ascribing the works of Jesus to Satan, and could only be committed by those who witnessed the public ministry of Jesus while He was on earth. But Christians may insult and/or offend the Holy Spirit in other ways today. Paul warned the Ephesians, "Do not grieve the Holy Spirit of God" (Eph. 4:30). Paul then added some specific ways to avoid this sin against the Holy Spirit. "Let all bitterness, wrath, anger, clamor, and evil speaking be put away from you, with all malice. And be kind to one another, tenderhearted, forgiving one another, just as God in Christ also forgave you" (Eph. 4:31,32).

The Principle of Commitment

A meaningful relationship cannot be developed without a commitment on the part of both persons to each other and a commitment to their relationship. Several of the identity terms for the Holy Spirit emphasize His commitment to us and our relationship with Him. When we recognize this, we should respond in like manner, committing ourselves to developing a healthy relationship with the Holy Spirit.

The Principle of Reverence
The identity names of the Holy Spirit reveal His divine nature. Thus, as God, the Holy Spirit should be treated with all the reverence and respect one would give the Father or Jesus. Treating the Holy Spirit as anything less than God in our response to His leading in our lives, our thanksgiving for His gifts or our worship of His Person demonstrates our failure to understand the implications of the identity names of the Holy Spirit.

The Principle of Sufficiency
When you are developing a relationship with another person, it is much easier to respond to that person positively if he or she is sufficiently meeting your personal needs. The identity names of the Holy Spirit are a reminder of the all-sufficiency of the Holy Spirit in His ministry in our lives. Some Christians find it helpful to take inventory occasionally and to identify specific needs God has met in their lives. We can come to a deeper appreciation of the value of our relationship with the Holy Spirit by reviewing how God has answered prayer, healed inner hurts, enabled us to minister effectively to others and helped us lead others to salvation.

---

*The original pronunciation may have been *Yahweh*. The word comes from four Hebrew consonants transliterated YHWH. Originally, Hebrew was written without vowels. Later, the vowels from *Adonai*, Hebrew for "Lord," were inserted. Hence, the term LORD (capital and small capitals) denotes the name *Jehovah*.

CHAPTER 6

Descriptions Given by God the Father

DESCRIPTIONS OF THE SPIRIT GIVEN BY THE FATHER	
1. The Promise of the Father	He would fulfill salvation.
2. The Procession of the Holy Spirit	He was sent to the world.
3. The Spirit of Your Father	He is identical in nature to the Father.

In any close relationship such as a family, people tend to be called by nicknames given them by other members of the family. Sometimes those names remain unknown to others outside the family and have special meaning only in the context of the relationship in which they were first assigned. Because this sort of thing often happens in human relationships such as families, athletic teams, fraternal organizations and churches, it should not be surprising that both God the Father and Jesus have special names by which they address the Holy Spirit. Also, certain names of the Holy Spirit tend to emphasize His relationship with the other two members of the Trinity. This chapter will consider some of the terms that relate the Holy Spirit to God the Father.

At least a dozen names of the Holy Spirit are used to describe His relationship to the Father. (Some are included for full reference, but were discussed earlier in the book. They will not be discussed here.) These names include the Promise of the Father (see Acts 1:4), Spirit of God (see Gen. 1:2), Spirit of the LORD (see Luke 4:18), Spirit of Our God (see 1 Cor. 6:11), His Spirit (see Num. 11:29), Spirit of the Lord GOD (see Isa. 61:1), Your Spirit (see Ps. 104:30), Your Holy Spirit (see Ps. 51:11), Spirit of Your Father (see Matt.

10:20), Spirit of the Living God (see 2 Cor. 3:3), My Spirit (see Gen. 6:3) and Spirit of Him Who Raised Up Jesus (see Rom. 8:11). In addition, variations of these names may also imply a relationship between God the Father and the Holy Spirit.

In seeking to analyze descriptive terms for the Holy Spirit, it quickly becomes obvious that many may belong to more than one grouping. This is true in part because of the nature of the terms. As the Author of Scripture, it was never the intent of the Holy Spirit to magnify Himself. Rather, His commitment was to magnify Christ (see John 16:13ff).

Two consequences of this commitment are usually apparent. First, many more names of Jesus appear in Scripture than names of the Holy Spirit—between seven and eight times as many. Second, many of the names of the Holy Spirit are used in more than one context. Thus, a single term might be described as an identity name, be related to the Father and/or the Son, reveal something of His character, and also describe an aspect of His ministry.

When the names of the Holy Spirit are examined in relationship to other members of the Trinity, it should not be concluded that the Holy Spirit is less than God. The Bible recognizes three Persons in the Godhead who are equal in nature, separate in person, yet submissive in duties.

The Trinity

Equal in Nature   Separate in Person
Submissive in Duties

When the Holy Spirit is described as though He were a possession of the Father, these names describe a relationship between two equals, just as two brothers may use the possessive pronoun to describe their relationship to each other. For one to speak of the other as "my brother" does not imply inferiority. They are equal in nature (i.e., they are both boys). Yet they are separate persons. In most cases, one will submit to the other's expertise, insight or perceived authority in the relationship. In this sense, one might be described as subservient in duty to the other, at least in certain areas. Although this illustration shows how the Holy Spirit is separate from the Father and Jesus, the illustration does not show the unity of the Godhead—they are One.

The Promise of the Father

Jesus described the Holy Spirit as "the Promise of My Father" (Luke 24:49) and "the Promise of the Father" (Acts 1:4). In both cases, the Holy Spirit is described in the context of prophetic teaching about the coming of the Holy Spirit in this age. On the Day of Pentecost, Peter abbreviated this title of the Holy Spirit and told his listeners, "For the promise is to you and to your children, and to all who are afar off, as many as the Lord our God will call" (Acts 2:39).

This promise of the Holy Spirit was significant in the Old Testament context in which it was given (see Joel 2:28). The ministry of the Holy Spirit was largely preparatory in the Old Testament. Only in the New Testament era has the reality of the abiding presence of the Holy Spirit and His continuing ministry in the life of believers been realized.

That does not mean the Holy Spirit did not have a ministry in the Old Testament. Actually, His work in the Old Testament was similar in several respects to His work today. First, He enabled people to become spiritual and to serve God. Second, He was active in restraining sin in the Old Testament just as He is in the New Testament (see Gen. 6:3; 2 Thess. 2:7).

As similar as the Old and New Testament ministries of the Holy Spirit are, some significant differences are also evident. The Old Testament ministry of the Holy Spirit was limited in its purpose, effect and quality. Relatively few people prior to Pentecost had an awareness of the ministry of the Holy Spirit in their lives. Those who did were not guaranteed of its continuity. On at least one occasion, David prayed, "Do not take Your Holy Spirit from me" (Ps. 51:11).

As the Promise of the Father, the Holy Spirit came on the Day of Pentecost, which marked the beginning of a new era in human history, particularly as it relates to the relationship between the Christian and the Holy Spirit. When a person becomes a Christian, he or she is regenerated, indwelt, filled and sealed by the Holy Spirit. (These various ministries of the Holy Spirit are examined more closely in chapter 2.)

As these ministries relate to the title "the Promise of the Father," they indicate a continuation of the Holy Spirit's Old Testament ministry into the New Testament, but in a much broader and more consistent manner. The New Testament Christian never needs to share David's fear that the Promise of the Father may depart. This Gift of God (see John 4:10; Acts 8:20) is given to Christians when they are converted, and abides with them forever.

THE PROCESSION OF THE HOLY SPIRIT

When Jesus taught His disciples about the coming of the Holy Spirit, He told them, "But when the Helper comes, whom I shall send to you from the Father, the Spirit of truth who proceeds from the Father, He will testify of Me" (John 15:26). Many of the names of the Holy Spirit include the use of a possessive pronoun, indicating a relationship between the Father and the Holy Spirit. Among other things, the use of these pronouns by the Father may imply what has been called the Procession of the Holy Spirit, which refers to the order or sequence of the Spirit's work.

Theologians have used the term "procession" for centuries to explain how the Father and Jesus relate to the Holy Spirit. The Greek word *ekporeuomai,* translated "proceeds," means "in the process" or "continually proceeding." This has resulted in the expression "the eternal procession" to describe the Holy Spirit as eternally coming, rather than just His coming at one time in history. Although Jesus only spoke specifically of the Holy Spirit proceeding from the Father, He suggested that the Spirit also proceeded from the Son when He described the Helper as the One "whom I shall send to you" (John 15:26).

The Holy Spirit is continually proceeding in order to minister to specific needs in our lives. This procession of the Holy Spirit demonstrates the compassionate concern our heavenly Father has for His children. Just as a human father constantly gives time, money and guidance to help his children grow to maturity, so our heavenly Father constantly gives the Holy Spirit to help us grow to spiritual maturity. The eternal procession of the Holy Spirit ought to be a constant reminder to Christians of the eternal compassion of the Father.

The Spirit of Your Father

The Holy Spirit is also described by the title "the Spirit of your Father" (Matt. 10:20). This description, along with other terms for the Holy Spirit that include the possessive pronoun, tends to emphasize the similarity of character between the Holy Spirit and God the Father. Just as people today may use the expression "the spirit of liberty" to describe something that is characteristically the same as liberty, so the term the Spirit of your Father describes the Holy Spirit as One whose nature is like that of God the Father. All that is true of the essential character of God the Father is also true of the Spirit of your Father.

What is God the Father like? The Bible describes God the Father as One who gives life to His children (see John 1:13), loves His children (see Rom. 8:15), protects His children (see Rom. 8:31), provides good things for His family (see Jas. 1:17) and teaches and trains His children (see John 14:26).

Likewise, the Holy Spirit is portrayed in Scripture as giving new life to the Christian (see John 3:8), expressing love in and through the Christian (see Gal. 5:22), protecting Christians by offering to lead them away from unnecessary danger (see Acts 20:23), giving spiritual gifts to Christians to equip them for effective ministry (see 1 Cor. 12:11) and teaching and training Christians (John 14:26). Everything God the Father does for the family of God, the Spirit of your Father also does for the believer.

Responding to the Father's Holy Spirit

The names of the Holy Spirit that are related to God the Father imply several principles in the Christian life. As we consider the Holy Spirit as the Promise of the Father, the coming of the Spirit on the Day of Pentecost is a reminder of the reliability of the other promises of God in Scripture. The nature of the Holy Spirit's relationship to Christians in this age ought to help us feel more secure in our relationship with God. The eternal procession of the Holy Spirit demonstrates the consistent concern God has for us. The similarity between the Spirit of Your Father and God the Father is a reminder that we too need to be like our heavenly Father (see Matt. 5:48). This similarity between the Christian and God the Father ought to extend to several areas of life, and is only possible as the Spirit of Your Father perfects His work in us (see Phil. 1:6).

The Principle of Reliable Promises
When Joshua called on Moses to rebuke two men because they had not gone outside the camp to prophesy as they had been instructed, Moses responded, "Oh, that all the LORD's people were prophets and that the LORD would put His Spirit upon them!" (Num. 11:29).

Throughout the entire Old Testament, this longing for a fuller relationship with the Holy Spirit was felt by those in Israel who walked with God. The highlight of the prophecy of Joel was the promise,

> And it shall come to pass afterward that I will pour out My Spirit on all flesh; your sons and your daughters shall prophesy, your old men shall dream dreams, your young men shall see visions (Joel 2:28).

This promise was considered so significant that Jewish scribes usually isolated the five verses containing it as a separate chapter in the brief prophecy of Joel.

Peter stood on the Day of Pentecost and announced, "But this [the pouring out of the Spirit] is what was spoken by the prophet Joel" (Acts 2:16). Many Jews may have wondered if the longing of Moses and the prophecy of Joel would ever become a reality in the life of the nation. But despite the apparent delay, the Promise of the Father did come in God's perfect timing. Once again, the promises of God proved reliable.

Many Christians can identify with the Jews' longing for the promised Holy Spirit. Like them, we sometimes find ourselves wondering if God's promise will ever be honored as we continue to seek the Holy Spirit's power. Sometimes we need to be reminded, "For all the promises of God in Him are Yes, and in Him Amen, to the glory of God through us" (2 Cor. 1:20). Every Christian has the Holy Spirit, who is called the Promise of the Father. His indwelling is a constant reminder that God honors His promises in His perfect timing.

But are we, who are indwelt by the Promise of the Father, as reliable in our word as He is? Sometimes circumstances over which we have no control may prevent our fulfilling all that we promised to do. When that happens, we want people to be understanding and not blame us. But what about the other times when for other less compelling reasons we forget or fail to do all we promised? That practice becoming a pattern in our lives indicates that the Promise of the Father is not being allowed to do His work in our lives. Jesus warned His disciples about making commitments beyond their ability and urged them, "But let your 'Yes' be 'Yes,' and your 'No,' 'No.' For whatever is more than these is from the evil one" (Matt. 5:37).

The Principle of a Secure Relationship

The Christian today does not have to pray like David, "Do not take Your Holy Spirit from me" (Ps. 51:11). The coming of the Promise of the Father on the Day of Pentecost marked a new era in the work of the Holy Spirit in the believer. Today, we can be secure in our relationship with the Holy Spirit, knowing He has taken up residence in our lives.

Understanding the security of our relationship with the

Holy Spirit ought to influence our living for and serving God. If we constantly had to please God in order to maintain our relationship with Him, that pressure would drain our energy and very soon our service would be marred by personal frustrations. But when we know our relationship with Him is secure, we are free to serve God out of a heart of gratitude. The result of this inner assurance is a motivation that we can do more for God.

One of the greatest hindrances to developing a healthy interpersonal relationship with another person is the pressure to live up to unreasonable expectations. When we base our concern for others on the condition of their meeting our expectations, we apply pressure that will inevitably destroy any relationship with them. Rather, we would do well to follow the example of the Holy Spirit, loving others unconditionally. Then as others feel secure in that relationship, we can be the kind of friend who helps them develop to their potential.

The Principle of Demonstrated, Consistent Concern

The eternal procession of the Holy Spirit demonstrates God's consistent concern for us. We recall that Jesus referred to the Spirit as the *parakletos,* meaning "one called along side to help." The Holy Spirit is our constant Helper who is ready, able and willing to assist us in every area of our lives. God the Father not only loves His children, but He has also demonstrated His love by sending His Spirit to help us.

Again, we can learn something about dealing with other people from our relationship with the Holy Spirit. People will tend not to be convinced of our love for them until they see our consistent concern demonstrated in some practical way. As we do things for others and assist them whenever and wherever possible, we give them the opportunity to experience the love of God flowing through our lives. In the process, we also establish credibility for our witness. Then, as we explain the love of God as revealed in the gospel, others are more open to responding to Christ as Savior because they have experienced the consistent concern of a Christian. This is the most effective means of reaching some people with the gospel. That may be why Jude called on the Early Church to demonstrate their consistent concern for others: "And on some have compassion, making a distinction" (Jude 22).

The Principle of Father/Son Likeness

As a boy matures in his family, it is not unusual for him to develop the habits and mannerisms he sees modeled by his father in the home. The same principle of father/son likeness ought to be at work in the family of God. Just as the Spirit of the Father is like God the Father, so Christians ought to become like their heavenly Father. Jesus called on His disciples, "Therefore you shall be perfect, just as your Father in heaven is perfect" (Matt. 5:48). The word translated "perfect" means perfect in the sense of complete, rather than perfect in the sense of being without sin.

From time to time, every Christian should take inventory of his or her progress in becoming like God the Father. The Bible describes various moral characteristics of God including integrity (see Num. 23:19), zeal (see Nah. 1:2), mercy (see Ps. 116:5), goodness (see Ps. 73:1), holiness (see Ps. 99:9), impartiality (see Acts 10:34), faithfulness (see 1 Cor. 1:9), righteousness (see Heb. 6:10), love (see 1 John 4:8), longsuffering (see Num. 14:18), graciousness (see Ps. 111:4; 1 Pet. 2:3) and compassion (Ps. 145:8).

Although many other attributes of God are identified in Scripture, the list above would be a good starting point to determine if you are allowing the Spirit of your Father to develop the character of God the Father in your life.

CHAPTER 7

References to the Spirit and Jesus

THE SPIRIT AND JESUS

The Spirit of Jesus Christ

1. The Spirit of His Son	He has the same nature as Jesus.
2. The Spirit of Jesus	He does the work of salvation.
3. The Spirit of Christ	He assists in the threefold anointed office of the Son.
4. The Spirit of Jesus Christ	He assists in the balanced ministry of the Son.

The Helper in the Life of Jesus Christ

1. The Spirit was involved in...	His virgin birth.
	His growth.
	His Ministry.
	Strengthening Him during the temptation.
	His miracles.
	His atoning work.
	Raising Him from the dead.
	The Ascension.

The Helper in the Life of Jesus Christ

1. The Holy Spirit is involved in...	Christ's ministry to believers.

ust as certain ways of referring to the Holy Spirit emphasize His relationship to God the Father, so other terms for Him tend to describe His relationship with Jesus. Some of these names or descriptions were given to the Holy Spirit by Jesus. Others were used by the apostles to describe the relationship between Jesus and the Holy Spirit. These references include the Spirit of Christ, the Spirit of Jesus, the Spirit of Jesus Christ, the Spirit of His Son and the Helper.

We have noticed that the name "Helper" is perhaps the

best-known name Jesus gave to the Holy Spirit (John 14:16,26). In some respects, all the names of the Holy Spirit given by Jesus may be summarized in this name.

The Holy Spirit may be considered the Helper in three senses. First, He is called "another Helper" (John 14:16), in that He follows Jesus, to whom this same name is applied (see 1 John 2:1). Second, He demonstrated Himself to be a faithful Helper throughout the life of Jesus on earth. Third, He is promised as the Helper that helps us today in our Christian life.

The Holy Spirit as Helper

1. Another Helper like Jesus
2. The faithful Helper in the life of Jesus
3. The promised Helper for Christians today

The Spirit of Jesus Christ

As we have said, when Jesus spoke of the Holy Spirit as *another* Helper, He used the Greek word *allos*, which means "another of the same kind or sort." This word is used in Scripture, for example, to refer to different bodies of flesh or different celestial bodies (see 1 Cor. 15:39-41)—things or people who are of the same sort. Thus, when this adjective is used to describe the Holy Spirit, it affirms that they are of the same nature. Jesus is the first Helper to be sent, and the Holy Spirit is the second. Several other titles of the Holy Spirit are used in Scripture to help remind Christians of the similarities between the Second and Third Persons of the Trinity.

The Spirit of His Son
The title the Spirit of His Son for the Holy Spirit stresses the complete unity of nature in the Trinity. The expressions

"son of" and "spirit of" are used in the Bible to describe similarity of nature. When Jesus is called the Son of God, this title implies He is by nature God. When the Holy Spirit is described as "the Spirit of His Son" (Gal. 4:6), the title implies that the Holy Spirit has the same nature as the Son, who has the same nature as God the Father. This is the most trinitarian name of God in Scripture applied to any individual Person of the Godhead. This title summarizes the teaching of Scripture on the equality and unity of nature in God.

Although I believe the name the Spirit of His Son refers to the Holy Spirit, I am also aware that many Bible teachers interpret the title to be a description of the nonphysical nature of Jesus Christ. Just as a person has body, soul and spirit, some interpret this phrase to mean the spirit that belongs to Jesus, not the Holy Spirit. They would interpret the names the Spirit of Jesus, the Spirit of Christ and the Spirit of Jesus Christ in the same manner.

The Spirit of Jesus

When the title "Spirit of..." is used to describe the Holy Spirit, the word following the preposition is often the key to understanding the meaning of that particular name. The meaning of the title "the Spirit of Jesus" (Acts 16:7, *NIV*) is wrapped up in the meaning of the name Jesus. Jesus means "Jehovah is Savior." It is used to describe the Second Person of the Trinity primarily in the context of His saving work (see Matt. 1:21).

The Spirit of Christ

The term "the Spirit of Christ" (Rom. 8:9) needs to be understood in the context of both the Old and New Testaments. The word "Christ" means "the anointed one," and was used to describe the threefold anointed office (i.e., those anointed to serve in the office of prophet, priest or king). When the title "Christ" is applied to Jesus, it affirms that He was the fulfillment of each of these three Old Testament offices. In this context, the Spirit of Christ implies that the Holy Spirit also has this threefold anointed ministry. It is a prophetic ministry in that it reveals the message of God to humanity (see 2 Pet. 1:21); a priestly ministry in that it offers an acceptable sacrifice for sin (see Heb. 9:14); and a regal ministry in that He rules in the broader kingdom of God (see Rom. 8:2).

In the New Testament, the expression "in Christ" is often used to describe the Christian's relationship to Jesus as one of union and communion. Again, this aspect of the meaning of the title Christ is also implied in the title the Spirit of Christ. The union and communion with God enjoyed by Christians is possible because of the indwelling Holy Spirit (see 1 Cor. 6:19). This means the Holy Spirit is the member of the Trinity with whom Christians tend to relate most directly in their union and communion with God.

The Spirit of Jesus Christ
Just as the title "Jesus Christ" is used in Scripture to illustrate the balance between His saving and His messianic ministry, so is the title "the Spirit of Jesus Christ" (Phil. 1:19). Paul used this title to emphasize the full provision and supply of Jesus Christ in his Christian life and ministry.

THE HELPER IN THE LIFE OF JESUS CHRIST

The Holy Spirit was involved in at least seven aspects of the earthly life and public ministry of Jesus. First, the Holy Spirit was involved in Jesus' virgin birth (see Luke 1:35). Second, the Spirit was involved in the maturing process of

Jesus as He grew into manhood (see Luke 2:40,45). Third, the public ministry of Jesus began with the descent of the Holy Spirit upon Him at His baptism (see Luke 3:21,22). Then the Holy Spirit led Jesus into the wilderness and filled Him so He could face temptation (see Luke 4:1).

Fourth, Jesus ministered in the power and anointing of the Holy Spirit (see Luke 4:14,18). Fifth, Jesus attributed His miracles to the work of the Holy Spirit (see Matt. 12:28). In His death, the Holy Spirit assisted Jesus in His atoning work (see Heb. 9:14). Sixth, Jesus was raised from the dead by the Holy Spirit (see Rom. 8:11). Finally, the Holy Spirit is involved in the postresurrection glorification of Jesus (see John 16:14).

The New Testament uses five different expressions describing the relationship between Jesus and the Holy Spirit during Jesus' ministry. First, Jesus was led by the Spirit (see Luke 4:1). Second, He was filled with the Holy Spirit (see Luke 4:1; John 3:34,35). Third, He was anointed by the Spirit (see Luke 4:18; Acts 10:38; Heb. 1:9). Fourth, He was empowered by the Holy Spirit (see Matt. 12:18). Finally, He rejoiced in the Spirit (see Luke 10:21). Each of these expressions imply a helping relationship with the Holy Spirit.

When Bible teachers seek to explain how Jesus became a man, they use the word *kenosis* to describe the self-emptying of Jesus in taking on human flesh (see Phil. 2:7). This emptying includes submitting to the limitations of humanity. Although Jesus never ceased to be God during His life on earth, He was nevertheless dependent upon the Third Person of the Trinity to accomplish much of the work of God. Although not denying the deity of Jesus, this truth illustrates His humanity.

THE HELPER IN THE CHRISTIAN'S LIFE

The Holy Spirit is active in the world today. Although at times one may wonder if anything is going right, and think the world is in total chaos, things are never as bad as they would be if the Holy Spirit were removed from the world. The Spirit is working to restrain sin in the world and to reprove sin in the unbeliever.

The moment someone is saved, a number of things take place in that person's life. The person is born again by the Holy Spirit, indwelt by the Holy Spirit, sealed with the Spirit and a host of other things almost too many to list. Many times Christians are not aware of all that takes place when they are saved until years later, but these things happen the moment they trust Christ as personal Savior. The Holy Spirit is the agent of regeneration.

The ministry of the Holy Spirit in our lives does not end at conversion, but continues beyond. He fills Christians as they yield to Him and allow Him to control their lives. He leads them and sheds light on the Scriptures, helping them to learn better the things of God. He gives them the fruit of the Spirit for character and the gifts of the Holy Spirit for Christian service.

HOW THE HOLY SPIRIT HELPS US LIVE FOR GOD

In other chapters of this book, some of these present ministries of the Holy Spirit are discussed as they relate to other specific names, titles and emblems of the Holy Spirit. The names of the Holy Spirit given by Jesus imply a number of principles that will help us cooperate with the Holy Spirit as He helps us live for God.

The Principle of Modeling Character

One way the Holy Spirit helps us to live for God is by modeling the character He wants to develop in our lives. As noted in the previous chapter, a number of the moral attributes of God are characteristic of the Holy Spirit. These are also character traits Christians need to develop in the Christian life. The Bible also calls this the fruit of the Holy Spirit (see Gal. 5:22-24), because they are character traits that are not only modeled by the Holy Spirit, but are also developed by the Holy Spirit in our lives. This is one of the helping ministries of the Holy Spirit.

The Principle of Eye-Opening Conviction

One aspect of the Holy Spirit's helping ministry in our lives is conviction. The word "conviction" is derived from two Latin terms meaning "cause to see." Conviction is the means by which the Holy Spirit opens our eyes to see what is right and wrong in our lives. When Jesus taught His disciples about the coming Helper, he noted: "And when He has come, He will convict the world of sin, and of righteousness, and of judgment" (John 16:8).

The sin that keeps people out of heaven is the sin of unbelief. All sin can be forgiven, but sin is not forgiven apart from faith. People who refuse to believe God are attacking His character, and God cannot save them in their unbelief. The Holy Spirit opens people's eyes so they can see their sin of unbelief "because they do not believe in Me [Jesus]" (John 16:9).

Jesus also taught that the Holy Spirit causes people to see righteousness, "Because I go to My Father and you see Me no more" (John 16:10). When Jesus was on earth, He stood as an example and reflection of the righteousness of God. His sinless life convicted people who saw their own unrighteousness. Today, it is the Holy Spirit who causes people to see themselves in relation to the righteousness of God. When that occurs in our lives, we will respond like Isaiah, who cried, "Woe is me, for I am undone! Because I am a man of unclean lips, and I dwell in the midst of a people of unclean lips" (Isa. 6:5).

The Holy Spirit also causes us to see the judgment that is a consequence of our sin, "Because the ruler of this world is judged" (John 16:11). Sometimes we tend to classify certain sins as more evil than others. Depending upon our cultural values, some sins may be more acceptable than others; but all sin is repulsive to God. Not everyone commits the same sins, but the Holy Spirit convicts people of sin of which they are guilty and "causes them to see" that their sin has been judged already. In this way, He shows them their need of a Savior and draws them to the place of salvation.

The Principle of Inner Fulfillment

A third way the Holy Spirit helps us in our Christian life and ministry is through inner fulfillment. This fulfillment is experienced by the Christian because of two aspects of the helping ministry of the Holy Spirit. First, the indwelling ministry of the Holy Spirit enables us to experience and appreciate our union with God. As "His Spirit who dwells in you" (Rom. 8:11), the Holy Spirit unites God and the Christian into a mysterious union. Our union with God is the basis of every aspect of our Christian life and ministry, which may be defined as God living and ministering His life through us.

The second helping ministry of the Holy Spirit is implied in the phrase, the Spirit of Christ. The Spirit of Christ enables us to enjoy communion with Christ. God made people to worship Him and enjoy Him forever. This means that people will have a greater sense of personal fulfillment in life when they are enjoying communion with God. This is realized as Christians are filled with the Holy Spirit and walk in the Spirit. To experience the fullness of the Holy

Spirit, the Christian needs to repent of sin and yield to God. As we have fellowship with God through His Holy Spirit, we enjoy the communion with God He intended humanity to experience from the beginning.

The Principle of Availability

Have you ever experienced the frustration of calling a government office to get information, only to be put on hold, or be transferred from person to person, and you end up talking to someone in the wrong department or talking to one who is not sure of the answer to your question? These descriptions of the Holy Spirit given by Jesus emphasize His availability as needed in our lives. When we turn to the Holy Spirit for help, we are never put on hold or transferred. Also, the help provided by the Helper is always just what we need to resolve the problem we face.

One of the characteristics of the Holy Spirit is that He is always and everywhere present at all times. When David asked, "Where can I go from Your Spirit? Or where can I flee from Your presence?" (Ps. 139:7), he had to conclude that the Holy Spirit was present everywhere (see Ps. 139:8-12). This attribute of the Holy Spirit guarantees that the Helper Jesus sent to help us is always at our side to assist as needed. In this regard, the Holy Spirit fulfills one of the chief prerequisites of a helper. He is available to help when needed.

The Principle of Personal Power

The Holy Spirit helps us by providing spiritual power to enable us in ministry. We are most effective in ministry when we use the gifts the Holy Spirit has given to us. These gifts are given to do the work He has entrusted to us in the power He makes available to us. Jesus did not commission His disciples to begin the task of world evangelism before they were endued or clothed with the power of the Holy Spirit (see Luke 24:49).

Sometimes children receive toys marked with three words that promise problems ahead: "batteries not included." Without batteries to energize these toys, they will not do what they were designed to do. Although they may look like the picture on the box, they fail to function like the toy our children see in the television commercial.

Like the toy without its batteries, many Christians fail to rise to their potential effectiveness because they are not energized with the power of the Holy Spirit. They may look like a Christian should look, but they fail to perform as a Christian should perform. They lack the power of the Holy Spirit to overcome sin in their lives and increase their effectiveness in ministry. Only as they yield more completely to God and allow the Holy Spirit to exercise greater control in their lives can they be energized by the power He offers.

CHAPTER 8

Descriptions of the Spirit's Character

DESIGNATIONS THAT REVEAL THE CHARACTER OF THE SPIRIT

Character Unique to God

1. The Breath of Life	His role in giving life to His creatures.
2 The Eternal Spirit	His role in giving eternal life.
3. The Spirit of Judgment	His role to discern.

Character Reproduced in Believers

1. Your Generous Spirit	His giving nature.
2. Your Good Spirit	His attribute of goodness.
3. Holy Spirit	His holy nature.
4. Spirit of Grace	His nature to forgive and to bestow blessings.
5. Spirit of Truth	His truthful nature.
6. Spirit of Wisdom	His omniscience.
7. Steadfast Spirit	His immutability.

One reason parents choose certain names for their children is based on their expectation or desire of what they hope their child will become. The meaning of a certain name may emphasize a particular character trait they would like to see developed in their child's life. Sometimes a Christian parent will select a biblical name for their child, hoping the child will mature to become a man or woman of God just like the one after whom they are named. Even when a child is given a family name, the particular name chosen is often selected because of some admirable characteristic in the life of the relative after whom the child is named.

When my first granddaughter was born, I was only 45 years old and felt I was too young to be called Grandpa or Grandfather by anyone, including my daughter and wife. "No one is going to call me Gramps...or any other name for old people," I announced vigorously.

My daughter taught my granddaughter to call me "Dr. Towns," obviously because that is what I was called by my students at Liberty University. The first few times she attempted to call me "Dr. Towns," people smiled or laughed. Because she was sensitive, she became self-conscious about addressing me at all.

My son-in-law calls me "Doc," and that is fine. Without any help, my granddaughter called me "Papa Doc" and the name stuck. The name reveals my occupation and character, yet it shows the affection of a granddaughter.

Also, naming people on the basis of discernible character traits often leads to nicknames. When a coach begins calling a certain player "Bulldog," he does so to draw out that player's tenacity. In a church, a lady who is particularly hospitable to others might earn the nickname "Miss Hospitality." At work, a certain person's creativity in dealing with problems on the job may be recognized when others refer to him or her as the in-house troubleshooter.

Many of the names of the Holy Spirit are names that draw our attention to His character or attributes. These names answer the question: What is the Holy Spirit like? The character names of the Holy Spirit include Breath of Life, the Eternal Spirit, Your Generous Spirit, Your Good Spirit, the Holy Spirit, the Spirit of Grace, the Spirit of Holiness, the Spirit of Judgment, the Spirit of Knowledge, the Spirit of Life, the Spirit of Love, the Spirit of Might, the Spirit of Power, the Spirit of Truth, the Spirit of Understanding, the Spirit of Wisdom and the Steadfast Spirit.

These character descriptions may be further broken into two classes. First, some of the character names of the Holy

Spirit draw attention to attributes that belong exclusively to God—for example, eternity. Second, many character names of the Holy Spirit describe some characteristic of God that should be reproduced to some degree in the life of the Christian. The character described by this second group of names is sometimes called "the fruit of the Spirit" because it is the character that is developed in the life of the Christian by the Holy Spirit.

Character that Is Unique to God

When the various character names of the Holy Spirit are used in Scripture, they focus attention upon one part of the personality of the Holy Spirit. In order to fully understand who the Holy Spirit is, it is important to realize that although a name may isolate a particular characteristic, the Spirit Himself possesses all of these character traits interwoven together. Thus, when we consider the Holy Spirit as the Breath of Life, it should not be forgotten that that life is also characterized by eternity, holiness, love, goodness and all of the other characteristics identified in the character names of the Holy Spirit.

The Breath of Life

When the Holy Spirit is described as "the breath of life" (Rev. 11:11) or "the Spirit of life" (Rom. 8:2), these titles emphasize the nature of God in His self-existence. Only God is able to live by Himself, independent of other life-support systems. Although people possess life, their life differs from that of God because its continuance is dependent upon the availability of oxygen in the atmosphere, nutrients in the food we eat, and the continued health of the body to digest that food and fight off disease. But when the Bible describes the Holy Spirit as possessing life, that life is sustained in itself and represents a quality of life unique to members of the Trinity.

The Eternal Spirit

The name "eternal Spirit" (Heb. 9:14) signifies that, as God, the Holy Spirit is without beginning and ending. Because we live within the limitations of time and space, our finite minds have a difficult time comprehending the nature of eternity. All other things had a beginning and most things have an end. Even the "everlasting life" we possess as Christians had a beginning in our experience, although it will be unending. God alone is "from everlasting to everlasting" (Ps. 90:2).

The Spirit of Judgment

The title "spirit of judgment" (Isa. 4:4) also identifies a characteristic of the Holy Spirit exclusive to God—the ability to make independent judgments. Several different words are used in Scripture to describe different kinds of judgments. People may exercise discernment and make judgments in some areas, but the ability to judge is severely limited. When we make judgments, they are valid only on the basis of some external standard (i.e., a law, biblical principle or precedent). Also, although we may be able to discern certain things, judging a person's motives is beyond our ability and is the exclusive prerogative of God. But the Spirit of Judgment can make right decisions in judgment without relying upon an external standard.

CHARACTER THAT IS REPRODUCED IN THE CHRISTIAN

Some of the Holy Spirit's character designations identify characteristics that apply to God in their most complete sense, but also represent character that is reproduced to some degree in the life of the Christian. Understanding each of these seven descriptions of the Holy Spirit will result in a better understanding of the primary work of the Holy Spirit in transforming our character (see Phil. 1:6).

Your Generous Spirit

The Holy Spirit is called "Your generous Spirit" in Psalm 51:12. Generosity is one of the character traits He seeks to develop in our lives. To be generous is to be liberal in our giving or sharing (see Rom. 12:8). Through His generous Spirit, God "freely give[s] us all things" (Rom. 8:32). As the Holy Spirit produces this character in us, we will also become increasingly generous in our willingness to give of ourself and resources to help others in need.

Your Good Spirit

The phrase "Your good Spirit" (Neh. 9:20) draws attention to His goodness. Although only God is good in the most complete sense of the word, goodness is the only character trait that appears on both of the biblical lists of the fruit of the Holy Spirit (see Gal. 5:21,22; Eph. 5:9). This suggests that goodness is something the Holy Spirit is committed to reproducing in our Christian lives.

The Holy Spirit

The name "Holy Spirit" is the most often used character name of the Holy Spirit in Scripture, occurring some 94 times in the Old and New Testaments. In addition, the holy character of the Spirit is emphasized in the name "Spirit of holiness" (Rom. 1:4).

Because the root meaning of holiness is "to separate or to cut off," holiness implies separation. In the context of our lives, this includes both separation *from* sin and separation *to* God. Holiness is the most communicable of all God's attributes. We can become holy because we were made in the image and likeness of God (see Gen. 1:26,27). We can only become holy as the Holy Spirit lives out His life through us.

The Spirit of Grace

A fourth transferable characteristic of the Holy Spirit is graciousness, a trait that is emphasized in the term "Spirit of grace" (Zech. 12:10). It is only by the grace or unmerited favor of God that people become Christians, so it is reasonable that Christians should respond by treating others graciously. When God and Christians treat others graciously, they do for others what is desirable yet undeserved. Only God is the complete personification of grace, but Christians should speak in such a way "that it may impart grace to the hearers" (Eph. 4:29).

The Spirit of Truth

"The Spirit of truth" (John 14:17) identifies truth or integrity as another characteristic of the Holy Spirit He is committed to developing in our lives. Truth is listed as an aspect of the fruit of the Holy Spirit (see Eph. 5:9). The Spirit of truth is the title given to the Holy Spirit in the context of leading the apostles into truth as they wrote the New Testament. One of the authenticating marks of the Scriptures is truth. In turn, truth and integrity ought also to be authenticating marks in the epistles the Holy Spirit is currently writing in our lives (see 2 Cor. 3:3).

The Spirit of Wisdom

The descriptions "Spirit of understanding" (Isa. 11:2) and

"Spirit of wisdom" (Exod. 28:3) emphasize the depth of wisdom and understanding that is characteristic of the Holy Spirit. Wisdom is seeing things from God's point of view, and involves applying known truth. The beginning of wisdom is the fear of the LORD (see Prov. 1:7), but we can also grow in wisdom through prayer. "If any of you lacks wisdom, let him ask of God, who gives to all liberally and without reproach, and it will be given to him" (Jas. 1:5). Wisdom is also developed in our lives as a result of the work of the Spirit of wisdom and the Spirit of understanding as He leads us and guides us in our everyday life.

The Steadfast Spirit

In Psalm 51:10, David prayed for a steadfast spirit on the grounds of the steadfastness of the Holy Spirit. This points to the stability that is characteristic of the Spirit. Those converted on the Day of Pentecost "continued steadfastly in the apostles' doctrine and fellowship, in the breaking of bread, and in prayers" (Acts 2:42). Christians today also need to develop stability in their commitment to biblical teaching, fellowship with one another, the observance of church ordinances and their personal and corporate prayer life. This stability is developed through the ministry of the steadfast Spirit reproducing Himself in our lives.

HARVESTING THE FRUIT
OF THE SPIRIT

When Christians use the expression "the fruit of the Holy Spirit," they are usually referring to nine specific character traits listed by Paul and called the fruit of the Spirit (see Gal.

5:21,22). Actually, Paul also used this descriptive expression to identify another list of three character traits produced by the Holy Spirit in the life of the Christian (see Eph. 5:9). When the two lists are compared, only one character trait, goodness, appears on both lists.

The word "fruit" is used throughout the Scripture to describe that which is produced by some living entity. The fruit of the vine is the grape that is produced in a healthy vineyard. The fruit of the womb is used to describe a child. In this analogy, the expression fruit of the Holy Spirit includes all the character produced by the Holy Spirit in the Christian life, not just the 9 or 11 character traits specifically mentioned by Paul.

Paul's use of the word "fruit" to describe Christian character suggests a relationship between developing character and harvesting produce in an orchard, farm or garden. The application of five specific gardening principles to the character names of the Holy Spirit will help us harvest the fruit of the Holy Spirit in our lives.

The Principle of Like Produces Like

In the very beginning, God created life on earth that has the ability to reproduce life. But that ability is limited. A plant or animal can only reproduce "according to its kind" (see Gen. 1:12,24). The gardener who plants seed in the garden knows what will grow because one of the laws of nature dictates that a plant can only reproduce "according to its kind." As a result, only potatoes will grow from potatoes, or melons from the seeds of a melon.

This law of reproduction in nature also has application in harvesting the fruit of the Holy Spirit. If like produces like, then only the Holy Spirit can produce spiritual fruit in our lives. This means we need to yield to the controlling influence of the Holy Spirit in our lives and to resist the influence of the world, the flesh and the devil. The fruit we produce in our lives will be like the seed we sow (i.e., the one to whom we yield to obey [see Rom. 6:16]).

The Principle of Soil Composition
In the parable of the sower and the seed, Jesus noted a relationship between the fruitbearing of the seed sown and the soil in which the seed was planted (see Matt. 13:8). Home gardeners know that certain plants grow better in certain kinds of soil. A cactus might be planted in a soil mixture composed largely of ashes and sand, but those who grow African violets use only the richest loam.

Just as a plant produces fruit as it draws what it needs from the soil in which it is planted, so Christians produce fruit as they draw what they need from Christ in whom they abide (see John 15:5-7), and from the Holy Spirit as they walk in the Spirit (see Gal. 5:16). When we fail to abide in Christ and walk in the Spirit, we become like the plant that is uprooted from its ideal soil environment. If the plant remains in that condition long, it will wither and die. If it remains in the right soil, it will blossom and produce fruit. So we produce the fruit of the Holy Spirit as we remain planted in the Holy Spirit.

The Principle of the Early and Latter Rain
To illustrate the need for patience, James reminded His readers, "See how the farmer waits for the precious fruit of the earth, waiting patiently for it until it receives the early and latter rain" (Jas. 5:7). The principle of the early and latter rain teaches that fruit is produced throughout a growing season that includes times of rain and sunshine. If it rains all the time, plants rot in the field. If it is always warm and sunny, they dry up and die. But the balance of

rain and sun at different periods in the growing season results in a fruitful plant and an abundant harvest.

The principle of the early and latter rain helps us understand how God uses various seasons in our lives, some apparently good and others apparently bad, to produce the spiritual character He is developing in our lives (see Rom. 8:28,29). If most Christians had their way, they would order a life to be lived in the sunny seasons when everything seems to be going well. Most of us become easily frustrated during the drippy, rainy seasons of life. When the outlook is overcast, we seem to get bogged down in the muck and mire of the mundane details of life. But the Holy Spirit knows just what seasons we need to mature and produce spiritual fruit. Just as a greenhouse farmer may darken the greenhouse if there is too much sun, or turn on the sprinkler system to water the plants, so the Holy Spirit controls our environment to produce spiritual fruit in our lives.

The Principle of Weeding

When Jesus told the parable of the sower and the seed, He noted that some seeds failed to mature into fruitbearing plants, because they were choked by the weeds that grew up around them (see Matt. 13:7). Every successful home gardener knows it is necessary to constantly weed the garden throughout the growing season if the full harvest is to be realized. When weeds begin to dominate the garden, it is unlikely that any of the vegetables planted will become as strong as they would be otherwise.

In the parable of the sower and the seed, Jesus compared the weeds to "the cares of this world and the deceitfulness of riches" (Matt. 13:22). In another parable, Jesus spoke of tares that were sown by the enemy (see Matt. 13:24-30, 36-43). Christians who desire to harvest the fruit of the

Holy Spirit in their lives should take care to weed their lives periodically of the anxiety, deceit and other sins that may hinder the development of Christian character.

The Principle of Pruning

An ongoing task in a vineyard or orchard is that of pruning. This involves cutting away the parts of the plant that do not produce fruit, so that the remaining plant will produce more fruit or stronger fruit. When Jesus described the relationship between Himself and His disciples in the context of a vine, He noted that the Father would prune the vine periodically to increase the productivity of its branches (see John 15:2). The primary sense in which the word "fruit" is used in this context is that of winning people to Christ, but a secondary meaning can be applied in harvesting the fruit of the Holy Spirit.

God may prune parts of your life to help you develop the kind of character He wants you to possess. James reminded the early Christians that "the testing of your faith produces patience" (Jas. 1:3). During these difficult times of pruning, we would do well to follow James's advice and "let patience have its perfect work, that you may be perfect and complete, lacking nothing" (1:4).

SECTION IV

The General Work of the Holy Spirit

CHAPTER 9

The Bible Authorship Names of the Holy Spirit

THE HOLY SPIRIT AND THE BIBLE

**How the Spirit Revealed
and Inspired Scripture**

1. The Spirit of the Holy God	His revelation in dreams and visions.
2. The Spirit of Revelation	His revelation of truth.
3. The Wind	His energy in inspiration.
4. The Spirits of the Prophets	His energy in the writing process.
5. The Spirit of Prophecy	His insurance of the message.
6. The Spirit of Truth	His revelation of content in Scripture.

**How the Spirit Helps Us
Understand Scripture**

1. The Anointing	He removes spiritual blindness.
2. The Fullness of God	He helps us understand.

The Bible is unique in the history of religious literature. It claims to be eternal in content and to offer the way of eternal life to those who believe its message. The Bible claims to be the actual words of God, and thus to be perfect, without error. Paul writes, "All Scripture is given by inspiration of God" (2 Tim. 3:16). The word translated "inspired" is *theopneustos*, which means "God-breathed," and describes the divine action of "out-breathing." The words of Scripture are "breathed out" by God.

What is the result of God's breathing out or inspiring the words of the Bible? A low view of inspiration claims the authors were lifted by God to write beyond their ability, as Shakespeare wrote in the spirit of inspiration and produced works that are among the greatest of all time. A high view of inspiration claims the message of the Bible and the words used by the authors are accurate and without error. After all, because God is perfect and can do no wrong, wouldn't He write a perfect book? The answer is yes.

The Holy Spirit is described as the Breath of God and the Wind of God. As such, when God inspired the Bible, He was merging the Holy Spirit with the spirits and words of the Bible writers. When we read the Bible, we have access to a perfect message of history and doctrine. When we read the Bible, we do more than take its message into our minds. We take the Holy Spirit into our hearts, because the Bible's words are the words of God and of His Spirit.

Addressing the relationship between the divine and human authors of Scripture, Peter explained, "For prophecy never came by the will of man, but holy men of God spoke as they were moved by the Holy Spirit" (2 Pet. 1:21). The phrase "moved by the Holy Spirit" means to be borne along or to be picked up and carried by the Holy Spirit. When the authors wrote, they were writing words the Holy Spirit wanted to be written.

Humans would not write the Bible if they could, and humans could not write the Bible if they would. Humans *would* not write the Bible, for in doing so they would have created a message of the perfect Son of God who condemns all, including themselves. Because God will judge sin, no rational people would write a book that would condemn themselves to hell. Rather, average people would write a book that reinforces the way they live. So no thinking person would write the Bible if he or she could.

In the second place, humans *could* not write a Bible if they would. Because of the limitations of imperfect humanity, it is impossible for an imperfect human having limited rational ability to conceive of an unlimited God who is all-powerful and eternal in attributes. Therefore, people could not have written the Bible if given the ability, nor would they have written the Bible if given the opportunity.

How the Holy Spirit Authored the Scriptures

Various names of the Holy Spirit help explain how He produced the Scriptures. These names are directly related to what Bible teachers call "revelation" and "inspiration." Revelation is the act whereby God gives people knowledge about Himself, which they could not otherwise know. Inspiration is the supernatural guidance of the writers of Scripture by the Holy Spirit, whereby they wrote the divine Word of God, transcribing it accurately and reliably. In both cases, these acts of God were primarily accomplished by the Holy Spirit.

Names Associated with Writing Scripture

1. The Spirit of the Holy God
2. The Spirit of Revelation
3. The Wind
4. The Spirits of the Prophets
5. The Spirit of Prophecy
6. The Spirit of Truth

The Spirit of the Holy God

Nebuchadnezzar called the Spirit who revealed truth to Daniel "the Spirit of the Holy God" (Dan. 4:8). The Spirit of the Holy God revealed to Daniel the meaning of visions and dreams, which could not be understood through means of divination or appeals to false gods. Nebuchadnezzar affirmed his confidence in Daniel's interpretive abilities when he said, "I know that the Spirit of the Holy God is in you, and no secret troubles you" (Dan. 4:9). More than 50 years later, on the eve of Babylon's destruction, another Babylonian King, Belshazzar, was reminded,

> There is a man in your kingdom in whom is the Spirit of the Holy God. And in the days of your father, light and understanding and wisdom, like the wisdom of the gods, were found in him; and King Nebuchadnezzar your father—your father the king—made him chief of the magicians, astrologers, Chaldeans, and soothsayers (Dan. 5:11).

Once again, Daniel was called upon to interpret the meaning of God's revelation, this time the handwriting on the wall.

The Spirit of Revelation

A second authorship name of the Holy Spirit is "the spirit of revelation" (Eph. 1:17). The Holy Spirit is the Spirit of Revelation in that He revealed truth to the apostles and prophets as they, with Him, wrote the Scripture. The word for "revelation" means an "uncovering." When Paul prayed that the Ephesians be given the Spirit of Revelation, he was requesting that the same Holy Spirit who revealed truth to him as he wrote would help the reader "uncover" or understand the message that was written.

The Wind

A third authorship name of the Holy Spirit is the emblem or picture of the Holy Spirit as "the wind." When Peter spoke of the authors of Scripture being "moved by the Holy

Spirit" (2 Pet. 1:21), he used a word that pictured a ship being moved along the waves by catching the wind in its sails. Just as the wind blows leaves or a kite in a certain direction, so the Holy Spirit "blew" the human writers of the books of the Bible in certain directions as they wrote. The result of this influence of the Holy Spirit was that the words written by the human authors were the very words God would have written had He chosen to take the pen Himself and not involve human personalities in the writing process.

The Spirits of the Prophets

God did not opt to exclude human personalities in the writing process, but rather used people to communicate His Word for us to read. One of the guiding principles of revelation is expressed in the biblical statement, "The spirits of the prophets are subject to the prophets" (1 Cor. 14:32). This statement probably indicates that the Holy Spirit's ministry of revealing truth and inspiring Scripture was always subject to the personality of the human author of Scripture.

Some may interpret this verse to mean the human spirit in the prophets was subject to the control of the prophets. As several commentators point out, however, it is more likely that the phrase "spirits of the prophets" means "the prophetic Spirit in the prophets." The verse implies that the Holy Spirit indwelling each prophet allowed the prophet some control. In writing Scripture, the Spirit supernaturally guided each human author to write the Word of God accurately and without error, but He allowed the writing style of the human author to shine through that Word. This explains how the four human authors of the four Gospels could describe an event, such as the feeding of the 5,000, and each one contribute differently to our understanding of that event. All four accounts are equally inspired and perfectly harmonious, but the personalities of the different authors caused them to treat the same event differently as they wrote what had been revealed by the Holy Spirit.

The Spirit of Prophecy

The title the Spirit of Prophecy emphasizes the role of the Holy Spirit beyond His guiding of the human authors to ensuring that the message itself was inspired. One of the governing motives of the Holy Spirit is to glorify Christ (see John 16:14); therefore, "The testimony of Jesus is the spirit of prophecy" (Rev. 19:10). As we read the Scriptures, we should read to learn what it teaches about Jesus (see Luke 24:44).

The Spirit of Truth

When Jesus explained to His disciples the work of the Holy Spirit in helping some of them contribute to the writing of the Scriptures, He said, "However, when He, the Spirit of truth, has come, He will guide you into all truth" (John 16:13). This title of the Holy Spirit emphasizes the inerrancy and integrity of the Scriptures. Because the Spirit of Truth led the human writers into all truth, Christians can read and study their Bibles today, confident that what they are reading is accurate and free from error.

HOW THE HOLY SPIRIT HELPS US
UNDERSTAND THE SCRIPTURES

The Holy Spirit has not only written the Bible, but He is also involved in helping us understand what He has written. Bible teachers call this ministry of the Holy Spirit "illumination." Illumination is the ministry of the Holy Spirit that enables us to understand and apply the spiritual message of the Scriptures. When a Christian opens the Bible and begins to discover the truths of Scripture, this ministry of the Holy Spirit enables him or her to understand the message of Scripture.

NAMES REFERRING TO THE SPIRIT'S HELP IN UNDERSTANDING THE SCRIPTURES

1. The Anointing
2. The Fullness of God

The Anointing

The title the Anointing is used in a context that emphasizes the assistance of the Holy Spirit in helping us understand the Bible: "But you have an anointing from the Holy One, and you know all things" (1 John 2:20). Some Bible teachers believe this title applies to the Holy Spirit in a twofold sense. First, we have an anointing of the Holy Spirit at conversion when we receive Him (see chapter 8). Second, we may have subsequent anointings of the Holy Spirit during times of personal revival (see chapter 11). In both cases, the ministry of the Holy Spirit as the Anointing helps us in our understanding of the truth of the Scriptures.

The Fullness of God

The Holy Spirit is also described as "the fullness of God" (Eph. 3:19). In this sense, the Holy Spirit helps us understand the Scriptures at the experiential level. By applying good study habits to reading and studying the Bible, anyone can draw out its truths and make conclusions concerning the meaning of what is written. But that does not necessarily result in any change in our Christian lives. Change takes place as the Holy

Spirit applies the Scriptures to our Christian experience. When God makes the Word of God real in the lives of Christians, they begin to understand the Scriptures experientially. This can only be accomplished by the Fullness of God.

HOW TO READ AND UNDERSTAND
THE HOLY SPIRIT'S BOOK

How people read and comprehend a book often depends upon their preconceived ideas about the author. If they have read another book by the same author, they tend to read the next book having certain specific expectations. Rather than judging the second book on its own merits, it is inevitably compared with the previous one. They conclude, "The first book was much better" or "The second book is much improved over the first." Readers tend to make judgments quickly about authors, based upon a single one of the author's books they have read. As a result, authors are soon cast into a mold that few are able to break, such as, "She is a mystery writer," or "He is a Christian life writer" or "A book by that author must be science fiction."

As Christians, our understanding of the authorship names of the Holy Spirit will influence the way we approach His Book, the Bible. But unlike many human authors, the Holy Spirit is not restricted in His Book to a single writing style or subject content. The Bible contains something of interest and value for everyone. Four principles relating to our appreciation of the author will influence the way we read and understand the Bible.

The Principle of the Author/God
The first guiding principle in reading the Bible is to consid-

er the Author, who of course is God. Because the Holy Spirit is also God, the Bible He inspired is nothing short of the Word of God. Those who appreciate the Bible as the Word of God will approach the Bible differently from those who view it merely as a piece of English literature or another religious book. When authors write a book, they invest something of themselves in that book. When God the Holy Spirit wrote the Bible, He invested something of Himself in that Book. As a result, the Bible is a unique book that must be spiritually discerned.

In reading and studying this spiritual book, the Bible, Christians should approach it in a spiritual frame of reference. Before seeking to hear from God, take a moment to consciously and intentionally yield yourself to God. Ask Him to make what you are about to read become real in your life. Pray with the psalmist, "Open my eyes, that I may see wondrous things from Your law" (Ps. 119:18). Then as you read the Bible as a yielded Christian, listen carefully to the voice of God through the Scriptures. Let God speak to you as you read His Word and let it accomplish its objectives in your life (see 2 Tim. 3:16).

The Principle of the Author/Teacher

Many books are written today by those who teach, and who have compiled their notes on a particular subject into a textbook they use in the classroom. When students take a course in which the teacher has written the textbook, they read the book differently than they might had they just picked up the book off a newsstand. When they are reading their teacher's book, they read every word thoughtfully, eager to understand all that has been written by their author/teacher. When possible, they may read reviews of the book or articles by others explaining it; but they will read the book first in light of what the teacher is teaching in the class.

The principle of the author/teacher suggests that Christians should read the Bible much as students read their teacher's textbook. This implies four things that should affect the way the Bible is read. First, read the Bible before reading books *about* the Bible. Studying other religious books is not wrong, unless they are books containing false teaching. But study the Bible first to get a foundation upon which the insights of other writers can be added later.

Second, read by having your whole attention on the Bible. Meditate on the words of Scripture and allow it to become a part of you (see Ps. 119:15). When a man asked R. A. Torrey to tell him in one word how he studied the Bible, Torrey responded, "Thoughtfully." Just as a student reads the textbook in the context of what the teacher is teaching in the classroom, so the Christian should read the Bible thoughtfully, carefully considering what the Holy Spirit has been teaching him or her in other areas of life.

Third, pay close attention to the words the Holy Spirit used to write His Book. If God inspired the very words of Scripture, the very words of Scripture are very important. The Bereans "searched the Scriptures" (Acts 17:11). The word "search" means to investigate, inquire, scrutinize or sift. Originally, the word "search" referred to the sifting of chaff from the grain. As we study the Bible, we should separate every word and study every word carefully and individually.

Fourth, read the Bible to understand what the Bible is saying. Do not read the Bible to find a proof text for a particular theological system. Rather, be diligent in your study of Scripture to let the Bible speak for itself (see 2 Tim. 2:15). Someone once said, "The Bible is 21, it can speak for itself."

The Principle of the Author/Friend
Perhaps you have had the opportunity to meet and develop a personal relationship with an author. Or maybe a

longstanding friend has written a book and given you a copy. We tend to read books written by our friends differently from books written by those we have never met. The principle of the author/friend suggests that our approach to personal Bible reading and study is enhanced by our personal relationship with the Holy Spirit.

First, when we view the Bible as a book written by our Friend, we will plan to read some of it every day, and all of it eventually. Some people just read parts of the Bible, but the Christian should study the whole Bible from Genesis to Revelation. The whole Bible has something to teach us about the Person and work of Jesus and how to live the Christian life (see Luke 24:27; 2 Tim. 3:16,17). Jesus taught from the whole Bible, and urged His disciples to do the same (see Matt. 5:17-19). The whole Bible was written by our Friend the Holy Spirit, so we will want to read all of it.

Second, we will want to read our Friend's Book systematically, to ensure we complete it and understand what is written. The early Christians read the Scriptures daily, setting a good example for Christians today (see Acts 17:11). Reading the Bible systematically implies (1) reading the Bible every day; (2) reading at the same time every day; and (3) following the same pattern or reading schedule every day.

Third, when we read the Bible as a book authored by a Friend, we tend to read it by allowing our own intimate knowledge of our Friend to color what we are reading. Perhaps a certain expression might pass unnoticed before you had a relationship with the author, but now it leaps off the page, having special meaning to you. As we grow in our relationship with the Holy Spirit, we will find ourselves increasing in our understanding of our Friend's Book.

The Principle of the Author/Helper
Sometimes we have opportunity to attend a seminar, work-

shop or conference where we receive help from an author/speaker. When that occurs, it is not unusual to want to purchase the author's books, particularly those books he or she has written that deal with the problem area in which we have already received some help. Then when we read that book, we read it not as we read other books, but rather to gain additional insights that can be applied to our lives.

The principle of the author/helper suggests that, as we experience the helping ministry of the Holy Spirit in our lives, we should be motivated to read the Bible to apply it to life. James urged the Early Church, "But be doers of the word, and not hearers only, deceiving yourselves" (Jas. 1:22). As you read the Scriptures, ask yourself the following questions:

- Is there some command to obey?
- Is there some promise to claim?
- Is there some sin to avoid?
- Is there some prayer to pray?
- Is there some challenge to accept?

An author writes a book, hoping it will be read. A reader reads a book, allowing knowledge of the author to influence an understanding of the book. The Holy Spirit wrote the Bible, intending for it to affect our lives. As you read the Bible this week, allow your growing knowledge of its divine Author to improve your understanding of and your response to its message.

CHAPTER 10

The Creation Names of the Holy Spirit

CREATION NAMES FOR THE SPIRIT

The Holy Spirit as Creator

1. The Brooding Dove   His constant attention to creation.
2. The Finger of God   His creative expression of beauty.
3. The Voice of the Lord   His power in creation.
4. The Breath of Life   His life in creation.

The Spirit's Work in Creation

1. The result of His work: The creation of order.
                                          The creation of design.
                                          The creation of beauty.
                                          The creation of life.
                                          The preservation of creation.
                                          The renewal of creation.

When God created the heavens and the earth, the Holy Spirit was involved in the creation process. Sometimes, the activity of the Holy Spirit in creation is described wrongly as a passive work. The first mention of the Holy Spirit in Scripture describes His work by using a word normally used to describe a bird brooding over its nest of eggs or young chicks: "And the Spirit of God was hovering over the face of the waters" (Gen. 1:2). But other statements in Scripture concerning the Holy Spirit's creative work make it clear He was more active than passive in creation. In his counsel to Job, Elihu attributed the work of the creation of life directly to the Holy Spirit. "The Spirit of God has made me, and the breath of the Almighty gives me life" (Job 33:4).

The Scriptures use a number of metaphors in reference

to the creative work of the Holy Spirit. These names include the Breath names, the Dove, the Finger of God, the Life names and the Voice names of the Holy Spirit. Merely because other Scriptures identify the involvement of another member of the Trinity in the same creative function does not minimize the role of the Holy Spirit. It merely illustrates the cooperative work of the Trinity in the act of creation.

In this chapter, we will consider several of these creation names of the Holy Spirit to better understand and appreciate His specific work in creation. This important teaching of Scripture has significant implications for our lives today.

THE HOLY SPIRIT AS CREATOR

As noted above, several names of the Holy Spirit imply His work in the creation of the world, including such names as "the Spirit of God" (Gen. 1:2). Although all the names of the Holy Spirit imply His actions as Creator, four names in particular may be viewed as summary names emphasizing His creative work.

THE CREATIVE NAMES OF GOD

1. The Brooding Dove   3. The Voice of the Lord
2. The Finger of God   4. The Breath of Life

The Brooding Dove
The first description of the Holy Spirit in Scripture describes Him in the context of a brooding dove. Although the emblem of a dove is not specifically mentioned in the con-

text of creation (see Matt. 3:16), His presence as a dove in creation is implied by the use of a particular Hebrew verb in Genesis 1:2. The verb *merachepheth,* translated "was hovering," pictures the brooding action of a dove who gently nestles its eggs and keeps them warm until they hatch, then continues to hover over its young until they can fly and find food for themselves.

This picture of the Holy Spirit as the Brooding Dove describes His work in parenting the new world into existence. The first mention of the Holy Spirit in the New Testament also describes the work of the Holy Spirit in the context of parenting. There the Scriptures describe Mary as being "found with child of the Holy Spirit" (Matt. 1:18). Some similarities between these two references of the Holy Spirit may be found, but the Holy Spirit's work in creation extended beyond what is normally considered in the context of parenting.

The Finger of God

Jesus used the expression "the finger of God" (Luke 11:20) to alert us to another way the Scriptures describe the work of the Holy Spirit in Scripture. David described the world God created as both "the work of Your fingers" and "the works of Your hands" (Ps. 8:3,6). Other names of the Holy Spirit related to this creative name include "the hand of God" (2 Chron. 30:12), "the hand of the LORD" (Job 12:9) and "the hand of the Lord GOD" (Ezek. 8:1).

Just as an artist uses hands or fingers in creating a painting or beautiful piece of pottery, so the finger of God or the hand of God is a reference to the creative nature of the Holy Spirit that adds beauty, scope and dimension to the world. The Holy Spirit is at work to make creation attractive, appealing and pleasing to mankind.

This is "anthropomorphic" language—describing the

divine in terms of the human. Scripture uses several such word pictures, speaking of the Holy Spirit creating life (see Job 12:9), bringing matter into existence (see Ps. 102:25), shaping the stellar heavens (see Ps. 8:3), gathering the physical land mass (see Ps. 95:5), creating man (see Ps. 119:73) and arranging the physical geography of the world (see Isa. 41:18-20). An understanding of the Holy Spirit's work in creation in this context should encourage a sense of celebration (see Ps. 92:4) and a humbling of one's self before the hand of God (see 1 Pet. 5:6).

The Voice of the LORD

Various "voice names" of the Holy Spirit also imply His involvement in creation, not so much in the phrases themselves as in other statements concerning creation. An appreciation of the creative work of the Voice of the LORD is foundational to a healthy and growing faith in God. "By faith we understand that the worlds were framed by the word of God, so that the things which are seen were not made of things which are visible" (Heb. 11:3).

This implies the involvement of the Holy Spirit in the creation of the world out of nothing (i.e., bringing matter into existence). It is significant in this regard how often the various voice names of the Holy Spirit are linked to physical manifestations in nature (see Pss. 18:13; 29:3-9; 77:18). When we hear His Voice directing our lives today, our response should be that of obedience rather than rebellion (see Ps. 95:7; Heb. 3:7).

The Breath of Life

The Holy Spirit is described as the Breath (see Ezek. 37:9), the Breath of the Almighty (see Job 33:4), the Breath of God (see Job 27:3), the Breath of Life (see Rev. 11:11), the Breath of the LORD (see Isa. 40:7) and the Breath of Your Nostrils (see Ps. 18:15). He is also described as the Spirit of Life (see Rom. 8:2) and by other names emphasizing His life-giving and life-sustaining ability.

All these names draw attention to that moment in history when "the LORD God formed man of the dust of the ground, and breathed into his nostrils the breath of life; and man became a living being" (Gen. 2:7). The relationship between the Breath names of the Holy Spirit and the beginning of human life was specifically identified by Elihu when he said, "The Spirit of God has made me, and the breath of the Almighty gives me life" (Job 33:4).

THE WORK OF THE HOLY SPIRIT IN CREATION

As noted previously, the Holy Spirit was actively involved in several aspects of the creation of the world. A comparison of the biblical teaching concerning this ministry of the Holy Spirit reveals His direct responsibility for at least six aspects of the creation, preservation, and renewal of this world. His involvement in creation resulted in the order, design, beauty and life of creation itself. His continuing creative role ensures both the present preservation and future renewal of creation.

Creation of Order

As we have noticed, the first mention of the Holy Spirit in Scripture describes His hovering over the primeval chaos and bringing a sense of order to the world (see Gen. 1:2). Isaiah described the Spirit of the Lord as measuring, calculating and weighing parts of the world as He brought it into existence (see Isa. 40:12-14). Also, the Holy Spirit is described as Creator of the heavens, which perhaps more than any other aspect of creation demonstrates the order of the universe (see Ps. 33:6).

Creation of Design

The Holy Spirit is also apparently responsible for the design in creation. "By His Spirit He adorned the heavens; His hand pierced the fleeing serpent" (Job 26:13). Many Bible teachers believe Job used the descriptive title "the fleeing serpent" as a reference to the Milky Way. If this conclusion is accurate, the creation of design in the heavens is attributed to the Holy Spirit. Although design is attributed to all three members of the Trinity, the Holy Spirit apparently shared in the planning of the creation much as an engineering team might share in the design of a bridge or a building.

When an engineer designs a structure, he does so with a particular object in mind. He intends that structure to accomplish the purpose for which it was designed. The purpose of the Holy Spirit is to bring glory to God (see John 16:14). The Holy Spirit accomplished His purpose in the design of creation in that "the heavens declare the glory of God" (Ps. 19:1).

Creation of Beauty

The statement by Job in Job 26:13 also implies the Holy Spirit's responsibility for the beauty of creation. In this sense, the work of the Holy Spirit goes beyond that of a design engineer to that of an architect. When an engineer designs a building or other structure, he is primarily concerned with function. When an architect designs a building, he is also concerned with form. By applying certain building code regulations to the design of a building, an engineer can draw four walls and a roof and prepare blueprints for a functional building. The architect may use those same regulations to design a similar building, but by the arrangements of doors and windows, the assignment of specific building materials, the shaping of the surrounding landscapes, and the selection of specific colors, he turns that functional building into a work of art. As the one responsible for the beauty of creation, the Holy Spirit has made a functional universe beautiful.

Creation of Life
As noted in the above discussion of the Holy Spirit as the Breath of Life, He is also responsible for the creation of human life (see Job 33:4). It is not inconsistent to consider the Holy Spirit as the One who shaped that lump of clay in the Garden of Eden, much as a potter shapes clay. The work of a human potter will ever remain inanimate. But the Holy Spirit breathed the breath of life into the first man and he became a living soul.

Preservation of Creation
The involvement of the Holy Spirit in creation reaches beyond the original creation to include the preservation of creation. The psalmist affirmed, "You take away their breath, they die and return to their dust. You send forth Your Spirit, they are created; and You renew the face of the earth" (Ps. 104:29,30). This implies the work of the Holy Spirit in sustaining life on earth today. If the Holy Spirit ceased in this work, death and corruption would immediately set in. Because of the Holy Spirit's work in the preservation of creation, a continual renewing and sustaining of life on earth is taking place.

Renewal of Creation
The final aspect of the Holy Spirit's work in creation involves the eventual renewal of creation at the return of Christ (see Rom. 8:21). In a certain sense, He is presently involved in this renewal process in transforming people into a new cre-

ation at conversion (see 2 Cor. 5:17), and in the continuing transformation of the converted (see Phil. 1:6). Yet in a more specialized sense, the Holy Spirit will be involved in the renewal of creation when it is released from the bondage of sin and sin's corruption, and is restored to its original character. This renewal of creation is part of the hope of the Christian that is tied to the victorious return of Christ.

THE RE-CREATIVE WORK OF THE SPIRIT IN OUR LIVES

When a person becomes a Christian, "he is a new creation; old things have passed away; behold, all things have become new" (2 Cor. 5:17). This re-creative work of the Holy Spirit in our lives is based upon the work of the Holy Spirit in creation. Several principles derived from the creation names of the Holy Spirit help us understand how the Holy Spirit accomplishes His work of re-creation in our life with God.

The Principle of Spiritual Renewal
The first principle is that of spiritual renewal. The re-created spiritual life of the Christian is a result of the Breath of Life communicating that life to us. Just as the Holy Spirit was able to turn lifeless clay into a living soul, so only the Holy Spirit is able to transform a repentant and believing sinner into a Christian who possesses spiritual life.

This principle is also implied by the picture of the Brooding Dove. A fertile egg will not hatch into a baby chick unless the parent bird keeps the eggs evenly warmed during the incubation period. By way of application, one who has heard the gospel and is willing to repent of sin and trust Christ for salvation can only be brought to that point through the ministry of the Holy Spirit. Although other factors may encourage people to trust Christ as Savior, ultimately it is the Holy Spirit who makes people a new creation in Christ.

Understanding this principle of spiritual renewal should affect the way we pray for others and ourselves. First, we should pray that the Holy Spirit will work through us and our efforts in reaching our friends with the gospel so that our outreach efforts will prove effective. Second, we should ask the Holy Spirit to use our Bible reading, fellowship with other Christians, and exercise of other spiritual disciplines such as worship, giving and so on, in His continuing work of re-creation in our lives. Only then can we be certain these practices are helping rather than hindering our spiritual growth.

The Principle of Spiritual Standards

The term Finger of God implies the principle of spiritual standards that also influence our Christian lives. Although many references to the finger or hand of God in Scripture tend to emphasize the miraculous power of the Holy Spirit, at least two remind us of this principle of spiritual standards. First, the law of God (i.e., the Ten Commandments) was originally written by the "finger of God" (Exod. 31:18; Deut. 9:10). Second, when God judged Babylon, He first caused His message of judgment to be written upon a wall with His finger (see Dan. 5:5). One of D. L. Moody's most famous sermons compared these two events and called upon the listener to realize that the judgment of God was based upon the standards in His law.

The principle of spiritual standards recognizes that the same Finger of God that fashioned the heavens has recorded a spiritual standard by which we should govern our lives. Usually, the manufacturer of a major appliance will publish a manual, directing the owner how to care and maintain the appliance. Similarly, our Creator has also placed in the Scriptures the information and directions necessary for "operating" our lives—rising to our highest potential and experiencing our greatest sense of fulfillment.

The Principle of the Sword of the Spirit

A third principle arising out of the creation names of the Holy Spirit is the principle of the Sword of the Spirit. If we believe the world was created by the Word of God, we will take advantage of "the sword of the Spirit, which is the Word of God," and use it as an effective tool in both our personal spiritual growth and in our battles for the Lord (see Eph. 6:17).

The Greek word *rhema*, which is translated "word" here, refers to a specific word that God brings to mind in a specific context. Sometimes, as you read your Bible, a specific verse seems to jump off the page, having meaning that addresses a particular need in your life. At other times, as you struggle to make a decision, the Holy Spirit may bring a verse to mind that helps you clarify the issues and make the right decision. These are examples of the Sword of the Spirit, which is the Word (rhema) of God (see Rom. 10:8).

As we recognize the value of this principle at work in our lives, we should be motivated in our personal Bible reading and memorizing. The Holy Spirit is able to bring a verse to mind only if we are already familiar with that verse through our Bible reading and have committed that verse to memory. It is therefore reasonable to conclude that our faithfulness in Bible reading and Scripture memorizing will help ensure a greater effectiveness of the Sword of the Spirit in the re-creation process of our lives.

The Principle of the Leading of the Spirit

Another principle rising out of the creation names is that of the leading of the Spirit. This principle is an extension of the two mentioned previously. If we recognize the principles of spiritual standards and the Sword of the Spirit, we will want to follow the leading of the Spirit in our lives through His witness within and through the clear teaching of the Bible. Also, the Holy Spirit can and does use spiritual counsel from others, unique circumstances in which we find ourselves and other means of leading in our lives.

The Principle of Spiritual Intervention

The final principle arising out of the creation names of the Holy Spirit is that of spiritual intervention. It is logical to assume there would have never been a world apart from its having been spoken into existence by God. Also, it appears the world would have remained in chaos apart from the work of the Holy Spirit in creation. As God has intervened in the past to accomplish His will, so He is at liberty to intervene in the future. The principle of spiritual intervention recognizes that there have been and continue to be times when God intervenes to accomplish what only He can accomplish.

When a person becomes a Christian, sometimes a significant change occurs in life that cannot be explained apart from the intervention of God. Also, Christians often experience changes in their circumstances that are beyond their control, but not beyond the control of the Holy Spirit (see Prov. 21:1). Third, sometimes the intervention of the Holy Spirit is so subtle that it may not be recognized as divine intervention but merely the next logical step in a series of events (see Acts 15:28). Recognizing the principle of spiritual intervention should make us more open to allowing God to make changes in our lives.

CHAPTER 11

---

*The Balanced
Ministry of the
Holy Spirit*

THE BALANCED MINISTRY OF THE HOLY SPIRIT

Seven General Descriptions

1. The Spirit of Access	His role in helping us to pray.
2. The Spirit of Indwelling	His presence in the believer.
3. The Spirit of Power	His helping us accomplish His will.
4. The Spirit of Unity	His role in bringing unity to believers.
5. The Spirit of Fruitfulness	His role in making believers effective.
6. The Spirit of Fullness	His role in giving us ability in our service.
7. The Spirit of Victory	His role in helping us overcome.

Grieving the Holy Spirit

1. Blaspheming the Holy Spirit	Rejecting Jesus Christ.
2. Lying to the Holy Spirit	Deceiving God.
3. Insulting the Holy Spirit	Delaying salvation.
4. Resisting the Holy Spirit	Rejecting the will of God.
5. Quenching the Holy Spirit	Putting the Spirit's influence out of your life.

The Holy Spirit is the Spirit of Christ (see Acts 16:7; Rom. 8:9; Gal. 4:6; Phil. 1:19; 1 Pet. 1:11). The Spirit therefore glorifies Christ. Whatever attention is given to Him in Scripture glorifies Christ. Jesus told His disciples that the thrust of the Holy Spirit's ministry was to glorify the Son: "He will glorify Me, for He will take of what is Mine and declare it to you" (John 16:14). As a result, an abundance of biblical material and songs exalt the name of Jesus. On the other hand, some feel that comparatively less attention is given to the person and work of the Holy Spirit, though Scripture frequently calls attention to His work (see Matt. 10:19,20; Luke 2:25-29; 12:11,12; John 7:39; 14:26; 16:13; Acts 2:2-4; 5:3,4; 10:9,13-15,19, 44-46; 11:5,7,8,12; 13:2; 15:28; 19:6; Rom. 8:5,16,26,27; 1 Cor. 2:13; 12:7-11; Gal. 4:6; 5:16-25; 6:8; 1 John 2:27). As a result, Christians often do not give Him His rightful place.

In the Holy Spirit's Book, the Bible, we are more likely to read about the accomplishments of the First or Second Persons of the Trinity than the Third Person of the Trinity. This does not mean the Holy Spirit is less important than others in the Godhead. Rather, it reflects His intent to exalt Christ and bring glory to the Father. It seems the Holy Spirit only mentions Himself in His book when it brings glory to Christ.

The book of Ephesians places more emphasis on the practical work and ministry of the Holy Spirit to the believer than perhaps any other place in Scripture. (The book of Acts is descriptive, and Romans 8 is theological.) The book of Ephesians contains perhaps the most comprehensive discussion on the growth and maturity of the believer through the balanced ministry of the Holy Spirit. Here Paul describes the Christian's new position "in the heavenlies," which is only possible through the ministry of the Holy Spirit.

In what may be the apostle Paul's most complete discussion of the ministry of the Holy Spirit, a number of descriptive terms for the Holy Spirit are stated or implied in Ephesians. These include the Spirit of Promise, the Spirit of Wisdom, the Spirit of Access, the Spirit of Indwelling, the Spirit of Revelation, the Spirit of Power, the Spirit of Unity, the Spirit of Feeling, the Spirit of Sealing, the Spirit of Fruitfulness, the Spirit of Fullness, the Spirit of Victory and the Spirit of Prayer. Some of these descriptive terms have already been discussed. In this chapter, seven titles that have additional truths to teach us will be discussed in the context of the Spirit's work in balancing and undergirding the maturing process in the Christian life.

THE HOLY SPIRIT'S UNDERGIRDING MINISTRY

In many respects, Paul's discussion of the Holy Spirit in Ephesians amounts to a summary of His ministry in the Christian life. Following are seven names or titles of the Spirit that are implied in this summary.

SEVEN IMPLIED NAMES OF THE SPIRIT

1. The Spirit of Access
2. The Spirit of Indwelling
3. The Spirit of Power
4. The Spirit of Unity
5. The Spirit of Fruitfulness
6. The Spirit of Fullness
7. The Spirit of Victory

The Spirit of Access
To give balance to the earthly life of the Christian, the Holy Spirit provides entrance "into the heavenlies." His implied name in this respect is the Spirit of Access (see Eph. 2:18). Through the Holy Spirit, Christians have access to the family of God in salvation and access to God by prayer. When we pray, we do so because of the ministry of "the Spirit of grace and supplication" in our lives (Zech. 12:10). Again, enjoying fellowship with other Christians is possible because of the Holy Spirit's role to give us new life when we are born again (see John 3:5). Therefore, the Holy Spirit may be described as the Spirit of Access.

The Spirit of Indwelling
The Holy Spirit may also be described as the Spirit of Indwelling (see Eph. 2:22). When a person becomes a Christian, he or she is immediately indwelt by the Holy Spirit. The biblical teaching concerning the indwelling of the Holy Spirit should motivate us to personal holiness (see

1 Cor. 6:15-20). But this teaching also reveals how it is possible for the Christian to live a holy life. The Christian life is the life of God living through us (see Gal. 2:20). Having the Holy Spirit indwelling every Christian makes it possible for every Christian to live a holy life.

What does the Holy Spirit do when He comes into our lives? Some think the effect is mere feeling or excitement. It is true that the Spirit brings great joy and peace into our lives (see Gal. 5:22). But Christians should never seek an experience or a feeling for its own sake. The Christian life is not emotional hysteria. Instead of seeking a feeling, we should seek Jesus Himself, asking Him to enter our lives (cf. John 14:23; Rom. 8:9 and Gal. 2:20). Feelings and excitement are not wrong. They are the inevitable by-product of the Holy Spirit's work in our hearts. We should enjoy the experiences the Holy Spirit brings, but not seek them apart from Him.

What does the Holy Spirit bring when He indwells our lives? He gives all that is good and spiritual.

WHAT THE INDWELLING SPIRIT GIVES

1. Eternal life	4. New desires
2. A new nature	5. The fruit of the Spirit
3. Spiritual life	6. Love and assurance

The Spirit of Power

Paul implied that the Holy Spirit could be described as the Spirit of Power when he prayed, "that He [God] would grant you, according to the riches of His glory, to be strengthened with might through His Spirit in the inner man" (Eph. 3:16). Because the Christian life involves God living through us, the Holy Spirit is the source of all spiritual power needed both to live for and to serve God. Just as an electric motor will not run if it is not plugged in, so

Christians will fail in their Christian lives if they are not plugged into the Holy Spirit, filled with His power and allowing Him to live through their lives.

The Spirit of Unity

Another implied title of the Holy Spirit in Ephesians is the Spirit of Unity (see Eph. 4:3). The Holy Spirit makes unity among Christians possible in at least two ways. First, He is the same Holy Spirit indwelling each Christian, empowering each to live a Christian life. This gives all Christians something in common, a basis for unity. Second, He is the one who has placed every Christian into a single Body, the Body of Christ. "There is one body and one Spirit" (Eph. 4:4). In this way, the Holy Spirit has established the conditions by which unity can be enjoyed. When a sense of unity is absent in a group of Christians, the Holy Spirit is being hindered. In such cases, believers may be fighting God, or simply refusing to allow the Holy Spirit to control their lives.

The Spirit of Fruitfulness

It has been suggested that the Holy Spirit could also be called the Spirit of Fruitfulness because He produces spiritual fruit in our lives. In Ephesians 5:9 we read: "(For the fruit of the Spirit is in all goodness, righteousness, and truth)." Just as fruit on a tree is the result of growth within the tree, so fruit in the Christian life is the result of the Holy Spirit working in and through us. How the Holy Spirit produces this spiritual fruit is discussed more fully in the chapter on the maturing names of the Holy Spirit (chapter 3).

The Spirit of Fullness

The description of the Holy Spirit as the Spirit of Fullness is based on the apostle's command, "Be filled with the Spirit" (Eph. 5:18). The fullness of the Holy Spirit is vital to the experience of living the normal Christian life. The tense of the Greek verb translated "be filled" carries the meaning of "be *continually* filled," demonstrating that experiencing the fullness of the Holy Spirit is a repeated experience for Christians. Rather than being controlled by the influence of the "spirits" of alcohol, Paul urged the Ephesians to allow God to control their lives through His Holy Spirit. "And do not be drunk with wine, in which is dissipation; but be filled with the Spirit" (Eph. 5:18). Notice the contrast between being drunk with the spirits of the bottle and the filling of the Spirit. The Christian does not get more of the Holy Spirit; rather, the Holy Spirit gets more of the Christian. Christians are filled with the Holy Spirit as they confess their sins to God (see 1 John 1:9) and yield completely to Him (see Rom. 6:13). Being filled with the Holy Spirit is an aspect of God's will for every Christian today.

THE FILLING OF THE SPIRIT IS...

1. Repeated
2. For service and holy living
3. Experiential
4. Available to all believers
5. For power in service and living

The Spirit of Victory

The Spirit of Victory is a title of the Holy Spirit implied in Ephesians 6:17,18. In Paul's discussion of the Christian armor, the Holy Spirit is mentioned twice, in ways that are most likely to contribute to victory in spiritual warfare. First, the Word of God is described as the Sword of the Spirit. This means that the Bible is the instrument the Holy Spirit uses to give believers victory. The sword of the Spirit is the only offensive weapon mentioned—most of the equipment described here is for the believer's defense. Yet no army experiences victory in a defensive mode. Hence, the necessity of the Sword of the Spirit.

Second, Paul concludes his illustration with an appeal to pray "in the Spirit." Paul returns to his theme of spiritual struggle, and praying in the Spirit is spiritual warfare. "For we do not wrestle against flesh and blood, but against principalities, against powers, against the rulers of the darkness of this age, against spiritual hosts of wickedness in the heavenly places" (Eph. 6:12).

GRIEVING THE HOLY SPIRIT

In light of the undergirding ministry of the Holy Spirit in the Christian life, it is important for the Christian to maintain a healthy relationship with Him. Paul warned the Ephesians of the danger of grieving the Holy Spirit, and urged them not to do so. The believer is told, "And do not grieve the Holy Spirit of God, by whom you were sealed for the day of redemption" (Eph. 4:30). This means the believer allows sin to remain in his or her life. This may be a hidden sin (to others but not to God), or what we consider a "small" sin (all sin is serious to God). A small sin may be a habit that is acceptable to others, so it does not convict us. But when the habit is wrong, it grieves the Holy Spirit.

In a sense, all sin grieves the Holy Spirit, but five sins in one way or another especially grieve the Holy Spirit.

GRIEVING THE HOLY SPIRIT

1. Blaspheming the Spirit
2. Lying to the Spirit
3. Insulting the Spirit
4. Resisting the Spirit
5. Quenching the Spirit

Blaspheming the Holy Spirit

The most serious sin against the Holy Spirit mentioned in the New Testament is described as blaspheming Him (see Matt. 12:31,32; Luke 12:10). This sin is more popularly described as "the unpardonable sin" or "the unforgivable sin." Not all Bible teachers agree on the specific nature of this sin, but one clue may be that it is first referred to when the Jews who witnessed the power of the Holy Spirit in the miracles of Jesus ascribed those miracles to Satan.

Historically, the sin of blaspheming the Holy Spirit involved the unbelief of those who rejected the miracles of God and the message of Jesus that the miracles substantiated. The "unforgivable" sin today is the final rejection of Christ as Savior during this life. God can forgive any sin, but He cannot forgive "unbelief," because belief is necessary for salvation.

Lying to the Holy Spirit

A second sin against the Holy Spirit is described as lying to or testing the Holy Spirit (see Acts 5:4,9). In the Early Church, a couple sold their land and made a significant financial contribution to the church from their profit. But in giving their money to the church, they attempted to convey the impression they were giving all the sales money to God, when in fact they kept back part of it for themselves. They were guilty of greed, fraud and lying to God. When confronted with their sin, both of them dropped dead. This event caused others to take seriously their relationship with God. It serves as a warning, even to this day, against attempting to deceive the Holy Spirit.

Insulting the Holy Spirit

A third sin against the Holy Spirit is described as insulting the Holy Spirit. The Hebrew writer asked:

Of how much worse punishment, do you suppose, will he be thought worthy who has trampled the Son of God underfoot, counted the
blood of the covenant by which he was sanctified a common thing, and insulted the Spirit of
grace? (Heb. 10:29).

This sin is identified in one of the five warning passages
of Hebrews. Many Bible teachers believe these passages
were specifically directed to unsaved persons who had
become a part of the Early Church, yet had not entered into
a personal relationship with God through Christ. This
teaching serves as a warning of the consequences of continued delay in responding to the gospel. Therefore, insulting the Holy Spirit may involve unnecessary delay in
receiving the gospel once one has realized his or her need
and been drawn to Christ by the Holy Spirit.

Resisting the Holy Spirit
A fourth way people grieve the Holy Spirit is through the
sin of striving with or resisting the Holy Spirit. God warned
the generation before the flood, "My Spirit shall not strive
with man forever, for he is indeed flesh" (Gen. 6:3). In the
New Testament, Stephen accused the Sanhedrin, "You stiffnecked and uncircumcised in heart and ears! You always
resist the Holy Spirit; as your fathers did, so do you" (Acts
7:51). This is a step beyond insulting the Holy Spirit and
involves some degree of active opposition to His leading in
a person's life. When God makes His will known to His people and they refuse to accept it, or challenge and reject it,
they are resisting the Holy Spirit.

Quenching the Holy Spirit
Allowing sin to remain in a believer's life grieves the Holy

Spirit. Allowing sin to control a believer's life and extinguish his or her testimony to others is called quenching the Holy Spirit. Paul warned, "Do not quench the Spirit" (1 Thess. 5:19). The word "quench" means to put out, as "quenching one's thirst," or putting out a fire. Because the Holy Spirit is God, in a sense, the Holy Spirit can never be quenched or put out of a person's life. God is everywhere. But people can minimize the influence of the Holy Spirit in their lives. Just as we can pour water on a fire until it no longer burns, so we can gradually extinguish God's influence in our lives. This is usually symptomatic of other problems in our lives, such as sin that is hindering our relationship with God or indifference to things that will strengthen us. As a result, the leading of the Holy Spirit is not as significant in our lives as it once was.

HOW TO AVOID SINNING AGAINST THE HOLY SPIRIT

In Paul's appeal for us not to grieve the Holy Spirit, he also suggested several specific things that can be done to keep from committing such sins against the Holy Spirit:

> Let all bitterness, wrath, anger, clamor, and evil speaking be put away from you, with all malice. And be kind to one another, tenderhearted, forgiving one another, just as God in Christ also forgave you (Eph. 4:31,32).

The Principle of Actively Searching for Barriers

The first principle that will help us avoid sinning against the Holy Spirit is to actively examine our lives for things that would destroy us. Sins against the Holy Spirit are rarely committed in isolation from other sins. Most often, Christians tend to grieve the Holy Spirit in their abusive treatment of other Christians. Therefore, Paul realizes that the first step in restoring the previous intimacy with the Holy Spirit is searching out sin in our lives and repenting of it—particularly any sin that has also hindered our relationship with other Christians.

The Principle of Applied Kindness
We should seek to be kind toward others, both toward those with whom we have a good relationship and those who have in some way offended us. This kindness was illustrated by Jesus on the cross in His dealing with the repentant thief. Earlier that day, the repentant thief had joined the other thief in mocking Jesus as He suffered on the cross. Then when the thief repented, Jesus responded to him with kindness of the sort we might think to be reflective of a relationship between two old friends. He was kind to the thief in spite of the way He must have felt at the time, and in spite of the thief's previous comments.

The Principle of Tenderheartedness
Our response to others should also be characterized by tenderheartedness. The word "tenderhearted" suggests the idea of a heart full of compassion for others. Compassion for others was a motivating factor in the life of Jesus (see Matt. 9:36), and it should also motivate His followers in their dealings with others. When we begin to recognize hurting people and to help them, it will change our attitude toward those who offend us and help us to avoid sinning against the Holy Spirit.

The Principle of Forgiveness
The principle of forgiveness will help us overcome the ten-

dency to grieve the Holy Spirit. We ought to forgive others, "just as God in Christ also forgave you" (Eph. 4:32). Only as we come to understand just how offensive sin is to God can we begin to understand the immensity of His love in forgiving us. "But God demonstrates His own love toward us, in that while we were still sinners, Christ died for us" (Rom. 5:8). Then as we begin to understand God's love, we will realize that the Holy Spirit has poured out that same love of God in our hearts (see Rom. 5:5). Therefore, we also ought to express that love by forgiving others who have wronged us.

The Principle of Deliberate Steps

How can we do all these things? The key is found in our walk with God. "Therefore be followers of God as dear children" (Eph. 5:1). Young children often desire to be like their parents or some other important person in their lives. They will deliberately imitate the unique mannerisms of their hero or role model. As Christians in the family of God, we too ought to desire to be like our Father in heaven, and seek to imitate Him. Only as we yield and allow Him to live through us can we overcome the old nature and apply these principles to avoid sinning against the Holy Spirit.

The Principle of Building Up Others

The final principle implied in Paul's appeal is nurturing others. When problems take place between Christians, it is too often characteristic to engage in subtle attacks against each other. But Paul's appeal is that Christians should engage in nurturing one another, having a view of building up each other in the faith.

Because it is the nature of sin to attack that which offends sin, we realize that our old nature will attack anyone who offends our old nature. It is the new nature of a Christian to forgive that which attacks our new nature. If we as Christians want to ensure against grieving the Holy Spirit, the focus of our energies should be directed toward nurturing others, including those who have offended us.

The description of the Holy Spirit in the Epistle to the Ephesians portrays His balanced ministry and emphasizes the important role He has in the Christian life. Therefore, we should be careful not to grieve Him by sinning against Him. Applying these principles to our lives will help us avoid falling into these sins

CHAPTER 12

Revival Names for the Holy Spirit

THE SPIRIT OF REVIVAL

Revival Names

1. My Blessing	His role in pouring out God's blessings upon believers.
2. The Fullness of God	His role in making believers aware of God's presence.
3. The Glory of the Lord	His role in making believers increasingly like God.
4. The Spirit of Life	His role in revitalizing the waning spiritual life.
5. The Spirit of Power	His role in energizing believers for ministry.

Outpouring Names

1. Rain Names	His outpouring upon a group.
2. The Anointing	His outpouring upon an individual.

I was converted in a revival that moved through the Presbyterian churches of Savannah, Georgia, in the summer of 1950. Two Bible college students were pastoring a mission church during the summer. They met for prayer on a screened porch of a garage apartment at five o'clock every morning. A little church that seated 200 had more than 300 in attendance evening after evening. Electricity was in the air when people started gathering each evening. They expected people to come to Christ, and it happened. I was converted July 25, 1950, at approximately 11:15 P.M., while praying by my bed at home.

Today, observers would call it an "atmospheric revival,"

yet it had a deep influence, because the change in my heart is still effective 43 years later. What happened was not just an emotional experience, but the anointing of the Holy Spirit on individuals and the outpouring of the Holy Spirit on a group of people. The word "revive" means to live again, and at this revival I felt that New Testament Christianity was alive again.

An evangelical revival is an extraordinary work of God in which: first, Christians repent of their sins as they become intensely aware of His presence; and second, people give a positive response to God in renewed obedience to His will. This results in both a deepening of their individual and corporate experience with God, and an increased concern for the spiritual welfare of both themselves and others within their community.

The Holy Spirit is the agent of new spiritual life, or revival, so it is not surprising that several of the terms Scripture uses to describe Him emphasize His work in revival. These names include the Anointing (the contemporary term for the filling of the Holy Spirit), My Blessing, the Breath of Life, Dew, the Enduement of Power, Floods on the Dry Ground, the Fullness of God, the Glory of the Lord, the Oil of Gladness, the Power of the Highest, Rain, Rivers of Living Water, Showers that Water the Earth, the Spirit of Glory, the Spirit of Life and the Spirit of Power.

THE HOLY SPIRIT AND REVIVAL

Although each of these ways of describing the Holy Spirit contribute to an understanding of revival, five of them may be considered as representative in describing His role in shaping the character of revival. These "names" are My Blessing (see Isa. 44:3), the Fullness of God (see Eph. 3:19), the Glory of the Lord (see 2 Cor. 3:18), the Spirit of Life (see Rom. 8:2) and the Spirit of Power (see 2 Tim. 1:7).

REVIVAL TERMS FOR THE HOLY SPIRIT

1. My Blessing
2. The Fullness of God
3. The Glory of the Lord
4. The Spirit of Life
5. The Spirit of Power

My Blessing

The Spirit's name My Blessing is implied throughout the Scriptures in describing revival (see Ps. 24:5; 133:3; Mal. 3:10). The expression "blessing of God" is often used by Christians to describe the benefits God pours out on His people, but ultimately the blessing of God is God Himself. During times of revival, Christians often have a renewed appreciation of who God is and the various blessings associated with His person and work. This is a result of the Holy Spirit's work in revival as God's Blessing.

The Fullness of God

When those who experience revival attempt to describe their experience to others, it is not uncommon for them to confess, "The place seemed filled with the presence of God" or "I sensed being filled with God until it seemed like I could not contain any more." As the Fullness of God, the Holy Spirit makes Christians intensely aware of God's presence during times of revival. Contemporary observers call this "atmospheric revival."

Paul prayed that the Ephesians "may be filled with all the fullness of God" (Eph. 3:19). In a sense, God is present everywhere and at all times. But it is easy for Christians to believe in His omnipresence, yet fail to recognize His presence in their daily lives. In revival, it is as though the Holy Spirit opens our eyes so we can see God's presence in our midst and allow Him to change our lives.

Results of God's Presence in Revival

Believers...
1. Expect God to work (faith).
2. Are stirred to pray more.
3. Are motivated to good works.
4. Search themselves for sin.
5. Repent and cleanse themselves.
6. Offer praise to God.

The Glory of the Lord

Another revival expression for the Holy Spirit often used to describe revival is the Glory of the Lord. Paul wrote:

> But we all, with unveiled face, beholding as in a mirror the glory of the Lord, are being transformed into the same image from glory to glory, just as by the Spirit of the Lord (2 Cor. 3:18).

The Glory of the Lord is based on the Old Testament Shekinah, an actual manifestation of the glory of God to Israel during the wilderness wanderings and in Solomon's Temple.

During revival, Christians once more gain a renewed vision of God in His glory and majesty through the ministry of the Holy Spirit. They sense their being in the presence of God in all His splendor. They respond as did Isaiah (see Isa. 6) or John (see Rev. 1) in recognizing their complete unworthiness in His presence. When they view God in His glory, they begin to see just how far short they have fallen (see Rom. 3:23) and they repent of their sin. Perhaps the phrase "glory to glory" is an actual description of a revival when God continues to pour His blessings (or His presence) upon those who wait for revival.

The Spirit of Life

As the Spirit of Life, the Holy Spirit is the agent of revival because He gives new life to the revived. "For the law of the Spirit of life in Christ Jesus has made me free from the law of sin and death" (Rom. 8:2). The word "revival" is derived from two Latin words that mean "to live again," and has two applications. First, revival is the return of New Testament Christianity to a group of people. Second, revival is a believer returning to his "first love" (Rev. 2:5)—the time when he was first converted.

One of the Hebrew words translated "revival" in the Old Testament is *chayah,* which is most often translated "living." Revival involves God's granting new life to dead or dying Christians and churches. This granting of life is a ministry of the Spirit of Life. Many Christians experience this revived life as they understand the Holy Spirit has placed them "in Christ" so He can live the Christian life through them.

The Spirit of Power

We have noted that although the phrase "spirit of power" in 2 Timothy 1:7 may refer to the Christian's spirit, the *source* of this power is the Holy Spirit. This term would have caused Timothy to recall the revival in Ephesus when "the word of the Lord grew mightily and prevailed" (Acts 19:20). During times of revival, Christians and churches are energized to do the work of God in a much more intense manner than may be the case normally. That is one reason why churches often experience numerical growth during revivals. When the energy of revival is channelled into productive ministry, God often blesses our efforts in evangelism by giving extraordinary results. The key to this success in ministry is the Spirit of Power at work in our lives.

REVIVAL AND THE OUTPOURING OF THE HOLY SPIRIT

Two terms are used in revivalistic literature to describe the experience of revival: "the outpouring of the Holy Spirit" and "the anointing of the Holy Spirit." Although experiences of revival are described in many ways, the expression "outpouring of the Holy Spirit" is usually a reference to the corporate spirit of revival in an area or among a group of Christians. In contrast, when revival comes to an individual, it is often described as an "anointing of the Holy Spirit."

THE OUTPOURING OF THE HOLY SPIRIT	THE ANOINTING OF THE HOLY SPIRIT
Revival of a group	Revival of a person

The terms "outpouring" and "anointing" refer to different degrees of the same ministry of the Holy Spirit. When the Holy Spirit comes upon one person, it is anointing. When the Holy Spirit comes upon many people, it constitutes an outpouring. Both of these phrases find their origin in the Scriptures and are consistently used in revivalistic literature to describe an intense experience with the Holy Spirit. Both expressions are also tied to the revival names of the Holy Spirit.

Outpouring Names of the Holy Spirit

1. Rain Names   2. The Anointing

Rain Names

Several of the revival terms for the Holy Spirit are tied to the picture of the Spirit watering the ground. These descriptive terms include "the dew" (Hos. 14:5), "floods on the dry ground" (Isa. 44:3), "a fountain of water" (John 4:14), "rain upon the mown grass" (Ps. 72:6), "rivers of living water" (John 7:38), "showers that water the earth" (Ps. 72:6) and "water" (Isa. 44:3).

In each case, the Holy Spirit is described symbolically as the means by which God pours out His blessing to revive and refresh Christians, much as rain is the means by which the earth is refreshed. These revival names should not be taken as denials of the personality of the Holy Spirit, but rather as descriptions that picture His influence in refreshing people who are spiritually thirsty, wilted or dying.

The Anointing

Another revival name of the Holy Spirit is "the anointing" (1 John 2:27), a term we also considered earlier. Some view this name exclusively as a saving name of the Holy Spirit because they feel the anointing causes people to understand spiritual truth. As such, the term refers to the illumination of the Holy Spirit.

But the Anointing can also be considered as a revival name. The anointing of the Holy Spirit is also a postconversion experience suggested by the contrast of the nature and effects of the anointing and regeneration. Because the Holy Spirit is the agent of regeneration, it is to be expected that similarities are found between regeneration and other ministries of the same Spirit. The differences serve to distinguish these various works.

Under the Levitical law two anointings were practiced: the anointing of blood and the anointing of oil. This was practiced at the cleansing of a leper (see Lev. 14) and the consecration of a priest (see Lev. 8). Both have typical application for the Christian life. The cleansed leper is a type of one who is cleansed from sin. And the New Testament identifies the believer as part of "a royal priesthood" (1 Pet. 2:9). This dual anointing represents the twofold experience of believers. They are first anointed with the blood of Christ (i.e., in regeneration), and then with the "oil" of the Holy Spirit in revival. David's desire to be "anointed with fresh oil" (Ps. 92:10) suggests that the anointing is a repeatable experience with the Holy Spirit.

SEVEN STEPS TOWARD AN OUTPOURING OF THE HOLY SPIRIT

What can be done to encourage an outpouring of the Holy Spirit so that we might experience His revival names? Some Bible teachers believe we will never experience another great outpouring of the Holy Spirit or, if a worldwide revival takes place, it will come from God alone and cannot be the result of seeking God through prayer.

Others, however, realize that God responds to the prayers of His people, governs His activities by certain laws, and will honor the promises of Scripture if we meet those conditions. Perhaps God will send a massive revival when His conditions are met (see 2 Chron. 7:14).

A survey of the biblical references to an outpouring of the Holy Spirit, or the pouring out of a blessing of God on

His people, suggests seven principles associated with these promises. When an individual Christian meets these conditions, he or she may experience the anointing of the Holy Spirit. When a group of Christians together meet these conditions, then God will pour out His Holy Spirit on them.

The Principle of Desire

The first precondition for revival is desire. God's people must want it. God has promised, "I will pour water on him who is thirsty, and floods on the dry ground; I will pour My Spirit on your descendants, and My blessing on your offspring" (Isa. 44:3). Here, as in other places in Scripture, God uses the imagery of thirst to identify an intense desire on the part of people for revival. God never sent revival to any people who did not first *want* a revival and/or the fruits of revival.

The Principle of Prayer

Prevailing and believing prayer is often mentioned as a precondition of revival in Scripture. Zechariah, the prophet, used the imagery of rain to describe the outpouring of the Holy Spirit, urging the people to, "Ask the Lord for rain in the time of the latter rain. The Lord will make flashing clouds; He will give them showers of rain, grass in the field for everyone" (Zech. 10:1; cf. Joel 2:23; Jas. 5:7).

Prevailing prayer has been so much a part of historical revivals that some writers regard revival as a prayer movement. The kind of prayer that is essential to produce revival blessing is that which prevails, and may be characterized as the prayer of faith.

The Principle of Repentance

Repentance of all known sin, which involves the humbling

of the believer, is another essential precondition of revival. "Turn at my reproof; surely I will pour out my spirit on you; I will make my words known to you" (Prov. 1:23). The Scriptures also declare:

> For thus says the High and Lofty One Who inhabits eternity, whose name is Holy: "I dwell in the high and holy place, with him who has a contrite and humble spirit, to revive the spirit of the humble, and to revive the heart of the contrite ones" (Isa. 57:15).

The Principle of Yielding

Perhaps the most frequently mentioned precondition of revival in Scripture is that of a recognition of the Lordship or Kingship of Christ. Many of the prophetic statements concerning the outpouring of the Holy Spirit refer to a time when the people recognize Christ as He returns to establish His Kingdom (cf. Isa. 32:15; Joel 2:27,29; Acts 2:17,18). On the Day of Pentecost, Peter affirmed the Lordship of Christ as he concluded his sermon, "Therefore let all the house of Israel know assuredly that God has made this Jesus, whom you crucified, both Lord and Christ" (Acts 2:36).

Recognizing the Lordship of Christ usually involves the practice of seeking God, surrendering to His will and repenting of known sin. In the Old Testament, people engaged in seeking God to obtain His blessing, as one might obtain a request from a king.

The Principle of Fellowship

The unity of the brethren is identified as a precondition of revival blessing in Psalm 133. God commands His blessing in the presence of a united people. Also, both the anointing of Aaron and the dew of Hermon in this psalm are emblems of the outpouring of the Holy Spirit in Scripture. The expression "with one accord" is often used to characterize the united fellowship of the revived Church in the book of Acts (see Acts 1:14; 2:1).

The Principle of Worship

Praise is associated with the blessing of God. According to the *Peshitta* (an ancient Syriac translation of the Scriptures) the psalmist writes, "Whosoever offers the sacrifice of thanksgiving glorifies me; and to him will I show the way of the salvation of our God" (Ps. 50:23, *Peshitta*). This was also the way the verse was translated in both the *Septuagint* and *Vulgate* translations of the Old Testament. More recent English translations such as the *New International Version* also translate the verse in a similar way. "He who sacrifices thank offerings honors me, and he prepares the way so that I may show him the salvation of God" (Ps. 50:23, *NIV*). It means God sends His revival blessing to those who properly worship Him.

If this reading of the verse is correct, it seems to teach that the "sacrifice of thanksgiving" (praise) is a precondition to God's manifesting His salvation. The word "salvation" should not be restricted to its soteriological sense, but, as is often the case in the Old Testament, probably refers to a broader blessing of God, including that of revival. This emphasis is consistent with an earlier statement in the Psalms: "But You are holy, Who inhabit the praises of Israel" (Ps. 22:3).

Notice that God lives in the presence of a worshiping people. Their praises invite the presence of God in a unique way. At the dedication of Solomon's Temple, the praises of God's people ushered in the presence of God in a most unique way.

Indeed it came to pass, when the trumpeters and singers were as one, to make one sound to be heard in praising and thanking the LORD, and when they lifted up their voice with the trumpets and cymbals and instruments of music, and praised the LORD, saying: "For He is good, For His mercy endures forever," that the house, the house of the LORD, was filled with a cloud, so that the priests could not continue ministering because of the cloud; for the glory of the LORD filled the house of God (2 Chron. 5:13,14).

The Principle of Giving to God

Scripture also associates the promise that God will pour out His blessing with the practice of giving to Him:

"Bring all the tithes into the storehouse, that there may be food in My house, and prove Me now in this," says the LORD of hosts, "If I will not open for you the windows of heaven and pour out for you such blessing that there will not be room enough to receive it" (Mal. 3:10).

Although the concept of "tithing" (i.e., giving 10 percent of our income to God) is interpreted differently among evangelical Christians today, sacrificial giving is an essential condition to be met in preparing for an outpouring of the Holy Spirit.

One reason some Christians do not properly give of their means to God is that they fail to understand the spiritual nature of biblical stewardship. Taking an offering is not just a means used by churches to raise money, although that is one purpose. The Scriptures identify several essential principles of financial stewardship. First, giving is a spiritual matter, not just a financial one (see Mal. 3:7). Second, failure to give money to God is a personal affront to Him (see Mal. 3:8). And third, God will withhold many blessings from His people if they do not give to Him (see Mal. 3:9).

God encourages His people to prove Him or test Him in the financial area of their lives (see Mal. 3:10). When they do so, they discover that God rewards them abundantly. First, He rewards their faith (see Mal. 3:10). Second, they are protected (see Mal. 3:11). Third, God gives them fruit in their lives (see Mal. 3:12).

From time to time, Christians ask God for revival. They seek renewed meaning to their faith. These seven principles make believers revival friendly, so that it is possible for them to experience the fullness of the revival terms for the Holy Spirit. As we meet these conditions in our lives, God will anoint us with the Holy Spirit, resulting in personal revival. If others join us in our effort to encourage revival, God will pour out His Holy Spirit on a larger group and effect a revival. If we want to experience revival in our personal lives, we can do something specific about it.

CHAPTER 13

The Pictorial Names
of the Holy Spirit

PORTRAITS OF THE HOLY SPIRIT

The Gallery of Religious Art

1. The Anointing   His role in setting us apart to God.
2. My Blessing   His role in blessing us with all spiritual blessings.
3. Fire   His role in presenting our worship to God.
4. Oil   His role in consecrating us to God.

The Gallery of Social Customs

1. A Deposit   His role in guaranteeing our salvation.
2. The Doorkeeper   His role in bringing us to the Good Shepherd.
3. The Enduement   His role in clothing us for ministry.

The Gallery of Nature

1. The Dew   His role in daily refreshing us.
2. A Dove   His role in bringing fruition.
3. Rivers   His role in filling to overflowing.
4. Wind and Water   His role in regeneration.

Some of the names of the Holy Spirit are highly symbolic in nature. These terms may be described as pictures that illustrate different truths about the Holy Spirit. These portraits of the Holy Spirit are hung throughout the Scriptures to help us understand a little about the nature of both His Person and His work. When considering these picture-names of the Holy Spirit, we should be careful not to come to conclusions that may be contrary to the clear teaching of Scripture. For example, pictures of the Holy Spirit as the Anointing Oil must not lead to the idea that He is actually a substance instead of a Person.

Despite their limitations, the picture-names of the Holy

Spirit contribute to our understanding of the Third Person of the Trinity. These names describe the Holy Spirit in a context that is more familiar to us than such abstract concepts as grace, love and holiness.

Among the various pictorial names of the Holy Spirit are the Anointing, My Blessing, a Deposit, the Dew, the Doorkeeper, a Dove, an Enduement (clothing), the Finger of God, Fire, Fountain, the Guarantee, the Oil, Rain, Rivers, Water and Wind. Each of these names were ascribed to the Holy Spirit in Scripture in a specific context. To this list, some Bible teachers would also add Eliezer, Abraham's servant who went out from Abraham the father to find a bride for Isaac (see Gen. 24). They see a parallel between Abraham's servant and the work of the Holy Spirit in gathering the Church, which is described as the Bride of Christ during this age.

Perhaps the best way to consider the various pictorial names of the Holy Spirit is to do so in the context of a museum or art gallery. In a large art gallery, various artifacts may be arranged in different groupings around a common theme. As we enter this museum devoted to the Holy Spirit, we will be viewing 11 portraits that are arranged in three separate galleries.

THE PICTORIAL NAMES OF THE HOLY SPIRIT

The Gallery of Religious Art	The Gallery of Social Customs	The Gallery of Nature
1. The Anointing	1. A Deposit	1. The Dew
2. My Blessing	2. The Doorkeeper	2. A Dove
3. Fire	3. The Enduement	3. Rivers
4. Oil		4. Wind and Water

A GALLERY OF RELIGIOUS ART

The first gallery in this museum may be described as the

gallery of religious art. Some of the pictorial names of the Holy Spirit are drawn from the religious setting of Israel's national religion. Four of these religious picture names are the Anointing, My Blessing, Fire and Oil.

The Anointing

It was customary in the religion of the Jews to set someone or something apart for God by an anointing with oil. The furnishings of the Tabernacle were anointed, as were people who were set apart for such roles as prophet, priest or king. In each situation, the anointing signified that the person or thing being anointed was set apart for the special service of God.

In the Old Testament context, only a few believers were filled with the Spirit for service. In the New Testament, in a certain sense, every Christian has "the anointing" (1 John 2:27). This means every Christian today has been set apart for God for some special service. You can do something for God, which only you can do for God. Christians should yield to the leading of the Anointing in their lives and use their spiritual gifts in the unique ministry opportunities prepared for them.

My Blessing

The second portrait in this gallery shows the priest with arms raised as he blesses the nation. This blessing is also a picture of the Holy Spirit (see Isa. 44:3). Many pastors today conclude their worship service by lifting their hands and reciting a benediction or blessing. When the priest offered His blessing on the people, it was not merely to conclude some aspect of worship but also to tell them of God's favor upon them. Even when this blessing occurred at the end of a religious ceremony, the granting of this blessing upon the people was often the beginning of the heartfelt celebration and worship of God from the people themselves.

Perhaps this would be a good point in our tour of the gallery to pause and consider the many blessings God has granted us in addition to His Blessing, the Holy Spirit. An old hymn urges Christians to "Count your blessings, name them one by one." When Christians follow the advice of this hymn writer and begin listing all the good things God has done for them, recalling these blessings is often the beginning of spontaneous thanksgiving to God for what He has done.

Fire

The third portrait of the Holy Spirit in this gallery is a picture of fire burning on the sacrificial altar. At first it appears to be an Old Testament altar for offering sacrifices to God. But on the Day of Pentecost, tongues of fire appeared over those gathered in the Upper Room as the Holy Spirit was poured out on them. The fire of God upon the altar was the means by which all that was offered to God ascended up to God and became "a sweet aroma to the LORD" (Lev. 1:9).

This, too, has an application in the Christian life. Christians may attempt to serve God in two ways. When they serve Him in the flesh, the fruit that results from those efforts may be described as corrupted: "fruit to death" (Rom. 7:5). But when we serve God in the Spirit, then that Holy Fire will cause those efforts to ascend before God and we worship and please Him.

Oil

The final portrait we shall consider in this gallery is that of a huge vat of oil. This was the freshly mixed, holy anointing oil. This, too, is a picture of the Holy Spirit (see Heb. 1:9). When the Holy Spirit is compared to this anointing oil, several similarities immediately become apparent. First, both are unique. The mixture of perfumes and spices used in the anointing oil were prohibited from any other use. So, also, the Holy Spirit is unique.

Second, notice the size of the vat holding the oil. This anointing oil was never mixed in small amounts. More oil was always available than one might expect would be necessary. The Holy Spirit is also unlimited in His supply. Third, the damp paddles lying in the corner of the picture indicate that the mixture has just been made. The anointing oil was always prepared as needed and was, therefore, always fresh when used. So, also, a freshness is evident in the ministry of the Holy Spirit in our lives.

A GALLERY OF SOCIAL CUSTOMS

As we leave the gallery of religious art, we come to a second gallery containing portraits of the Holy Spirit drawn from social customs. Three of the pictures hanging on the walls of this room deserve special attention as we continue our tour. These portray the Holy Spirit as a Deposit, a Doorkeeper and an Enduement or Clothing.

A Deposit
The first picture in this gallery portrays two people sitting at a table, one passing the other a document and a bag of coins. It was customary in the first century to offer a deposit as a guarantee of the person's commitment to honor a contractual agreement. The apostle Paul drew on this cultural practice when he described "the Spirit in our hearts as a deposit" (2 Cor. 1:22). At the moment a person is converted, the Holy Spirit is given as "the guarantee of

our inheritance until the redemption of the purchased possession, to the praise of His glory" (Eph. 1:14). The ministry of the Holy Spirit in our lives is a constant reminder (guarantee) of future blessings God also intends to bestow upon us.

The Doorkeeper

The next picture is that of a Doorkeeper at the gate of a sheepfold. "To him the doorkeeper opens, and the sheep hear his voice; and he calls his own sheep by name and leads them out" (John 10:3). Jesus is the Shepherd calling His sheep. The doorkeeper is the Holy Spirit who opens the door of salvation so people can become Christians, then opens doors of service so that Christians can lead others to Christ. Concerning Lydia, the Bible says, "The Lord opened her heart to heed the things spoken by Paul" (Acts 16:14). This portrait also illustrates the similar work of Jesus as, "He who opens and no one shuts, and shuts and no one opens" (Rev. 3:7).

An Enduement

The final picture in this gallery is that of a wardrobe filled with various styles of clothing. Jesus implied that the Holy Spirit was the Enduement of Clothing when He told His disciples, "But tarry in the city of Jerusalem until you are endued with power from on high" (Luke 24:49).

Just as one dresses in a certain way prior to taking on a certain task, so Christians should be clothed in the power of the Holy Spirit before attempting to serve God. One would not expect a mechanic to wear a three-piece suit as he goes to the garage to work on a car, or a bank manager to address his board wearing bib-overalls. Today, special wear is available for tennis, golf or bike riding. People dress in appropriate clothes to help rather than hinder them in their jobs. Perhaps the large number of garments portrayed in this picture serves as a reminder of how few Christians have taken seriously the need to be clothed in the Holy Spirit.

A GALLERY OF NATURE

The third and final gallery of this museum is a gallery of nature. This gallery includes several landscapes and pictures portraying the wonders of nature around us. These pictures also have something to tell us about the Holy Spirit.

The Dew
The first picture in this gallery is a landscape. It is a morning scene of a grassy meadow on the side of a mountain. As you look closely, you can see the large drops of dew still clinging to the blades of grass and flower petals in the meadow. That dew is a picture of the Holy Spirit. The Holy Spirit wrote, "I will be like the dew to Israel" (Hos. 14:5). Just as the morning dew symbolizes the freshness of the morning, so the Holy Spirit makes all things fresh and new in our lives.

A Dove
The next picture is set in the branches of a tree. As you look closely, a dove is sitting in its nest. Although the eggs are hidden from view, it is obvious that the mother dove is waiting for those eggs to hatch.

The Holy Spirit was described as a dove at the baptism of Jesus. "And immediately, coming up from the water, He saw the heavens parting and the Spirit descending upon

Him like a dove" (Mark 1:10). The dove, symbolic of the Holy Spirit, gently came upon the Savior. Long before this scene, the Bible portrayed the Holy Spirit brooding over the waters of the newly created earth. "And the Spirit of God was hovering over the face of the waters" (Gen. 1:2). This portrait of the dove serves to remind us of His role in creation, His beauty and His gentle character.

Rivers

The third picture in this gallery is another landscape. It portrays a winding river across a dry field. The vegetation on the banks of that river appear healthy and green, although the rest of the field seems to be suffering the effects of drought.

Jesus promised that the Holy Spirit would be like rivers of living water. "He who believes in Me, as the Scripture has said, out of his heart will flow rivers of living water" (John 7:38). This picture serves to remind us that the source of life is the Holy Spirit, who will constantly spring up within us.

Wind and Water

The final picture is that of a storm. As we ponder this picture, we see large trees bending in the wind, and rain pelting to the ground from the clouds above. The wind and water portrayed in this picture are portraits of the Holy Spirit. The wind is not seen, but its effects are evident. We cannot see the Holy Spirit in the salvation experience, but His effects are evident. "So is everyone who is born of the Spirit" (John 3:8). The rain that is falling upon the earth in this scene is the means by which the dry earth is refreshed, just as the Holy Spirit refreshes Christians. "He shall come down like rain upon the mown grass, like showers that water the earth" (Ps. 72:6).

ARRANGING A PERSONAL GALLERY
OF HOLY SPIRIT PORTRAITS

Many people today have hobbies that involve collecting and displaying things that are important to them. These collections may include such things as stamps, coins, baseball cards, antiques, salt and pepper shakers or porcelain dolls. Other people collect art, such as oil paintings, prints or carvings. Still others collect slides or pictures of the family. Collecting and displaying such items are governed by certain principles that may also be applied to arranging a personal gallery of Holy Spirit portraits in your life.

The Principle of Authenticity

Nothing is more frustrating to a collector than to acquire something, only to learn later it is not genuine. This can have devastating effects as we arrange our personal gallery of portraits of the Holy Spirit. We need to be careful that all that is evident in our lives is the product of the Holy Spirit rather than some other spirit. Our Christianity needs to be genuine. John's advice for first-century Christians is good advice for today, also: "Beloved, do not believe every spirit, but test the spirits, whether they are of God; because many false prophets have gone out into the world" (1 John 4:1). That which is authentic of the Holy Spirit will affirm the Lordship of Jesus in your life, and cause others to have a higher regard for Him.

The Principle of Balanced Arrangement

As is apparent from the study of the various names of the Holy Spirit, many different ministries of the Holy Spirit are evident in our lives. Just as a collector arranges art objects, considering an eye to balance and positioning that befits the art, so Christians should give thoughtful attention to balancing these ministries of the Spirit. Sometimes Christians become so excited about one aspect of the Holy Spirit's ministry, they neglect other areas that are just as important. As you consider the various ministries of the Holy Spirit, be sure to let Him work in every area of your life. This is a part of Christian maturity. The word "maturity" means complete or well-rounded. The Christian should be complete or balanced in doctrine, character, service, giving, worship and Bible study.

The Principle of Visibility

The principle of visibility recognizes the desire of collectors to display their collection so that others can see it. As you consider your personal relationship with God, much of the Spirit's work is no doubt recognizable to you. The question is: What has the Holy Spirit done in your life that is evident to others? As we gather portraits of the Holy Spirit in our lives, we need to live in such a way that those portraits become visible to others.

The Principle of a Growing Collection

The one consistent thing about collectors is that they all collect. Something inside them keeps them searching for more. This means they make occasional additions to the collection, resulting in periodic rearrangements of the display.

This will also take place in our gallery of the Holy Spirit. The Holy Spirit is still working in our lives, helping us become like Jesus (see Phil 1:6). Therefore, new portraits will always be added as long as we continue to allow the Holy Spirit to maintain control, and as long as we continue growing in Christ.

What does your gallery of the Holy Spirit look like? Paul described his converts as "an epistle of Christ, ministered by us, written not with ink but by the Spirit of the living God, not on tablets of stone but on tablets of flesh, that is, of the heart" (2 Cor. 3:3).

These studies have focused on the names of the Holy Spirit recorded in the written Word of God, the Bible. Had they been based upon that which the Holy Spirit Himself has written into your life, how might it have been different? May God help each of us as we develop our own unique galleries of the Holy Spirit.

Appendices

The Names, Titles and Emblems of the Holy Spirit

The Anointing (1 John 2:27)
My Blessing (Isa. 44:3)
O Breath (Ezek. 37:9)
The Breath of the Almighty (Job 33:4)
The Breath of God (Job 27:3)
The Breath of Life (Rev. 11:11)
The Breath of the LORD (Isa. 40:7)
The Breath of Your Nostrils (Ps. 18:15)
A Deposit (2 Cor. 1:22)
Like the Dew to Israel (Hos. 14:5)
A Different Spirit (Num. 14:24)
Divided Tongues, as of Fire (Acts 2:3)
The Doorkeeper (John 10:3; *New English Bible,*
cf. Acts 16:14)
A Dove (Mark 1:10)
The Enduement of Power (Luke 24:49, implied)
The Eternal Spirit (Heb. 9:14)

An Excellent Spirit (Dan. 5:12)
The Finger of God (Luke 11:20)
Floods on the Dry Ground (Isa. 44:3)
A Fountain of Water (John 4:14)
The Fullness of God (Eph. 3:19)
Your Generous Spirit (Ps. 51:12)
The Gatekeeper (John 10:3, *RSV*)
The Gift of God (John 4:10; Acts 8:20)
The Gift of the Holy Spirit (Acts 2:38)
The Glory of the Lord (2 Cor. 3:18)
God (Acts 5:4)
Your Good Spirit (Neh. 9:20)
The Guarantee of Our Inheritance (Eph. 1:14; cf. 2 Cor. 5:5)
The Hand of God (2 Chron. 30:12)
The Hand of the LORD (Job 12:9; Isa. 41:20)
The Hand of the Lord GOD (Ezek. 8:1)
He/Himself (John 14:16,26; Rom. 8:16,26)
Another Helper (John 14:16)
The Helper (John 14:26)
The Holy One (Job 6:10)
His Holy One (Isa. 10:17)
The Holy Spirit (Luke 11:13)
His Holy Spirit (Isa. 63:10)
Your Holy Spirit (Ps. 51:11)
The Holy Spirit of God (Eph. 4:30)
The Holy Spirit of Promise (Eph. 1:13)
The Holy Spirit Sent from Heaven (1 Pet. 1:12)
The Holy Spirit Who Is in You (1 Cor. 6:19)
The Holy Spirit Who Dwells in Us (2 Tim. 1:14)
The Lord (2 Cor. 3:17)
A Mighty Voice (Ps. 68:33)
A New Spirit (Ezek. 11:19)
The Oil of Gladness (Ps. 45:7; Heb. 1:9)
One Spirit (1 Cor. 12:13; Eph. 2:18; 4:4)
The Power of the Highest (Luke 1:35)

The Promise (Acts 2:39)
The Promise of My Father (Luke 24:49)
The Promise of the Father (Acts 1:4)
The Promise of the Holy Spirit (Acts 2:33)
The Promise of the Spirit (Gal. 3:14)
Rain upon Mown Grass (Ps. 72:6)
Rivers of Living Water (John 7:38)
The Same Spirit (1 Cor. 12:4,8,9,11)
The Same Spirit of Faith (2 Cor. 4:13)
His Seal (John 6:27; 2 Tim. 2:19)
The Seal of God (Rev. 9:4)
The Seal of the Living God (Rev. 7:2)
His Seed (1 John 3:9)
Seven Eyes (Zech. 3:9; 4:10; Rev. 5:6)
Seven Horns (Rev. 5:6)
Seven Lamps of Fire Burning Before the Throne (Rev. 4:5)
The Seven Spirits Who Are Before His Throne (Rev. 1:4)
The Seven Spirits of God (Rev. 3:1; 4:5)
The Seven Spirits of God Sent Out into All the Earth
(Rev. 5:6)
Showers that Water the Earth (Ps. 72:6)
A Sound from Heaven, as of a Rushing Mighty Wind
(Acts 2:2)
The Spirit (Num. 27:18)
His Spirit (Num. 11:29)
My Spirit (Gen. 6:3)
Your Spirit (Ps. 104:30)
The Spirit of...
     Adoption (Rom. 8:15)
     Burning (Isa. 4:4)
     Christ (Rom. 8:9; 1 Pet. 1:11)
     Counsel (Isa. 11:2)
     Deep Sleep (Isa. 29:10)
     Elijah (2 Kings 2:15; Luke 1:17)
     Your Father (Matt. 10:20)

The Fear of the LORD (Isa. 11:2)
God (Gen. 1:2)
Our God (1 Cor. 6:11)
Glory (1 Pet. 4:14)
Grace (Zech. 12:10; Heb. 10:29)
Him Who Raised Up Jesus (Rom. 8:11)
His Son (Gal. 4:6)
Holiness (Rom. 1:4)
The Holy God (Dan. 4:8,9,18; 5:11)
Jesus (Acts 16:7, *NIV*)
Jesus Christ (Phil. 1:19)
Judgment (Isa. 4:4)
Knowledge (Isa. 11:2)
Life (Rom. 8:2)
The Living Creatures (Ezek. 1:21)
The Living God (2 Cor. 3:3)
The LORD (Judg. 3:10)
The Lord GOD (Isa. 61:1)
Love (2 Tim. 1:7)
Might (Isa. 11:2)
Power (2 Tim. 1:7)
Prophecy (Rev. 19:10)
The Prophets (1 Cor. 14:32)
Revelation (Eph. 1:17)
A Sound Mind (2 Tim. 1:7)
Stupor (Rom. 11:8)
Supplication (Zech. 12:10)
Truth (John 14:17)
Understanding (Isa. 11:2)
My Understanding (Job 20:3)
Wisdom (Exod. 28:3; Deut. 34:9)
His Spirit Who Dwells in You (Rom. 8:11)
The Spirit Who Is from God (1 Cor. 2:12)
The Spirit Whom He Has Given Us (1 John 3:24)
A Steadfast Spirit (Ps. 51:10)

The Voice of the Almighty (Ezek. 1:24)
The Voice of the LORD (Ps. 29:3,4,5,7,8,9)
His Voice (Ps. 95:7; Heb. 3:7)
His Voice (Most High—Ps. 18:13)
The Voice of Your Thunder (Ps. 77:18)
Water (Isa. 44:3)
The Wind (John 3:8)
My Witness (Job 16:19; cf. Heb. 10:15)

Total: 126

APPENDIX 2

The Sevenfold Name of the Holy Spirit

THE SEVEN NAMES OF THE SPIRIT IN ISAIAH
ISAIAH 11:2

1. The Spirit of the LORD	His identity name, describing who He is.
2. The Spirit of Wisdom	His ability to discern people and motives.
3. The Spirit of Understanding	His ability to distinguish the authentic from the counterfeit.
4. The Spirit of Counsel	His ability to make right decisions.
5. The Spirit of Might	His ability to carry out His decisions and purposes.
6. The Spirit of Knowledge	His knowledge about the Godhead.
7. The Spirit of the Fear of the LORD	His work in helping people approach God.

We have noted in this book that the Holy Spirit is the forgotten or unknown Person of the Trinity. The Father and Son are clearly focused because most people can identify with a Father or Son. But a spirit is difficult to envision.

People tend to think of something like Casper the Friendly Ghost on television, or an influence, such as the "spirit of the times" or "spirit week" at college. People do not think of a spirit as a real thing.

But think of the Holy Spirit as a real person. For example, envision a construction worker. The work of God in salvation has been compared to constructing a building. The Father is the architect or engineer who plans the project. The Son is the foreman or construction superintendent who gets the job done. And the Holy Spirit is the workman who actually does the work of salvation. This means the Holy Spirit does the work in preparing the ground (the heart), then builds the house (salvation) and keeps the building in repair (progressive sanctification).

Although the names or titles for the Holy Spirit considered in this book come from the Scriptures, most of the arrangement is by the author. However, at least one significant grouping of the Holy Spirit's names or titles has been arranged by the Holy Spirit Himself. Isaiah 11:2 lists seven names or titles given to the Holy Spirit. This list of seven names is more than tautology or mere repetition for emphasis. The seven descriptions are purposefully presented to portray the Spirit who will rest upon the Messiah (i.e., Jesus Christ):

> The Spirit of the Lord shall rest upon Him, the Spirit of wisdom and understanding, the Spirit of counsel and might, the Spirit of knowledge and the fear of the Lord.—Isaiah 11:2

Notice carefully that the Spirit who will rest on the Messiah is described as (1) the Spirit of the LORD; (2) the Spirit of Wisdom; (3) the Spirit of Understanding; (4) the Spirit of Counsel; (5) the Spirit of Might; (6) the Spirit of

Knowledge; and (7) the Spirit of the Fear of the LORD, or the Spirit of Reverence.

This sevenfold representation of the Holy Spirit is not a complete description of who He is—more than a hundred other names of the Holy Spirit are listed in Scripture. But this list gives insight to the person and work of the Holy Spirit.

This sevenfold list of names is unique in that although this "name-group" occurs in the Old Testament, the full meanings of each name are revealed in the New Testament. Most would expect the opposite. It has been calculated that only 90 direct references to the Holy Spirit are listed in the Old Testament, compared to 263 similar references in the New Testament. This means the New Testament, having three times as many references to the Holy Spirit, is usually more descriptive of the Holy Spirit than the Old Testament.

THE MEANING OF THE SEVEN NAMES

In the context of Isaiah's prophecy, these names of the Holy Spirit have specific reference to the anointing of the Holy Spirit, which rested upon Jesus during His public ministry. In a broader sense, each of these names emphasizes some aspect of the character and work of the Holy Spirit in our lives today.

Some Bible teachers have compared this sevenfold arrangement of the names of the Holy Spirit with the gold lampstand in the Tabernacle (see Exod. 25:31-40). In this comparison, the first name, the Spirit of the LORD, is compared with the central light in the lampstand. The other six names are compared to the three pairs of branches coming out from the lamp. Note that two of these names relate to intellectual ability (the Spirit of Wisdom and the Spirit of Understanding), two relate to practical activity (the Spirit of

Counsel and the Spirit of Might) and two relate to relationship with God (the Spirit of Knowledge and the Spirit of the Fear of the Lord).

The Spirit of the Lord

The Spirit of the Lord may be viewed as the primary name of the Holy Spirit in Isaiah's list, and as such the name that introduces the other six descriptions. Although the other names describe some aspect of what the Spirit does, or His ministry, the name Spirit of the Lord describes who He is. In this context, the use of this title alerts the reader to remember that each of the following names should be understood in the context of God's wisdom, understanding, counsel, might, knowledge and reverence, rather than that of man.

The Spirit of Wisdom

Wisdom is the ability to discern the true nature of things underneath appearances. Therefore, this title of the Holy Spirit suggests His ability to discern the true nature of people and their motives.

It is possible for Christians to hide sin in their lives, and to serve God by having wrong motives, fooling those around them into believing they are living in complete fellowship with God. But the Spirit of Wisdom cannot be fooled by the images we portray. Instead, He is able to see through our masks and discern our inner nature and motives. When the Holy Spirit illuminates the lives of Christians, they would do well to confess their sin and yield to the Spirit in obeying Him so as to resolve their spiritual problem.

The Spirit of Understanding

Understanding includes the ability to distinguish the differences between or among things despite their similarities. A counterfeit copy of an art masterpiece may be done well enough to fool many who appreciate good art, but a legitimate art critic is able to discern the subtle differences in color, paint texture and brush stroke that distinguish the counterfeit from the original.

The name Spirit of Understanding also seems to overlap the meaning of the name Spirit of Wisdom, and to suggest the Spirit's ability to discern between that which is genuine and counterfeit in our lives. Christians should take inventory in their lives from time to time and ask the Spirit of Understanding to expose the counterfeit in their lives and help them replace it with reality in their relationship with God.

The Spirit of Counsel

The word "counsel" refers to the ability to make right decisions and adopt right conclusions. The name Spirit of Counsel reminds us of the Holy Spirit's ability in decision making. This term reminds Christians of the need to seek the leading of the Holy Spirit in making personal decisions in their lives. When this is done, the Holy Spirit will guide us in our decision making according to the principles of the Word of God and His intervention in our circumstances of life. Also, the Spirit of Counsel may direct His counsel to us through other people who act as channels for the message He has for us. Christians should take advantage of all the principles of decision making as they are led daily by the Spirit of Counsel.

The Spirit of Might

"Might" refers to the power or energy necessary to carry out those decisions made with the aid of the Spirit of Counsel. The name Spirit of Might reminds Christians of the Holy

Spirit's ability to accomplish what He has decided to do. An appreciation of this truth is the basis for developing great faith in God (see Rom. 4:21). Once, when a Christian lady was introduced by her pastor as having great faith in God, she corrected his statement and confessed, "I have a little faith in a great God." We grow in faith as we recognize the greatness of the Spirit of Might in His ability to perform what is promised.

The Spirit of Knowledge

Some Bible teachers believe the words "of the LORD" should be applied to both of the last two names of the Holy Spirit in this listing. This means that the knowledge referred to here is "the knowledge of the LORD." Acquiring this knowledge is a continuing process. After spending three years with Jesus, Philip was rebuked with the question, "Have I been with you so long, and yet you have not known Me, Philip?" (John 14:9). Christians today will grow in their knowledge of God as they rely upon the ministry of the Spirit of the Knowledge of the LORD. This growing knowledge of who God is will also result in greater spiritual insight in other areas of our lives (see Prov. 9:10).

The Spirit of the Fear of the LORD

The last of these seven names of the Holy Spirit is the Spirit of the Fear of the LORD. The expression "fear of the LORD" is an Old Testament phrase describing a lifestyle of reverential trust in God (see Pss. 34,37). Some Bible teachers call this "the Spirit of Reverence."

The name the Fear of the LORD reminds Christians of the work of the Holy Spirit in helping us approach God with reverence in our prayer to and worship of God. Also, when we have proper respect for who God is, this will motivate us to abstain from sinful habits and attitudes that are offensive to God. This is only possible through the ministry of the Spirit of Reverence in the Christian life.

THE SPIRIT AND THE NUMBER "SEVEN"

The fact that Isaiah 11:2 includes *seven* terms for the Holy Spirit is not coincidental. Throughout the Scriptures, which were authored by the Holy Spirit, He is described by expressions such as Seven Eyes, Seven Horns, Seven Lamps Burning Before the Throne, the Seven Spirits Who Are Before His Throne, the Seven Spirits of God and the Seven Spirits of God Sent Out into All the Earth.

Throughout the Scriptures, certain numbers seem to be used in such a way as to suggest a significance beyond the apparent use of counting. The Hebrew word *shevah* (seven) seems to imply fullness, satisfaction or having enough. Some Bible teachers describe the number *seven* as the number of perfection, because various lists of seven appear in Scripture as apparently representative of the whole. Perhaps Isaiah assigns seven descriptive titles to the Spirit because He is perfect in Himself, is whole or completes the Godhead as the Third Person.

Seven Horns
The description of the Holy Spirit as Seven Horns suggests His *strength*. The apostle John saw the Lamb by the throne of God in heaven "having seven horns and seven eyes, which are the seven Spirits of God sent out into all the earth" (Rev. 5:6). In the Near East, the horn was considered a symbol of strength. This was probably due to the use of

horns by rams and cattle in defending themselves or attacking another animal.

When Israel went into battle, it was customary to call the army to battle by blowing a ram's horn. Perhaps blowing the horn served as a challenge to the army to demonstrate their strength in battle just as the ram demonstrated its strength with its horns.

Seven Eyes

The phrase "Seven Eyes" is used in describing the Holy Spirit in both the Old and New Testaments (see Zech. 3:9; 4:10; Rev. 5:6). Although God is Spirit and does not possess a physical body, the Scriptures often use anthropomorphisms to describe what God is like. An anthropomorphism is a description of God that portrays God as though He had the body of a person (Grk. *anthropos*). The focus in these descriptions is usually upon a single part of the body that implies some truth about God. Here, the term "eyes" suggests the insight of the Holy Spirit, and His understanding of all He sees. Zechariah explained, "They are the eyes of the LORD, which scan to and fro throughout the whole earth" (Zech. 4:10).

Seven Lamps

A third description of the Holy Spirit seen by John in his vision was "seven lamps of fire burning before the throne, which are the seven Spirits of God" (Rev. 4:5). This imagery emphasizes the work of the Holy Spirit in searching out and exposing all that is contrary to the nature of God. Lamps of fire were placed around homes in the first century to provide interior lighting, much as light fixtures do in contemporary homes. When something was lost, a person would use a lamp as a flashlight to search for the item. Lamps were also used to cast light on an object for close examination to expose flaws or counterfeits. The title Seven Lamps implies the similar work of the Holy Spirit in our lives.

Seven Spirits
When John referred to "the seven Spirits who are before His throne" (Rev. 1:4; 3:1; 4:5; 5:6), he was emphasizing the role of the Holy Spirit in His full governmental action. The Seven Spirits of God are identified both in the context of being before the throne in heaven (see Rev. 1:4; 4:5) and in the midst of the churches on earth (see Rev. 3:1; 5:6). The throne represents the rule of God in heaven. Portraying the same Seven Spirits also on the earth suggests the extension of that rule of God to earth. This descriptive reference reminds us that the Holy Spirit overrules and governs in the affairs of our lives.

*Names, Terms and Titles of Christ in Scripture**

A (21 terms)
The Advocate with the Father (1 John 1:2)
An Alien unto My Mother's Children (Ps. 69:8)
Alive for Evermore (Rev. 1:18)
The All and in All (Col. 3:11)
The Almighty Which Is (Rev. 1:8)
The Alpha and Omega (Rev. 1:8)
An Altar (Heb. 13:10)
The Altogether Lovely (Song of Sol. 5:16)
The Amen (Rev. 3:14)
The Anchor of the Soul (Heb. 6:19)
The Ancient of Days (Dan. 7:9)
The Angel of God (Gen. 21:17)
The Angel of His Presence (Isa. 63:9)
The Angel of the Lord (Gen. 16:7)
The Anointed of God (1 Sam. 2:35; Ps. 2:2)
Another King (Acts 17:7)

The Apostle of Our Profession (Heb. 3:1)
The Ark of the Covenant (Josh. 3:3)
The Arm of the Lord (Isa. 53:1)
The Author of Eternal Salvation (Heb. 5:9)
The Author of Our Faith (Heb. 12:2)

B (32)
The Babe of Bethlehem (Luke 2:12,16)
The Balm in Gilead (Jer. 8:22)
A Banner to Them That Fear Thee (Ps. 60:4)
The Bearer of Glory (Zech. 6:13)
The Bearer of Sin (Heb. 9:28)
The Beauties of Holiness (Ps. 110:3)
Before All Things (Col. 1:17)
The Beginning (Col. 1:18)
The Beginning of the Creation of God (Rev. 3:14)
The Beginning and the Ending (Rev. 1:8)
The Beloved (Eph. 1:6)
My Beloved Son (Matt. 3:17)
The Better (Heb. 7:7)
The Bishop of Your Souls (1 Pet. 2:25)
The Blessed and Only Potentate (1 Tim. 6:15)
The Blessed for Evermore (2 Cor. 11:31)
The Blessed Hope (Titus 2:13)
The Branch (Zech. 3:8; 6:12)
The Branch of the Lord (Isa. 4:2)
The Branch of Righteousness (Jer. 33:15)
The Branch Out of His Roots (Isa. 11:1)
The Bread of God (John 6:33)
The Bread of Life (John 6:35)
The Breaker (Mic. 2:13)
The Bridegroom of the Bride (John 3:29)
The Bright and Morning Star (Rev. 22:16)
The Brightness of His Glory (Heb. 1:3)
The Brightness of Thy Rising (Isa. 60:3)

Our Brother (Matt. 12:50)
A Buckler (Ps. 2:7; 18:30)
The Builder of the Temple (Zech. 6:12,13)
A Bundle of Myrrh (Song of Sol. 1:13)

C (40)
The Captain of the Host of the Lord (Josh. 5:14,15)
The Captain of Their Salvation (Heb. 2:10)
The Carpenter (Mark 6:3)
The Carpenter's Son (Luke 4:22)
A Certain Nobleman (Luke 19:12)
A Certain Samaritan (Luke 10:33)
The Chief Cornerstone (Eph. 2:20; 1 Pet. 2:6)
The Chief Shepherd (1 Pet. 5:4)
The Chiefest Among Ten Thousand (Song of Sol. 5:10)
A Child Born (Isa. 9:6)
Child of the Holy Ghost (Matt. 1:18)
The Child Jesus (Luke 2:27,43)
The Chosen of God (1 Pet. 2:4)
Chosen Out of the People (Ps. 89:19)
Christ (Matt. 1:16)
The Christ (1 John 5:1)
Christ Come in the Flesh (1 John 4:2)
Christ Crucified (1 Cor. 1:23)
The Christ of God (Luke 9:20)
Christ Jesus (Acts 19:4)
Christ Jesus Our Lord (2 Cor. 4:5)
Christ a King (Luke 23:2)
Christ the Lord (Luke 2:11)
Christ Our Passover (1 Cor. 5:7)
Christ Risen from the Dead (1 Cor. 15:20)
The Chosen of God (Luke 23:35)
A Cleft of the Rock (Exod. 33:22)
A Cluster of Camphire (Song of Sol. 1:14)
The Comforter (John 14:16-18)

A Commander to the People (Isa. 55:4)
Conceived of the Holy Spirit (Matt. 1:20)
The Consolation of Israel (Luke 2:25)
The Corn of Wheat (John 12:24)
Counselor (Isa. 9:6)
The Covenant of the People (Isa. 42:6; 49:8)
The Covert from the Tempest (Isa. 32:2)
The Covert of Thy Wings (Ps. 61:4)
The Creator (Rom. 1:25)
The Creator of the Ends of the Earth (Isa. 40:28)
A Crown of Glory (Isa. 28:5)

D (17)
My Darling (Ps. 22:20)
David (Matt. 1:17)
The Day (2 Pet. 1:19)
The Daysman Betwixt Us (Job 9:33)
The Dayspring from on High (Luke 1:78)
The Daystar to Arise (2 Pet. 1:19)
His Dear Son (Col. 1:13)
That Deceiver (Matt. 27:63)
My Defense (Ps. 94:22)
The Deliverance of Zion (Joel 2:32)
My Deliverer (Ps. 40:17)
The Desire of All Nations (Hag. 2:7)
Despised by the People (Ps. 22:6)
The Dew of Israel (Hos. 14:5)
A Diadem of Beauty (Isa. 28:5)
The Door of the Sheep (John 10:7)
Dwelling Place (Ps. 90:1)

E (17)
Mine Elect (Isa. 42:1)
Eliakim (Isa. 22:20)
Elijah (Matt. 16:14)

Emmanuel (Matt. 1:23)
The End of the Law (Rom. 10:4)
The Ensign of the People (Isa. 11:10)
Equal with God (Phil. 2:6)
The Eternal God (Deut. 33:27)
That Eternal Life (1 John 1:2)
The Everlasting Father (Isa. 9:6)
An Everlasting Light (Isa. 60:19,20)
An Everlasting Name (Isa. 63:12)
Thy Exceedingly Great Reward (Gen. 15:1)
His Excellency (Job 13:11)
The Excellency of Our God (Isa. 35:2)
Excellent (Ps. 8:1,9)
The Express Image of His Person (Heb. 1:3)

F (38)
The Face of the Lord (Luke 1:76)
The Fairer than the Children of Men (Ps. 45:2)
Faithful (1 Thess. 5:24)
Faithful and True (Rev. 19:11)
The Faithful and True Witness (Rev. 3:14)
A Faithful Creator (1 Pet. 4:19)
A Faithful High Priest (Heb. 2:17)
A Faithful Priest (1 Sam. 2:35)
The Faithful Witness (Rev. 1:5)
A Faithful Witness Between Us (Jer. 42:5)
A Faithful Witness in Heaven (Ps. 89:37)
My Father (Ps. 89:26)
A Father of the Fatherless (Ps. 68:5)
The Feast (1 Cor. 5:8)
My Fellow (Zech. 13:7)
The Finisher of the Faith (Heb. 12:2)
The First and the Last (Rev. 1:8)
The Firstbegotten (Heb. 1:6)
The Firstborn (Heb. 12:23)

The Firstborn Among Many Brethren (Rom. 8:29)
The Firstborn of the Dead (Rev. 1:5)
The Firstborn of Every Creature (Col. 1:15)
Her Firstborn Son (Luke 2:7)
The Firstfruit (Rom. 11:16)
The Firstfruits of Them That Sleep (1 Cor. 15:20)
Flesh (John 1:14)
The Foolishness of God (1 Cor. 1:25)
Foreordained Before the Foundation of the World
(1 Pet. 1:20)
The Forerunner (Heb. 6:20)
Fortress (Ps. 18:2)
The Foundation Which Is Laid (1 Cor. 3:11)
The Fountain of Life (Ps. 36:9)
The Fountain of Living Waters (Jer. 17:13)
The Free Gift (Rom. 5:15)
The Friend of Publicans and Sinners (Matt. 11:19;
Luke 7:34)
A Friend That Sticketh Closer than a Brother (Prov. 18:24)
The Fruit of the Earth (Isa. 4:2)
The Fruit of Thy Womb (Luke 1:42)
Fullers' Soap (Mal. 3:2)

G (47)
The Gift of God (John 4:10)
A Gin (Isa. 8:14)
A Glorious High Throne from the Beginning (Jer. 17:12)
A Glorious Name (Isa. 63:14)
Glory (Hag. 2:7)
My Glory (Ps. 3:3)
The Glory as of the Only Begotten of the Father (John 1:14)
The Glory of God (Rom. 3:23)
The Glory of His Father (Matt. 16:27; Mark 8:38)
God (Rev. 21:7)
God Who Avengeth Me (Ps. 18:47)

God Blessed Forever (Rom. 9:5)
God Who Forgavest Them (Ps. 99:8)
Our God Forever and Ever (Ps. 48:14)
The God of Glory (Ps. 29:3)
The God of Israel (Ps. 59:5)
The God of Jacob (Ps. 46:7)
The God of My Life (Ps. 42:8)
The God of My Mercy (Ps. 59:10)
God in the Midst of Her (Ps. 46:5)
God Manifest in the Flesh (1 Tim. 3:16)
God of My Righteousness (Ps. 4:1)
God of My Salvation (Ps. 18:46; 24:5)
God of My Strength (Ps. 43:2)
God with Us (Matt. 1:23)
A Good Man (John 7:12)
The Goodman of the House (Matt. 20:11)
Good Master (Matt. 19:16)
The Good Shepherd (John 10:11)
The Governor Among Nations (Ps. 22:28)
Great (Jer. 32:18)
The Great God (Titus 2:13)
A Great High Priest (Heb. 4:14)
A Great Light (Isa. 9:2)
A Great Prophet (Luke 7:16)
That Great Shepherd of the Sheep (Heb. 13:20)
Greater (1 John 4:4)
A Greater and More Perfect Tabernacle (Heb. 9:11)
Greater than Our Father Abraham (John 8:53)
Greater than Our Father Jacob (John 4:12)
Greater than Jonah (Matt. 12:41)
Greater than Solomon (Matt. 12:42)
Greater than the Temple (Matt. 12:6)
Guest (Luke 19:7)
Our Guide Even unto Death (Ps. 48:14)
The Guide of My Youth (Jer. 3:4)

The Guiltless (Matt. 12:7)

H (41)
The Habitation of Justice (Jer. 50:7)
Harmless (Heb. 7:26)
An He Goat (Prov. 30:31)
The Head of All Principality and Power (Col. 2:10)
The Head of Every Man (1 Cor. 11:3)
The Head of the Body, the Church (Col. 1:18)
The Head of the Corner (1 Pet. 2:7)
The Health of My Countenance (Ps. 42:11)
The Heir (Mark 12:7)
Heir of All Things (Heb. 1:2)
My Helper (Heb. 13:6; Ps. 30:10)
The Helper of the Fatherless (Ps. 10:14)
A Hen (Matt. 23:37)
The Hidden Manna (Rev. 2:17)
My Hiding Place (Ps. 32:7)
A Hiding Place from the Wind (Isa. 32:2)
The High and Lofty One Who Inhabiteth Eternity
(Isa. 57:15)
An High Priest (Heb. 5:5)
An High Priest After the Order of Melchizedek (Heb. 5:10)
An High Priest Forever (Heb. 6:20)
My High Tower (Ps. 18:2)
The Highest Himself (Ps. 87:5)
An Highway (Isa. 35:8)
Holy (Isa. 57:15)
Thy Holy Child Jesus (Acts 4:27)
Thine Holy One (Acts 2:27)
The Holy One and Just (Acts 3:14)
The Holy One of Israel (Ps. 89:18)
That Holy Thing Which Shall Be Born of Thee (Luke 1:35)
Holy to the Lord (Luke 2:23)
Our Hope (1 Tim. 1:1)

The Hope of Glory (Col. 1:27)
The Hope of His People (Joel 3:16)
The Hope of Israel (Acts 28:20)
The Hope of Their Fathers (Jer. 50:7)
The Horn of David (Ps. 132:17)
The Horn of the House of Israel (Ezek. 29:21)
An Horn of Salvation (Luke 1:69)
An House of Defence (Ps. 31:2)
An Householder (Matt. 20:1)
Her Husband (Rev. 21:2)

I (5)
I Am (John 18:6)
The Image of the Invisible God (Col. 1:15)
Immanuel (Isa. 7:14)
Innocent Blood (Matt. 27:4)
Isaac (Heb. 11:17,18)

J (18)
The Jasper Stone (Rev. 4:3)
Jeremiah (Matt. 16:14)
Jesus (Matt. 1:21)
Jesus Christ (Heb. 13:8)
Jesus Christ the Lord (Rom. 7:25)
Jesus Christ, the Son of God (John 20:31)
Jesus of Galilee (Matt. 26:69)
Jesus of Nazareth (John 1:45)
Jesus of Nazareth, the King of the Jews (John 19:19)
A Jew (John 4:9)
John the Baptist (Matt. 16:14)
Joseph's Son (Luke 4:22)
The Judge of All the Earth (Gen. 18:25)
The Judge of the Quick and the Dead (Acts 10:42)
A Judge of the Widows (Ps. 68:5)
The Just One (Acts 7:52)

This Just Person (Matt. 27:24)
The Justifier of Him Who Believeth (Rom. 3:26; Acts 13:39)

K (22)
Thy Keeper (Ps. 12:15)
The Kindness and Love of God (Titus 3:4)
Another King (Acts 17:7)
The King Eternal (1 Tim. 1:17)
The King Immortal (1 Tim. 1:17)
The King in His Beauty (Isa. 33:17)
The King Forever and Ever (Ps. 10:16)
The King Invisible (1 Tim. 1:17)
The King of All the Earth (Ps. 47:7)
The King of Glory (Ps. 24:7,8)
The King of Heaven (Dan. 4:37)
The King of Israel (John 1:49)
King of Kings (Rev. 19:16)
The King of Peace (Heb. 7:2)
The King of Righteousness (Heb. 7:2)
King of Saints (Rev. 15:3)
The King of Salem (Heb. 7:2)
The King of Terrors (Job 18:14)
King of the Jews (Matt. 2:2)
The King Who Cometh in the Name of the Lord (Luke 19:38)
The King's Son (Ps. 72:1)
The Kinsman (Ruth 4:14)

L (58)
A Ladder (Gen. 28:12)
The Lamb (Rev. 17:14)
The Lamb of God (John 1:29)
The Lamb Slain from the Foundation of the World
(Rev. 13:8)
The Lamb That Was Slain (Rev. 5:12)
The Lamb Who Is in the Midst of the Throne (Rev. 7:17)

The Last (Isa. 44:6)
The Last Adam (1 Cor. 15:45)
The Lawgiver (Jas. 4:12)
A Leader (Isa. 55:4)
The Life (John 14:6)
The Lifter Up of Mine Head (Ps. 3:3)
The Light (John 1:7)
The Light of Men (John 1:4)
The Light of the City (Rev. 21:23)
The Light of the Glorious Gospel of Christ (2 Cor. 4:4)
The Light of the Knowledge of the Glory of God (2 Cor. 4:6)
The Light of the Morning (2 Sam. 23:4)
The Light of the World (John 8:12)
The Light of Truth (Ps. 43:3)
A Light to Lighten Gentiles (Luke 2:32)
A Light to the Gentiles (Isa. 49:6)
The Lily Among Thorns (Song of Sol. 2:2)
The Lily of the Valleys (Song of Sol. 2:1)
The Lion of the Tribe of Judah (Rev. 5:5)
The Living Bread (John 6:51)
The Living God (Ps. 42:2)
Lord (*despotes*; 2 Pet. 2:1)
Lord (*kurios*; John 13:13)
Lord (*rabboni*; Mark 10:51)
Lord Also of the Sabbath (Mark 2:28)
My Lord and My God (John 20:28)
The Lord and Savior (2 Pet. 1:11)
Lord Both of the Dead and Living (Rom. 14:9)
The Lord from Heaven (1 Cor. 15:47)
Lord God Almighty (Rev. 16:7)
The Lord God of the Holy Prophets (Rev. 22:6)
Lord God of Israel (Ps. 41:13)
Lord God of Truth (Ps. 31:5)
Lord God Omnipotent (Rev. 19:6)
The Lord God Who Judgeth Her (Rev. 18:8)

The Lord Holy and True (Rev. 6:10)
Lord Jesus (Rom. 10:9)
Lord Jesus Christ (Jas. 2:1)
The Lord Mighty in Battle (Ps. 24:8)
The Lord of All the Earth (Josh. 3:11)
The Lord of Glory (1 Cor. 2:8)
The Lord of the Harvest (Matt. 9:38)
The Lord of Hosts (Ps. 24:10)
O Lord Our God (Ps. 8:1,9)
Lord of Lords (1 Tim. 6:15)
Lord of Peace (2 Thess. 3:16)
The Lord of the Vineyard (Matt. 20:8)
The Lord of the Whole Earth (Ps. 97:5)
The Lord's Christ (Rev. 11:15)
The Lord's Doing (Matt. 21:42)
The Lord Strong and Mighty (Ps. 24:8)
Lowly in Heart (Matt. 11:29)

M (42)
Magnified (Ps. 40:16)
Our Maker (Ps. 95:6)
A Malefactor (John 18:30)
The Man (John 19:5)
A Man Approved of God (Acts 2:22)
A Man Child (Rev. 12:5)
The Man Christ Jesus (1 Tim. 2:5)
A Man Gluttonous (Matt. 11:19)
The Man Whose Name Is the Branch (Zech. 6:12)
The Man of Sorrows (Isa. 53:3)
The Man Whom He Hath Ordained (Acts 17:31)
Manna (Exod. 16:15)
Marvelous in Our Eyes (Matt. 21:42)
The Master (*didaskalos*; John 11:28)
Master (*epistates*; Luke 5:5)
Your Master (*kathegetes*; Matt. 23:10)

The Master of the House (*oikodespotes*; Luke 13:25)
Master (*rabbi*; John 4:31)
The Meat Offering (Lev. 2:1)
The Mediator (1 Tim. 2:5)
The Mediator of a Better Covenant (Heb. 8:6)
The Mediator of the New Covenant (Heb. 12:24)
The Mediator of the New Testament (Heb. 9:15)
Meek (Matt. 11:29)
Melchizedek (Gen. 14:18)
A Merciful and Faithful High Priest (Heb. 2:17)
His Mercy and His Truth (Ps. 57:3)
Mercy Seat (Heb. 9:5)
The Messenger of the Covenant (Mal. 3:1)
Messiah (Dan. 9:25)
Mighty (Ps. 89:19)
The Mighty God (Isa. 9:6)
The Mighty One of Jacob (Isa. 49:26; 60:16)
The Minister of Sin (Gal. 2:17)
A Minister of the Circumcision (Rom. 15:8)
The Minister of the Heavenly Sanctuary (Heb. 8:1-3)
A More Excellent Name (Heb. 1:4)
The Morning Star (Rev. 2:28)
The Most High (Ps. 9:2; 21:7)
The Mouth of God (Matt. 4:4)
The Mystery of God (Col. 2:2)

N (5)
A Nail Fastened in a Sure Place (Isa. 22:23)
A Name Above Every Name (Phil. 2:9)
A Nazarene (Matt. 2:23)
Thy New Name (Rev. 3:12)
A Nourisher of Thine Old Age (Ruth 4:15)

O (9)
An Offering and a Sacrifice to God (Eph. 5:2)

The Offspring of David (Rev. 22:16)
Ointment Poured Forth (Song of Sol. 1:3)
The Omega (Rev. 22:13)
His Only Begotten Son (John 3:16)
The Only Begotten of the Father (John 1:14)
Only Potentate (1 Tim. 6:15)
The Only Wise God (1 Tim. 1:17)
An Owl of the Desert (Ps. 102:6)

P (40)
Our Passover (1 Cor. 5:7)
The Path of Life (Ps. 16:11)
A Pavilion (Ps. 31:20)
Our Peace (Eph. 2:14)
The Peace Offering (Lev. 3:1)
A Pelican of the Wilderness (Ps. 102:6)
A Perfect Man (Jas. 3:2)
The Person of Christ (2 Cor. 2:10)
Physician (Luke 4:23)
The Pillar of Fire (Exod. 13:21,22)
The Place of Our Sanctuary (Jer. 17:12)
A Place of Refuge (Isa. 4:6)
A Plant of Renown (Ezek. 34:29)
A Polished Shaft (Isa. 49:2)
Poor (2 Cor. 8:9)
My Portion (Ps. 119:57)
The Portion of Jacob (Jer. 51:19)
The Portion of Mine Inheritance (Ps. 16:5)
The Potter (Jer. 18:6)
The Power of God (1 Cor. 1:24)
Precious (1 Pet. 2:7)
A Precious Cornerstone (Isa. 28:16)
The Preeminence (Col. 1:18)
A Price (1 Cor. 6:20)
The Price of His Redemption (Lev. 25:52)

A Priest Forever (Ps. 110:4)
The Priest of the Most High God (Heb. 7:1)
A Prince and Savior (Acts 5:31)
The Prince of Life (Acts 3:15)
The Prince of Peace (Isa. 9:6)
Prince of Princes (Dan. 8:25)
The Prince of the Kings of the Earth (Rev. 1:5)
The Prophet (John 7:40)
A Prophet Mighty in Deed and Word (Luke 24:19)
The Prophet of Nazareth (Matt. 21:11)
A Prophet Without Honor (Matt. 13:57)
One of the Prophets (Matt. 16:14)
The Propitiation for Our Sins (1 John 2:2)
Pure (1 John 3:3)
A Purifier of Silver (Mal. 3:3)

Q (2)
Of Quick Understanding (Isa. 11:3)
A Quickening Spirit (1 Cor. 15:45)

R (53)
Rabbi (John 3:2)
Rabboni (John 20:16)
Rain Upon the Mown Grass (Ps. 72:6)
A Ransom for All (1 Tim. 2:6)
A Ransom for Many (Matt. 20:28)
The Red Heifer Without Spot (Num. 19:2)
My Redeemer (Job 19:25)
Redemption (1 Cor. 1:30; Luke 21:28)
The Redemption of Their Souls (Ps. 49:8)
A Refiner's Fire (Mal. 3:2)
Our Refuge (Ps. 46:1)
A Refuge in Times of Trouble (Ps. 9:9)
A Refuge for the Oppressed (Ps. 9:9)
A Refuge from the Storm (Isa. 25:4)

Our Report (Isa. 53:1)
A Reproach of Men (Ps. 22:6)
Their Resting Place (Jer. 50:6)
A Restorer of Thy Life (Ruth 4:15)
The Resurrection, and the Life (John 11:25)
The Revelation of Jesus Christ (Rev. 1:1)
Reverend (Ps. 111:9)
A Reward for the Righteous (Ps. 58:11)
Rich (Rom. 10:12)
The Riches of His Glory (Rom. 9:23)
The Riddle (Judg. 14:14)
Right (Deut. 32:4)
The Righteous (1 John 2:1)
A Righteous Branch (Jer. 23:5)
The Righteous God (Ps. 7:9)
The Righteous Lord (Ps. 11:7)
My Righteous Servant (Isa. 53:11)
The Righteous Judge (2 Tim. 4:8)
A Righteous Man (Luke 23:47)
Righteousness (1 Cor. 1:30)
The Righteousness of God (Rom. 10:3)
A River of Water in a Dry Place (Isa. 32:2)
The Rock (Matt. 16:18)
The Rock That Is Higher than I (Ps. 61:2)
The Rock of Israel (2 Sam. 23:3)
A Rock of Offense (Rom. 9:33)
The Rock of My Refuge (Ps. 94:22)
The Rock of His Salvation (Deut. 32:15)
The Rock of Our Salvation (Ps. 95:1)
The Rock of Thy Strength (Isa. 17:10)
The Rod (Mic. 6:9)
A Rod Out of the Stem of Jesse (Isa. 11:1)
The Root of David (Rev. 5:5)
A Root of Jesse (Rom. 15:12; Isa. 11:10)
A Root Out of Dry Ground (Isa. 53:2)

The Root and Offspring of David (Rev. 22:16)
The Rose of Sharon (Song of Sol. 2:1)
A Ruler (Mic. 5:2)

S (95)
The Sacrifice for Sins (Heb. 10:12)
A Sacrifice to God (Eph. 5:2)
My Salvation (Ps. 27:1)
The Salvation of God (Luke 2:30; 3:6)
The Salvation of Israel (Jer. 3:23)
A Samaritan (John 8:48)
The Same Yesterday, Today, and Forever (Heb. 13:8)
A Sanctuary (Isa. 8:14)
A Sardius Stone (Rev. 4:3)
The Saving Strength of His Anointed (Ps. 28:8)
Savior (Titus 2:13)
The Savior of All Men (1 Tim. 4:10)
The Savior of the Body (Eph. 5:23)
The Savior of the World (John 4:42; 1 John 4:14)
The Scapegoat (Lev. 16:8; John 11:49-52)
The Sceptre of Israel (Num. 24:17)
The Sceptre of Thy Kingdom (Ps. 45:6)
The Second Man (1 Cor. 15:47)
Secret (Judg. 13:18)
The Secret of Thy Presence (Ps. 31:20)
The Seed of Abraham (Gal. 3:16)
The Seed of David (Rom. 1:3; 2 Tim. 2:8)
The Seed of the Woman (Gen. 3:15)
The Sent One (John 9:7)
Separate from His Brethren (Gen. 49:26)
Separate from Sinners (Heb. 7:26)
The Serpent in the Wilderness (John 3:14)
My Servant (Isa. 42:1)
A Servant of Rulers (Isa. 49:7)
My Servant the Branch (Zech. 3:8)

A Shadow from the Heat (Isa. 25:4)
The Shadow of the Almighty (Ps. 91:1)
The Shadow of a Great Rock (Isa. 32:2)
A Shelter (Ps. 61:3)
My Shepherd (Ps. 23:1; Isa. 40:11)
Shepherd of Israel (Ps. 80:1)
Our Shield (Ps. 84:9)
Shiloh (Gen. 49:10)
Shoshannim ("lilies"; Pss. 45; 69 [titles])
A Sign of the Lord (Isa. 7:11)
Siloam (John 9:7)
Sin (2 Cor. 5:21)
A Sinner (John 9:24)
A Snare to the Inhabitants of Jerusalem (Isa. 8:14)
The Son (Matt. 11:27)
His Son from Heaven (1 Thess. 1:10)
A Son Given (Isa. 9:6)
The Son of Abraham (Matt. 1:1)
The Son of David (Matt. 1:1)
The Son of God (John 1:49)
The Son of Joseph (John 1:45)
The Son of Man (John 1:51)
The Son of Mary (Mark 6:3)
The Son of the Blessed (Mark 14:61)
The Son of the Father (2 John 3)
The Son of the Freewoman (Gal. 4:30)
The Son of the Highest (Luke 1:32)
The Son of the Living God (Matt. 16:16)
The Son of the Most High (Mark 5:7)
A Son over His Own House (Heb. 3:6)
The Son Who Is Consecrated for Evermore (Heb. 7:28)
My Song (Isa. 12:2)
A Sower (Matt. 13:4,37)
A Sparrow Alone Upon the House Top (Ps. 102:7)
That Spiritual Rock (1 Cor. 10:4)

A Star Out of Jacob (Num. 24:17)
My Stay (Ps. 18:18)
A Stone Cut Out of the Mountain (Dan. 2:45)
A Stone Cut Without Hands (Dan. 2:34)
The Stone of Israel (Gen. 49:24)
A Stone of Stumbling (1 Pet. 2:8)
The Stone Which the Builders Refused (Ps. 118:22)
The Stone Which the Builders Rejected (Matt. 21:42)
The Stone Which Was Set at Nought (Acts 4:11)
A Stranger (Matt. 25:35)
My Strength (Isa. 12:2)
The Strength of Israel (1 Sam. 15:29)
The Strength of My Life (Ps. 27:1)
A Strength to the Needy in Distress (Isa. 25:4)
A Strength to the Poor (Isa. 25:4)
Strong (Ps. 24:8)
A Strong Consolation (Heb. 6:18)
A Stronghold in the Day of Trouble (Nah. 1:7)
A Strong Lord (Ps. 89:8)
My Strong Refuge (Ps. 71:7)
My Strong Rock (Ps. 31:2)
A Strong Tower (Prov. 18:10)
A Strong Tower from the Enemy (Ps. 61:3)
A Stronger than He (Luke 11:22)
A Stumbling Block (1 Cor. 1:23)
The Sun of Righteousness (Mal. 4:2)
A Sure Foundation (Isa. 28:16)
The Sure Mercies of David (Isa. 55:3; Acts 13:34)
A Surety of a Better Testament (Heb. 7:22)
A Sweet-smelling Savor (Eph. 5:2)

T (20)
A Tabernacle for a Shadow (Isa. 4:6)
The Tabernacle of God (Rev. 21:3)
Teacher (Matt. 10:25)

A Teacher Come from God (John 3:2)
The Temple (John 2:19)
The Tender Grass (2 Sam. 23:4)
A Tender Plant (Isa. 53:2)
The Tender Mercy of God (Luke 1:78)
The Testator (Heb. 9:16,17)
The Testimony of God (1 Cor. 2:1)
A Thief (Rev. 16:15)
This Treasure (2 Cor. 4:7)
The Trespass Offering (Lev. 5:6)
A Tried Stone (Isa. 28:16)
The True Bread from Heaven (John 6:32)
The True God (Jer. 10:10)
The True Light (John 1:9)
The True Vine (John 15:1)
The True Witness (Prov. 14:25)
The Truth (John 14:6)

U (7)
Undefiled (Heb. 7:26)
Understanding (Prov. 3:19)
The Unknown God (Acts 17:23)
The Unspeakable Gift (2 Cor. 9:15)
The Urim and Thummin (Exod. 28:30)
The Upholder of All Things (Heb. 1:3)
Upright (Ps. 92:15)

V (7)
The Veil (Heb. 10:20)
The Very God of Peace (1 Thess. 5:23)
Very Great (Ps. 104:1)
A Very Present Help in Trouble (Ps. 46:1)
The Victory (1 Cor. 15:54)
The Vine (John 15:5)
The Voice (Rev. 1:12)

W (25)
A Wall of Fire (Zech. 2:5)
The Wave Offering (Lev. 7:30)
The Way (John 14:6)
The Way of Holiness (Isa. 35:8)
The Weakness of God (1 Cor. 1:25)
A Wedding Garment (Matt. 22:12)
The Well of Living Waters (John 4:14)
The Well of Salvation (Isa. 12:3)
A Winebibber (Matt. 11:19)
Wisdom (1 Cor. 1:25)
The Wisdom of God (1 Cor. 1:24)
A Wise Master Builder (1 Cor. 3:10)
Witness (Judg. 11:10)
My Witness (Job 16:19)
The Witness of God (1 John 5:9)
A Witness to the People (Isa. 55:4)
Wonderful (Isa. 9:6)
Wonderful Counselor (Isa. 9:6)
The Word (John 1:1)
The Word of God (Rev. 19:13)
The Word of Life (1 John 1:1)
A Worm and No Man (Ps. 22:6)
Worthy (Rev. 4:11; 5:12)
That Worthy Name (Jas. 2:7)
Worthy to Be Praised (Ps. 18:3)

X (2)
X (The Greek letter *Chi*, the traditional symbol of Christ,
    since it is the first letter of the title "Christ" in Greek.)
X (as an Unknown Quantity; see Rev. 19:12)

Y (2)
The Yokefellow (Matt. 11:29,30)
The Young Child (Matt. 2:11)

Z (4)

Zaphnath-Paaneah (Gen. 41:45)
The Zeal of the Lord of Hosts (Isa. 37:32)
The Zeal of Thine House (John 2:17; Ps. 69:9
Zerubbabel (Zech. 4:7,9)

Total Names and Titles: 669

*From *The Names of Jesus* by Elmer L. Towns (Denver, CO: Accent Publications, 1987), adapted.

APPENDIX 4

*The Preeminent Pronouns of Christ in Scripture**

Who Art, and Wast, and Shalt Be (Rev. 16:5)
Him That Bringeth Good Tidings (Nah. 1:15)
He Who Brought Us Up (Josh. 24:17)
He Who Created (Rev. 10:6)
He That Cometh (Luke 7:19; Matt. 11:3)
He That Cometh After Me (John 1:15,27)
He Who Cometh Down from Heaven (John 6:33)
He That Cometh in the Name of the Lord (Matt. 21:9)
He That Cometh into the World (John 11:27)
Who Coverest Thyself with Light (Ps. 104:2)
Who Crowneth Thee with Lovingkindness (Ps. 103:4)
He That Was Dead and Is Alive (Rev. 2:8)
Who Dwelleth in Zion (Ps. 9:11)
He Who Fighteth for You (Josh. 23:10)
He That Filleth All in All (Eph. 1:23)
Who Forgiveth All Thine Iniquities (Ps. 103:3)
This That Forgiveth Sins (Luke 7:49)

Who Girdeth Me with Strength (Ps. 18:32)
Who Giveth Me Counsel (Ps. 16:7)
He That Hath the Bride (John 3:29)
He Who Hath His Eyes Like a Flame of Fire (Rev. 2:18)
He Who Hath His Feet Like Fine Brass (Rev. 2:18)
Thou Who Hearest Prayer (Ps. 65:2)
Who Healeth All Thy Diseases (Ps. 103:3)
He That Is Higher than the Heavens (Eccl. 5:8)
He That Holdeth the Seven Stars (Rev. 2:1)
He That Is Holy (Rev. 3:7)
Who Laid the Foundations of the Earth (Ps. 104:5)
Who Layeth the Beams of His Chambers in the Waters
(Ps. 104:3)
Thou Who Liftest Me Up from the Gates of Death (Ps. 9:13)
He That Liveth (Rev. 1:18)
Him That Liveth Forever and Ever (Rev. 10:6)
Him That Loveth Us (Rev. 1:5)
Who Maketh His Angels Spirits (Ps. 104:4; Heb. 1:7)
Who Maketh the Clouds His Chariot (Ps. 104:3)
He That Openeth (Rev. 3:7)
Who Hast Power over These Plagues (Rev. 16:9)
Who Redeemeth Thy Life from Destruction (Ps. 103:4)
Thou Rulest the Raging of the Sea (Ps. 89:9)
He That Sanctifieth (Heb. 2:11)
Who Satisfieth Thy Mouth with Good Things (Ps. 103:5)
Thou Who Saveth by Thy Right Hand (Ps. 17:7)
Who Saveth the Upright in Heart (Ps. 7:10)
He Who Searcheth (Rev. 2:23)
Whom Thou Hast Sent (John 17:3)
He Who Hath the Seven Spirits of God (Rev. 3:1)
He Who Hath the Sharp Sword with Two Edges (Rev. 2:12)
He That Shutteth (Rev. 3:7)
He Who Sitteth in the Heavens (Ps. 2:4)
Him That Sitteth on the Throne (Rev. 6:16)
Who Stretchest Out the Heavens Like a Curtain (Ps. 104:2)

He Who Testifieth (Rev. 22:20)
He That Is True (Rev. 3:7)
Him That Was Valued (Matt. 27:9)
He Who Walketh in the Midst of the Seven Candlesticks
(Rev. 2:1)
Who Walketh upon the Wings of the Wind (Ps. 104:3)

Total: 56

*From *The Names of Jesus* by Elmer L. Towns (Denver, CO; Accent
Publications, 1987), adapted.

The Names of the LORD God (Jehovah Elohim; Kurios ho Theos) in Scripture

This Holy LORD God (1 Sam. 6:20)
The LORD God...Abounding in Goodness (Exod. 34:6)
The LORD God...Abounding in Truth (Exod. 34:6)
Lord God Almighty (Rev. 4:8)
The LORD, the Everlasting God (*Jehovah El Olam;*
Gen. 21:33)
The LORD God (*Jehovah Elohim;* Gen. 2:4)
The LORD God of Abraham, Isaac, and Israel (1 Kings 18:36)
The LORD, the God of David Your Father (2 Kings 20:5)
The LORD God of Elijah (2 Kings 2:14)
The LORD God of Your Fathers (*Jehovah Elohe 'Abothekhem;*
Exod. 3:15)
The LORD, the God of All Flesh (Jer. 32:27)
The LORD God of Gods (*El Elohim Jehovah;* Josh. 22:22)
The LORD God...Gracious (Exod. 34:6)

The LORD *Is* the Great God (Ps. 95:3)
The LORD God of Heaven (Gen. 24:7)
The LORD, the God of Heaven and the God of Earth
(Gen. 24:3)
The LORD God of the Hebrews (Exod. 3:18)
The LORD *Is* God of the Hills (1 Kings 20:28)
The Lord God of the Holy Prophets (Rev. 22·6)
The LORD God of Hosts (*Jehovah Elohim Tseba'oth;*
2 Sam. 5:10)
The LORD God of Israel (*Jehovah Elohe Yisra'el;* Exod. 5:1)
The Lord God Who Judges Her (Rev. 18:8)
The LORD *Is* a God of Justice (Isa. 30:18)
The LORD *Is* the God of Knowledge (1 Sam. 2:3)
The LORD God of My Lord the King (1 Kings 1:36)
The LORD God...Long-suffering (Exod. 34:6)
The LORD God of My Master Abraham (Gen. 24:12,27,42,48)
The LORD God Merciful (Exod. 34:6)
The LORD, God Most High (*Jehovah El Elyon;* Gen. 14:22)
The Lord God Omnipotent (Rev. 19:6)
The LORD *Is* the God of Recompense (*Jehovah El Gemuloth;*
Jer. 51:56)
The LORD, God of My Salvation (*Jehovah Elohe Yeshu'athi;*
Ps. 88:1)
The LORD, the God of Shem (Gen. 9:26)
The LORD, the God of the Spirits of All Flesh (Num. 27:16)
The LORD God of Truth (*Jehovah El 'Emeth;* Ps. 31:5)
The LORD *Is*...God of the Valleys (1 Kings 20:28, implied)

Total: 36 names

The Name God (Elohim) in Scripture

Almighty God (*El Shaddai*; Gen. 17:1)
God Who Avenges Me (*El Nekamoth*; Ps. 18:47)
The Eternal God (Deut. 33:27)
The Everlasting God (Isa. 40:28)
The Faithful God (*El Emunah*; Deut. 7:9)
God-Who-Forgives (*El Nose'*; Ps. 99:8)
God (*Elohim*; Gen. 1:1)
The God of Abraham (Gen. 31:42)
God Almighty (Gen. 28:3)
The God of the Armies of Israel (1 Sam. 17:45)
The God of Bethel (Gen. 31:13)
The God of All Comfort (2 Cor. 1:3)
The God of Daniel (Dan. 6:26)
The God of the Earth (Rev. 11:4)
God My Exceeding Joy (*El Simchath Gili*; Ps. 43:4)

The God of All the Families of Israel (Jer. 31:1)
The God of My Father (Gen. 31:5)
The God of Your Father Abraham (Gen. 26:24)
The God of His Father David (2 Chron. 34:3)
The God of the Gentiles (Rom. 3:29)
The God of Glory (*El Hakabodh*; Ps. 29:3)
God, the God of Israel (*El Elohe Israel*; Gen. 33:20, alt.)
The God of Gods (Deut. 10:17)
The God of All Grace (1 Pet. 5:10)
God in Heaven (*Elohim Bashamayim*; Josh. 2:11)
The God of Heaven (Ezra 5:12)
The God of Heaven and Earth (Ezra 5:11)
The God of the Hebrews (Exod. 5:3)
God *Is* My Helper (*Elohim 'Ozer Li*; Ps. 54:4)
The God of Hope (Rom. 15:13)
God of Hosts (*Elohim Tsaba'oth*; Ps. 80:7)
God of the House of God (*El Bethel*; Gen. 35:7, alt.)
The God of Isaac (Gen. 28:13)
The God of Israel (*Elohe Yisra'el*; Exod. 24:10)
The God of Jacob (*Elohe Ya'akob*; 2 Sam. 23:1)
The God of Jerusalem (2 Chron. 32:19)
The God of Jeshurun (Deut. 33:26)
The God of the Jews (Rom. 3:29)
God Who Judges the Earth (*Elohim Shophtim Ba'arets*; Ps. 58:11)
The God of Judgment (Mal. 2:17)
My God, My King (*Eli Malki*; Ps. 68:24)
The God of the Land (2 Kings 17:26)
The God of My Life (*El Khayyay*; Ps. 42:8)
The God of the Living (Matt. 22:32, implied)
The God of Love (2 Cor. 13:11)
The God of Our Lord Jesus Christ (Eph. 1:17)
God Most High (*El 'Elyon;* Gen. 14:18)
God Most High (*Elohim 'Elyon*; Ps. 57:2)
The God of Nahor (Gen. 31:53)

The God of Patience (Rom. 15:5)
The God of Peace (Rom. 15:33)
The God of My Praise (Ps. 109:1)
God *Is* a Refuge for Us (*Elohim Machaseh Lanu*; Ps. 62:8)
God of My Righteousness (*Elohe Tsidqi*; Ps. 4:1)
God My Rock (*El Sela'*; Ps. 42:9)
The God of My Salvation (*Elohe Yish'i*; Ps. 18:46)
The-God-Who-Sees-Me (*El Roi*; Gen. 16:13)
The God of Shadrach, Meshach and Abed-Nego (Dan. 3:29)
The God of My Strength (*Elohe Ma'uzi*; Ps. 43:2)
A God of Truth (Deut. 32:4)
The Great God (Deut 10:17)
A Holy God (*Elohim Qedoshim*; Josh. 24:19)
A Jealous God (*El Qanna*; Exod. 20:5)
The Living God (*El Khay*; Josh. 3:10)
My Merciful God (*Elohe Khasdi*; Ps. 59:10)
The Mighty God (*El Gibbor*; Jer. 32:18)

Total: 66 names

The Names of the Lord (Jehovah) in the Old Testament*

Adonai Jehovah—The Lord GOD (Gen. 15:2)
Hamelech Jehovah—The LORD, the King (Ps. 98:6)
Jehovah—The LORD (Exod. 6:2,3)
Jehovah Adon Kol Ha'arets—The LORD, the Lord of All the Earth (Josh. 3:13)
Jehovah Bore—The LORD Creator (Isa. 40:28)
Jehovah Ma'oz Khayyay—The LORD the Strength of My Life (Ps. 27:1)
Jehovah Khereb—The LORD...the Sword (Deut. 33:29)
Jehovah Eli—The LORD My God (Ps. 18:2)
Jehovah 'Elyon—The LORD Most High (Ps. 7:17)
Jehovah 'Oz-Lamo—The LORD the Strength of His people (Ps. 28:7)
Jehovah Gibbor Milchamah—The LORD Mighty in Battle (Ps. 24:8)
Jehovah Maginnenu—The LORD Our Defence (Ps. 89:18)
Jehovah Go'el—The LORD Thy Redeemer (Isa. 49:26; 60:16)
Jehovah Hashopet—The LORD the Judge (Judg. 11:27)
Jehovah Hoshe'ah—The LORD Save (Ps. 20:9)

Jehovah 'Immekha—The LORD Is with You (Judg. 6:12)

Jehovah 'Izuz We Gibbor—The LORD Strong and Mighty (Ps. 24:8)

Jehovah Jireh—The-LORD-Will-Provide (Gen. 22:14)

Jehovah Kabodhi—The LORD My Glory (Ps. 3:3)

Jehovah Qanna—The LORD, Whose Name *Is* Jealous (Exod. 34:14)

Jehovah Keren-Yish'i—The LORD the Horn of My Salvation (Ps. 18:2)

Jehovah Machsi—The LORD My Refuge (Ps. 91:9)

Jehovah Magen—The LORD, the Shield (Deut. 33:29)

Jehovah Ma'oz—The LORD...My Fortress (Jer. 16:19)

Jehovah Melech 'Olam—The LORD King Forever (Ps. 10:16)

Jehovah Mephalti—The LORD My Deliverer (Ps. 18:2)

Jehovah Meqaddishkhem—The LORD Our Sanctifier (Exod. 31:13)

Jehovah Metsudhathi—The LORD...My Fortress (Ps. 18:2)

Jehovah Misgabbi—The LORD My High Tower (Ps. 18:2)

Jehovah Makheh—The LORD That Smiteth (Ezek. 7:9)

Jehovah Nissi—The LORD Our Banner (Exod. 17:15)

Jehovah 'Ori—The LORD My Light (Ps. 27:1)

Jehovah Rophe—The LORD That Healeth (Exod. 15:26)

Jehovah Ro'i—The LORD My Shepherd (Ps. 23:1)

Jehovah Sebaoth—The LORD of Hosts (1 Sam. 1:3)

Jehovah Sal'i—The LORD My Rock (Ps. 18:2)

Jehovah Shalom—The LORD Our Peace (Judg. 6:24)

Jehovah Shammah—The LORD Is There (Exek. 48:35)

Jehovah Tsidqenu—The LORD Our Righteousness (Jer. 23:6)

Jehovah Tsuri—O LORD, My Strength (Ps. 19:14)

Jehovah 'Uzam—The LORD Their Strength (Ps. 37:39)

Jehovah Moshi'ekh—The LORD Thy Savior (Isa. 49:26; 60:16)

Total: 42 names

*From *The Names of Jesus,* by Elmer L. Towns (Denver, CO: Accent Publications, 1987), adapted.

APPENDIX 8

The Names
of God in the Book
of Psalms

This list of the names and descriptive titles ascribed to God in the book of Psalms is based upon the *New King James Version*. As various translators may use various English words to translate the Hebrew text, this list may differ from that compiled by those using another translation. Also, this list includes only the first instance where the name is used to clearly identify God or may be viewed as a descriptive title of God without seriously violating the normal rules of biblical interpretation. Because these names are often repeated in other psalms, some psalms are not represented on the list. The name of God appears in every Psalm, but this list does not attempt to include every reference to every name. This list includes 232 names and descriptive titles of God.

1:6	LORD (*Jehovah*)
2:4	He who sits in the heavens

3:2	God (*Elohim*)
3:3	a shield for me
	My glory (*Kabodhi*)
	the One who lifts up my head
4:1	God of my righteousness (*Elohe Tsidqi*)
5:2	My King
5:11	Your name
7:1	LORD my God (*Jehovah Elohim*)
7:9	the righteous God
7:10	Who saves the upright in heart
7:11	a just judge
7:17	the name of the LORD Most High (*Jehovah 'Elyon*)
8:1	LORD, our Lord (*Jehovah Adonai*)
	You who set Your glory above the heavens
9:2	Most High (*Elyon*)
9:9	a refuge for the oppressed
	A refuge in times of trouble
9:13	You who lift me up from the gates of death
10:14	the helper of the fatherless
10:16	The LORD *is* King forever (*Jehovah Melech 'Olam*)
14:6	the LORD *is* his refuge
14:7	the salvation of Israel
16:5	the portion of my inheritance
	my cup
17:7	You who save those who trust *in You*
18:1	LORD, my strength
18:2	The LORD is my rock (*Jehovah Sel'i*)
	my fortress (*Metsudhathi*)
	my deliverer (*Mephalti*)
	My God, my strength
	My shield
	the horn of my salvation (*Keren-Yish'i*)
	my stronghold (*Misgabbi*)
18:3	*who is worthy* to be praised
18:18	my support

18:30	a shield to all who trust in Him
18:32	God who arms me with strength
18:46	the God of my salvation (*Elohe Teshu'athi*)
18:47	God who avenges me (*El Nekamoth*)
19:14	O LORD, my strength (*Jehovah Tsuri*)
	my redeemer
20:1	the name of the God of Jacob
20:5	the name of our God
20:7	the name of the LORD our God
20:9	Save, LORD (*Jehovah Hoshe'ah*)
22:1	My God, My God (*Eli Eli*)
22:3	Who inhabit the praises of Israel
22:9	He who took Me out of the womb
22:19	My Strength
23:1	The LORD *is* my shepherd (*Jehovah Ro'i*)
24:8	The King of glory
	The LORD strong and mighty (*Jehovah 'Izuz We Gibbor*)
	The LORD mighty in battle (*Jehovah Gibbor Milchamah*)
24:10	The LORD of hosts (*Jehovah Sebaoth*)
27:1	The LORD *is* my light (*Jehovah 'Ori*)
	my salvation
	The LORD *is* the strength of my life (*Jehovah Ma'oz Khayyay*)
28:1	O LORD my Rock (*Jehovah Tsur*)
28:7	The LORD *is* the strength of His people (*Jehovah 'Oz-Lamo*)
28:8	the saving refuge of His anointed
29:3	The God of glory (*El Hakabodh*)
29:10	King forever
30:4	His holy name
30:10	my helper
31:2	my rock of refuge
	a fortress of defense

31:5	O LORD God of truth (*Jehovah El 'Emeth*)
32:7	my hiding place
33:20	our help and our shield
35:3	I *am* your salvation
35:5	the angel of the LORD
37:39	their strength in the time of trouble (*'Uzam*)
38:22	O Lord, my salvation (*Adonai*)
40:17	my help and my deliverer
41:13	the LORD God of Israel (*Jehovah Elohe Yisra'el*)
42:8	the God of my life (*El Hayyay*)
42:9	God my Rock (*El Sela'*)
43:2	God of my strength (*Elohe Ma'ozi*)
43:4	God my exceeding joy (*El Simchath Gili*)
45:3	O Mighty One
46:1	A very present help in trouble
46:7	the God of Jacob (*Elohe Ya'akob*)
47:2	a great King over all the earth
47:9	the God of Abraham
48:14	Our God forever (*Elohenu 'Olam*)
50:1	The Mighty One, God the LORD
50:6	Judge
53:6	the salvation of Israel
54:4	God *is* my helper (*Elohim 'Ozer Li*)
57:2	God Most High (*El Marom*) who performs *all things* for me
58:11	God who judges in the earth (*Elohim Shophtim Ba'arets*)
59:5	LORD God of hosts (*Jehovah Elohim Tseba'oth*) the God of Israel (*Elohe Yisra'el*)
59:9	my defense
59:10	My merciful God (*Elohe Yisra'el*)
59:11	O Lord our shield
59:16	refuge in the day of my trouble
59:17	The God of my mercy
60:12	He who shall tread down our enemies

61:2	the rock that is higher than I
61:3	a shelter for me
	a strong tower from the enemy
62:7	The rock of my strength
62:8	God *is* a refuge for us (*Elohim Machaseh Lanu*)
65:2	You who hear prayer
65:5	the confidence of all the ends of the earth
65:6	Who established the mountains by His strength
65:7	You who still the noise of the seas
66:20	Who has not turned away my prayer
67:6	God, our own God
68:4	Him who rides on the clouds
	YAH
68:5	a father of the fatherless
	a defender of widows
68:8	God, the God of Israel (*El Elohe Yisra'el*)
68:19	*Who* daily loads us *with benefits*
68:24	my God, my King
68:33	Him who rides on the heaven of heavens
68:35	He who gives strength and power to *His* people
71:7	my strong refuge
71:16	Lord God
71:22	O Holy One of Israel
72:18	the LORD God, the God of Israel
	Who only does wondrous things
72:19	His glorious name
73:26	the strength of my heart
	my portion forever
74:12	my King from of old
76:1	great
76:12	awesome
77:14	the God who does wonders
78:35	the Most High God their redeemer
80:1	O Shepherd of Israel

	You who lead Joseph like a flock
	You who dwell *between* the cherubim
81:10	I *am* the LORD your God
	Who brought you out of the land of Egypt
83:18	You, whose name alone is the LORD
	the Most High over all the earth
84:2	the living God
84:11	a sun and shield
86:5	good
	ready to forgive
	abundant in mercy
86:15	a God full of compassion
	gracious
	Longsuffering
	abundant in mercy
88:1	LORD God of my salvation (*Jehovah Elohe Yeshu'athi*)
89:17	the glory of their strength
89:26	my Father
	the rock of my salvation
90:1	our dwelling place
91:1	Almighty
91:9	The LORD, *who is* my refuge (*Jehovah Machsi*)
	your habitation
93:4	The LORD on high
	mightier than the noise of many waters
	(mightier) than the mighty waves of the sea
94:2	O Judge of the earth
95:3	the great God
	the great King above all gods
95:6	the LORD our Maker
97:5	the Lord of the whole earth
98:6	the LORD, the King (*Hamelech Jehovah*)
99:8	God-Who-Forgives (*El Nose'*)
103:3	Who forgives all your iniquities

	Who heals all your diseases
103:4	Who redeems your life from destruction
	Who crowns you with lovingkindness and tender mercies
103:5	Who satisfies your mouth with good *things*
103:8	merciful and gracious
	Slow to anger
	abounding in mercy
104:2	Who cover *Yourself* with light as *with* a garment
	Who stretch out the heavens like a curtain
104:3	Who makes the clouds His chariot
	Who walks on the wings of the wind
104:4	Who makes His angels spirits
104:5	*You who* laid the foundations of the earth
106:21	God their Savior
	Who had done great things in Egypt
106:48	the LORD God of Israel
108:13	He *who* shall tread down our enemies
109:1	O God of my praise
109:21	O GOD the Lord
113:5	Who dwells on high
113:6	Who humbles Himself to behold...in the heavens
114:8	Who turned the rock *into* a pool of water
115:15	the LORD, Who made heaven and earth
118:14	my strength and song
119:57	my portion
121:4	He who keeps Israel
121:5	your keeper
	your shade at your right hand
123:1	You who dwell in the heavens
124:1	the LORD who was on our side
124:6	the LORD, Who has not given us *as* prey to their teeth
132:2	the Mighty *God* of Jacob

135:5	above all gods
135:21	the LORD out of Zion, Who dwells in Jerusalem
136:2	the God of gods
136:3	the Lord of lords
136:4	Him who alone does great wonders
136:6	Him who laid out the earth above the waters
136:7	Him who made great lights
136:10	Him who struck Egypt in their firstborn
136:13	Him who divided the Red Sea in two
136:16	Him who led His people through the wilderness
136:17	Him who struck down great kings
136:23	Who remembered us in our lowly state
136:25	Who gives food to all flesh
136:26	the God of heaven
140:7	the strength of my salvation
142:5	My portion in the land of the living
144:1	Who trains my hands for war
144:2	My loving kindness
	My high tower
	the One in whom I take refuge
	Who subdues my people under me
144:10	*The One* who gives salvation to kings
	Who delivers David His servant from the deadly sword
146:6	Who keeps truth forever
146:7	Who executes justice for the oppressed
	Who gives food to the hungry
147:8	Who covers the heavens with clouds
	Who prepares rain for the earth
	Who makes grass to grow on the mountains
149:2	their Maker